Return to
The
Little
French
Guesthouse

Return to The Little French Guesthouse

helen pollard

Bookouture

Published by Bookouture

An imprint of StoryFire Ltd.
23 Sussex Road, Ickenham, UB10 8PN
United Kingdom

www.bookouture.com

ISBN: 9781786810489
eBook ISBN: 9781786810472

For Amy and Tom

You are both a source of pride
and delight to me – every day of my life.

CHAPTER ONE

I knew there would be many unusual things in my new remit as manager of Rupert's guesthouse, but I hadn't guessed seeing the guests naked would be one of them.

It was early morning, just a couple of days into my new life at *La Cour des Roses*. I'd made myself an espresso – first things first – and taken it outside. With my feet bare so I could feel the grass between my toes and the refreshing dew against my skin, I pottered down the lawn, past beds of ornamental grasses and begonias and daisies, weeping willows, stepping stones leading off to secret arbours and seating spots, until I reached the chicken run, surrounded by shrubs and trees.

Draining my coffee, I donned flip-flops – bare feet were all very well, but nature lost its appeal when you found yourself toe-deep in chicken poop – and let the half-dozen fussing birds out of their safe house, giving them breakfast and water.

Backing out, I said a polite 'Good morning' to Gladys, one of our guests, who had wandered down after me.

'Morning, Emmy. I thought I'd come out for a little peace and quiet before breakfast.'

I nodded my understanding. Gladys was an elderly lady holidaying with her daughter – an overbearing, middle-aged woman with a brusque manner. She didn't take after her mother, a gentle soul whose company I enjoyed very much.

'Clare's planning our day,' she explained wearily. 'I'm sure it will be lovely.' She fingered the draping leaves of a weeping pear as we wended our way back up the garden, the skin across the back of her hands paper-thin. 'I love this colour, don't you? Almost silvery.'

'Yes. Beautiful. Gladys, why don't you tell Clare that you're tired and you'd like to spend the day here? You could relax and enjoy the garden.'

Gladys gave a short laugh then put on an unconvincing smile. 'Don't worry. I like sightseeing, and I can't complain with Clare doing all the hard work.'

Hearing a clatter of shutters, it was a natural reaction for both of us to glance up at the house. How could I have known we should've looked anywhere but there? If only I'd had a great big cappuccino instead of a tiny espresso, and lingered over it at the bottom of the garden. If only I'd taken my time admiring the silvery weeping pear leaves. If only I'd linked arms with Gladys to steady her as we walked.

Because there stood Geoffrey Turner in all his glory.

He'd pulled aside the voile curtains to open the shutters and unfortunately the bedroom windows were tall and low slung on the upper storey of the house . . . As was Geoffrey Turner. It wouldn't have been so bad if he'd been young, fit and tanned – but mid-fifties, white and pot-bellied was not a sight I wanted to see on an empty stomach.

My mouth dropped open in shock. As did his. The voile curtains were hurriedly tugged shut – although since the whole point of voile is that it's practically see-through, *that* didn't help much. And by then, it was a tad too late.

I heard a gasp from Gladys. Unsurprisingly, she hadn't been watching her feet. She tripped over the edge of a flowerbed, stumbled and fell. I caught one of her arms, but she landed with the other awkwardly underneath her.

Crouching, I waited for her to catch her breath. 'Gladys, are you all right?'

She tried a wobbly smile. 'I'll be fine, Emmy. I just need to get myself back up.' But as she used both hands to push, she yelped in pain.

I didn't want to risk hurting her by tugging her around. 'I'll go and get Clare.'

Gladys managed a wan smile. 'Didn't think a naked man could have such a dramatic effect at my age!'

With an answering smile, I shot off to the house and up the stairs to their room.

Clare, her hair wet from the shower, expressed immediate alarm and came running out, helping me to lift her mother so we could walk her to the kitchen and sit her on a chair.

'What hurts, Mother? Have you broken something?' Clare's voice was brittle with anxiety, her hands fluttering at her sides.

'There's no need to fuss,' the old lady said, although she was still shaken. 'Nothing hurts other than my pride and my wrist.'

I fetched her a glass of water and then took a bag of peas from the freezer, wrapping them in a clean tea towel and placing them on her arm.

'What made you fall? Did you trip over something?' Clare demanded.

I glanced at her in alarm. Surely she wasn't going to complain about the dangers of flowerbeds in the garden? Although since she'd already commented on the stairs being too numerous for her mother, the shower too powerful and the shutters too heavy, I wouldn't be surprised.

Gladys was obviously worried about the same thing. 'No, I just wasn't looking where I was going.' In a misguided attempt to lighten the fraught atmosphere, she added, 'One of the guests appeared naked at the window. It diverted my attention somewhat.' She gave a little chuckle.

Her strategy backfired.

'*What? Who* was naked at the window? You mean he was *exposing* himself to you?'

Gladys winced. 'It was only Geoffrey, and he wasn't exposing himself. He opened the shutters and . . .'

'It's the same thing!'

'Oh, for goodness' sake, Clare, of course it isn't! I'm sorry I mentioned it. It was an accident, and it's not as if I haven't seen it all before.'

'How's your wrist?' I asked her, out of genuine concern but also in an attempt to change the subject. I lifted away the peas to look.

Another ill-chosen distraction.

'It's swollen! It could be broken! We need to call an ambulance,' Clare decided.

That threw me for six. 'An ambulance?' I refrained from adding "What on earth for?" although I kept it in reserve.

'My mother's seventy-eight. She could have broken her arm and goodness knows what else. Cracked a hip or her collarbone. And how do we know she won't go into shock?'

Conscious that the other guests would begin pottering down for a so far non-existent breakfast any minute, I glanced over at Gladys. The poor woman looked as though she wanted an ambulance called about as much as I did.

'Your mum doesn't think she's done any more damage than hurting her wrist. I'm sure when Rupert gets back from walking the dog, he'll be happy to sort out a doctor's appointment or even run her to A&E, if you like. I don't think there's any need for an ambulance at this stage.'

Clare's mouth set in a stubborn line. 'Who's the customer here? I want you to call an ambulance and I want you to do it now!'

I looked at Gladys, but she only gave me a pained look back.

'Fine. No problem.' Plastering on a smile, I reached for the phone . . . and a sense of déjà vu punched me right in the gut.

I didn't know the number to dial. Again.

Memories of Rupert tumbling from his chair with a suspected heart attack flooded my brain – but I wasn't a holidaymaker any more. This was my job now. Why hadn't I thought to learn something like that as soon as I came back here?

Because you've spent the past few weeks handing in your notice, finishing up at work, packing up all your worldly goods and driving them to France – and you weren't to know this would happen.

I took the phone into the hall, ostensibly for quiet, but in reality to rummage through Rupert's ragged phone book. It was hopeless. Why would he write the number down? He already knew it. As should I. Pulling my mobile from my pocket, I resorted to the internet, but I was interrupted mid-search.

'What's taking so long?' Clare stormed into the hall as Pippa and Angus started down the stairs. Rudely, she glanced over my shoulder. 'You're having to look the number *up*?'

'Yes, well, I . . .'

'I don't believe it! You *run* this place and you don't know the number to call for an ambulance?'

'I've only been here a couple of days and I . . .'

'That's no excuse!'

She was right. 'Well, I know it now, so . . .'

It was at this moment that Geoffrey Turner and his wife made an appearance. I was surprised he dared, but I supposed he could hardly sit in his room and starve.

'And *you*!' Clare jabbed a finger in his direction, her face pinched, an angry red flush across her cheekbones. 'You ought to be ashamed of yourself!'

Geoffrey straightened his shoulders. 'My apologies, but it was an accident. I was half asleep and I'd forgotten the sill was so low . . .'

'Exposing yourself to an old lady like that! Disgusting!'

'*Exposing* myself? How should I know anyone would be in the garden so bloody early in the morning?'

Geoffrey's wife Mary shrank against the wall, looking from Geoffrey to Clare with undisguised horror at the turn the morning was taking.

Clare was undeterred. 'My mother is on her way to the hospital because of you! Or she would be, if the so-called manager of this place knew how to phone for one.'

I took a deep breath. 'I have the number now, so if everyone would be quiet for a moment . . .'

But Geoffrey's eyes had narrowed dangerously. 'You don't know the number for an ambulance?' No doubt he was happy to seize on my shortcomings to distract from his own.

'I *do* know the number,' I insisted. 'It only took me a minute to look it up.'

'A minute can make all the difference in an emergency.'

'It's a sprained wrist, not a stroke!' I snapped, exasperated. *Oops.*

The final set of guests were tentatively heading down the stairs – whether for breakfast or free entertainment, I wasn't sure.

'What if it wasn't?' one of them piped up helpfully.

I had no answer to that . . . and I was painfully aware that Geoffrey was not the man to pick a fight with. A well-known travel blogger, I'd thought he was quite a coup for us. While I was winding things up at work, I'd come across his number and remembered dealing with him when I'd worked on an account for a hotel chain a couple of years before. Knowing there was a gap in Rupert's bookings, I'd contacted him and offered him a free stay in return for an honest review, imagining how he would wax lyrical about the classy guesthouse, the delicious food, the beautiful garden . . .

I had left my home, job, friends and cheating ex-boyfriend in the UK for a glorious new existence in the Loire Valley, and Geoffrey Turner was supposed to be the beginning of making *La Cour des Roses* more successful, more profitable . . . And if word got around that I could do that for this place, who knew where that might lead?

Yet there I stood, just three days in, with a roomful of shrieking guests and Geoffrey Turner as red as one of Rupert's beetroot chutneys.

When Rupert appeared in the doorway, dog in tow, his face relaxed after his morning constitutional, I could have kissed him.

Everyone started talking at once – Clare shouting about guests that exposed themselves to old ladies and his manager's incompetence in medical emergencies, versus Geoffrey's robust denial of the former but agreement with the latter, amidst my desperate attempts to placate and explain.

'Right! Thank you all!' Rupert held up his hands in a shushing gesture, while his canine companion wisely slunk off to her basket at the far end of the hall. 'If you'd like to go into the kitchen for breakfast, Emmy will tend to you as always.'

He ushered them through and went over to Gladys, still stationed on the kitchen chair, looking pale. 'Now then, Gladys, let's take you into the lounge where it's quieter and decide what we're going to do, shall we?'

Clare wasn't having this at all. 'I've already told you I want an ambulance!'

Rupert's chest expanded as he filled his lungs with a calming breath. 'I understand your concern, Clare, but I think your mother would be far more comfortable in a car. It means we can set off immediately, and it's less upsetting for her, don't you think?'

I could see the desire to get her own way warring with Rupert's common sense. All eyes were upon her.

'Fine. If you insist.' She wheeled around to glare at Geoffrey Turner. 'But I expect *him* to leave! I don't see why we should have to share our holiday accommodation with a pervert!'

Geoffrey reddened. 'And I don't see why I should have to share mine with a shrieking shrew!'

Rupert blanched. As did our audience. To add to the merriment, the phone rang. I glared at it with trepidation, still dreading potential conversations in French – I fared better in person, when I could lip-read and people could tell if I wasn't following them and slow down.

I snatched it up as Rupert took Gladys and Clare through to the hall, and tried my best to capture it between one shoulder and ear while ferrying juice and milk from the fridge to the table in a vain effort to get breakfast underway.

'*Bonjour. La Cour des Roses.*'

'Hello, is that Gloria?'

Relieved to hear the very English voice, I said, 'No. This is Emmy Jamieson. Can I help?'

'Is Gloria available?'

'She's no longer here, I'm afraid. What can I do for you?'

'Oh.' A tut of dismay. 'It's Gloria I've been dealing with.'

'I'm the manager here, and I'm happy to help. May I ask who's calling?'

'Julia Cooper. I'm ringing about the Thomson booking in September,' she announced, as though I should know all about it.

From what I remembered when I'd glanced ahead at the reservations, September wasn't exactly booked up, and I didn't remember seeing a Thomson on it. Still, I didn't want to play dumb at this stage. 'Lovely to speak to you. How can I help?'

'I wanted to let you know that there will be five airbeds altogether. As I said to Gloria, we're happy to supply them. We'll expect you to provide linen and duvets as agreed.'

The spoon I was using to transfer yogurt to a glass bowl remained suspended in mid-air. 'Airbeds?'

'Two in one of the rooms, one in one *gîte* and two in another *gîte*. As for travel cots, we only need one setting up in the one *gîte* without airbeds, as far as I know.'

'Ah. Right. Okay.' Dropping the spoon, I glanced around the kitchen for a notepad, but the granite worktops only held breakfast goods. I grabbed a lone pen from the windowsill and resorted to scribbling notes around the edge of the label on the yogurt carton.

'You do know about the Thomson booking?'

'I'm so sorry, but I've only been here a few days, Mrs . . . Ms? Cooper.'

'Mrs, but Julia is fine. Might as well be on first-name terms. We'll be speaking quite often, I'm sure.'

We will? I already had questions clamouring to be answered, but she sounded like she might be an irritable sort, and if we would be speaking often, there was no point in getting on the wrong side of her. Yet. And feeding our current guests might not go amiss right now.

'I'm sorry to sound vague, Julia. I'll make sure Rupert brings me up to speed on your booking. And I'll let him know about the airbeds and travel cot. I'm sure we'll have it, but would you give me your phone number, in case I have any questions for you?'

'Better safe than sorry, I suppose.' She told me her mobile and landline, adding, 'I'm sorry to hear that Gloria's no longer there. She was most helpful.'

She was? Crikey!

We said our goodbyes, and I stared at the phone. *Airbeds? Really?*

As I replaced it in the hall, Rupert was leading Clare and Gladys outside. Hardly a good time to ask about the Thomson booking, and besides, I had more pressing concerns.

I grabbed his arm. 'What am I going to do about Geoffrey?' I hissed, as Clare solicitously led her mother across to Rupert's car.

'I'll try to talk some sense into Clare. She might calm down once we've got her mother sorted. But you'll have to deal with Geoffrey.'

'What about eggs?'

He gave me a blank look. 'Eggs?'

'What if anyone asks for eggs? Mine always turn out like rubber.'

Rupert huffed out an impatient sigh. 'Tell them the hens didn't lay. Tell them they saw Geoffrey Turner naked and it put them off.'

He went after Clare and Gladys while I reluctantly returned to the kitchen, its efficient but warm mix of wood, granite and gadgetry failing to comfort me now that I was solely in charge of it.

I chopped fruit into a large glass bowl, added orange juice to keep it fresh and took it across to the large pine table under the sloping roof, along with the yogurt and jars of local preserves. Finally, I placed croissants, brioche rolls, *pains au chocolat* and *pains aux raisins* (my personal favourite) in a basket and surveyed the result. One thing I was sure about – there was nothing I would change about breakfast.

When I had no further excuses, I enquired as to whether anyone would like anything cooked. Glancing across at Geoffrey, desperately trying to forget the fact that I'd seen his private parts dangling at the window half an hour earlier, I could only pray that nobody requested sausages.

As I cleared up afterwards, I mulled over whether to tackle Geoffrey about his . . . well, his tackle, but decided the subject was best left alone. Since I could hardly force a guest – let alone a prominent travel blogger – to leave over a genuine accident, I had to trust that Rupert's persuasive charm and Gladys's entreaties would win Clare over.

Geoffrey poked his head around the kitchen door. 'Have you got a first aid kit? Mary's scraped her elbow.'

'Do you need me to come?'

'Not at all,' he said hurriedly. 'Only a scratch. Just lend me your kit, would you?'

He had a keen gleam in his eye – one I hadn't seen before – and I didn't like it. When I fetched the kit and handed it to him, the surprise on his face was transparent, although he was quick to hide it. Was he *testing* me, to see if I knew where the kit was?

With the kitchen cleared, I fired up the laptop and brought up the September spreadsheet to see what Julia Cooper had been on about. There were bookings, but not as many as I'd like. This puzzled me, because Rupert had once told me that September was popular with those wanting to visit when places were quieter. Certainly, there was no mention of Julia Cooper or a Thomson anywhere.

No doubt Rupert would know all about it. Since I couldn't ask him until he got back, I made myself a much-required coffee. I patted my thigh and the dog came dashing from the hall to follow me out to the garden, where I settled in a chair for five minutes' peace. She placed her head on my knees so that I could stroke her velvet fur and play with her ears.

'How am I going to get us out of this mess, then?' I asked her.

Her only answer was to heave a sigh and gaze at me with those huge, sad eyes.

Gloria was my new love. Not, you understand, the Gloria who was Rupert's estranged wife and who'd seduced and run off with my boyfriend, Nathan, earlier that summer, while we were holidaying at *La Cour des Roses*, but Rupert's newly-acquired, black Labrador.

A local farmer had found her wandering his land, looking thin and unkempt, and when the vet could find no form of identification – either chip or tattoo – she'd ended up at the local animal shelter. For Rupert, hankering after a dog and no longer held back by his pet-hating estranged wife, it was love at first sight.

Nobody knew her name, and in his own twisted way, he'd named her Gloria. This, of course, was a name I couldn't stomach, so I'd taken to using various doggy endearments, and she didn't seem to mind. If she was a dog of discernment, she'd probably prefer it.

The vet estimated that she was about five years old, and she was loyal, affectionate and appealing – everything the original Gloria wasn't. The only thing they had in common besides the name was that she was anybody's for a belly rub.

CHAPTER TWO

'I'm so glad you two get along,' Rupert said fondly from behind us, making me jump.

I spun around. 'You're back early. You've only been gone a couple of hours.'

He plonked himself down on the grass next to the dog, making me smile. He couldn't have done that a while back – the ligament he'd damaged falling off a bar stool during the angina attack meant he could barely walk at one point. With his angina under control now, and me here to limit his stress – in theory – he was looking a darned sight better than when I'd left him a few weeks ago. He was leaner, and I presumed walking the dog was good for him. Even his face was slimmer, and he'd begun to grow a short-cropped beard, silver-grey to match his hair, which he was wearing a little longer, allowing the natural wave to show. I wasn't fully decided about the beard, but it hid his slightly sagging jowls, so I was reserving judgement until I could review the finished product.

'How's Gladys?' I enquired.

'As we thought. Lightly sprained wrist. That daughter of hers needs locking up. All that hysteria!'

'I'm sorry I didn't know the number for the ambulance.'

He plucked idly at the short-cropped lawn, playing with the blades of grass before letting them fall. 'Don't worry about it. We should probably have a notice up in the hall. In the rooms and *gîtes*, too.'

'I'll sort it. I might have it printed on my forehead for good measure. Oh, and by the way – Julia Cooper. Thomson booking. September. Airbeds. What's going on?'

His face was a total blank. 'Run that by me again.'

I did, but the result was the same. 'No idea what you're talking about.'

I relayed my conversation with Julia Cooper as near to verbatim as I could manage.

Rupert shook his head. 'No. I'm none the wiser. Is it on the spreadsheet?'

'I looked but I couldn't see it. I'll go get the laptop.'

'Sun's too bright. Easier to go in.'

In Rupert's den, he lowered himself onto the captain's chair at the desk, leaving me to enjoy the little leather sofa, and stared at the screen. 'Did you ask her what date?'

'No. She made it sound as though I should know all about it, and I didn't want to come across as a total idiot. I assumed you'd know.'

He waved a finger at the laptop. 'No, but there are a few gaps, so a booking would be good – if we knew when the hell it was.'

'Don't worry. I'll phone her back and explain as best I can.'

Rupert ineffectually shuffled a few sheets of loose paper around on the leather-topped desk. 'There must be something here, somewhere. Even Gloria can't have taken a booking and not written it down, surely?'

I gave him a look. 'You're not asking me to place money on that, are you?' I frowned. 'When we transferred all the crap from the diary weeks ago, you seemed fairly booked up, but now there are quite a lot of gaps. This month too. Why?'

Rupert sighed heavily. 'The honest truth? I think Gloria was losing interest big time, Emmy. All that stuff we transferred? Not all of it made sense. I've had the odd complaint that we'd never got back to people about enquiries. And some of the bookings Gloria had in the diary as a done deal turned out to be only provisional. I had a couple of no-shows, and when I contacted them, they said they hadn't had confirmation, so they'd booked elsewhere.' He shrugged. 'It isn't all down to Gloria, though. We've had a few genuine cancellations – they're par for the course in this business.'

'Okay. Well, I'm here now and I intend to do something about that. We'll see what we can rescue for this year, fill a few gaps if we can, and it definitely won't be happening next year. As for this Thomson thing, I know bits of paper were Gloria's method of choice, but I'll search the e-mails just in case.'

He nodded, a resigned air about him that I didn't like.

I decided to risk a little probing. 'Have you heard from Gloria?'

He grunted. 'Haven't *spoken* to her. She e-mailed to say she was staying in the Kensington flat, which I already knew through you, when you told me Nathan had moved to London.'

'Ten years of marriage, and she sent you an *e-mail*?'

'I could remind *you* that you had a five-year relationship and only got a note, Emmy.'

'True. But we've spoken since. Or had the odd slanging match anyway. We had to, what with renting out the flat in Birmingham.'

'Hmmph.' He moved the antique blotter around on the desk, then a brass paperweight. 'I can't believe the two of them are shacked up together in *my* flat. It makes me sick to my stomach. It's bad enough, her running off with someone, but to use my own property . . . Although I don't suppose it's *my* flat any more, is it? Hasn't been since we got married.'

'Did she . . . Did she say anything about divorce in her e-mail?'

'No.' His tone was abrupt. 'And neither did I.'

That puzzled me. 'But a few weeks ago, you told me you wanted to know where you stood.'

'I *did*. But I think several weeks' absence and one short e-mail clarifies that on an emotional front from Gloria's point of view, don't you? As for the financial front, I'd rather not precipitate anything. If you hadn't noticed, it's peak season and I could do without inviting something I haven't time to deal with. Gloria's getting free use of the flat for now – as is your delightful ex-boyfriend – and she hasn't cleared out the joint bank account. As for everything else, I moved it all pretty sharpish, so if she wants more, she'll have to make it official. And I can put up with the trepidation of not knowing how and when, for now, compared with dealing with the actuality.'

I could understand that. No point in prodding a nest of vipers unless you had to. But I wasn't sure that was the full story. He looked so much healthier, but he had been a bit quiet since I'd been back. 'Do you miss her, Rupert?'

He thought about it, but then his face closed. He shrugged. 'No use crying over spilt milk, as they say. Life goes on, and we have a business to run.'

Understanding this was his signal that he would say no more on the subject, I stood. 'Right. Let me check the e-mails, and I'll let you know if I find anything.'

'Thanks, Emmy. But . . . airbeds?' He shook his head. 'Ah, well. At least you'll have plenty to tell Alain this evening.'

I smiled. Alain was Rupert's half-English, half-French, caramel-eyed accountant. A kiss we'd shared in the pouring rain had nothing whatsoever to do with my decision to move to France, of course, but that didn't stop me being disappointed that he was currently catching up with relatives near Paris. 'Not tonight. He has some family get-together.'

'Everything going all right between you two?'

Subtle as a brick. Since Rupert had decided we were made for each other, he'd taken playing matchmaker to a whole new level.

'Fine, thank you. Within its limitations.'

'Must be awkward for him,' Rupert muttered. 'Playing nicey nicey with his brother when the bastard ran off with his wife.'

'It was a long time ago. He's over it, he says – as far as you can get over something like that. He once told me he'd had a lucky escape. I gather Sabine is on the bossy side.'

Rupert snorted. 'Oh, and you're not?'

'Ah, well, he hasn't had a proper chance to find that out yet, has he?'

A search of the e-mails revealed a small string of correspondence between Gloria and Julia Cooper – filed in Miscellaneous as opposed to Reservations, in Gloria's usual, haphazard manner. There were a few tentative enquiries from Julia, one referring to phone calls that Gloria had clearly not deemed important enough to tell Rupert about, and a final one from Julia, long and involved, giving me both a fighting chance and a heart attack at the same time.

The good news was that Julia had booked all three *gîtes* for the middle two weeks of September – although from the looks of the names and dates, they would not necessarily be fully occupied the whole time – and then all four rooms in the guesthouse over varying dates in the middle of that fortnight. From the number of Thomsons, I assumed it was a family gathering of some kind. And the figure Julia confirmed she would pay for the privilege looked pretty generous to me, especially if we were struggling for bookings that month.

The bad news was that there was also a long list of requests and demands, which presumably made sense to Gloria at the time if they had been discussed on the phone, but which made far less sense to me than I would like. They ranged from buffet lunches (which I had never known Rupert to provide) to a cake (for what occasion, it wasn't made clear), a caterer (why would they need a caterer?) and then mention of the airbeds and travel cots with numbers to be confirmed . . .

Some of these guests would arrive in only two weeks' time, the bulk of them just a few days later, and yet I had no idea which of these demands Gloria had actioned – if any – and which were or weren't to be included in the price quoted.

Gloria's reply to Julia Cooper? *Thank you for your e-mail. No problem. All in hand.*

I looked at the date of her reply and my heart sank. It had been sent when Nathan and I were on holiday at *La Cour des Roses* – and when Gloria had had her hands full with other things. Namely Nathan.

When I showed Rupert what I'd found, his response was to run a hand across his stubbly beard. 'Damn.' He looked again at the reservations spreadsheet. 'We already have a booking at the guesthouse right in the middle of this. And one of the *gîtes* is occupied. I added them in after Gloria left. I had no idea that all this should have been blocked out.'

'You're not a mind reader, Rupert.' I straightened my spine. 'It's too late to do any more today – we have a guest meal to cook. But we need a division of labour tomorrow. I'll phone Julia Cooper in the morning to get a better picture of what Gloria's let us in for. You need to go through the den and the e-mails to ascertain whether Gloria set anything in motion. You'll know what to look for better than me. As for the double-booked guests, I'll have to contact them and explain we need to move them if possible – offer to pay any charges they'll incur changing their flights or ferries.' I winced. 'Do you want me to cancel my afternoon with Sophie tomorrow?'

Sophie – my new French girlfriend since my breakdown in her salon after Nathan's desertion – was desperate to catch up, and she had put aside her precious midweek closing day to take me somewhere nice.

'No. You haven't seen her for weeks. A few hours won't make any difference. But what are you going to say when Julia Cooper asks why you don't know any of this? Or if she asks you to confirm it's all underway?'

I made a face. 'Lie. And if necessary, grovel.'

As I concentrated on the jobs Rupert dared allow me to do in the kitchen – chopping, mixing; things that even I couldn't get wrong – I damped down panic as I thought about the downturn the day had taken. Geoffrey Turner's nakedness, Clare's temper, Gladys's arm, Geoffrey's attitude at my incompetence. Julia Cooper, double bookings, Gloria's administration skills (or lack thereof). Oh God. Geoffrey's imminent review. And to think I'd woken that morning full of the joys of spring – or rather, summer.

I needed this to work. All of this. I needed to ensure *La Cour des Roses* was not only the going concern it always had been, but that it could thrive enough for Rupert to pay me what he'd promised. When we'd discussed it, both of us were under the impression the place was on an even keel. The gaps I'd spotted since, and Rupert's admission that Gloria had been seriously mucking things up – Julia's call was confirmation of that, if we'd needed it – didn't fill me with confidence.

Even though I was living rent-free, my salary was only enough to get by and run my car. I was reliant on rent to cover the mortgage for the flat in Birmingham, and I needed to make a start at getting my own business off the ground for additional income. I had *some* savings to tide me over if that took a while, but they wouldn't last forever.

I thought about the way my work colleagues had looked at me askance when I'd told them I was passing over a promotion in order to move to France; my mother's worry that it might not work out for me; Nathan's response to the news. The idea that I might have to crawl back home with my tail between my legs was not one I relished.

But I'd never been one to crumble in the face of a challenge – even if days like today were not what I'd had in mind for my first week – and Rupert was relying on me to shoulder the workload and relieve his stress. Heaven help me.

Our three guest meals a week usually had a real dinner party feeling, but that night, unsurprisingly, the atmosphere was definitely on the chilly side. Gladys was pale and in pain, while Clare was over-solicitous, constantly making reference to the fall and shooting daggers at Geoffrey as she did so. He, in turn, became more morose as the evening wore on, while his wife looked like she would rather be anywhere else. By the end of the evening, our other two couples looked the same, despite the glory that was Rupert's baked camembert with French bread, chicken in a creamy mushroom-and-brandy sauce with steamed vegetables, then fruit salad with homemade brandy snaps. It was a relief when everyone decided on an early night.

'That was a nightmare!' I told Rupert as we cleared away.

'Ninety-five per cent of the time, it goes with a swing. Look on the bright side.'

'That's not easy when Geoffrey Turner's involved.'

'Emmy, you worry too much.'

But I continued to do just that as I trooped around the outside of the house to my room.

I loved the way Rupert had done it out for me. The walls were a restful, creamy yellow, and Rupert had eschewed his usual favouring of antiques – due to lack of time to source them – and gone with simple and modern wooden furniture. Even with a double bed, drawers, wardrobe and dressing table, there was space for a reading nook in the form of a small, upholstered chaise longue by the large window, which overlooked the small orchard. The rugs, cushions and bedding were various shades of calming green. The en suite was plain and white, but he'd added cheery towels and accessories, and I was well suited.

He'd even had a window converted into a door, so I could come and go as I pleased –the internal door led straight into Rupert's private lounge, something he couldn't do much about. But he'd had a lock fitted, for which we both held a key, and we'd agreed it would only be used in an emergency.

I undressed, brushed my teeth, and climbed between the crisp sheets, stretching as the cotton cooled my skin. With Geoffrey Turner and his potential review still preying on my mind, I reminded myself of one of my mother's favourite sayings: *What will be, will be.*

If the shriek woke me from a deep sleep, it must have been loud enough to wake the dead in the main part of the guesthouse.

I shot out of bed, slapped on the bedside light and glanced at the time. Two o'clock in the morning. What the . . . ?

Clattering next door suggested Rupert had also staggered out of bed. A bark from the dog. An admonishment to shut up and go back to bed from her master.

Throwing on a thin robe, I scrabbled in my drawer for the key to our adjoining door. As I raced into Rupert's lounge, I nearly broke my neck hurdling over the black Lab, camouflaged in the dark room. Repeating Rupert's instruction to go back to bed, I closed the door on her and took the stairs two at a time, my mind dreaming up all sorts of scenarios. Had someone seen a rat? Perhaps someone had had a heart attack?

There was quite a kerfuffle up on the landing. Everyone had come out of their rooms in varying states of undress, and Rupert was in the middle of the scrum, trying to ascertain what had happened. The commotion was centred around Gladys, and Clare was noisily lambasting Rupert and anyone who would listen.

'What kind of establishment do you run here that allows people to break into our room in the middle of the night, stark naked, eh? Look at my mother! Frightened the wits out of her!'

'But who broke in? Who was naked?' Rupert asked desperately.

'That *pervert* down the hall.' Clare pointed an accusatory finger at the Turners' closed door.

Taking a quick census, I realised the Turners were the only ones absent. Leaving Rupert to deal with the mêlée, I went along to their door and tapped quietly.

Mary opened it an inch.

'May I come in?'

She opened the door just wide enough to allow me through, as though she expected a riot of angry guests to barge in after me. I stepped in, glancing at the neat array of toiletries on the polished dark wood dressing table.

'Where's Geoffrey?'

Mary was tight-lipped. 'In the bathroom.'

'May I ask what happened?'

'He sleepwalks sometimes. Not very often,' she hastened to add, her eyes shifting quickly to the closed bathroom door.

'Isn't that rather a hazard in his occupation?'

'It only started a couple of weeks ago. He was put on some new medication and it's disrupted his sleeping patterns.' Her chin lifted defiantly. 'I always lock the door, just in case.'

'And tonight?'

Her shoulders slumped. 'I forgot. He must have wandered into the corridor, then thought he was coming back to bed and gone into the wrong room.'

I nodded. I couldn't imagine a well-known travel blogger would deliberately set out to expose himself to his fellow guests.

'The thing is, Mary, that might give someone a start, but it wouldn't be the end of the world if he wasn't . . .'

'I *know!*' she wailed. 'After you saw him at the window, I *told* him he should wear something to bed. But he doesn't like to overheat.'

I thought about Clare's temper overheating, and wondered why she had to have been allocated the room right next to Geoffrey's.

'I'll go and explain.'

Back in the corridor, Clare's face was pinched, her robe pulled tightly around her, her arms folded defensively across her bust.

Rupert was still trying to calm her down.

'There's a perfectly innocent explanation,' I told them. 'Apparently, Geoffrey sleepwalks sometimes . . .'

'His wife should lock him in, then. We'll certainly be locking our door from now on!'

'She usually does, but she forgot.'

'I don't believe in coincidence,' Clare said. 'Twice in one day? I don't think so. I want him out tomorrow, or we'll be taking this further, do you understand?'

At this, Gladys spoke up. 'Well, I for one have had enough excitement. Let's drop it for now and let these good people get some sleep, shall we? I'm sorry I woke you all.'

Everyone shuffled off. When they were all safely back in their rooms – the click of Gladys and Clare's lock ringing out loud and clear – Rupert and I made our way downstairs.

In his lounge, Rupert rubbed at his face. 'What a night!'

The dog came over to lean against him, seeking reassurance as to what all the fuss was about.

'Nothing for you to worry about, Gloria,' he told her.

She whined anyway.

'Great. Now she needs to pee. I'll let her out. You get some sleep, Emmy.'

Back in my room, I threw myself back into bed to contemplate what the hell I'd let myself in for. At least Geoffrey couldn't have the cheek to write a bad review after this. Could he? If only Clare hadn't been, well, *Clare*.

Lying on my side, I stared at my phone on the bedside table. It would have been so nice to talk to Alain right now. To see if he could stop me worrying and make me laugh. But I didn't think he'd appreciate a task like that at two thirty in the morning.

* * *

Unsurprisingly, everyone was rather bleary-eyed the next morning.

I took orders for hot drinks while Rupert over-compensated by being ridiculously cheery, whistling as he prepared eggs – laid by his own chickens – in whatever style his guests requested. One couple, however, was noticeably absent.

'Where are the Turners?' I whispered out of earshot of the others – and most especially out of earshot of Clare.

'Probably daren't show their faces. Not after Geoffrey showed everything else.'

'Not funny, Rupert.'

'They'll be waiting until the coast is clear.'

As the table emptied, I glanced at the wall clock. 'Should I go and see if they're all right?'

'Maybe they went out for breakfast, so they wouldn't have to face anyone.'

I went across to the window. No sign of their car in the courtyard. 'You're right. That must be it.'

'See? I told you not to worry.'

When we'd cleared everything away, I went upstairs to do my daily room check – make the beds, quick dust and sweep, check the flowers for wilting, wipe the bathroom over, lob bleach down the loo. Since I knew the Turners were already out, I started with theirs.

It was empty. Not a single possession.

I went back downstairs to tell Rupert.

He shook his head. 'That's a shame.'

'It's more than a shame, Rupert. Geoffrey's blog is read by thousands of people, and he's been belittled and driven from the place by a fellow guest.'

'Maybe he should try wearing some ruddy boxer shorts at night, then.'

'You're not taking this seriously!'

'I am, Emmy, and I know you feel responsible, because it was your idea to bring him here. But what happened had nothing to do with us. Maybe we should be grateful he left of his own accord, otherwise we'd have Clare on our backs. And maybe he should sort out his medication before his next port of call.'

Back upstairs, I stripped the bedding and cleaned the bathroom . . . but despite my efforts, there was an odd smell. I opened the windows, checked the drawers for left items, then opened the large antique wardrobe. The smell was much stronger in there. I sniffed and wrinkled my nose. It smelled of . . . Oh dear. Gingerly, I felt at the base. It had been wiped, but the wood was still damp.

I went back downstairs. 'Do you know how to get the smell of urine out of wood?'

Rupert spun around. '*What?*

'Geoffrey's sleepwalking was worse than we thought. He peed in the wardrobe.'

'What the hell for? There's a perfectly good en suite in there!'

'The door to which is next to the large wardrobe door.'

'No wonder they left! Have you mopped it out?'

'Looks like they did, but the smell has impregnated the wood. Any ideas?'

Rupert burst out laughing. 'No idea whatsoever. Maybe Madame Dupont will know.'

And so, when Madame Dupont arrived for her cleaning stint, I took her upstairs to show her the damp patch. Since my French didn't stretch to bodily functions yet, I resorted to pointing at the bathroom door, the word '*toilette*' and some crude miming of a Frankenstein-style sleepwalker, followed by a man whizzing. It did the trick.

'When are the next guests due?' she asked.

'Saturday.'

She patted my cheek. '*T'inquiète pas, Emie.*'

Ten minutes later, she had hung bunches of freshly cut lavender from the rail in the wardrobe – why hadn't I thought of that? – and placed a shallow tray of ground coffee in the base.

'To absorb the smell,' she explained.

It was a waste of good coffee, if you asked me. But, like a mind reader, she laughed and told me she'd found the stash of cheap stuff Gloria used to foist on the guests, but which Rupert or I wouldn't touch.

'Might as well be useful for something,' Madame Dupont pointed out.

I grinned, unsure as to whether she was referring to the coffee or Gloria.

CHAPTER THREE

Closeted away in the den, I steeled myself to phone Julia Cooper.

'Hello, Julia? Emmy Jamieson from *La Cour des Roses* here. I'm sorry to trouble you, and this is a little awkward, but I was looking into your booking for September and wondered if you wouldn't mind filling me in a little? I have your e-mails, but since I'm new here, I thought it sensible to double-check everything.'

'What about Mr Hunter?'

Urgh. 'He is aware of the booking, of course . . .' *Well, he is now.* '. . . but since Gloria's no longer here, we wouldn't like to think we might not have all the information we should have.' *Any would be good, actually.* 'So would you mind taking me through it all? Start at the beginning, and help me fill in any blanks?' *Of which there are many.*

A sharp intake of breath. 'Very well, but I hope there aren't going to be any problems, Emmy. I'm sure Mr Hunter knows all this, but in a nutshell, my parents – Frank and Sylvia Thomson – have their golden wedding anniversary in a few weeks' time. The family decided on a reunion and celebration over a long weekend, and we chose *La Cour des Roses* because of the jazz festival.'

'The jazz festival?'

'At Saint-Martin. My parents are *huge* jazz fans. They met at a jazz concert, and the festival is only a week or so before their actual anniversary.'

'Well, that sounds perfect,' I enthused. 'I'm *so* pleased you chose us for your special trip.'

'I hope the reservations aren't a problem? Everyone has flights and channel crossings booked. We even have one group coming from Australia.' Her voice hitched. 'This can't go wrong now, Emmy. It's taken me months to get everyone organised.'

'I'm sure,' I soothed, gritting my teeth and thinking about the double bookings. 'Looking at your e-mail, the guest room dates are clear, but I'm a little confused that you've booked all three *gîtes* for a fortnight, even though you said it's just a long weekend?'

'Gloria told me the *gîtes* run Saturday to Saturday, so to have them for our long weekend, I had to book them for a full fortnight. Some of the family are coming for just a few days – those who can't get much time off work or have older kids in school. Some are making a proper holiday out of it – my brother from Australia, for example. So those staying longest will be in the *gîtes,* the rest in the guesthouse.'

'And the airbeds?' I dared.

'You don't have quite enough accommodation, so Gloria said it would be fine to use airbeds. That won't be a problem, will it?'

'Ha. Ah, no, not at all, as long as your guests are willing. Now, the e-mail mentions a cake . . .'

'The anniversary cake. I assume Gloria already ordered it?'

'Of course . . . but as I intend to double-check *all* our arrangements, would you mind telling me what specifications you gave her?'

Another sigh. 'Big enough for all of us, but not too big – we don't want to transport any home. One layer only. Some element of gold for the anniversary. No cream – it upsets my mother's stomach. No nuts – one of the children has a nut allergy. Tasteful, not tacky. Gloria said she had that in hand.'

I wasn't sure 'tasteful, not tacky' was what Gloria did best, but I kept that to myself. 'And the caterer?'

'For the party on the Monday night, naturally.'

'I . . . see.' I was too busy scribbling furiously, and not concentrating hard enough on my acting skills.

Julia's voice became shrill. 'You really don't know anything about this, do you?'

Okay, bugger the acting. A little grovelling was in order. 'I'm so sorry, Julia, but it was Gloria who dealt with all the administrative tasks here . . .' *Like filing her nails.*

'Are you saying none of this is booked?'

And perhaps a little lying. 'No, not at all. Mr Hunter is looking into it and we're positive it's all been set in motion, but I just need to make sure that what you think is happening and what we think is happening match perfectly.' I stared at Rupert's teetering bookshelves, feeling that this conversation was in much the same state.

She sighed. 'Fine. The jazz festival at Saint-Martin runs from Friday evening to Sunday, so we'll be dipping in and out of it on those days. We're having the golden wedding anniversary party in the garden on the Monday night, before some of us go home on the Tuesday. Your caterers should be booked for that, but if you're double-checking, we requested upmarket French party and finger food, and waiting staff – one to circulate with food, another at the bar. Gloria said *La Cour des Roses* would provide all the drinks, including champagne for the speeches.' A hint of suspicion crept into her voice. 'Since, as you say, that's already booked, I'd like to see a confirmed menu from your caterers as soon as possible.'

'I'll get Rupert onto it. And the buffet lunches . . . ?'

Another tut. 'Naturally, you will be providing breakfast for the guests in the house. But Gloria said you'd provide lunch for the house guests for the three days of the jazz festival, since we'll be coming and going and won't be able to have any evening meals. That way, we can eat before we set off, and grab a snack at the festival in the evenings.'

'Well, Julia, that all sounds in order.' *Like hell.* 'I'll speak to Mr Hunter and send you a confirmation e-mail within the next day or two, laying out everything the way we understand it, for both our peace of minds.' I couldn't bring myself to ask the burning question I had in mind. What did the figure on that e-mail relate to? Who was paying for all this?

But it seemed Julia had the same thing on *her* mind. 'When you do, Emmy, I would be grateful if you could also send an estimate for the caterer and the cake. It'll help me plan ahead. The rest *is* included in the price I agreed with Gloria. I hope that's not going to change.' A definite warning tone.

'We wouldn't dream of it. We're so looking forward to having you here, and we'll do everything in our power to make it an occasion to remember.'

'I appreciate it. Although I can't say I appreciate having to explain it all again.'

'I know, and I apologise, but we want to get it right for you. I'll speak to you soon.'

I flung the phone on the desk and flopped my head back, my mind reeling and my hands shaking slightly. This was so much bigger than I'd imagined. I couldn't *believe* Gloria had agreed to it all and not even bothered telling Rupert. It said a great deal about the state of their marriage before she left.

I found him in the kitchen, rubbing butter into flour – for shortbread, my taste buds hoped – and humming obliviously. The sun was bright through the open windows, warming the stone floor and sparkling on the wine glasses on the shelf. I made sure he was sitting down before I broke the happy news. His reaction was the same as mine, only with more inventive expletives.

'We need to decide who's doing what,' I said firmly.

'I thought you were going out with Sophie soon?'

'I have half an hour.'

His face fell.

Once I'd agreed to sort the cake, extra bedding, and all future communications with Julia, and bullied Rupert into all food-related tasks and some investigative work finding out where Gloria had got to with everything, I took a deep breath. 'Dare I ask about health and safety regulations, with regard to airbeds cluttering up floors in rooms?'

'You leave all that to me, Emmy.' By which he meant he was ignoring them and hoping for the best.

'Hmm.' I raised my eyebrows at him.

A knock at the patio doors.

'Sophie!' Delighted, I rushed over to give her a hug.

'*Bienvenue*, Emmy. I'm *so* happy you decided to come to France.' She kissed me and then Rupert on both cheeks. 'I'm a little early. I hope you don't mind?' She smiled, her dimples flashing in her pretty face, her hair in its perfect wavy blonde bob.

'Not at all,' Rupert reassured her. 'Emmy was about to submit me to more managerial misery and I didn't fancy it.'

At the sound of a new voice, the dog deserted her basket in the hall and came bounding through to inspect the visitor.

'And who is this?' Sophie asked, delighted at the effusive welcome.

'This is Gloria, Rupert's new acquisition.'

'I . . . see. She's lovely.' She fussed with the dog, then looked up at Rupert. 'I was hoping to take Emmy to Chenonceau today, but it's quite a drive, so we'd be back late. Is that a problem?'

'Not at all. Take her away for as long as you like.' He gave me a pointed glare. 'I have plenty to be getting on with. Off you go, the pair of you.'

I grabbed my bag and followed Sophie to her car.

The minute we were inside, she let out a disbelieving laugh. 'He called his *dog* after his *wife*?'

I held up my hands in a 'what can you do?' gesture.

She glanced at me sideways as we set off. 'You look tired. Is everything all right?'

I forced a smile, and spent most of the journey telling her about Geoffrey Turner and Julia Cooper. She laughed and sympathised in equal measure, somehow making the load seem so much lighter.

'Well, at least you won't be bored for your first few weeks here,' she pointed out.

'That's true.' I decided it was time to change the subject. 'So, where are you taking me?'

'You hardly did any sightseeing when you were here on holiday, and that was a terrible shame, so I decided it was time you visited a *château*. Chenonceau is my favourite.'

When we got there and parked, she dragged a rucksack out of the boot. 'Lunch,' she explained. 'There's a picnic area over there. I presume you haven't eaten yet?'

Startled, I glanced at my watch. It was already early afternoon. I'd been so busy, I hadn't noticed. 'You are so thoughtful. I'm starving!'

Laughing, she led me to a picnic bench under a tree, the car park hidden from sight by a hedge, and took out a baguette, cheese, tomatoes, traditional black peppercorn *saucisson* and nectarines. Simple fare, but it tasted so good, sitting in the shade with a friend and watching the other tourists.

'You look incredible, as usual,' I told her. 'Did you have a good holiday?'

'It was okay. A family visit more than a holiday, and it meant spending two weeks with my parents.' She made a face. 'But my cousins have a villa by the sea, so I can't complain.'

'I should think not! No holiday flings?'

'Ha! With my parents around? Hardly!' She pouted. It only made her look sexier than ever. 'I don't seem to be able to meet anybody that . . .' She stopped, her pretty brow creasing. 'Something about ships.'

I wracked my brain. 'Anyone that floats your boat?'

'That's it! In my salon, I only see women. And my friends are nearly all in couples now. It feels awkward sometimes, still being single. You won't believe who I've been seeing a lot of, in the absence of available men.'

I leaned forward, agog. 'Who?'

'Ellie Fielding.'

'*What?*'

'She came to have her hair cut at my salon after we met at Rupert's when you were here last time, and we got on so well. Since she's only over the road in town, we started to have coffee sometimes in our lunch break.'

'Really?' I wasn't sure what Sophie had in common with a middle-aged English estate agent. I'd only met Ellie a couple of times and found her a little scary, although I had warmed to her by the end of my stay.

'We should get together, the three of us,' Sophie went on. 'She's fun, I promise.'

When we'd put Sophie's rucksack back in the car, we paid at the entrance and began to walk up the long approach to the *château*, lined with trees, tall and straight like sentries. I felt a sense of anticipation I hadn't had since I was a kid, when we were going somewhere and I just *knew* it was going to be good.

Past two stone sphinxes guarding either side of the path, the grounds opened out onto an area of manicured lawns and perfectly pruned trees. When we reached a long, single-storey white stone building with tables and smart parasols outside, Sophie asked, 'Quick coffee?'

I was anxious to see the *château* – I could see glimpses of its white walls and grey turrets – but I was equally anxious to sit here in this perfect spot. 'Isn't it getting late? Shouldn't we get on?'

Sophie laughed. 'You English and your boring opening hours. We are in France, Emmy, and it is August. The castle is open into the evening. Don't worry.'

She went in to fetch coffee while I sat at a table watching little birds hop about snatching crumbs, and gazed out across the lawns, smooth as bowling greens.

'This was once the stables,' Sophie explained when she came back and caught me studying the building.

'Crikey. Posh stables! How old is the *château*?'

'I think it was built in the early 1500s. It is known as the "*Château des Dames*" because three women had it built and added to it over the years. And during the revolution it was protected by a woman too. She saved the chapel by turning it into a store for wood.'

'My mother would like all that.'

'Is she a feminist?'

'Oh, she'd hate to be labelled, but she believes in independence, and she takes no nonsense from anyone, believe me.'

'What did she say about you coming to France?'

'She thinks I'm very brave.' I made a face. 'After the past couple of days, I think she means foolhardy.'

'You can only do your best, Emmy. These problems at *La Cour des Roses* – they are not your fault.'

'I know. But it's my job to fix them.'

She frowned. 'I know you want to do well, to show Rupert what you can do, but . . .'

'It's not just a matter of showing Rupert. I do want to do my best for *La Cour des Roses* – that benefits both of us – but it's more than that. If I can build up a reputation locally as someone who has a good eye for what's needed, for fixing problems and improving things, that might help with my own business eventually.'

'What are you planning?'

'Initially, an online holiday letting agency for *gîtes* in the area. But once I'm settled and my French has improved, I'd be happy to use my marketing experience to work on some kind of freelance basis.'

'Aren't there a lot of accommodation agencies already?'

'Yes – but mine will be specialised to this area only. I spoke to a company in the UK who do something similar, and they stand out because they insist on quality over quantity. Amazing photos, impressive blurbs. Loads of local information and expertise. They personally inspect every property, and they use a professional photographer.'

'Sounds expensive.'

'Yes, but they're doing well. There are studies showing that too much choice is very stressful. So when you use a site that offers you hundreds of properties, it's like finding a needle in a haystack. And not every property owner is as honest as they might be in their descriptions. With mine, people will book something, knowing I wouldn't list it if I wouldn't stay there myself. I want to stand out from the crowd, and I want to get it right. I've spoken to my brother, Nick, and he's working on the website for me. He's not a website specialist, but he *is* a computer genius. Makes a fortune in London. He's offered me his services for free, bless him.'

Sophie raised her coffee cup. 'That's lucky!' She took a sip.

'It certainly is. So it's just a question of getting that going, writing tourist info for the site . . . and finding clients.'

Sophie nodded. 'How will you do that?'

I smiled, taking in the perfect blue sky with its dreamy wisps of white cloud. 'Initially, I intend to take advantage of my first client to tout for me. Rupert knows every man and his uncle out here.'

Sophie bounced in her seat. 'And Ellie! I bet she could help you. I *told* you we should get together with her!'

'Maybe you're right.'

We finished our coffee and set off towards the *château*. I glimpsed formal gardens, but my focus was on the building itself – and oh my, what a building. It didn't take long to work out why this was Sophie's favourite. Elegant architecture of pale stone, grey roof . . . and it extended all the way across the River Cher upon perfect arches. I gasped.

'Gorgeous, isn't it?' Sophie smiled. 'We'll get a better view from the gardens, but we should do the interior while it's so hot out here.'

A long hall of cream stone, a guards' room lined with tapestries, the chapel she'd told me about, Louis XIV's living room with heavy gilt-framed portraits. An imposing white staircase led to bedrooms filled with brocade and tapestries.

'These flowers are spectacular,' I said to Sophie, pointing to a huge antique urn of large, white lilies, contrasting gorgeously against the green foliage. There had been an opulent fresh flower arrangement in almost every room, something I found surprising and beautiful. I peered closer. 'I can't believe they're all real. It must cost them a fortune!'

Sophie laughed. 'We are in a French *château*, Emmy. It is all about fine living and riches!'

We went all the way down the narrow stairs into the kitchens, with their heavy wooden dressers and walls festooned with copper pans. The camera on my phone had never worked so hard in its life.

It was all impressive, but it was the long gallery that really took my breath away. Once a ballroom, it spanned the length of the *château* across the river, its ceiling wooden and its floor laid with black and white tiles. Potted trees stood like sentries in recesses between arched windows that looked out over the river.

I could have spent all day at those windows, gazing at the view and catching the breeze, but we reluctantly left it behind to explore the gardens. Perfect lawns, ornamental trees, climbing roses, flowerbeds of pinks, purples and white held in their patterns by miniature hedges . . . I'd never been a fan of formal gardens, but I had to admit that these were something to admire.

Sophie gave me a nudge as we walked. 'So, are you going out with that handsome accountant of mine now?'

'Not yet. He's away visiting family, so we're still at the phone-call stage.'

'Did you speak to him much when you were back in England?'

'Not at first. He didn't want to influence my decision.'

Sophie smirked. 'I hope you didn't spoil his good deed by telling him you'd already been influenced?'

I laughed. 'No. But then Rupert got heavy-handed with his persuasion techniques, and Alain felt the need to intervene and offer advice, so we began to e-mail and phone.'

'It's a shame he was away when you came back.'

I sipped water from a bottle, considering. 'Maybe it's not a bad thing. It gives me a chance to get settled first.'

'Gives you a chance to try phone sex, too. Before you move on to the real thing.'

'We don't know each other well enough for that yet!'

She gave me a cheeky grin. 'That's why it could be fun.'

I drifted for a moment as my mind pondered the possibilities, and my pulse pepped up the pace. Hmm . . .

'What are you thinking about?' she asked me knowingly.

I sighed. 'He suggested an online date tonight, since we can't have a real one yet. I'm nervous, I suppose. I've got used to the distance of the phone.'

'Emmy. You once had dinner with him. You spent a day at the zoo with him. You kissed him.'

I melted a little at the memory. 'I know. But that was weeks ago. What if it's not the same? That connection we felt. What if it isn't there any more?'

'Oh, it'll be there. I believe in you two.'

I barked out a laugh. 'That's because you're a hopeless romantic!'

'I know. I can't help it. It's a curse.'

From the far end of the gardens, our view looking back at the *château* was captivating, not least because the entire structure was reflected in a mirror image on the surface of the river, its opposite bank lush with trees.

'Thank you for bringing me here,' I told her. 'It's so beautiful.'

'You're welcome. I've had a wonderful day.'

On the drive home, she asked me, 'Will you write about Chenonceau? For your website?'

'Yes. The idea is to give my own impression of a place, then provide relevant links.' I smiled. At least something had gone well today.

It was early evening by the time we got back, and I was feeling sleepy from the car ride, but I still had my online 'date' with Alain ahead.

I ate a light supper, showered to wake myself up, and then, feeling ridiculous, I chose a flattering top and carefully applied make-up, although I now had an established tan, so I didn't need much. It might not be a proper date, but there was no point in scaring the poor bloke off across the airwaves.

Good job he wasn't going to see my baggy jim-jam bottoms with the dodgy elastic.

As I waited for him to appear on my laptop screen, nerves fluttering like butterfly wings in my stomach, I sent a silent thank you to Sophie. My day at Chenonceau meant that at least I would have plenty to talk about. Although there was certainly no shortage of other topics after the past couple of days.

When Alain's handsome face came into view and I saw the way it lit up at the sight of mine – his smile curving his lips and reaching his warm brown eyes, crinkling the laugh lines there – the fluttering in my stomach settled into a pleasant hum.

'Hi.'

'Hi yourself.'

We stayed like that for a long moment, grinning inanely at each other.

'How was your family thing last night?' I finally asked him.

'Fine. There were a lot of us there. Cousins, aunts, uncles. It's nice to see them again.'

I thought about what Rupert had said yesterday. 'But it must be awkward for you?'

'I think it's more awkward for them. They greet Adrien and Sabine and the kids, make a huge fuss of them, then realise I'm there on my own – again – and that's when they remember *why* I'm on my own. I get forced bonhomie or awkward "Still single, Alain?" questions for a while, but after several glasses of wine, everyone relaxes. I'm used to it.'

'I'm surprised you don't take someone with you, just to shut them up.'

'I've thought about it, but there's enough play-acting in the family.' He smiled. 'Maybe next time, I can do that and be genuine about it.'

My pulse raced. That slight accent of his was enough to make me want to accompany him anywhere he chose. 'Maybe.'

'What have you been up to?'

I laughed. 'Honestly, Alain, you won't believe it!' I told him about Geoffrey's shenanigans, imitating Clare's shrill voice and crinkling my nose at the smell in the wardrobe.

'Well, there's a baptism of fire in guesthouse management for you.' His amusement turned to a frown. 'But you're worried about what he might say in his review?'

I loved him for that insight – that he understood the importance of what had happened, instead of dismissing it like Rupert. I loved that he understood its significance to me personally.

'Rupert says he's hardly likely to broadcast it, but I'm worried he might pick up on the other stuff. Being harangued by another guest. Me not knowing the emergency number.'

'Cut yourself some slack, Emmy. You'd barely just arrived! And Rupert could be right – he might not review at all.'

'But if he does, and it's crap, it'll be my fault.'

Alain gave me a disparaging look. 'What, for trying to do your job by using your contacts in a positive way to improve Rupert's business?'

Oh, I could do with a hug from this man right now.

'No. For inviting a naked blogger.'

We both burst into laughter, and I thought, if we could laugh like this with miles between us, what would we be like when we were together?

'You look beautiful tonight,' he told me. 'I wish I was there with you instead of huddled in my old bedroom here. Alternatively, I wish you were huddled in my old bedroom here with me.'

Behind him I could see white walls, shelves crowded with books and a faded poster of a man leaning back as he blew into a saxophone. His bed was covered with a blue throw and looked in need of a little rumpling, if you asked me.

'Me, too.'

His lips twitched. 'Won't be long now.' His expression became serious. 'I can't wait to see you, Emmy.'

A fuzzy feeling of anticipation flooded my veins. 'Change the subject. To something that doesn't make me want to leap in the car and drive to Paris.'

'Okay. Is the guesthouse busy?'

'Not as busy as it should be.'

He frowned. As Rupert's accountant, that was bound to concern him. 'What do you mean?'

I told him about Julia Cooper and Gloria's utter lack of interest.

He shook his head. 'That bloody woman!'

'I've said worse today, believe me.'

He looked at me for a long moment. 'You can do it, Emmy.'

How did he *do* that? How did he know exactly when I was having a crisis of confidence? 'Yeah. We'll get through it. The amount they're paying seems generous, so it'll be worth it, assuming I don't lose the guests that have been double-booked.'

'I'm sure you can be persuasive, when you want to be.' He gave me a long look that made my stomach flip. 'And, you know, that jazz festival is pretty popular. If this works out, maybe you could use it next year to attract other jazz enthusiasts.'

'Oh? Have you ever been to it?'

'Quite a few times.' He seemed about to say something else, but changed his mind.

'Do you like jazz, then?'

He laughed, a sound that wrapped around me like soft velvet. 'I wouldn't attend a jazz festival if I didn't, would I? How about you?'

'I can honestly say I know nothing about it.'

'Maybe that's an area I can educate you in some time.'

I stared at my screen. That man could educate me in *anything*. 'Maybe.' Feeling a little hot under the collar, I aimed for safer ground. 'Sophie took me to Chenonceau today.'

'Did you love it?'

I broke into a wide smile. 'What's not to love?'

'There are so many places I haven't been to for ages. It would be great to revisit them with you.'

We both fell quiet as we contemplated the possibilities ahead.

'When are you due back?' I broke the silence.

'Ten days yet.' He sighed. 'I'm sorry I was away when you arrived.'

'Me too. But it'll be great to see you when you do get home.'

'I'll speak to you soon. Try not to worry about everything.' He blew me a kiss.

I stared at the blank laptop screen for a few long moments after he'd gone.

CHAPTER FOUR

I woke the next morning full of new hope. After my 'date' with Alain, I'd curled up with my laptop on the chaise longue in the soft glow from the standard lamp and written up my impressions of Chenonceau, choosing a few photos to go with it. I liked the idea of giving my own account of a place and what I'd particularly liked about it. I could leave all the facts and figures and opening times to the official sites that already did it so well, by providing links to them. Why reinvent the wheel? My job was to entice people to the Loire region to stay in one of the properties I featured.

It occurred to me that there was nothing to stop me writing about my day at the zoo with Alain weeks ago (minus the personal interaction) when I got chance, and I already knew Pierre-la-Fontaine quite well.

It seemed that, between them, Alain and Sophie had unwittingly done a pretty good job yesterday, convincing me I'd made the right decision by moving out here. I already had three good friends in Rupert, Sophie and Alain . . . and the potential of more with Alain. There were wonderful places to visit, I had my business to work on, and although *La Cour des Roses* was turning out to be more of a challenge than I'd anticipated, at least I wouldn't get bored.

My phone pinged with a text as I started on breakfast. It was from Alain.

Hope you got some beauty sleep (not that you need any) and that you have a good day today. I enjoyed 'seeing' you last night. Can we do it again tomorrow?

I texted back a big, fat *Yes*.

To add to my good mood, Clare and Gladys were leaving today. Clare had sported a smug expression ever since Geoffrey and Mary's unexpected departure the day before, whilst Gladys's sparkle had continued to wilt. I didn't expect to see them again.

As for the other couple who were leaving, would they be back? Would they recommend us? A lot of Rupert's bookings were down to repeat business and word of mouth, and I didn't want to lose that.

I was clearing up when Ryan poked his head around the patio door. 'Emmy, hi!' When I went across to him, he enveloped me in a friendly hug. 'Welcome back!'

'Thanks. How are you?'

'Fine. Busy time of year. Everything insists on growing at a ridiculous rate. I can barely keep up with it. How do you like your room?'

'I love it. Thank you.' It was Ryan who Rupert had strong-armed into doing the work on it. 'It must have nearly killed you, doing that on top of all your gardening jobs!'

Ryan leaned against the doorframe, a clear blue sky behind him, a light breeze ruffling his blonde hair. 'Rupert was obsessed with getting it done quickly. I didn't want him to stress. He . . . He told me about his angina.'

'Well, thank you. For my room, and for looking out for Rupert.'

'You're welcome.' His lips twitched. 'Rupert tells me you're currently involved long-distance with a certain accountant?'

'That man is *such* a gossip!'

Ryan grinned. 'Alain's a decent bloke, Emmy – and God knows, you deserve one, after that idiot, Nathan.'

I smiled as I watched him head off to his green-fingered jobs. Our few days of romping after Nathan deserted me had been therapeutic at the time – but at that point, I'd assumed I was unlikely to see him again. I'd been worried about things being awkward between us when I came back, but I'd clearly been worrying for nothing. It seemed our friendship was intact, and as casually comfortable as I could wish for it to be.

I went to find Rupert. He was in the den, a coffee at hand as he riffled through papers on the desk, the breeze from the window occasionally trying to lift them off altogether and forcing him to use the brass paperweight.

'Did you have a good day with Sophie yesterday?' he asked.

'Fabulous. It's an amazing place.'

'Yes, it is. You should make sure you get out and about a bit.'

I nodded my wholehearted agreement, then laughed. 'Did you know that Sophie and Ellie have become friendly lately? It sounds like they're as thick as thieves.'

'Really? I wouldn't have imagined it, I must admit.'

'You'd think they'd be such opposites.'

'Maybe that's why they get on – they complement each other, bringing different sides to the friendship. Although that theory didn't work out with Ellie and Gloria. They started opposites and stayed opposites.'

'Ellie and *Gloria*?'

'Indeed. We got to know Ellie through buying this place, and as you can imagine, she was helpful with all sorts of practical advice. Ellie's only a few years older than Gloria, so Gloria homed in on her as a potential best mate. But after a year or so, they stopped meeting up – although we still had mutual social circles. I was sorry it didn't work out.'

'Oh? Why?'

He chuckled, sipping at his coffee, then blotting a drip on the desk with a loose receipt. 'I was hoping Ellie's no-nonsense approach would be a good influence on Gloria, but it was not to be.'

'Hmm. Shame.' *Doubt Ellie sees it that way, though.* 'Any joy on the Thomson front yesterday?'

'As far as I can tell, Gloria hadn't done anything about anything.' He gave me a direct look. 'I think she didn't realise what it entailed when she took the booking. And by the time she did, Nathan was here and . . . Well, I'll contact some caterers today. At least it's for a Monday night. I don't think we'd have stood a chance at such short notice if it was on a Friday or Saturday.'

'Okay. I'll send an e-mail to Julia, and I'll see what I can do about the double bookings.'

Rupert made a face. 'Good luck.'

Luck was half on my side. One set of guests was initially irate – naturally enough – but because they were retired, they were flexible and willing to alter their crossings by a few days at our cost. The other set were livid, tied in to the dates they had booked off work, and would be taking their custom elsewhere. I tried offering a compensatory discount if they booked with us next year, but it was clear from the conversation that they had no intention of ever booking with us again.

Feeling sick at heart but unable to help myself, I checked Geoffrey Turner's blog for anything damaging. Nothing . . . yet. The suspense was killing me.

When I came to e-mail Julia, I noticed she'd used a business e-mail address, and it occurred to me I might be better armed to fight the good fight if I knew more about her, so I did a little nosing around on the internet. *Very* interesting. Julia Cooper ran a business that specialised in organising residential leisure courses; painting, crafting, writing, cooking – you name it, they could find you a course to attend.

My initial reaction was to be daunted. It meant that Julia Cooper would be exacting, critical, demanding . . . I stared at my screen, tapping a pencil against my lips. Hmm. That would be one way of filling gaps in low season at *La Cour des Roses* next year, wouldn't it? And it certainly wouldn't do any harm to ensure that Julia's booking ran as smoothly as possible after its rocky start; impress her with the location and accommodation and hospitable hosts. Food for thought, anyway. I would have to make a few changes around here, to make sure *La Cour des Roses* was the best it could be in the time available before the Thomsons landed.

I was upstairs in the middle of my daily room check when Pippa came haring along the landing in a bikini as though her life depended on it.

'What's the matter?' I asked her with some alarm.

'It's out on the roof terrace!'

'What's out on the roof terrace?'

'A dead bird! I went to sunbathe, and there it was.'

'Oh. Er. Okay.' Maybe she had a bird phobia? 'I'll come and move it for you.'

She shuddered. 'Thank you. I . . . I'll go out on the patio instead.'

Shaking my head, I went along to the end of the landing, where the door opened onto the roof terrace on top of Rupert's private single-storey extension. In the doorway, I hesitated. This was the one place I hadn't yet surveyed with improvements in mind. I hadn't been out there since the fateful night I'd caught Nathan and Gloria at it like bunnies.

Nothing had changed. The view across the countryside was still spectacular. The tiles still absorbed the sun so that they warmed your feet through the soles of your sandals. There were pots of flowers – presumably tended by Ryan, since I suspected Rupert no longer ventured up there, for the same reason as me – and an old wrought-iron table. The sun loungers lounged in their usual spot.

I squeezed my eyes tightly shut, wishing away an image of Nathan and Gloria laid out on the nearest one. Crumpled clothing and murmurs of illicit lust.

When I opened them again, I saw the source of Pippa's misery. A large bird – possibly once a pigeon, but no longer recognisable – was spread across the tiles in a mass of feathers and bones and blood and guts. Perhaps it had fallen foul to a bird of prey of some kind? A bird of prey with no table manners, that was for sure.

Feeling sick, I went to fetch rubber gloves, newspaper and something to scrape off the remains, then brought up a bucket of soapy water to wash down the tiles. The experience did nothing to improve my opinion of that roof terrace at all.

When I got back downstairs, Madame Dupont was pressing bedlinen in Rupert's private lounge, where he kept his super-duper industrial-looking steam machine. As I ferried the newly pressed items upstairs to the gigantic wooden *armoire* up on the landing, I wondered why all the clean linen was stored up there. It was hardly convenient for the *gîtes*.

'Madame Dupont, why do we keep the linen for the *gîtes* upstairs?' I asked her when I went to collect another armful.

'Perhaps Madame Hunter thought my poor old legs needed the exercise.'

'Well, I don't think it's very . . .' I wanted to say sensible, but didn't know the word. I settled for 'very good.'

'But there is nowhere else, *Emie*. There is not enough space in the *gîtes*.'

'Hmm.' Out in the hall, I pointed to a large wooden bench chest. 'What's in there?' I opened it and rooted around. I didn't know the French word for 'old tat' but when I held up a broken flip-flop and a doormat with a large hole in the middle, my message was clear enough. 'It's not near the *gîtes*, but it would save you climbing the stairs if we had some up there and some in here. What do you think?'

She patted my arm. 'I think you are very thoughtful, *Emie*.'

I emptied the chest out onto the hall floor, made an executive decision about its evicted contents – bin, bin or bin – and lined it with a clean sheet. When she'd finished with the pressing machine, we both went upstairs to pull everything out of the armoire in an untidy heap, ready to divide it up.

Something crackled at the back, and I tugged out a polythene clothing bag.

I gasped. Could it be . . . Gloria's wedding dress? And if so, was *this* how much sentimentality she felt for it, to leave it crumpled and musty at the back of a cupboard?

Exchanging a glance with Madame Dupont, I pulled it out of the polythene and hooked it over the cupboard door. It was tasteful, understated and clingingly skinny. A pale coffee colour, silky soft, no fuss.

Staring at its soft folds, I wondered what I would have chosen if Nathan had proposed, but I stopped that train of thought as soon as it started. If we *had* got married, no doubt my wedding dress would also be languishing at the back of a cupboard as our relationship deteriorated and finally imploded.

'It's very beautiful,' I murmured. So beautiful that even I had to admit that Gloria must have looked spectacular in it.

Madame Dupont harrumphed. 'It is a shame the lady who wore it was not beautiful in here.' She placed a hand over her heart.

'What should I do with it?'

'You must show Monsieur Hunter, *Emie*. Ask him.' She glanced at her watch. 'I will help you put all this away, but then I must go.'

I gave her a talk-about-rats-leaving-a-sinking-ship look, but she ignored me and set off downstairs with an armful of sheets for the hall chest.

Once she'd scuttled home, I went to find Rupert. He was in the garden playing with the dog, who seemed to have an endless capacity for ball retrieval, as did her master.

'Rupert. Have you got a minute?'

Over they trotted, a man and his dog, already inseparable. I gestured for him to follow me upstairs, pleased to see that the canine half of the duo waited patiently in the hall.

'I found this. What do you want to do with it?'

A heavy silence surrounded us as Rupert stared at the dress. He reached out to touch it, but changed his mind and drew his hand back. 'Gloria looked stunning in this.'

'I can imagine.' I waited politely as he drifted off into his memories.

It lasted all of sixty seconds. 'No use to either of us now, though, is it?' He unhooked it and took it downstairs, leaving me to follow.

'What will you do with it?'

When he turned, I was relieved to see a twinkle in his eye. 'Ceremonial burning? Shredding? We could take a pair of scissors to it each – you have as much right as I do, I reckon.'

'That's a gorgeous dress, Rupert. I couldn't do that.'

'I'll stick it in the back of my wardrobe for now. It'll give it a change of scene. Got a minute?'

I followed him into his lounge, where he flung the dress across the sofa. Crossing to the bookshelf, he plucked out a cream photograph album, opened it and handed it across to me.

Gloria on her wedding day. She *had* looked stunning. The dress accentuated her skinny frame, and she had been in her mid-thirties then, ten years younger than when I'd met her. Her hair was still bleached blonde, but in a trendy, choppy cut, with a simple headdress of coffee-and-cream rosebuds. No flounce, just utter class.

'I can see why you fell for her,' I said gently, then turned the page to a photo of the two of them. '*And* her for you. You scrubbed up pretty nicely for a middle-aged duffer. How old were you? Fifty?'

'Hmmph. Fifty and foolish.'

'Yes, well, hindsight's a wonderful thing.' I handed back the album. 'How about lunch?'

We raided the fridge for cheese, fat olives and plum tomatoes, and had them with the ubiquitous French bread, enjoying the airy cool of the kitchen. So far, I'd resisted having a glass of wine with lunch – I suspected it could be a slippery slope – but after the wedding dress episode, I decided to make an exception. Rupert settled for sparkling water. He seemed to have cut back a bit on his drinking lately, and I was grateful – for the sake of my liver as well as his.

'Could try selling it online,' Rupert mused.

'Well, it's not *specifically* a wedding dress. It could be a bridesmaid dress or an evening dress, but . . .' I busied myself with slicing a peach.

'Spit it out, Emmy.'

'What if Gloria wants it back?'

Rupert spluttered, spraying me with breadcrumbs. 'Emmy. When my wife walked out with your spineless boyfriend, she took every last thing of value that she could fit into that sports car of hers. Jewellery, designer dresses, the lot. What she left behind, I assume she didn't want. If she thought so little of our wedding that she left that dress stuffed in the back of a *cupboard . . .*'

'I'm sorry. That she did that.'

He shrugged, his anger spent. 'She built up a lot of resentment the last few years, and some of the blame for that has to lie with me. We were happy at first, flitting between London and Majorca. The rot only set in with *La Cour des Roses.*'

I looked around at my new home: paradise. 'She never liked it here?'

'I think she only went along with it because she could see that I was getting bored and needed something to occupy me.

She once told me she'd assumed it would be temporary. That the novelty would wear off.'

'But it didn't.'

Rupert shook his head, tearing off a great hunk of bread. 'No. And I began to make good friends here.'

'But Gloria didn't?'

'No. She tried, but the kind of people we were mixing with are the kind of people who have no other side to them, who don't like pretence.'

I nodded as I thought about the people I'd met last time I was here - Ellie, ageing hippie photographer Bob, Alain, laid-back Ryan, loveable old Jonathan. I couldn't imagine any of them meshing with Gloria in any meaningful way.

'Gloria has spent her life putting on a front,' Rupert went on. 'For customers at the restaurant she managed, putting a brave face on things when her first marriage failed.' He leaned back and shook his head. 'When we bought this place, I hoped she would relax and realise there are good things in life that don't involve spending money.' He gestured around us and towards the open patio doors to the lawn, where colourful blooms burst from every flowerbed. 'But for her it was just another excuse to put on a front as mistress of the house.' He sighed. 'I don't think anyone seriously *dis*liked her – not until her spectacular departure, anyway – but they didn't love her. She was all sweetness and light when she first met people, so by the time they got to know us both, they put up with her for my sake, I think. Jonathan's a prime example. The reason we started to meet in town on market day is because he didn't want to bump into Gloria here. When she was away in London or Paris, I couldn't budge him from lounging around in the garden with a beer or two.'

I thought about what he'd said before, about Gloria trying – and failing – to make friends with Ellie. 'Do you think she might have been lonely?'

'Maybe. And I was complacent enough to believe that our marriage was enough for her.' He gave me a direct look. 'I was shocked when she went, but I wasn't surprised. Does that make sense?'

'I think so.'

I didn't know what to say next, and when the telephone rang, I answered it with relief.

'Emmy? Julia Cooper here.'

'Good afternoon, Julia. How can I help?'

Gathering who it was, Rupert scuttled off, grabbing the full bag out of the bin on the way as a valid excuse, and left me to it. Coward.

'Thank you for your e-mail this morning,' Julia said. 'But as I was reading it, I realised there was no mention of the tent and the caravans.'

Thank God this wasn't a video call. My face must have been quite a picture. 'Tent? Caravans?'

'Indeed. Didn't you . . . Didn't you know about them?'

'I'm so sorry, but no. I don't remember seeing anything on your e-mails.' *Not that it's my fault you didn't mention them when I asked you to go over all the details.* When the silence stretched awkwardly between us, I decided it was time to be semi-honest and hope that Rupert would forgive me. 'I'm afraid relations were a little strained before Gloria left *La Cour des Roses*, and not all information was properly shared. I apologise that it's having this impact on you. But I would be grateful if you could get me up to speed on the . . . On the caravans.'

She clicked her tongue. 'I asked Gloria if it would be okay for two groups to come in their caravans. Three people in one, two in another. There will also be a tent with four people – which will need to be pitched on grass, obviously. I hope you're not going to tell me any of that will be a problem?'

'If Gloria agreed to it, then naturally, we will honour that.' My mind raced. I thought about how many factions were now coming, and how many vehicles that would mean. 'Parking might be an issue. Some of you might have to use the lane, and some of you might have to block each other in. But as you're all from the same party, I'm sure it will work out.'

She murmured agreement. 'Don't forget they'll need access to an outside tap for water. And somewhere suitable for chemical toilet waste.'

Toilet waste? I stared helplessly through the kitchen window at the sun glaring off the gravel in the courtyard. 'We'll sort something out. I'm so glad you called. And once more, apologies for the communication issues. If you think of anything else, please feel free to ring any time.'

I took a deep, calming breath as I hung up, but dread settled upon me. That made it thirty-four people, including kids, and where exactly were we going to put a tent and two caravans? Feeling a bit sick, I risked pushing myself over the edge, checking Geoffrey Turner's site on my phone. Still nothing. I thanked God for small mercies.

Rupert was at the back of the house, inspecting shutters and flicking off peeling paint while the dog pranced around, chasing butterflies. He indicated the paint flakes showering the ground beneath the windows. 'These are beginning to go. I wonder if Ryan might want some extra work at the end the season before he goes back to the UK. He should prefer doing these in the balmy autumn months here, compared with freezing his arse off on a rainy British building site. What do you think?'

'I think we have bigger problems than repainting the shutters.'

As I relayed the phone conversation to him, his jaw fell by degrees.

'What the hell does she think this is, a ruddy campsite? Bloody Gloria.' When the dog pricked up her ears, he said, 'Not you, you daft mutt.'

We trooped round to the courtyard, where he eyed the space. 'The tent will have to go on the grass, maybe in the orchard, but there's no stretch of grass with access directly from the courtyard for the caravans. They'll have to stay on the gravel. One on either side of the exit, I reckon. That way, they can use the outside tap around your side of the house. As for chemical toilet waste, I'm at a loss.'

'What about hiring a portable toilet and putting it in that corner of the courtyard? It would be perfect for the tent, and the caravans could use it for disposal?'

'I'll look into it.' He heaved a sigh. 'That nice big figure we looked at the other week? It's diminishing by the minute. So far, we're down by five new duvets for the airbeds, and a ruddy toilet.'

As I helped Rupert prep for the guest meal that evening, my phone pinged. A text from Alain.

What are you doing?

I texted back. *More chopping vegetables. It's all he trusts me with. Meringues are beyond me.*

They're beyond me too. Any progress today?

One double-booking pacified. The other a lost cause, I'm afraid. Julia's added two caravans and a tent.

Should be interesting.

What are you doing?

Promised my niece and nephew I'd read to them before bedtime.

I smiled as an image of Alain curled up reading to small children came into my head. It wasn't something I'd thought about before. *Do you enjoy that?*

They're sweet, cuddly and still relatively innocent. Can be monsters, but not too manipulative yet. I can hand them over if they won't go to sleep afterwards. Best of all worlds.

Rupert looked across at me, pointing at my chopping board with his spoon. 'Will those vegetables be finished before midnight, or are you going to carry on sexting all evening?'

I glared at him and turned back to my phone. *Sorry. The boss is getting cross. Got to go.*

Say hi to Rupert from me. Speak to you tomorrow.

'He says hi,' I dutifully told Rupert.

'All that, just for a "Hi"?'

That evening's guest meal was a darned sight pleasanter than the previous one – not that that would be hard.

Our two sets of new arrivals were happy not to have to schlep out to find a restaurant after their long journey – especially when provided with something like tonight's prawn-and-salmon terrine, pork tenderloin in Dijon mustard and lentil sauce with vegetables, and homemade meringues drizzled with raspberry coulis. My waistline was only grateful that Rupert didn't offer such delights every night of the week.

Alice and Duncan, Hugh and Bronwen were friends who had booked together – a foursome who were up for a laugh. And Pippa and Angus kindly refrained from mentioning recent events, bless them.

The table was set with matching cloth and napkins – although I thought the white linen was brave, with bottles of white *and* red wine in the middle. The wine glasses gleamed in the soft lighting that was keeping the dusk outside the windows at bay; the mingling aromas of Rupert's cooking lingered in the air, tantalising our taste buds between each course.

'I wish we weren't leaving soon,' Pippa said wistfully. 'It's so nice here. Heaven knows we've stayed at some strange places over the years.'

My heart lifted at the thought that she wasn't holding the recent Turner shambles against us.

'Angus, do you remember that weird one in Fort William?' she went on.

'Do I? The bedframe, headboard and built-in bedside tables were all red leather. When we were . . . you know . . . it felt like we were in a porn film!'

Pippa slapped him, but she was smiling. 'The mirrors along the entire wall of fitted wardrobes didn't help. Angus was convinced they were two-way, with a hidden camera behind them.'

'Didn't dare do it again once I'd got that idea in my head. Made me feel rather inhibited.'

Everyone laughed, Pippa looking both embarrassed and delighted with his confession.

'We were once in a place in North Wales that was like an undertaker's,' Hugh told us. 'The room was chock-full of artificial flower arrangements. One was even free-standing on a pedestal in the corner.'

Bronwen wrinkled her nose in disapproval. 'You wouldn't think it would be so distressing, but it was, and I couldn't put my finger on why. Then I realised they were like those formal arrangements you get in funeral parlours.'

Hugh shuddered. 'I could barely sleep. I kept expecting a headless corpse to jump out of the wardrobe in the middle of the night. And it didn't help that the owner was really tall and thin, with dark hair in a widow's peak like some kind of vampire.' His expression was sheepish, but his eyes twinkled at the memory.

Alice smiled. 'We stayed in a place where the heating consisted of something made out of a length of plastic pipe that you plugged in.'

Rupert shook his head. 'How do these places get away with that? I have regulations coming out of my ar— I mean, out of my backside. Can't move for 'em.'

'Ah well, we're going back a bit,' Duncan explained. 'But even so.'

Alice started to laugh. 'I hand-washed my knickers and spread them over it to dry. It got so hot, it singed them!'

When the others expressed alarm, with deep laugh lines fanning out from the corners of her eyes she explained, 'They *were* cheap nylon. We were happy with cheap thrills in those days, weren't we, Duncan?' She gave her husband a cheeky grin.

'Yes, well, those cheap thrills weren't so funny when I ended up on the floor,' he grumbled, his balding head gleaming under a nearby wall light.

'The mind boggles!' Rupert muttered drily.

'It was a twin room. Being young and keen, we pushed the beds together, only they were different heights. Some time in the night, they drifted apart – and muggins here had been lying in the middle, over the join.'

'Ha!' Alice could barely speak for laughing. 'He got stuck right down the gap, both arms and legs still up on the bed and the rest of him firmly wedged on the floor in the middle!'

'I think I can top that one,' Rupert joined in. 'When I was a youngish bachelor in my first flat, I decided to impress the ladies with black satin sheets.'

Pippa snorted with laughter, causing wine to shoot up her nose and making everyone laugh before he'd even got started.

Rupert wagged his finger reproachfully at her. 'We're talking mid-eighties here, Pippa. Things like that were the height of sophistication back then. Anyway, there they were, smooth and shiny on the bed. And I was wearing red satin boxers to further impress.'

There was another tipsy giggle from Pippa and an inelegant snort from Hugh.

'My quarry – long-legged and beautiful – was sitting in the bed waiting for me. Full of enthusiasm, I took a run-up to the bed, launched myself onto it, satin met satin, and I went flying right across and off the other side. Concussed myself on the bedside cabinet.'

The sound of delighted laughter filled the kitchen, making me feel ridiculously happy. Whatever happened with Geoffrey Turner, he couldn't take *this* away.

It was well after midnight by the time Rupert and I had cleared away. As I was about to collapse into bed, out of habit I checked my mobile on the bedside table before turning it off.

Three missed calls from Nathan.

CHAPTER FIVE

I rose at five thirty after bugger-all sleep. What the hell did Nathan want?

Making use of my time, I sat with my laptop at my bedroom window. Still no review on the Silver Fox blog. I e-mailed my Chenonceau page to Nick, then decided that since the website wouldn't be sorted for a while – poor Nick had paid work to get on with, after all – I should get started on a leaflet giving bullet points of what I intended the agency to be and do, maybe detailing extra marketing services I could offer. It would be useful for Rupert and me to have on us, in case someone showed an interest, and it would be easy to e-mail if necessary.

At seven, I sorted out the chickens and began on breakfast. I would phone Nathan as soon as I had the table ready.

He beat me to it. 'Em. Where the hell have you been? I tried calling you all last night.'

'Sorry. I was busy, and then it was too late to call you back.'

'Busy doing what?' he asked suspiciously.

'Working. What's up?'

'Well, I'm glad you're swanning about sunning yourself in France while I'm up to my ears in phone calls here.'

Hearing guests on the stairs, I bit back a response. 'Hold on a minute.'

Smiling at Pippa and Angus, I told them to help themselves, then apologised and took myself off to the bottom of the garden.

'What's wrong?' I asked him, once I was out of earshot.

'The flat, that's what's wrong. Thank you so much for nominating me as the contact for the agents.'

I took a deep breath. 'We are both down as contacts, Nathan, but we discussed this. Since you are in the UK, you have to be the first point of call. I can hardly come all the way back to Birmingham for a dripping tap, can I?'

'It's hardly a dripping tap, Em. We have no tenants.'

'*What?* But it was all agreed! The agent said . . .'

'The couple they'd found changed their minds.'

'They can't do that!'

'Yes, they can. They hadn't signed the contract yet.'

'Oh, for God's sake. That agent gave me the impression it was all signed, sealed and delivered.'

'Well, it wasn't quite, it turns out.'

'Will he get someone else?'

'He's making it a priority, whatever that means. In the meantime, the mortgage is due, and there'll be no rent to cover it. Make sure your half is in on time, Emmy.'

I didn't like his tone. We'd kept an account open for the sole purpose of dealing with the flat, and that involved trust on both sides. 'I could say the same to you.'

'I'll keep up my end of the bargain. I ought to be taking a fee for dealing with all this crap.'

The nerve! 'Let's call it quits for the crap you put *me* through, shall we?'

I clicked off the phone and stood for a long time, staring at nothing.

Oh, this was not good. I'd based my finances on the mortgage being paid by the rent. Now there was no rent, I might have to dip into my savings. What if we couldn't get anyone? The rental agents had assured us it was a desirable property, but even a couple of months would make a big dent in money I didn't want to touch.

I thought about what Nathan had said, about me swanning about in the sun. If he'd been standing there in front of me, I might have throttled him. He was earning good money in London and living rent-free with Gloria in a flat that belonged to the man he stole her from. And although I, too, was living rent-free, it was on a far more moderate wage. I simply didn't have the disposable income to cover mortgage payments.

My stomach felt heavy and sick. I couldn't afford for the flat to stand empty. If that was going to happen, I might have to persuade Nathan to sell – and who knew how long that would take?

The minute breakfast was out of the way, I shut myself in Rupert's den to phone the letting agents. The call was as unsatisfactory as I'd thought it would be – a confirmation of what Nathan had said. In a tone that brooked no nonsense, I laid it on thick about requiring tenants as a matter of urgency, or we would have to look at switching agencies or perhaps even selling. They got the message.

'Everything okay?' Rupert asked me as I came out. 'I passed by the den and you sounded rather . . . forceful.'

No point in hiding it. I told him.

He blew out a breath. 'Damn. I honestly thought it was a great idea to rent that flat out. A sale is so much more complicated when you've just split up, and it takes time. And I thought it would be good for you to stay on the property ladder in the UK, just in case.'

I shot him an alarmed look.

He immediately patted my hand. '*Not* because I might go bankrupt overnight or sack you for the Backfiring Blogger Balls-up. I won't change my mind, Emmy. I want you here, and I can afford to pay you what we agreed as long as we keep steadily busy – which, I admit, seems to be a bit of a battle at the moment. But I'm enjoying more time with the dog and less worry and hard work in my old age. I only thought that keeping a foothold in the UK would give *you* peace of mind, in case you decide you don't like it out here.'

I glanced through the patio doors at the glorious garden and remembered that Alain's return was just over a week away. 'I can't see that happening any time soon, Rupert.'

'Well, then. You've already been proactive, phoning the agents. Keep at them. I'm sure Nathan will do the same. If they have both of you on their backs, they might make more effort.'

'I will. Did you get anywhere with the caterers yesterday?'

'I've spoken to several on the phone. They were all unimpressed with the short notice, but I have meetings with a couple later today.' He slapped his forehead. 'Although the numbers I gave them will be wrong, what with the ruddy campers, won't they? How many is that now?'

'Thirty-four, if you count a baby and a toddler.'

He sighed. 'Okay. At least I know before I meet with the caterers. No more temporary dwellings she hasn't told us about?'

I laughed. 'Not as far as I know. I'll go into town and order the cake. Any recommendations?' There was more than one *pâtisserie* in Pierre-la-Fontaine – there was more than one of anything that involved food in the town – and I could do without trawling them all.

'The last time I had to order something for a guest, I used the one a few doors up from Sophie's salon, same side of the street.'

'Okay. Thanks.'

Full of pioneering spirit, I drove into town, almost swerving the car into a ditch when I noticed a bird of prey hovering over a field, no doubt hoping for a juicy field mouse. Too big for a buzzard. Maybe a kestrel? Not that I was any kind of expert.

I parked up and walked to the main square, where a combination of being pleased with my take on Chenonceau that I'd finished that morning and a desire to put off braving the *pâtisserie* meant that I spent the first half hour taking photos of the white and cream buildings in the main square, the town hall, the colourful flowers surrounding the stone fountain, and jotting down notes.

Glancing towards the top of the square, I thought about catching up again with Rupert's friend Jonathan at their favourite café next market day and smiled. I wondered if Jonathan would follow through on his previous threats to claim me as his Girl Friday if I ever came over here. No doubt I would find out soon enough.

Finally out of excuses, I took a deep breath, stepped into the *pâtisserie* and started my mission.

I managed a confident greeting and to get the idea across that I needed to order a special cake. But it turned out that confectionary could be a minefield in a foreign language. Size, type of cake, type of filling, type of icing, colours, trim, decoration, ribbon . . . and there I was, thinking I'd been clever because I'd looked up beforehand how to say it was for a fiftieth wedding anniversary and couldn't have any cream or nuts due to allergies.

The middle-aged lady behind the counter was friendly and unfailingly polite, and the process was mercifully aided by photos she had on a tablet, so I could accept and reject their various features. Her patience was finally rewarded with my order – the price of which did nothing for my blood pressure until I reminded myself it was Julia who would be paying for it – but I left feeling exhausted and rather deflated.

The deficiency in my language skills was beginning to seriously sink in. I got by at the market and in cafés, where they were used to tourists. I barely needed to speak at all at the supermarket. I managed with Madame Dupont because it didn't matter if I got it wrong – we just laughed and muddled through. But I was still nervous of answering the phone, and my experience in the *pâtisserie* had shown that I wasn't anywhere near as competent as I'd hoped.

On the way back to the car, I walked passed Ellie Fielding's estate agency, wavered for a moment, thought about what Sophie had said, and stepped inside.

Philippe, Ellie's business partner, was deep in conversation on the phone, but he waved at me.

'Emmy!' Ellie bounced up from her chair, came dashing over and startled me by kissing me warmly on each cheek. 'I'm so glad you decided to come to France.'

'Thank you.'

She glanced at her watch. 'Do you have time for a quick coffee? I have an appointment in half an hour, but I could do with a shot of caffeine. The woman I'm meeting is deluded. She thinks that because of the last recession she can get a house with a pool and acres of land at 1972 prices.'

I smiled. Ellie pulled no punches. 'I'd love a coffee. Thanks.'

She led me to a nearby café, not far from Sophie's salon and the fountain. It was crowded, but I liked the buzz. We ordered and Ellie sat back, beanpole thin and towering over me even when seated, the sun glinting off her vibrant red, short-cropped hair.

'I bet Rupert's chuffed that he finally got the right-hand woman he was so keen to tempt back?'

I let out a self-deprecating laugh. 'He might not be so keen at this rate.' When our coffees were placed in front of us, I filled her in on our naked wanderer.

'Your idea was sound,' Ellie said. 'It was just an unfortunate set of circumstances. Have you seen a review yet?'

'No. It's making me a nervous wreck, checking every two minutes. The idea was to have him telling everyone how great *La Cour des Roses* is, obviously, but I have a nasty feeling that isn't the way he'll go.'

Ellie tactfully changed the subject. 'Our mutual, overly romantic friend Sophie tells me that romance is on the horizon with the town accountant?'

'He's not back for another week yet, but maybe. I hope so.'

Ellie laughed. 'Sophie was rather more definite about the prospect.'

'Yes, well, I might be wise not to get too optimistic on that score. I could be back home with my tail between my legs at this rate.'

Ellie frowned. 'What do you mean? You only just got here!'

I told her about Nathan's phone call that morning.

'What an arse!' Ellie declared.

The waiter arrived with our coffees, then scurried off, either run off his feet or sensibly frightened by Ellie's intent expression.

'He was with you for five years, and he doesn't trust you to cough up?'

'I don't blame him for worrying about it. *I'm* worried. A couple of months or so I can live with. I have savings. But it's not viable in the long term, is it?'

'What about this business of yours? What did you have in mind?'

I glanced at a holidaying family choosing postcards outside the nearby newsagent's and smiled as the father happily plucked an English newspaper from a rack, goggled at the price and put it back. A little nervously – Ellie was a shrewd businesswoman – I explained.

'Sounds good,' she said. 'Not too much outlay at the start, other than your time and your brother's. But how will you get *gîte* owners to sign up? They might not want to pay if they already use other sites, and if you're so small at first.'

'I won't charge to list, so owners pay nothing up front – only a percentage if they get a booking through the site.'

'Ah. So new customers haven't got anything to lose by advertising with you?'

'That's the idea.'

'Only problem is, you could be looking at the early season next year for any income that way.'

'I know. I didn't think that mattered. But if we don't get any tenants soon, it will.'

Ellie thought about it. 'Can't do anything about the delayed income. But the sooner you get set up, get people interested and on the books in readiness for next year, then knowing it's in the bag will make all the difference, surely? Make you feel more secure about your prospects?'

'I suppose so.'

'Hmm. I might be able to get the word out for you.'

She gave me the predatory smile that used to terrify me, but that I now knew was her potential-business-in-the-offing expression – only this time it was *my* potential business. She was turning out to be quite a sweetie, Ellie Fielding.

'Philippe and I have sold plenty of properties to Brits over the years. I can't pass their details on to you, obviously, but *we* could send an e-mail extolling your virtues. You know, "Hi there, it was a pleasure doing business with you, by the way, we thought you might like to know that a local businesswoman is starting a new venture that may be of interest to you, blah blah blah."'

'That's so good of you, Ellie. Are you sure Philippe won't mind?'

'This is a small town. Businesses are happy to support each other. And it never harms us to be able to recommend services if clients are dithering. If someone's thinking of buying, but worrying about letting out their property, something like that might tip the scales. You'd have to let me know the set-up in more detail, and then I could start recommending you to new clients, too.'

'The website's still a work in progress, so I've started working on a leaflet summing up what I'm about.'

Ellie smiled encouragement. 'Well, then, get it finished, woman! Here's my business card. E-mail it to me ASAP.' She stood. 'Right. Better go put this brainless woman in the picture about the current property market.'

As I drove back, I decided three main priorities had come out of the morning.

I needed to get on with the leaflet – I didn't want Ellie's offer and enthusiasm to peter out. I could make sure I kept up with writing tourist info for the website. And I needed to do something to improve my French. If I was going to make a proper go of it here, 'getting by' was no longer an option.

The minute I walked in, Rupert tetchily informed me that my mother had phoned. Twice.

'Is there an emergency?' I asked him, alarmed.

'In your mother's eyes, yes. She's not happy about all this texting, Emmy. Apparently, it's not good enough. She expects a proper conversation today, or else.'

'Urgh.'

'She also wants to know why you didn't answer your mobile.'

'I was probably driving or in the shop. Anything else I should know?'

He scrubbed at his beard. 'Yes. She doesn't expect to speak to you any less than she did when you were in the UK. There's no excuse for it, in this day and age.'

I shook my head. 'When I lived in the same city as her, she was perfectly happy with the odd phone call and the occasional personal appearance. That woman has a selective memory.'

'A mother's prerogative. Go and get it done, Emmy, and save us both from any more earache.'

Taking bread and cheese with me, I gravitated to my chaise longue at the open window and did as I was told. A proper online video chat. As Mum required a full rundown of my first week, it was a long session.

'So, Emmy, any sign of a new romantic attachment yet?' she enquired nonchalantly.

My brow furrowed. I hadn't said anything to her about Alain – the woman would put the Spanish Inquisition to shame. 'Why do you ask?'

'Is a mother not allowed to enquire after her daughter's love life?'

'Depends what agenda she has.'

'My *agenda*, Emmeline Jamieson, is to ensure that my daughter is well and possibly even happy after her previous boyfriend behaved like a total arse. Is that too much to ask?'

I laughed. 'No, I suppose not.'

'So?'

I toyed with denial, but Mum always *knew*, somehow. 'There may be,' I hedged.

'*May* be? What's that supposed to mean?'

'It means I would prefer not to go into details at this time.'

Mum tutted. 'You'd make a great politician!' She waited, and when no further information was forthcoming, said, 'Well?'

I stared at the familiar backdrop of the family lounge behind her: the sofa that had been the site of a hundred cushion battles with my brother, the twenty-year-old family portrait in pride of place on the wall behind it. 'I may be starting to see someone soon,' I admitted.

'Too cryptic. Who is this someone?'

'His name is Alain.'

'Is he French?'

'Half-French, half-English.'

'How did you meet him?'

'He's Rupert's accountant.'

'How old is he?'

'Thirty-six.'

'He's not married or with a partner? And if not, why not, at that age?'

'Mum! He's divorced.'

'Hmm.' She mulled this over. 'Children?'

'No.'

'What did you mean you *may* start to see him? Either you are or you aren't.'

'He's away at the moment. We've been chatting on the phone and online.'

Uh-oh. Sure enough . . .

'Oh, so you can make time to speak to a man you're not even dating yet, but not to speak to your own mother?'

'I would have phoned, Mum. It's been like a madhouse here.'

'And this Alain. Is he—'

'No, that's enough for today.'

'I was only going to ask, Emmy, if he's likely to treat you better than the last one.'

I bristled. 'I wouldn't be thinking about getting involved with him if I didn't believe that, would I?' But then I relented. Anything for an easy life. 'Alain is a genuinely nice bloke. But don't read anything more into it than that at this stage, okay?'

'I won't.'

A likely story. By the end of the evening, my father, brother and Aunt Jeanie would be in the picture, at the very least.

With that ordeal out of the way, I made my regular check of Geoffrey Turner's blog. I was so used to doing it with no result that I hadn't even bothered to steel myself this time.

I nearly choked on my cheese.

THE SILVER FOX TRAVELLER

at

La Cour des Roses, near Pierre-la-Fontaine, Maine-et-Loire

#WishYouWereAnywhereButHere

La Cour des Roses is in a swoon-worthy spot, a natural sun-trap nestled amidst the rolling farmland and vineyards of the Loire Valley. Its gardens are beautifully planted with mature oaks, weeping pears, delicate willows, fragrant herbs and colourful annuals in bright pinks, purples and oranges. The welcoming patio is well maintained with potted geraniums and plenty of space for all. From the roof terrace, you can gaze upon the bucolic view, sipping iced tea in the hot sun or a rich red wine under a star-filled night sky. The guesthouse itself is a typical converted French farmhouse of creamy stone and blue-painted shutters.

But I'm afraid, dear readers, this is where my praise ends. Let's step inside.

Hulking antiques are at odds with dreary, cheap prints of generic French countryside and assorted kitsch such as decorative eggs and anorexic ballerina figurines, no doubt purchased at a local flea market by a decorator with a split personality disorder.

The guest lounge is uninhabitable, with no redeeming features. Frankly, it defies the Trade Descriptions Act. The chairs are stiff and uncomfortable, the décor is as above, and there's an added hint of the Arctic. How any French room manages to be so cold in August, I do not know.

In contrast, our room may as well have been sitting over the fiery pits of Hades. The electric fan provided was noisy and inadequate, and even with all possible measures taken to keep cool, sleep was elusive. Our mattress was too soft, and the voile curtains – besides affording little privacy – had no blackout ability, forcing us to close the shutters at night, rendering the room stuffy.

Yes, they gave us darkness, but don't think we got a lie-in with the army of chickens clucking from the crack of dawn. Speaking of nuisance animals, *La Cour des Roses* is also home to a giant, malodorous Labrador, who lumbers about communal areas being 'friendly' to the unsuspecting, frightened and allergic.

The complimentary bathroom toiletries were in large glass bottles – no doubt a twee attempt to make them look homemade. Judging by the smell, they had been filled with the cheapest supermarket rubbish imaginable. I didn't enjoy smelling like a marzipan fruit basket.

And on to the dining . . . The host, Rupert Hunter, provides breakfast daily and three guest meals a week, supplying recommendations for local restaurants on other nights. I suspect the average tourist might not mind his gastronomic offerings. But while it was not traditional British fare, it was not *très français*, either. Perhaps Mr Hunter is aiming to cater to everyone's taste by trudging along the middle ground, but the result has a dismaying lack of identity. If I stay at a French guesthouse, I expect skilled French cuisine, not some half-baked cross-channel hybrid. At one point, I was served some kind of fish mousse and thought I'd slipped through a wormhole back to the 1970s.

Mealtimes are – most unfortunately – a communal affair, and Mr Hunter presides with his own brand of verve and humour, although I warn you, his overbearing personality may not be to everybody's taste. I'm sure the idea is everyone will get along famously in a jolly holiday atmosphere, but our personal experience of clashing personalities – vociferously clashing personalities – made us most uncomfortable, to the point where we had to leave early. The proprietors seemed reluctant to intervene in the matter.

On the subject of ineffectiveness, I was dismayed to witness a request for an ambulance delayed because Ms Jamieson had no idea how to call for one. It beggared belief.

In summary, *La Cour des Roses* should, in theory, be a charming enough place to visit, but in practice . . . the risk is yours.

CHAPTER SIX

If I were a cartoon character, there would have been steam coming out of my ears, with accompanying shrill whistles.

I took the laptop through to Rupert, herding him into his private lounge first, in case his language was too colourful when he read the review.

His language wasn't colourful. He remained unnervingly quiet.

'It's so *unfair*!' I flopped my head back against the chair, banging it a little harder than intended. 'He's twisted everything!'

Rupert made no effort to comfort me in my distress, causing my heart to sink further. He blamed me, I knew he did.

'He's made a huge deal about me not knowing the emergency number, but failed to say it only took me a minute to find it. He makes it sound like a life was in jeopardy. This is just completely subjective. I don't even believe he didn't like the food – or the shampoo. He never said anything at the time. There's only *one* decorative egg, and I have no idea what ballerina figurine he's on about. I thought I'd got rid of that kind of thing. As for the dog . . .' My shoulders slumped. 'He's right about the dog.'

'Emmy . . .'

But I was on a roll. 'And why were there "vociferously clashing personalities"? Hmm? I see he doesn't bother mentioning it was because he flashed an elderly woman. *Twice*!'

'He's hardly going to mention that, is he? Calm down. You're giving me a headache.'

Rupert moved over to the kettle at his little kitchenette to make us a cup of tea, while I stared at the words on the screen, willing them to metamorphose into something more palatable – but they remained resolutely horrid.

'Maybe not that many people will see it, Emmy. And of those who do, there can't be *that* many who would have happened to be considering coming here. We're only a drop in the ocean, really.' He handed me a mug. 'As for the things he complains about, there's a fair few we can fix. Those pictures, for example. I suspect you had half an eye on them already.'

I grunted. 'That's what annoys me.'

'As for the problems with other guests, with any luck, people will see his experience as unfortunate – a one-off.'

'Except his two-star rating is emblazoned right across the top. It's *huge*! Oh, this all my fault!'

'Of course it isn't your fault!' he snapped. 'Shit happens. Now get rid of that martyred expression, put on that scary marketing one you possess instead, and tell me what we can do about it. We have a right to reply, surely?'

'Absolutely not.'

'*What?*'

'It inevitably makes it worse. It can escalate things. Best just to leave it be.'

Exasperated, Rupert stood and began to pace the length of his lounge – no dreary prints here, I noticed, but rather acceptable original landscapes. 'So a man can wander naked in my guesthouse and pee in my wardrobe, and we can't give our side of the story?'

'No. Think about it, Rupert. A guest expects confidentiality. They don't expect you to tell the world about their personal habits after they've left. If you say anything about Geoffrey's, they won't trust you not to say anything about theirs, will they?'

'So what *can* we do?'

I took several deep breaths. 'I've already done laminated notices with the emergency numbers. But we need to get that mutt of yours on the website. Cute photos. If anyone *has* got a problem with her, at least they can't say they didn't know.' I sighed. 'That means I need to e-mail everyone who's already booked and let them know about her, just in case.'

Rupert's mouth dropped open. 'You're kidding.'

'What if someone has a phobia or an allergy? And then . . .' I drummed my fingers on the table. 'We can't do anything about this blog. Those who read it will make their own minds up. But Geoffrey's bound to put a short version of this on popular review sites as well. That's where we *can* do something. We need to get as many positive reviews as possible to counteract it.'

'And how do you propose to do that?'

'Every time a guest leaves, ask them if they'd be kind enough to leave one.'

'What if they didn't have a good stay?'

'Accidentally-on-purpose forget to ask – but most guests love it here, you know they do.'

'Then why did we need the ruddy blogger?' Rupert asked sulkily.

'Because we need *more* people to love it. You have me to pay now. We have gaps in the bookings. We need to extend the season. We have to reach beyond loyal guests, word-of-mouth and the local tourist board. When I get a chance, I'll set us up on social media. Post photos of breakfast and dinners, the house and grounds, even the dog. But as for reviews . . . We could send an e-mail a few days after people leave, thanking them for choosing us and reminding them that reviews are appreciated.' I brought up a popular site on the laptop and turned it so he could see. 'Your average rating is good, but the *number* of reviews isn't high. Your customers don't think to leave one. I could e-mail everyone who's stayed this season. Thank them, say we hope they'll repeat the experience, and tell them how much we'd appreciate a review.'

'Can't hurt. It'll be a lot of work for you, though, setting up the e-mail list.'

'It's what you're paying me for. And we'll be able to use it in future.'

Dragging my laptop to the den, I spent the remainder of the afternoon creating an e-mail list of past customers, starting with the most recent and working my way back to the beginning of the year. It was a pig of a job and gave me a headache, but I persevered, then sent out my begging-for-a-review e-mail. I knew only a percentage would bother, but whatever we got would be worth it. The Silver Fox's review could do a lot of damage, sitting on those websites, unchallenged by enough positive reviews. Which might mean fewer bookings. Which I couldn't allow, if I wanted to earn some sort of living here.

Rupert popped his head around the door. 'Are you all right? I haven't seen you for hours.'

'Yeah. I wanted to get this done.'

'Aren't you supposed to be speaking to Alain tonight? Do you want something to eat?'

I looked at the time on my screen. 'I had no idea how late it was. But I'm not hungry.'

'I know you feel responsible, Emmy, but I don't want you making yourself poorly over this. How about I defrost some homemade soup for you?'

I gave him a grateful smile. 'That sounds perfect. Thank you.'

Alain had already seen the review. I was touched that he'd kept an eye out for it, knowing I was so worried.

'What do you think?' I asked him.

'It's mean and small-minded.'

'It's more than that. It's distorted!' My voice hitched.

Alain nodded. 'It's a real hatchet job.' He gave me a puzzled look. 'You must have dealt with stuff like this all the time in your last job, Emmy.'

'Of course! But this feels more personal. There's . . . There's more at stake. I gave everything up to be here, Alain. I don't want it to go wrong.'

'I know. I wish I could give you a hug right now.'

'I wish you could, too.'

His voice became more matter-of-fact. 'I presume you have a comeback strategy?'

I told him how I'd spent my afternoon. 'I don't know why Rupert didn't already have an e-mail list,' I grumbled.

'The poor bloke was too busy doing all the things Gloria couldn't be bothered to do, I should imagine.'

Alain reached for a mug of tea at his side, and as I watched the way he folded his long fingers around it, I found myself wondering how they would feel caressing me.

'Everything okay?' Alain asked.

I jumped out of my reverie. 'Er – fine. I – er . . .' *Think of something, Emmy, quick.* I hesitated, wondering whether I should tell him about Nathan and the flat. And then I figured there was no point in having an accountant for a friend if you couldn't tell him your financial worries.

'What do you think?' I asked when I'd explained.

'I think it's unlucky, but it's too early to worry about it yet. Surely it won't make that much difference to you in the short term?'

'No, as long as it *is* only short term. I can manage, but it wasn't what I'd planned. My savings were for setting up my business or for other things here. I don't want to fritter them away on mortgage payments from my old life.'

'I can understand that. We'll keep fingers crossed for now, okay?'

I laughed. 'Is that an official accountancy strategy?'

'Of course.'

'Well, apart from your impressively detailed accountant's advice, I have another favour to ask.'

'Oh? Will I enjoy it?'

'Not necessarily. I was wondering if you'd consider helping me with my French. It's years since I did it at school. I've bought books and CDs, but I'm struggling to find the time and it's boring and it's never going to be up to scratch at this rate. I need help with it. You know, colloquialisms and stuff.'

'I'm more than happy to help you with that, and whatever else you need or want besides.' He allowed a dramatic pause that had my pulse racing. 'Once I get back, maybe we should set up something specific. An hour each date. Otherwise, you'll keep putting it off.'

'Okay. Sounds good.' Although I could think of better things to do on our dates.

'And don't put yourself down, Emmy. You're doing all right so far.' When I began to shake my head, he said sternly, 'You manage to communicate with Madame Dupont, so you can't be too rubbish.'

'I know, but I don't get enough practice here at *La Cour des Roses*.'

'Okay. There are two different ways to approach this, and we need to do both. First, you can't ignore the basics. Grammar . . .'

'Urgh.' I glanced at the language books I'd bought, still pristine on my little bedside table. 'Grammar?'

'Yes. We need to work out what you remember, what you don't and what you were never taught in the first place. Learning a language is like building a wall. If you don't make the bottom rows straight and sturdy, the rest will be flimsy and you'll always feel insecure. It will make you feel so much more comfortable and confident. I promise.'

'Okay. Will I like the second approach better?'

He laughed at my hopeful expression. 'Maybe. You need to absorb the language into your consciousness. Have the car radio on a news channel. If you're meeting up with Sophie, ask her if you can speak in French for part of the time. Same with me.'

'With you?'

'Yes. We need to get you comfortable and fluent.'

'Oh, Alain, no. I'm not ready.'

'You never will be unless you get on and do it. I promise not to make fun of you, and I won't correct everything – I'll just help with words you don't know and let you babble on, okay?'

When I remained decidedly *un*babbly, he simply lapsed into French. 'What did you do today? Who's staying at *La Cour des Roses*?'

'Okay . . .' Shy and embarrassed, I did my best, while he gently corrected and supplied vocabulary.

And, oh my goodness, how sexy was Alain when he spoke French?

I shook my head to clear it, gritted my teeth and persevered. After ten minutes, Alain told me I was tired and I'd had enough.

I refrained from telling him that I would never have enough of listening to him speak French. I could feel a cold shower coming on.

My alarm jolted me out of a dreamless sleep. I stretched and climbed out of bed, pottering over to the window to watch the early morning light filter through the leaves of the trees in the orchard.

I loved being round the back of the house like this – my own little hideaway. I loved taking my coffee breaks in a beautiful garden with a dog's head in my lap, instead of a crowded city or the tension-filled kitchenette in the office.

The guest meal tonight meant three courses of Rupert's glorious cooking – despite what Geoffrey Turner thought.

And then I remembered it was Saturday, a day of hard labour. I'd only done a couple of these so far, while I was on holiday – not the usual tourist activity in the Loire region, I grant you – and I knew I would be exhausted by the end of it. But maybe that was just what I needed right now. Honest physical work, with no time to brood on tenants and bloggers and Thomson task lists.

Once I'd set up breakfast, I glanced at the shopping list and groaned. This was one of the things I intended to change about Saturdays, but for today I was stuck with it. Leaving the guests to Rupert – other than eliciting a promise for a review from Pippa and Angus who were leaving and declared they would be back – I got off so that I could be back by mid-morning.

Dumping the shopping in the kitchen for Rupert to get started on welcome baskets, I walked over to the long building of cream and grey stone, once a barn but now housing the *gîtes*. Cars were still being loaded outside two, but the third was empty, its wooden door wide open.

As I approached, half a dozen little birds shot out of the vine that clambered over the doorway, chattering crossly and making me jump. Passing through the doorway, I spotted small bunches of grapes hidden amongst the foliage. I'd disturbed them from stealing their breakfast.

Madame Dupont was scrubbing the oven, her back to me. Her floral dress was garish but of a cool, summery material – unlike her thick support stockings. I didn't know how she could stand to wear them. It was nearly thirty degrees already.

'*Bonjour*, Madame Dupont.'

She whirled around. '*Bonjour, Emie.*'

We settled into a work routine, Madame Dupont continuing with the oven while I started on the fridge. I wrinkled my nose. Someone had been adventurous in their choice of local cheeses.

'Rupert said you'll have to visit your sister again. How is she?'

Worry etched her wrinkled forehead. 'She has severe arthritis and diabetes.'

'I'm so sorry.' At least her sister's conditions sounded similar in French to English, otherwise I'd have had no idea what I was commiserating over. 'That must be hard for you. Is she married?'

'*Veuve.*' When I shook my head in non-comprehension, she explained. 'Her husband died. And her children moved away – one to Paris, the other down south – so when she is very bad, I go to help for a day or two.'

'That's good of you.'

'And good of Monsieur Hunter to allow me to fit my work around it. But I told my sister I can never go on a Saturday. Too much to do here!'

Her capacity for work never ceased to amaze me. She must have been over seventy.

'When will Alain be back from Paris?' she asked me, a mischievous glint in her eye.

The woman was the centre of the local gossip grapevine and a dreadful meddler. Rupert came a close second. It was like having my very own cheerleading team of two.

'In a week,' I answered vaguely, aware that whatever I told Madame Dupont I was imparting to the entire Loire valley.

She flashed me a semi-toothless smile. 'You need someone nice after your last boyfriend.'

I couldn't argue with her there.

After the second *gîte*, we took a break, drinking *thé au citron* at one of the patio tables at the back. It was so peaceful out here, each *gîte* separated from its neighbour with large, pale yellow roses on the trellises between, a wooden gate at the end of each little patio leading out to the large lawn area for the *gîte* occupants to use, the grass curving away from the building and around towards Rupert's own garden, a tall hedge shielding it from the courtyard and making it a quiet sunbathing spot or a safe play area for kids.

We were sitting with our faces lifted to the sun, sipping tea and enjoying the quiet, when a motor fired up, making me jump.

Madame Dupont laughed. 'That will be Ryan.'

He manoeuvred the mower along the strip of lawn beyond the gates. Shirtless in the summer heat, frayed denim shorts, hair streaked blonde by the summer sun . . . You'd have to have stopped breathing to not be moved by the sight, but appreciation was one thing and feelings were another. We'd agreed to remain friends after those few mad days for good reason. Neither of us had been looking for a relationship at the time, and although Ryan was one of the nicest guys on the planet, his casual, easy-going nature wouldn't work for me in the long term. And then there was the small fact that he was seven years younger than me.

We exchanged a friendly wave.

'Come on,' Madame Dupont said with a wink. 'We can't sit about staring at that beautiful young man all day.'

When the third *gîte* was done, I drove Madame Dupont home to her ramshackle cottage to save her elderly legs, kissed her goodbye, winced at the racket from the ugly black chickens in her yard, then headed back to start on the vacated guest rooms – after which I collapsed in a heap in the kitchen, where Rupert dutifully supplied me with a huge mug of Earl Grey tea.

'Mmm.'

'Glad to be back?'

'Oh, yes. I *love* cleaning.' I fixed him with a glare. 'About this Saturday morning shopping. I can go to the supermarket any day of the week. Why Saturday?' I spied Geoffrey Turner's decorative egg on the counter and twirled it round on the granite. It was one of the few ornaments I had kept of all of Gloria's tat: a decoupage peacock feather pattern of iridescent blues, greens and gold. Was it really hideous kitsch?

'Habit, because of the guest meal and welcome baskets. I used to shop while Gloria helped Madame Dupont with the *gîtes* and rooms.'

I doubted such labour was evenly divided between the two women. I stopped the spinning egg and wondered where Gloria's ballerina was, or if Geoffrey had simply made it up. 'It doesn't make sense any more. You have the dog to walk, and we're too busy. I'll shop on weekdays from now on, fresh stuff only. I do *not* want to see anything on the list that could have gone on your weekly online order. Understand?'

'I can't believe I'm *paying* to be bossed around like this.'

'Well, you can pay me back by bossing me around this kitchen. What's on tonight's menu?'

'Caesar salad, poached salmon in hollandaise sauce with buttered green beans and garlic potatoes, apricot tart. No doubt far too eclectic and nowhere near French enough for Geoffrey Turner.'

'Ha! I doubt tonight's guests will agree with him. Any progress on catering for the Thomsons?'

'One was far more expensive than the other for a similar menu, so I went with the more reasonable one. They have a good reputation. They're sending me a proposed menu and official quote on Monday. I'll forward it to Julia as soon as I get it.'

'Good. So that's the cake and the party food sorted. I can tell you now, my French doesn't stretch to portable toilets. I'm leaving that to you.'

As we worked side by side, I marvelled – as ever – at the fact that I could play any practical part in producing the delicious food that would be relayed to the table this evening. I was in a good mood when the phone rang.

'I'll get it,' Rupert said as he glanced across and saw that I was busy mangling apricots in my attempt to pit them.

'*La Cour des Roses*? Yes, Rupert Hunter speaking. Yes, I remember your booking, and we look forward to . . . Cancel? Is there a problem? I . . . Yes, I have seen it, but . . .' He turned his back to me and my heart sank.

'Mr Webster, that was just one man's experience, and we feel it was not at all representative of . . . Yes, I do appreciate that, but . . . I can't persuade you to change your mind? Then I'm sorry. Yes. Goodbye.'

I stared at him as he put the phone down, a fresh apricot squashed to a pulp in my hand. 'What? Tell me.'

'The Websters have cancelled. A whole week.'

'Why?'

'They saw the Silver Fox's review.'

'Shit.' I released the apricot mush from my hand onto the chopping board. 'Charge them.'

'What?'

'They can't cancel at the last minute like that.'

'He made it clear he expected no charges. Not only that, but he wants his deposit back.'

'And you agreed to that?'

'Not happily or willingly, but yes, I did.'

'But . . .'

'There's no point in getting in a fight over this, Emmy. I can't go over there and prise the balance out of the man's wallet, can I? And if I don't return his deposit, he could take it further. He could contact the Silver Fox and we could end up with some kind of campaign being waged against us. I think the safest thing to do is to let it lie. Could you put that fruit knife down? You're beginning to scare me.'

I complied. 'Oh Rupert, I'm so sorry.'

He shook his head. 'It really isn't your fault, Emmy.'

'This is ridiculous! It's one thing Geoffrey Turner slagging us off to all and sundry, and us losing potential clients. But to lose *existing* clients . . . This is serious stuff. I've a good mind to e-mail the bastard and request that he take down his review on the basis that it's biased and doesn't reflect the *full* details of his stay.'

Rupert just looked at me.

'All right, I know. Escalation, blah blah blah. I *hate* this!'

Rupert began to laugh.

'What?' I snapped. 'What can possibly be so funny?'

'You stamped your foot, Emmy. You actually stamped your foot like a toddler.' He took the wine out of the fridge. 'I recommend a very large glass of this.'

I took his recommendation to heart. And then repeated it, for good measure. It certainly helped me enjoy the guest meal.

Our new guests consisted of Ruby and Charles Jackson, and also Violet and Betty, two delightful old dears who had made me laugh as they drove carefully into the courtyard with Violet peering comically over the top of the steering wheel and Betty battling with a large map. They immediately took to Rupert – and I immediately warned him that he would have to moderate his language for the duration of their stay.

That evening was a fascinating exhibition of good-willed restraint on the part of our fun foursome, who held back on further tales involving their past sexual exploits, and Rupert carefully editing his own anecdotes. In the end, it was Ruby and Charles who saved the day by telling us about their once-in-a-lifetime trip to Australia the previous year – PG-level entertainment enjoyed by all.

Over coffee, I smiled contentedly. Amiable guests. Fab food. Only a few days until I could throw myself into Alain's arms. This was a fine life, if I let it be.

CHAPTER SEVEN

'I'm not happy, Emmy, and I hope you have a good explanation.'

'Ah. Er. Morning, Julia.' As yet unaided by caffeine, my mind raced with no destination in mind. 'Explanation for what?'

'I got a call late last night from my daughter – which I could well have done without, just before I went to bed. Robert and I have barely slept!'

'Is there a problem with the booking?'

'I'll say there's a problem. She was searching for *La Cour des Roses* on the internet, and what do you think she found?'

My heart sank right down to my feet as my brain guessed what was coming next.

'The Silver Fox Traveller. Two stars, Emmy. Two stars! When I think how much we're paying you! Your website *screams* about what an idyllic place it is. Well, the Silver Fox didn't find it idyllic, did he?'

'No, but to be fair . . .'

'I'm not in the mood to be fair, Emmy. I'm in the mood to be convinced that none of the things he mentions in his review are going to be a problem when we get there, or heaven help me, I'll have to consider pulling the plug on this whole thing. And believe me, that will hurt me a darned sight more than it will hurt you. But I'll do it if I have to.'

I thought about the figure she was paying us. The planning and the time and the stress that Rupert and I had already put into it.

The rooms and *gîtes* empty for nearly a fortnight with very little chance of filling them. I felt sick to my stomach.

'I have no doubt I can reassure you, Julia.' I took the phone into the den for privacy and sank into the chair at the desk. This was going to be a long call.

'Right. Noisy chickens . . .'

Crikey. She obviously had the review in front of her and intended to work her way through the entire thing.

'There are only a few, at the bottom of a very long garden, and they're locked away at night. No roosters to wake you at dawn, I promise. We've never had any other complaints.'

'Hmm.' A pause, as she no doubt scanned the review. 'Dreary pictures are the least of my worries.'

I tried a light chuckle. 'I'm not keen on them myself. They were already on my to-do list.'

'The lounge, however, does not sound at all adequate.'

'I agree it isn't ideal, and that's also on my list. I can't refurnish it before you come, but I will make it as hospitable as I can. I'm hoping the weather stays fine enough for you all to gather on the patio and in the garden, but the little lounges in the *gîtes* are lovely for smaller groups.'

'Hmmph.'

I winced. That one wasn't going down too well.

'Soft mattresses?'

'I'm sure you'll appreciate, Julia, that it's very hard to accommodate everyone. All our mattresses are medium, and we feel that's the only way to go.'

'Fair enough. Voile curtains?'

'Shutters are by far the best black-out method. Voile because people like an airy feel to their room in the daytime.'

'I'm not happy about these cheap toiletries at all. We're paying good money . . .'

That *did* get my goat. I'd spent hours on those the last time I was here. 'I can assure you that the bottles are for aesthetic and environmental reasons, and the toiletries in them are of a very high quality. When you arrive, I'd be happy to show you what we put in them.'

'Maybe. Now, I know evening meals aren't relevant in our case, but even so . . .'

'Julia, I must say that the Silver Fox was most unfair on that score. Rupert produces beautiful food.' I described what we'd had the night before. 'I can personally guarantee that whatever he serves is always fresh and delicious.'

'And the fact that this Silver Fox was apparently driven out by other guests?'

'Well, that shouldn't be relevant in your case, as you're all family.' *Although that isn't always a given.* 'I can't give details – the dispute was of a personal nature . . .' *Literally.* 'But it was a set of circumstances unlikely to ever be repeated.' *Hopefully.* 'I strongly believe it has nothing to do with your booking, or indeed any of our future guests.'

'And the ambulance?'

Urgh. 'The honest truth? I'd only been here two days and I didn't know the number.' I heard her suck in a breath. 'It took me just one minute to find it, and I won't forget it now! But it was only a sprained wrist.'

'I see.' Her tone softened a little. 'Now. This dog. I looked again at your website and suddenly she's right there, photos and all. She wasn't when I booked.'

'I know.' I made a mental note that I had yet to e-mail all our future bookings about her. As if I didn't have enough to be getting on with. 'The Silver Fox was right about that, so we rectified it straight away. Will she be a problem?'

'Not with the people. I am concerned about the dogs we're bringing, though.'

'You're bringing dogs?'

'Yes. Two. Didn't I tell you?'

'Er, no.' In need of comfort, I moved from the captain's chair to the squishy leather sofa, where I could flop my head back.

'Don't worry, they'll be in one of the caravans. But now I'm worried about how they'll get along with Mr Hunter's dog. *Gloria.*'

Ah, she'd spotted that, had she? 'I'll speak to Rupert. I'm sure it will be okay, but if they can't get along, we'll contain our dog, okay?'

'Fine.'

'Have I allayed your fears, Julia? I really hope so.'

'In the main. The fact is, I feel I don't have much choice but to go ahead with the booking at this stage. Heaven knows where we'd find somewhere else big enough. But I can't say I'm happy, Emmy. My dealings with *La Cour des Roses* have hardly been a smooth process. My main contact leaving, information not being passed on, having to repeat myself. I'm a busy woman. And now this review. I can't begin to tell you how ill that made me last night. Have you any idea what it's like, trying to gather an extended family together like this?'

'I can only apologise, and . . .' I closed my eyes for a moment and prayed that Rupert would forgive me. 'I'd like to find some way to compensate you for your trauma. How about if we extend breakfast to *all* your guests on the days you're all here? So, the five days, Friday through to the Tuesday? The *gîtes*, the caravans, the tent? We can't fit everyone in the kitchen, but we could put extra seating out on the patio and you could all come and go as you please. What do you think?'

Seconds ticked by. 'I think that is a generous offer which I am more than happy to accept. Thank you.'

I puffed out my cheeks in silent relief. It didn't last long.

'Have you sorted out the band yet?'

I rested my face against the cool leather arm of the sofa in despair. 'The band?'

'Didn't we discuss the band?'

'No, Julia. I'm sorry, but I would have remembered.'

'That must have been a conversation I had with Gloria, then. Maybe I forgot to put it on my e-mail. I *would* apologise, especially in light of your generous breakfast offer, but at the end of the day, Gloria should have passed that information on to you.'

'Yes, she should have. So . . . a band?' *Shoot me now.*

'I need you to book a jazz band for the party night. Someone playing at the festival. Small – size is an issue, obviously.'

Obviously.

'And we want an intimate atmosphere, something mellow. No brass blasting out or anything screechy.'

Thank goodness for that.

'Er. Wouldn't you be better doing that? You must know more about it than me . . .'

'Actually, Emmy, I know very little about jazz. My parents' enthusiasm didn't rub off on me, alas. And I just can't fit it in. There are others in the family who take an interest, but they wouldn't be any the wiser about the bands on a French programme, would they? I'm sure you could ask around. Send me the details of who you've booked, will you? Oh, and that means we need a marquee.'

Could this get any worse? 'For . . . ?'

'For the band, Emmy. If it rains, we can hardly bring them into the house, can we? We'd all be deafened. The bar could go under there, too. Don't worry, we'll be paying for all this.'

I should hope so.

'Okay, Julia.' I thought about Alain. He'd been to the festival in the past. Maybe he might have some clue how I could go about this. 'How are you managing to keep a surprise like this from your parents?'

'We told them that Robert and I are bringing them to France for a few days, but they don't know about the jazz festival or the party or the rest of the family coming.' She chuckled. 'Mum did think it was strange that other family members happen to be away at the same time. She said it was a good job we'd invited her, because there would be nobody around back home at this rate!'

'Are you expecting to keep the party from them until the last minute?'

'No. I would have liked to, but one of the kids is bound to give it away once we all get together.' She laughed at my sigh of relief. 'So you don't need to worry about that side of things, Emmy, but thank you for checking.'

'You're welcome.'

We hung up, and I went over a mental checklist of all the horrific crimes against holidaymakers Geoffrey Turner had accused us of. I tried to calm myself with the fact that he'd exaggerated, and anything real was in hand. I wouldn't mind knowing where that damned ballerina figurine was, though.

I went back through to the kitchen, where Rupert was clearing up on his own.

'Are you all right?' he asked. 'You've been gone ages.'

'Julia Cooper.'

He listened carefully as I told him everything. 'You did the right thing, Emmy, offering that breakfast sweetener. The woman's right – her whole booking has been a shambles. It's the least we can do.'

'It's going to seriously eat into our profits.'

'Can't be helped. Better than losing the whole booking, or having them badmouth us all over the place. Good girl.' He patted my hand. 'By the way, Sophie rang. She and Ellie are taking you out for the afternoon.'

'Oh, Rupert, I can't. What about this stupid band and the marquee and . . .'

'A couple of hours away won't do you any harm. You're a nervous wreck. I'll deal with the marquee. You've got a while before Sophie comes, if you want to look into the jazz thing, okay?'

'Okay.'

I sloped off to my room, where I allowed myself five minutes of pure self-pity: pouting, hugging my pillow, the whole works.

When the five minutes were up, I fired up the laptop and sent an e-mail to everyone who was booked in over the next couple of months, warning them about the dog and including a link to the relevant page on the website, hoping the cute photos would sway anyone on the doubtful side.

Then I brought up the website for the jazz festival – all in French, naturally – and found a programme of bands expected to play. I might as well have been looking at a list of Latvian authors. It meant nothing to me. I simply had no idea where to start, and the only thing I was utterly convinced about was that it was well beyond my job description as manager of a small guesthouse.

As a distraction technique, I pulled up a couple of popular review sites to see if my begging e-mail to past guests had reaped any rewards yet. My heart lifted to see a couple of new reviews – both short but complimentary.

Five stars: *Excellent food, excellent customer service, lovely accommodation.*

Four stars: *Beautiful, clean room. Nice food. Guest lounge a disappointment.*

I *really* needed to talk to Rupert about that lounge.

Geoffrey's review was still far too prominent for my liking, but then I noticed another low rating next to it. What the . . . ?

Don't stay here if you want any kind of customer service. The management do not back up their customers in times of difficulty, and have no idea how to deal with medical emergencies. Clare Jones.

Since I'd already done self-pity, I segued into panic. The feeling of being overwhelmed was so great, my chest felt tight, my throat constricted, my lungs compressed.

What on earth had possessed me to think I could switch from a career in marketing to running a guesthouse in a foreign country? So far, my efforts had made things worse, not better. Bookings were lower than when Rupert had enticed me out here.

I knew a lot of that was Gloria's fault, but it didn't change the facts. We'd had a further cancellation because of the Silver Fox and a near miss with Julia. And the way things were going, with every single phone call bringing new, unwanted challenges, this Thomson thing was going to be the death of me.

If I couldn't do what I wanted for *La Cour des Roses*, how could I expect to make a go of setting up my own business? It was one thing having bright ideas for improving other people's businesses – I'd been doing that all my working life – but running my own was on a whole new level. That expression about biting off more than you could chew felt rather apt at the moment.

Deserting the laptop, I went through my outside door and lay on the grass in the shade of an apple tree, shielding my eyes from the dappled sunlight with my arm, forcing myself to breathe steadily. This little area always felt like the perfect hideaway at times of stress, and sure enough, it did the trick. I dozed a little, and allowed my mind to empty. It felt good, and after a while I felt ready to face the world. Well, Sophie and Ellie, anyway.

When Sophie called for me, Ryan was lugging his kit through to the garden.

'Hello, ladies.'

'Hi, Ryan.'

I glanced at Sophie. The twinkle in her eyes had suddenly become a lot twinklier.

'This is Sophie,' I told him. 'She owns the hairdressing salon at the bottom of the square. Or have you two already met?'

'We haven't officially had the pleasure.' Ryan came over to shake her hand. 'Although I think I saw you at the farewell party Rupert held for Emmy a few weeks ago?'

'Yes, I was there.' Sophie never took her eyes off Ryan's. 'I spotted you, too.'

Long seconds stretched before Ryan broke eye contact. He smiled, teeth white against his tanned face, streaked blonde hair flopping across his forehead, and I heard Sophie's sharp intake of breath. 'Hope to see you again some time.'

As he moved away, Sophie fanned her face. 'Now him, I *would* bother about,' she stated, and as we drove to Ellie's, she proceeded to grill me over everything I knew about him.

I recited Ryan's biography as I knew it, and heaved a sigh of relief that I'd never confided in her about what we'd got up to in the bushes. And then, being me, I worried whether I *should* tell her. If they were as interested in each other as the sparks had suggested, would she expect me to? *Urgh.*

As we pulled up at Ellie's house, I decided against it for now. Nothing may ever come of it. And if they did become an item, Ryan might not want her to know. It was his decision, too. And there was always the chance she could take it the wrong way – that it might seem like I was just passing him on to her, like a used car. As ever, I opted for safety.

Ellie's house was out on a country road, at what I guessed was the point of a triangle between *La Cour des Roses* and Pierre-la-Fontaine, and it stood very much alone, surrounded by fields.

'I like my solitude,' she explained as she got in the car and caught me gaping. 'I get enough interaction at work.'

'Where are we going?' I asked as Sophie set off again, enjoying the breeze through the open car window.

I could see tall crops over some of the roadside hedges, but I noticed that some of the fields had already been harvested. Giant rolls of golden hay dotted the fields, basking in the sunshine – a glorious sight without those ugly black bin bag-type covers used in the UK to fend off the rain.

'Saumur,' Sophie told me. 'It's not far, and it will give you an idea of a larger French town. You can write about it for your website.'

'You shouldn't feel you have to take me places and act as my tour guide.'

'Oh? Would you make the time to do this if I didn't? No. You would work, work, work at *La Cour des Roses*.'

'And you need content for your site so you can get it up and running,' said Ellie.

They had good points. 'Well, thank you.'

'Anyway, I enjoy getting out and about myself. It's too easy not to make the effort,' said Sophie.

It was only twenty minutes to Saumur. We found a parking space on the roadside at the river and strolled along the wide street, the Loire on one side and grandiose, columned buildings of cream stone on the other.

'What's that?' I pointed at a fancy building adorned with intricate stonework and fluttering flags.

'The *Hôtel de Ville*,' Ellie said.

'A hotel? Very fancy!'

'Not a hotel. It's the town hall.'

'But in Pierre-la-Fontaine, the town hall is the *Mairie*, isn't it?'

'One of the vagaries of French.' Ellie rolled her eyes in Sophie's direction.

'Well, there's a nugget of confusing information that I won't retain.'

We turned into narrower, cobbled streets and did a little window shopping until lunch called. We chose a place with trendy rustic décor and just enough shade to sit outside, and shared a platter of *charcuterie* and cheese and a bottle of wine.

'How is Rupert doing nowadays, do you think?' Ellie asked me. 'I've seen him a few times since Gloria left, but he's a bit of a closed book. I worry about him, but I don't feel it's my place to delve too deeply.'

As I sipped my wine, I weighed up how much I could say without giving away confidences. 'I think he's got used to the idea that she's gone. And I think he's resigned to the idea that she'll file for divorce, but he's not chasing that up for now.'

'Don't blame him!' Ellie said. 'That's going to be expensive.'

'I think it was awful, the way she left him,' Sophie commented. 'If she was unhappy, she should have spoken to him about it, not run off with someone like that.'

I shrugged. 'Perhaps she tried to, in her own way, and he didn't listen or try to read between the lines. I think Rupert knows he should have paid more attention to the fact that she wasn't happy at *La Cour des Roses*.'

'But if she didn't want to be there, why did she marry him?'

'Because when she first met him, Sophie, *La Cour des Roses* didn't exist,' I explained. 'They had a flat in London and a house in Majorca, and Gloria was happy with that . . . But then Rupert came here and fell in love with the place and wanted a project.'

Ellie eyed the wooden board of goodies the waiter placed in the middle of the table, then began to transfer her choices to her plate, indicating we should do the same. 'Gloria was less suited to the rural location,' she explained. 'Not enough shops, and – as you've gathered – she doesn't like to work too hard.'

'But Rupert seems like such a nice man,' Sophie said quietly.

'He is,' Ellie asserted. 'He's a great character. Warm, funny, sociable, loyal to his friends. Soft as putty under that gruff exterior.'

I raised an eyebrow at such praise from Ellie.

'Then why would he marry someone like Gloria?' Sophie asked.

Ellie made a face. 'Lord knows. Mid-life crisis?'

'Partly that,' I chipped in. 'Mutual attraction. She *is* attractive for her age,' I insisted when Ellie was about to argue. 'I've seen photos of her when they got married. She was a stunner.'

Ellie held her little finger in the air and waggled it. 'And she had him wrapped around this, pretty sharpish.'

I glanced across the way at two men manoeuvring themselves out of a tiny antique shop, carrying a tall chest of drawers of highly polished wood, puffing as they hefted it to the end of the narrow street and a waiting van.

When I turned back, Sophie had a puzzled look on her face.

'I assumed nobody liked Gloria because she slept with your boyfriend, Emmy, and because she left Rupert. But now I get the impression that nobody liked her before that, either.'

'They liked Rupert, so they put up with Gloria.' Ellie confirmed what Rupert had told me. 'She wasn't always unpleasant – she knew how to play hostess – but I found her vacuous at best and bitchy at worst.'

I frowned at her. 'But Rupert told me that you and Gloria were friends at first.'

'Gloria wanted to be, so I went along with it for a while. I could see that she was at sea with the move and the renovations and the guesthouse. She had all these grand ideas, but it turned out she didn't enjoy her new role there. She told me once that she'd liked her job as a restaurant manager, but she worked long hours and so when Rupert proposed, she thought it was the answer to her prayers. When he bought *La Cour des Roses*, she thought it would be fun at first, but then reality set in. I think she felt old before her time, away from the thick of things. I felt sorry for her, but then . . .' Ellie seemed about to say something else, but only shrugged. 'Well. We weren't each other's cup of tea. We had nothing in common.' She deftly changed the subject. 'So, Emmy. When's Alain due back?'

'Next weekend.'

'And you'll definitely be seeing each other? Dating?'

'Dates have been mentioned. He's going to help me with my French.'

Ellie snorted, her wine halfway to her mouth. 'Now *there's* a euphemism I haven't heard before.'

Sophie giggled. 'I would offer to help you with your *French,* but I don't think it would be the same, somehow.'

When I glared at them both, Ellie took pity. 'We'd better go easy on her, Sophie. It's all looking a bit tentative at the moment. When it gets more robust, *then* we'll rib her mercilessly.'

'Rib?' Sophie rubbed at her ribcage, asking 'What is this "rib"?' and making us both laugh.

'Do you want to walk up to see the *château*?' Ellie suggested when we'd paid the bill. 'Get rid of some calories?'

Since she was thinner than a runner bean, I didn't see why calories were an issue for her, but they probably were for me, so I was happy to go along with the idea.

We made our way through the town and up to the castle, walking around its walls of cream stone and admiring its grey roof and pointed turrets, taking in the view across to the river with its arched bridge. Sophie and Ellie were immensely patient while I took photographs. It was gorgeous. It would be the perfect addition to my website.

CHAPTER EIGHT

I'd enjoyed my afternoon with Sophie and Ellie very much – a well-timed distraction – but by the time I spoke to Alain that evening, I was all wound up again over everything that was going wrong and everything I had to do.

We were talking online – it seemed to have become an unspoken agreement after that first time; a kind of graduation from phone calls and on to the next stage – and it meant I couldn't hide my agitation.

'Are you still upset about the review?' he asked with concern. 'I understand why, but it's only one man's opinion, Emmy.'

'You didn't see the other one?' I directed him to the site where Clare's review sat simmering.

He slipped on his reading glasses to peer closer at the screen. They made him look like some kind of sexy professor in need of loving attention.

Desire hit me like a punch to the gut. 'God, you look sexy in those!'

Oops.

'What? I mean, er, really?' he stammered. It was kind of cute.

'Yeah. But I didn't mean to say that out loud.'

He grinned, finished reading Clare's brief but deadly missive, then took his glasses off, tossing them to one side.

When I put on an exaggerated pout, his lips twitched. 'I can put them back on again, if you like.'

'That's okay. I fancy you without them as well.'

'Glad to hear it.'

'So, what do you think?'

'About you fancying me with or without my glasses on?'

I rolled my eyes. 'The review.'

'I think you're right to do what you've done. Smother it with good ones. Once they start rolling in, these will have much less impact.'

'I hope so. I don't like their impact so far.' I told him about the Websters' cancellation and my dicey conversation with Julia Cooper.

'But you persuaded her. And bribed her with breakfast goods. Well done, you.'

'Yes, well, that's not all she wants. Now there are dogs and a marquee, *and* she wants me to find her a jazz band from the festival for the party. I tried to look into it this morning, but it meant nothing to me. It's hopeless!' The feeling of being overwhelmed that I'd had that morning washed over me in a fresh wave.

Alain gave me a considered look. 'Tell me what you've fixed so far, between you and Rupert.'

'Who's in what accommodation and when. The cake. The caterer. Duvets for airbeds. Where the tent and caravans will go.'

'Well, I don't think that's bad going in just a few days, considering you were starting from scratch, do you? What's left to do?'

'Marquee. Toilet waste.'

Alain grinned. 'Let's leave those to Rupert, shall we?'

'Dogs not getting on.'

'Can't do anything about that till they get there. What else?'

'This wretched band! I don't know where to start!'

'You should start by asking someone to help you. And that someone would be me. I told you, I've been to the festival before. Let me bring up the programme.'

On went the glasses again.

Sigh.

'I can't say I know all these bands, by any means. But I would suggest that you aim for those in the less popular time slots. They'll be the ones who'd be keen for an extra gig. So – not those playing Friday night or Saturday night. Maybe the afternoon or Sunday ones instead. And as Julia said, you need a small band. I do recognise a couple of these. Why don't I go through this later tonight and e-mail you the names I think look most likely? Then you'll need to look online to see if there are any clips of them playing, so you can judge whether they produce the kind of sound you want blasting through the grounds.'

I watched the breeze ruffling the leaves outside my window, then jumped as the dog came bounding into sight, let loose by Rupert for an evening gambol. I grinned as she raced around the trees like a manic skier on a slalom run. 'If you like jazz, wouldn't you be better doing that?'

He shook his head. 'It sounds to me like the Thomsons might be a mixed bunch – some into jazz, some not, but all getting into it for the sake of the guests of honour. You know nothing about jazz, right?'

'Damn right.'

'So you'll be a good judge of whether it's the kind of music non-jazz lovers could enjoy as background music at a party.'

I blew out a long breath. 'Thank you.' My voice was small. 'I know it's not your problem.'

He rolled his eyes. 'If it makes you look as woebegone as that, then it *is* my problem. I prefer to see you smiling.'

'Sorry.'

'Don't be sorry. Just take things one at a time and you *will* get there. I know you've had a crap week, and you're seeing this Thomson thing as negative right now, but it's not. A group of thirty-four people have chosen *La Cour des Roses* for one of the biggest events their family will experience. You and Rupert are going to make it fantastic for them. And if they like it, some of them may come back for a proper stay some time.'

There was a child's shriek in the distance, followed by a loud giggle.

Alain grinned. 'Bedtime for the little horrors. They're too excited about Paris tomorrow. Mum and Dad have told them they'll take them on a boat. I'd better go and see if their uncle can have a calming influence on them.' He winked. 'I'll send you that e-mail later. Night, Emmy.'

'Night.'

If he worked his calming influence on those kids the way he'd worked it on me, they would be settled in minutes.

He was right. I'd built all the different strands of the Thomson party into one big mountain, without taking stock and realising we'd already scaled quite a bit of it already. The jazz band was the worst hurdle, and when I got his e-mail, I'd do what he suggested and make a start.

Every time I spoke to him, I was reminded that I had a future here to look forward to, if I could make it work. *La Cour des Roses*, my agency, my language skills . . . It was a lot to contemplate and to implement, but that was what I'd come out here to do. I wasn't about to give up yet.

Alain's promised e-mail was sitting in my inbox the next morning. He'd sent it at one in the morning, bless him, but I couldn't do anything about it right away. Monday was market day. I did, however, make time for a desultory phone call with the letting agents in Birmingham. No, they hadn't found tenants yet, and did I realise it had only been three days since I last called them?

'Are you thinking of going into town today, ladies?' I asked Violet and Betty over breakfast. The long wooden table was set with all the usual breakfast goodies, as well as bright orange slices of heavenly sweet cantaloupe melon, which Rupert had bought from a roadside stall on one of his walks with the dog. The kitchen windows were flung wide and the bright sun hadn't yet managed to chase away a light, refreshing breeze.

'Rupert has promised to let us follow him in, so he can show us where to park,' Violet told me. 'We're worried about it being busy because of the market.' Her lined brow furrowed at the thought, highlighting the face powder she used so liberally.

I smiled. This was why Rupert's business was so successful, usually. He didn't just provide bricks and mortar and good food – he always went several steps beyond what might be expected.

'No sign of the Jacksons yet?'

I heard a snigger from the direction of the oven, where Rupert was plating scrambled eggs for Violet and Betty. I even thought I heard a giggle from the ladies themselves. Yesterday, the Jacksons had arrived for breakfast at the last possible minute of Rupert's generous hours – Charles Jackson dishevelled and out of breath, Ruby Jackson's cheeks as flushed as her name might suggest – proclaiming they had 'slept in'.

It looked like it could become a pattern. As everyone was finishing up, they did the same again, rushing in with out-of-breath apologies. They were clearly morning people.

When Rupert had settled the dog by the open window in his lounge, we met Violet and Betty in the courtyard. Rupert drove sedately so they could keep up. I looked over at him as we dawdled past a field with a combine harvester growling and grinding its way through a golden crop. I thought about him pottering about, throwing sticks for his beloved dog, laughing with the guests. Since the moment with the wedding dress, he had seemed to be okay. A bit tetchy sometimes, but that was just his way. Even so, he and Gloria had been married for ten years – they'd been *in love*. I was well over Nathan, but I knew now that I hadn't ever been in love with him. Could Rupert really be recovering so well so quickly? I wanted to ask, but with Rupert it was best to pick your moments carefully.

We pulled into town and parked on a quiet street further away from the centre than usual so Betty and Violet could park without difficulty. My arm muscles groaned as I thought about the extra distance I would have to carry the bags later.

Like a tour guide, Rupert corralled his charges and led them along the streets to the main square. Violet and Betty were rapt as he pointed out the best shops, cafés and stalls.

'Those two have a major crush on you, Rupert Hunter,' I told him when they had tottered off and we bypassed the trinkets and clothes to get to the food stalls at the top end. 'You've got them hanging on your every word.'

'They're welcome to have a crush, as long as they don't try anything on.' He shuddered. 'They must be a good fifteen years older than me.'

'That didn't stop your wife sleeping with my boyfriend, did it?'

'Hmmph. Did us both a favour.' He gave me a sly look. 'You wouldn't be whispering sweet nothings over the airwaves with a gorgeous French accountant otherwise, would you?'

'It's not all sweet nothings,' I said defensively. 'He's going to help with trying to find a jazz band.'

'Well, we need all the help we can get with that,' he admitted. 'I should have thought of Alain the minute you mentioned it.'

'Because he's been to the jazz festival before?'

Rupert barked out a laugh. 'He hasn't just *been* to it, Emmy. He's played there.'

'Played there?'

'Saxophone.' He gave me a puzzled look. 'Didn't you know?'

'No. He didn't say. He just said he'd try to help.'

'Ah. Well, he's a modest soul, our Alain. He's never been one to advertise these things. It's just a leisure thing for him, I think – a way to relax.'

I nodded and smiled at the idea of Alain's long fingers playing an instrument. Any instrument.

I pulled myself back. 'So. Which stalls today?'

'Cheese, sausage and . . . Oh, you have got to be kidding me.'

I followed his gaze to my favourite market stall – favourite, in that it was fascinating and of an era I'd thought long gone. Girdles, corsets, stout bras and granny pants that I didn't imagine *anyone* wore any more. And who was browsing there, paying particular attention to a pair of snug-looking pants with a waistband so high it would reach right up to their matronly bosoms? Violet and Betty.

Sniggering, we shuffled past before they could see us.

Pierre-la-Fontaine was heaving, and the queues at the stalls were long with holidaymakers keen to try local produce, so our shopping was laboured.

But our post-shopping coffee was what I looked forward to most, because we would bump into Jonathan. He was – as ever – propping up the bar inside the café, easy to spot by his shock of white hair.

'Rupert. And the lovely Emmy. Welcome back!' He embraced us both.

Jonathan preferred to stay inside, where he could enjoy the down-to-earth company of the regulars. I welcomed the cool interior with its dark wood wall panelling, matching tables and chairs, the TV above the bar, the chatter of locals catching up on market day – but I did insist we sit at a table.

When the barman placed a squat cup of steaming coffee in front of me, I sighed with nothing short of utter contentment.

'Happy?' Jonathan asked me with a smile.

'Mmm. Happy.' I sipped, glorying in the taste. There was no doubt about it – the French knew how to make coffee.

'Rupert's not driving you mad yet?' Jonathan jabbed his friend in the chest.

'It'll be the other way around,' Rupert pointed out. 'She's just getting back into her stride. She's already ordering me about. Soon she'll be changing everything, insisting on this, that and the other.'

'Isn't that why you coerced her into coming out here?'

Rupert gave me a fond look. 'Yup. Doesn't mean I can't grouse about it, though, does it?'

'So, now you're back, any chance of a few errands, Emmy? I'll slip you a bit of cash.'

Rupert spluttered on his coffee. 'God. It'll be like bob-a-job week all over again.'

I stared at him. 'What the hell's "bob-a-job week"?'

Rupert and Jonathan exchanged grins, and Rupert explained. 'When we were lads, Emmy – *much* longer ago for Jonathan than for me – bob-a-job week was when cubs and scouts went from door-to-door asking if anyone had a job they wanted doing for a bob. That's a shilling. If you weren't invited in by some dubious old bloke eagerly anticipating his favourite week of the year, you were used as slave labour by people who thought it perfectly acceptable to get a small child to wash their car, mow their lawn and clean out their tropical fish tank for less than the price of a pint of beer.'

My eyes widened. 'And your parents were happy about that?'

'These were times when parents were happy to allow their kids to play in the park and woods for hours on end without word of their whereabouts, as long as they weren't cluttering up the house,' Jonathan pointed out. 'Times when bread and dripping constituted a meal, bananas and custard were an exotic treat and, once a year, you were lucky if you didn't get a piece of coal as the booby prize in your birthday game of pass the parcel.'

Rupert snorted. 'Bearing in mind that the party games mainly consisted of kids sitting on each other's laps and groping each other wearing blindfolds.'

'Golden times, I'm sure,' I said drily.

'In any case,' Jonathan pointed out, 'If it was bob-a-job week, our parents were too busy exploiting whichever uniformed little terrors knocked on *their* door to worry about what we were up to.'

I decided to get back on track, before they could traumatise me with any more tales of their childhoods. 'So, you were saying, Jonathan? About errands?'

He coughed and cleared his throat. 'Oh, yes. I know you want to set up your own business, but for now, I thought you could start with the odd errand for me. Can't pay you much, but . . .'

'Well, that wasn't the kind of business I was hoping to set up . . .' I began, but stopped as his face fell. Jonathan already had to put upon his friends, spreading out requests for favours so he didn't annoy anyone too much. The fact that he was offering to pay something – hopefully more than a shilling – suggested he needed more help than he was letting on. 'What do you need me to do?'

Jonathan beamed, happy to have his minimum-wage Girl Friday. He wanted to know, could I go round once a week to do some spring cleaning? His cleaner would only do the basics. Could I phone him before I went shopping, in case he hadn't managed to get out? And if his leg was playing up so he couldn't drive, could I take him to do his shopping or to an occasional medical appointment? I stopped myself asking why he didn't get a taxi, because I suspected I already knew the answer – that he couldn't afford them on a regular basis.

As he talked, I wondered how I'd gone from the prospective owner of my own holiday accommodation site to scrubbing skirting boards and cleaning out cupboards . . . But if the poor man needed it doing, he needed it doing.

As we left the café, I picked up a colourful leaflet from a table near the door. 'What's this?'

'A fête here in town,' Rupert told me as we made our way to the car. 'They hold it every year.'

'What kind of fête?'

'Craft stalls, food stalls, entertainment, the usual. It has a really nice atmosphere.'

'Do a lot of tourists come?'

'Yes, but that's not specifically the aim. It's organised by and for the townspeople, but tourists are welcome to join in and always do. It's good for local businesses.'

I paid the flyer more attention. 'Don't we have a gap next weekend? I'll check when we get back.'

On the drive home, Rupert asked, 'Are you okay, doing all that for Jonathan? I know it isn't what you had in mind.'

'It's fine. We'll see how it goes.'

'You know he won't pay you much.'

'I know, but if I don't do it, someone else will have to. I get the impression he's struggling and this is his way of admitting it. I feel guilty about him paying me, but I don't want to hurt his feelings at this stage. I'm happy to help.'

'You're a warm-hearted girl, Emmy.'

'Ha! You mean I'm a total sap!'

'That too. I have to say, what you're planning sounds like a far better use of your marketing talents. Talking of which, quite a few people are impressed by the great job you did updating my website. Some of them haven't got one, and some have but it's crap. I said you might be interested.'

'I could do that kind of thing in the quieter months. But you need to be careful not to oversell me. I'm not a web designer. I managed to titivate yours, but if someone wants a professional job doing, they should go to a professional.'

'Except that would cost them a professional sum of money,' he pointed out as we took the turning into *La Cour des Roses*. 'Most people aren't willing to cough up much, so you'd be a halfway house.'

I climbed out of the car, opened the boot and lifted out some of the bags. As I walked to the door, I noticed with sadness that the climbing roses around it had finished for this season, their petals littering the ground beneath. 'Well, I wouldn't turn it down at this stage.'

After lunch, I looked at the flyer again and brought up the bookings on the laptop.

'The weekend of that fête, Rupert, we have a room free.'

'So?'

'I wanted to e-mail loyal customers about last-minute vacancies anyway. If I do it today, there might be *someone* who fancies this coming weekend. I could use this to tempt them.'

'It's hardly the tourist attraction of the year, Emmy.'

'That could be the point, though, couldn't it? Traditional, small-town French life at its best. Tell me your most loyal customers, and I'll send them a list of last-minute dates and offer a twenty per cent discount.'

He opened his mouth to object, then closed it again. 'You're going to tell me that eighty per cent is better than nothing, aren't you?'

'Yes.'

'Won't it encourage people not to book in future? To wait for special offers?'

'Not if we only target regular guests who know you're usually busy. But we need to agree which dates are free. I don't want to send this out and then find out you had something on the back of a shopping list that I don't know about. And while I've got your attention . . .'

He groaned.

'I want to speak to you about the guest lounge. Geoffrey Turner hated it, and another reviewer has commented on it. Haven't you asked yourself why nobody goes in it?'

'The bedrooms are spacious and comfortable. The garden is glorious. People eat in the kitchen. The rest of the time, they're out and about. Maybe they don't feel the need?'

'Let's assume there *is* a need. You're a guest here. It's pissing down outside. Your wife has flu and needs to rest quietly in your room. Where do you go?'

'The lounge is there if they want it, Emmy.'

I dragged him to his den and gestured around the room. 'Initial impression. Three words.'

'Cosy. Welcoming. Comfortable.'

I led him across to the guest lounge. 'Same here. Imagine the rain's beating down outside.'

'Large. Formal. Uninviting. Hmm. I don't suppose I saw it that way before. I don't come in here much.'

'Exactly!' I looked at him curiously. '*Why* is the lounge this way, when the rest of the house isn't?'

He shuffled his feet. 'That was down to . . .'

'Don't tell me. Gloria.'

At the sound of her name, Gloria left her basket in the hall and came over to join us.

'Did you *have* to call your dog Gloria?'

'It seemed like a good idea at the time.'

I shook my head. 'Why did Gl— . . . your absent wife do this?'

'She wanted it to be a formal dining room – little tables like they have sometimes in B&Bs back in the UK – but I thought it would be stuffy and awkward, with people not daring to speak above a whisper. I wanted a cheerful atmosphere. So I had the kitchen done the way it is now, even though Gloria disagreed with guests eating in the kitchen.'

For once, I felt a pang of sympathy for his errant wife. And yet Rupert had been proved right. The dining area lent itself to a friendly atmosphere – usually – and it was easier for him than ferrying everything through like a waiter.

'And this was the compromise?'

'Yes. If she couldn't have her dining room, she wanted an elegant after-dinner coffee room.'

I thought about what usually happened – people talking and laughing around the table until late, with no intention of budging.

Why would you budge from a room with a great atmosphere to one that had none whatsoever?

I tried to picture it differently. 'Gloria's idea wasn't so terrible in principle.'

Rupert looked surprised. 'Really?'

'The trouble with eating in the kitchen is that we can't start washing up and scrubbing out pans while people are there. We have to sit and play host until the last guest decides they need their bed. It makes it an awfully late night for us.'

'So you're suggesting we encourage people to come in here after dinner?'

'Not while it looks a funeral parlour, no. But if we made it welcoming, eventually we could. Get rid of that ugly sideboard and the torturous seating. Two large sofas facing each other, squidgy and comfortable, with a coffee table in between. And over there, four armchairs in a circle with a small coffee table in the middle. Move the bookshelf from the hall into here. That will make the hall more spacious, too. Plants. Lamps. Rugs. Cushions.'

Rupert winced. 'My wallet's weeping already.'

'You don't have to redecorate, just refurnish. I bet a lot of guests are disappointed with this lounge. Nathan and I were. I think it would be a good investment.'

Rupert scrubbed a hand across his face. 'Okay. Let's do it.'

I made a face.

'What's wrong? I'm agreeing with you, and you're still not happy?'

'We're too busy for that much disruption at the moment. I'll make it as homey as I can, for now – Julia Cooper will have something to say about it, if I don't – and you can think about furniture and how much you're willing to spend, once things quieten down. It's not an instant fix. We need to get it right.'

I was about to ask him if he knew the whereabouts of my nemesis, the ballerina, but I thought better of it. Rupert had just given me permission to turn this ghoulish Victorian parlour into an inviting space to relax, and I needed to seize the moment. But first . . .

'And while we're on the subject of lounges . . .'

Rupert looked aghast. 'It's a whole subject now?'

'When Julia complained about Geoffrey's review, I told her the *gîtes*' lounges are lovely.'

'They are.'

'Not the middle one, Rupert. Neither Madame Dupont nor I can get those walls properly clean. You can still see the crayon marks.'

Rupert grunted. 'I knew I should've charged that ruddy family.'

I hid a smile. The first time I'd seen the full mural of trains, faded but still evident despite Madame Dupont's efforts with various cleaning potions, I'd found it as charming as I'd found it annoying. 'Can we get it painted before they come?'

'*What?* You must be joking! It's booked up till the weekend before they land!'

'I know. But one group doesn't arrive till midweek. That gives us a few days.'

'I usually do the decorating myself in the winter,' Rupert grumbled.

'I don't think you can leave this one that long. It looks a mess. We've been lucky nobody has said anything so far. But Julia Cooper will, the mood she's in. Can you get someone in, just this once? You've too much on to do it yourself.'

'And what about the place stinking of paint when the Thomson lot arrive?'

'Whoever you use can get started that weekend, work fast – and keep the windows wide open. I really think it needs to be done, Rupert.'

He gave a sigh. 'Okay. I'll look into it.'

My victory half-won, I moved back to our original topic. 'As for *this* lounge.' I gestured at the bookshelf in the hall. 'That first.'

'We'll never shift that!'

'No, but I can hear a motor in the garden and I assume it's attached to a Ryan.'

We collared the poor lad – who I suspected regretted making an appearance – to help us move the bookshelf into the lounge. That done, both he and Rupert made a hurried departure before I could find more heavy lifting for them to do.

When I'd replaced all the books, I took down the two dreary prints and appropriated several nicer pictures from Rupert's lounge and my own room, borrowing hammer and nails and hoping to God that I didn't pierce anything electrical. I would have to think of something more permanent later – perhaps something involving Rupert's friend Bob and his photography skills – but this would have to do for now.

I stole throws from Rupert's sofa and my room to make the sofa more inviting, and used a lacy tablecloth as a runner for the forbidding sideboard.

Rupert's lounge was a bit denuded now, but I didn't think he'd mind. I even peeped into his bedroom to see if there was anything I could nick. The last time I'd been in there, not long after Gloria left him, I'd been horrified by the pink, lace and floral décor she'd subjected the poor man to. So I was pleased to see that he'd treated himself to respectably masculine denim-style bedding, and the walls were now plain white.

Good for Rupert.

Still, he would be losing his bedroom chair and floor lamp to make a little reading corner in a barren corner of the guest lounge.

A couple of extra cushions here, a footstool and a little coffee table from Rupert's lounge there, and I glanced around with a huge amount of satisfaction. It still had a long way to go, but it was a start.

Tired but satisfied, I created a separate e-mail list of regulars from the names Rupert had given me and sent them our last-minute offers, and after a quick supper, I worked my way down Alain's list of half a dozen or so bands, researching each online as he'd suggested. As I did so, I thought about his day in Paris, including the family boat trip on the Seine, and sulked.

A little fizz of apprehension started in my stomach. Alain was coming in less than a week. And while part of me wanted him right here, right now . . . Was Sophie right – that we were meant for each other? Or had the kiss we shared been just a holiday fantasy? We'd built it up so much, over e-mail and on the phone. Could the reality really live up to the promise? What would we do together? Would we have anything to say?

I jolted myself out of my contemplation and tried to concentrate on the task at hand. I rejected two bands because the clips I found were too loud for my liking, and began to see why Alain had made me do this. If I didn't like the music, a multi-generational group of guests might not, either. Of the other five, I could only find clips for four, and they were okay, although I was well aware that a five-minute sample wasn't necessarily representative.

I went to bed exhausted but satisfied.

In the morning, I decided I'd been neglecting my own goals, and since I'd worked until bedtime on the jazz band, I settled down in the cool of my room by the open window to work on the leaflet I'd promised Ellie. When it was done, I e-mailed it to her, then printed it off to show Rupert.

He was in his bedroom, filling boxes with what looked like the clothes Gloria had left behind.

'Having a clear-out?' I asked cautiously.

'Yes. It's very therapeutic.'

'I can imagine.' I noticed the wedding dress stuffed in a box and winced.

He saw me, and gestured at it. 'When you found that the other day and we were talking about it . . . It made me realise that even if I don't want to set anything legal in motion yet, there are things I can be doing. Like this. I know she's gone, so what's the point of opening the wardrobe every morning and seeing her stuff?'

I nodded. A man had to do what a man had to do, I supposed. 'Will you . . . throw it out?'

'Not yet. I just need it to be out of sight and out of mind, I suppose. I'll put it in an outhouse for now. Decide what to do about it at the end of the summer, if I haven't heard from her.' He saw the leaflet in my hand. 'Did you want me?'

'Yes.' I showed it to him. 'What do you think?'

'Neat. Concise. Sums up the basics and has all your contact details.'

'I don't suppose you know a decent printer in town, do you?'

'There's a place up near my café that'll do it for you. You can use the one here, though, if you want.'

'No, I might as well get them properly done. Thanks anyway.'

I left him to his cathartic clear-out, pleased that he felt comfortable enough with Gloria's departure to finally decide to move forwards.

I was making progress on all fronts, Rupert was healing, and I was finally feeling close to an even keel. But by mid-morning, I was back to feeling like I was knitting a jumper that the cat kept getting its claws into and unravelling.

The phone rang and Rupert took the call. I wasn't paying attention, but when I glanced over as he hung up, he looked downcast. 'Another cancellation.'

I sighed. 'Don't tell me – they saw Geoffrey's review?'

'Yes.'

'I would throttle that man if I could! What's the point of trying to make things better if we're going to have no guests left at this rate?'

Five minutes later, Rupert took a call from the *pâtisserie* I'd ordered the cake from. They were extremely apologetic, but their craftsman couldn't possibly fit in the extra order and they should never have agreed to it. To make up for this error, they had contacted another *pâtisserie* in town and explained our requirements. The new place was willing to take it on but expected me to visit them in person to confirm my requirements and pay a deposit. Could I go in tomorrow morning?

Oh, joy. I'd had enough trouble with edible gold leaf and organza ribbon the first time.

I snuck away to my room and flopped on the bed, where I tried to call Kate – the best friend I'd inconsolably left behind in the UK – but it went straight to voicemail. I knew Sophie would be working, so after briefly considering pestering Nick (not always clear on how to handle upset women) and then my mum (liable to jump on a plane to come and coddle me in person), I called Alain.

'I'm actually in the house – can't we Skype?' he said.

'I don't want you to see me if I burst into tears. I'm not pretty when I cry.'

I told him about the second cancellation, and he consoled me, but I was still feeling pretty beaten up when we said our goodbyes. One step forward, two steps back. I knew I was being too negative, but sometimes it felt as though my whole existence in France was at risk, and each little thing that went wrong pushed me closer to my non-life back in the UK.

CHAPTER NINE

When Madame Dupont arrived for her shift, she was so late that it was well after lunch, and she was all hot and bothered.

'I am so sorry! Some of my chickens got out! I found a hole in the fence. I've been chasing them up and down the lane all morning!'

'Did you find them all?' I asked her, concerned.

'I found five. I don't know if more went missing. I didn't have time to count them.' She puffed out her wrinkled cheeks. 'Have you ever tried to count that many chickens in a yard as big as mine when they're all moving?'

'I'll help you later, if you like.'

She patted my hand. 'You have enough to do here. If I've lost a few, then I have. That's life.'

'What will you do about the fence?'

'I nailed some old wood over it for now.' She mimed to help me out.

As we drank our lemon tea later, she asked me, 'When is Alain due back?'

'Sunday afternoon.'

Her eyes twinkled. 'You will be happy to see him again, *Emie*?'

'Of course!' I didn't add that I was as nervous as an adolescent – not that I had that kind of vocabulary in my possession anyway.

'Will he take you out to a restaurant? Or will you go to his house?'

'I'm not sure,' I told her, slightly puzzled by this avid curiosity.

'Maybe you could cook for him?'

'Oh, no. I don't think so.' I tried to hide my horror at the idea. I was loath to admit to the old woman that I couldn't cook unless it involved a microwave and removing plastic packaging.

Madame Dupont tutted and wagged her finger at me. '*Emie*, you impress a man by pleasing his *estomac*.' She rubbed hers as she spoke, to make sure I understood.

I doubted my cooking would impress him, but I didn't want to go down in the old lady's estimation. 'Er, maybe. We'll see.'

It was late afternoon and she was pulling on her old cardigan and getting ready to leave when the knock came at the door.

I opened it to find Alain standing there, as tall and handsome as ever in light cotton chinos and a polo shirt, with those soft brown eyes the colour of demerara sugar and that fabulous smile.

My mouth dropped open.

'Hi.'

'Hi.'

His fingers were tapping agitatedly at his thigh, and I suspected he was as nervous as me. The realisation made me relax a fraction.

Madame Dupont shook her head at me. '*Bonjour*, Monsieur Granger. Come in, come in! You are several days early!'

'Yes. I . . . I wanted to be back home.' He stepped into the hall and kissed her cheeks, then smiled at me.

It was heart-melting, and I smiled back . . . until I realised I was wearing my cleaning cut-offs and a plain old T-shirt.

Rupert came through from the kitchen. 'Alain! Good to see you!'

They shook hands, and the dog came over for her share of attention. While Alain fussed over her, Madame Dupont pulled me aside.

Her smile was broad. 'You should cook for Alain on your first proper date together. Show him what you are capable of.' When I still looked doubtful at the prospect, she patted my cheek. 'Don't worry. I will bring something for you tomorrow morning that he will like.'

'But I don't even know when we . . .'

'Relax, *Emie*. He will want to see you. And I will bring something, okay?'

If it made her happy, where was the harm? Perhaps a nice country casserole that I could pass off as my own?

I smiled my thanks. 'That's very kind of you, Madame Dupont.'

When I'd waved her off, I stood in the hall for a moment, gathering my wits. Over the phone, Alain and I had been safe to chat, laugh, grumble, flirt – and I realised I was grateful for that time we'd had getting to know each other better without the pressure of *being* together. Now he was back, it was the real deal – something that excited me and terrified me at the same time.

Taking a deep breath, I followed Alain and Rupert into the kitchen.

'Good trip?' Rupert asked him.

'Fine, thanks. As family visits go.'

Rupert nodded in sympathy, while Gloria ran around everybody's legs, getting in the way, her tail battering our legs to death.

'How many times have I told you, that dog shouldn't be anywhere near the kitchen?' I scolded.

Rupert gave an exaggerated look around him. 'Unless my age is affecting my eyesight, I can't spot any guests in here at the moment, can you?'

'One dog hair found in the soup, Rupert. One. That's all it takes.'

'Fine. Gloria! Hall! Basket!'

She sat in slavish devotion at his feet.

I shook my head. 'Hopeless.'

Alain was trying not to laugh. 'You lot are made for each other, do you know that?'

Rupert grunted and tickled Gloria behind the ear. 'Talking of being made for each other, are you two going to kiss or am I going to have to bang your heads together?'

Embarrassed, we politely kissed continental-style on each cheek.

'Oh, for crying out loud. And I thought *I* was rubbish at that stuff! Bugger off, the pair of you. You're making me depressed. Go out in the garden or something!'

We did. Out of range of the meddling matchmaker we knew and loved, I breathed in the scent from the lavender that lined the courtyard and willed myself to relax.

Alain stopped me on the patio. 'You look beautiful, Emmy.'

'Thank you. I . . . Why did you come back so early? I only spoke to you this morning!'

'I decided that you and Rupert needed some moral support. And I couldn't wait any longer to do this.'

He reached out and caught me in his arms, then touched his lips to mine, tentative at first . . . but not for long. Our lips fit together as perfectly as I remembered, only this time, there was nothing to hold us back. No sense of regret that I was returning to England; no reluctance to start something we couldn't finish. This kiss was allowed to have promise and possibility . . . and oh, it was sweet.

'That's more like it!' Rupert had come out to pry and cheer us on. Gloria barked her approval.

Alain shook his head in friendly despair. 'Let's go and get ourselves some privacy.' Picking up a lounger and indicating for me to do the same, he dragged it right down to the bottom of the garden, where we set them side by side. We settled ourselves and he took my hand, twining his fingers in mine.

'How are you?' he asked.

'Tired. Happy that I came. Stressed. Wondering if I'm a bit insane.' It was nice and private down here, hidden away from the house and almost enclosed by shrubs and trees, the gentle fussing of the chickens nearby a relaxing background accompaniment – no matter what Geoffrey Turner thought.

'All understandable. You've had quite a time of it since you got here. It'll settle down soon.'

'God, I hope so.'

'How did you get on with the jazz band?'

I made a face. 'Two sounded awful – not that I'm any judge. So I'm down to five.' I narrowed my eyes at him. 'And you haven't been totally honest with me.'

He raised an eyebrow. 'In what way?'

'You said you liked jazz. You didn't tell me you *played*.'

Was it my imagination or did he blush slightly? 'I do like jazz. It was just a slight omission.'

I cocked my head to one side, studying his face. 'Why didn't you tell me you played the sax?'

'I . . . didn't think it was particularly relevant.'

'Liar.'

'Okay. Well. It's not something I shout about, that's all. It's for my own amusement.'

'Okay.' I touched my lips to his. 'Tell me why you like jazz, and what you like about it.'

'My dad loves it, so I was brought up with it. Oscar Peterson, Lionel Hampton. As for sax players, Stan Getz was the one who made me gravitate towards the saxophone. Andy Hamilton cemented it.' He laughed when I looked at him blankly. 'I mainly like the mellow stuff. I don't like it when it gets too experimental and weird, and I find the traditional sets a bit stiff and . . . unyielding. I have CDs. If you come round, I'll educate you.'

Mmm . . .

'Talking of which,' he said, cutting off the drift of my thoughts, 'I don't suppose you're free tonight?'

I shook my head regretfully. 'New arrivals. Guest meal.'

'Tomorrow?'

'I could be free tomorrow.'

'Good. That'll give me a chance to unpack and settle back in.'

'You haven't even unpacked yet?'

'No. I came straight here to see you.'

Wow.

'I don't know what you had in mind, Emmy, but maybe we could go for a walk, then out for dinner? Or I could cook something at my place?'

My heart skipped a beat. If we were alone at his place, what would that mean? A civilised evening over pasta and a glass of wine? A teenaged snog and grope on the sofa? An adult foray into the bedroom?

'Any of that sounds good,' I told him, reminding myself to breathe.

Alain smiled. And you see, that was the problem right there. That smile. I might do *anything* when he smiled at me like that.

I remembered Madame Dupont. 'Except I have to cook for you.'

'Why?'

'Because Madame Dupont decreed it, and I'm too lily-livered to stand up to her. And she'll quiz me about it afterwards. It's a long story, and not all is clear yet.'

He laughed. 'Okay. How about if I pick you up late afternoon? We can go to my place and I'll let you cook.'

'Wouldn't it be easier if I drive to you?'

'No, I'll pick you up. That way you can relax, not worry about getting lost, maybe have a glass of wine or two.'

'Will you be plying me with alcohol so you can take advantage of me?' I enquired innocently.

He gave me a look that shot straight to my lower portions and turned them into molten heat. 'Will you need alcohol?' He leaned across and planted a light kiss on my lips. 'You look tired.'

'Sorry. I'm knackered.'

'We don't have to make conversation,' he pointed out, his hand straying from my shoulder to skim down the side of my rib cage to my hip.

My breathing stepped up a notch as he drew me closer to him. I melted into the kiss in a dreamlike state, not thinking, only feeling. His lips were so right on mine, his hands belonged on me . . .

'Don't mind me. Just thought I'd bring you some tea.'

Rupert. And his sidekick. She came bounding up, slobbered over Alain's chest, then leapt up and plonked herself full stretch across both our laps.

'Can't you *train* this dog?' I asked him.

'She's just being friendly.'

'There's friendly and there's intimate, Rupert. Not all the guests like dogs to this extent.'

He placed the tray of tea on the ground next to us. 'If you were *guests*, I wouldn't let her do that. Then again, I wouldn't expect the guests to set up a double lounger at the bottom of my garden to canoodle on. That's what the rooms are for.'

'We weren't canoodling. We were . . .'

Alain laughed. 'We were canoodling. There's no other word for it.'

His laughter was infectious, and I had to join in. This delighted Gloria so much that she leapt off us and ran a full lap of the garden, barking excitedly.

Alain leaned in close. 'My place tomorrow. No arguments.'

His eyes were intent on mine. Rupert, the garden, the dog all melted away as I lost myself in their cinnamon depths. He wasn't getting any arguments from me.

'Go fetch your laptop.' He broke the spell. 'We'll try to find contact details for those bands you thought might be okay, and we'll e-mail them.'

'In French?'

His lips twitched. 'If they're French, I would imagine so.'

I smiled. 'I *knew* you'd come in useful.'

The next morning, to my relief, I saw more reviews had started trickling in, all on the complimentary side. If the flow continued, it would be enough to make *La Cour des Roses* look respectable again. When I was sure things were going in the right direction, I showed Rupert.

'Listen to this: "We couldn't have asked for a more beautiful place to stay. The garden was a vision, the food was superb, the bedroom everything we could have wished for, and the host couldn't do enough for us." Five stars. Someone who stayed back in May.'

'Thank God for that.' Rupert smiled sympathetically. 'You've done a great job turning this around, Emmy.'

'Hmmph. I haven't stopped thousands of people from reading Geoffrey's review.'

'No, but it's forced us into doing *this*. Anyone who looks will see all these now. That will work out in our favour, in the long run.' He gave me an enquiring look. 'Seeing Alain tonight?'

'Yes. Is that okay?'

'I'm not your keeper, Emmy. Of course it is.'

When Madame Dupont appeared mid-morning, she was bearing, as promised, her offering for my welcome home meal with Alain.

It was a dead chicken. *Very* dead – as in no head, but with feathers, feet and everything else unfortunately still attached.

I deserved an acting award, really I did. Firstly, for not vomiting on the spot. Then for managing to beam broadly, express sincere thanks for her kind gift and assure her that it would be a wonderful treat for Alain – the perfect way to impress him with my culinary skills.

My thanks were mostly genuine. Rupert had once told me that Madame Dupont kept chickens to feed her extended family. She didn't dole them out lightly, so the fact that I'd been presented with one was very touching. Still, a nice *cassoulet* would have given out the same message.

Happy that her offering had been so well received, she pottered off to begin on her chores upstairs, while I wandered into the kitchen, holding the dead fowl at arm's length.

Rupert stared. 'What the . . . ?'

'Madame Dupont gave me a chicken,' I stated numbly.

'So I see. You're honoured.' The corners of his mouth twitched. 'What are you going to do with it?'

'In theory, I'm going to cook it for Alain in order to impress him with my culinary expertise and please him by appealing to his stomach.'

'And in practice?'

'God knows. She . . . She said she chose a young one, so it can be cooked today. I think.'

Rupert nodded. 'When they're older, you have to leave them a while or they won't be tender.' He looked at me sternly. 'You know you have no choice but to go ahead, Emmy, don't you? What if Madame Dupont bumps into Alain and asks him whether he enjoyed it?'

'I could bin this one and go to the supermarket for chicken breasts and you could make me a nice sauce to take with me and then Alain would tell her that the chicken was delicious, thank you – because it was – and she would be pleased and impressed with me and none the wiser?'

'You can't do that.' He grinned. 'You know how to pluck it? De-gut it?'

I swallowed back my breakfast, which was considering making a reappearance. 'Do you?'

'I do,' he told me proudly. 'I've been on the receiving end of several chickens over the years. The first time, I had to stop Gloria from running screaming from the house until after Madame Dupont left. *Then* she ran screaming from the house, while I researched what the hell to do with it. It was a mess, but I got better at it.' He indicated a far corner of the granite worktop. 'Shove it over there and cover it with something. I'll do it later this morning.'

'You're sure you don't mind?'

'Can't see a way around it if we're going to honour Madame Dupont's gesture, appease your guilt and appeal to Alain's stomach. And then there's the chicken to consider. If you throw it away, it's given its life for nothing, hasn't it?'

'I hadn't thought of that.' I blanched. 'How am I going to eat it, knowing that?'

'For goodness' sake, Emmy, where do you think supermarket chickens come from? Man up a bit, love.'

'Urgh. Well. Thanks, Rupert.'

I went outside for fresh air, wandering mindlessly to the bottom of the garden, only to end up at the chicken run, where I had to tell myself that I was imagining the baleful looks they gave me.

After dealing with the new *pâtisserie* in town and leaving my leaflet with the printer Rupert had recommended, I grabbed a sandwich from the *boulangerie*, ate it on a bench near the fountain, enjoying the cool mist that drifted my way, then made my first visit to Jonathan's. He lived in a small, pale blue terrace on the road leading out of the far side of Pierre-la-Fontaine. The paint was peeling on the windowsills – another sign that Jonathan was not too flush financially.

I knocked, opening the door when I heard a welcoming yell. It opened directly into the lounge, and my eyes widened in surprise. I'd expected small, poky rooms, but the place had been renovated to make one large, open-plan room with a kitchen area at the far end.

'Welcome to my humble abode.' Jonathan hoisted himself from his armchair. 'Cup of tea?'

'I'll make it.'

'No, I'll do it. You have a look around, upstairs and down, so you know what's what.'

I went upstairs first. Two smallish bedrooms, one Jonathan's and the other piled with junk. A bathroom that could do with replacing but was nevertheless clean.

I went back downstairs. There were some appealing landscapes on the walls, and the mantelpiece and shelves were filled with shells, photos and ornaments. I lifted a few to look at them.

'Mementos from trips,' Jonathan explained as he handed me a mug of tea, then went back for his. He could only carry one at a time because of his stick.

I moved on to the photos. One of Jonathan and Bob at *La Cour des Roses* made me smile. I'd got the impression the last time I was here that Bob spent half his life running around after Jonathan, but they were obviously good mates, too. There were photos of places Jonathan had visited. And one of Jonathan when he was quite a bit younger, his hair grey rather than white, with another man, their heads close together, both smiling at the camera.

'Who's this?'

Jonathan smiled. It transformed his face. 'Matthew. The love of my life. He died twelve years ago. Cancer.'

'Oh, Jonathan, I'm so sorry. How long were you together?'

'Ten years. I met him soon after I moved over here. I knew he was the one, Emmy, from the minute we set eyes on each other in the market square. He was an artist.' He gestured at the paintings on the walls.

'These are his? They're beautiful.'

'Yes, they are. He was.' Jonathan chuckled. 'We made enough to get by, with him selling his artwork to the tourists, and my pension. We travelled around, enjoyed our time together.'

'You must miss him.'

'More than I can say, Emmy. More than I can say. But we were lucky that we met each other at all, and I have my little house and my friends now. Life could be a lot worse.'

I nodded. 'So. What do you need me to do around here?'

'Well, as you can see, it's only small and it doesn't take the cleaner long to do a quick whizz round. But she's getting on and she can't do anything unreachable or backbreaking. Skirting boards, tops of the kitchen cupboards, mouldy grouting, that kind of thing. Then there's all that junk in the spare room. I'm not daft, Emmy – I know you didn't come over here to set yourself up as a cleaner. But I would appreciate a spring clean over the next few weeks. I don't know who else to ask. I can't do it myself and . . . to be honest, it's beginning to depress me.'

I glanced around, noticing the layer of glued-on dust atop the skirting boards, the woodwork that needed a good scrub. 'I'm fine with it, Jonathan. Honest.' And it would give him some company in his own home that he wouldn't have otherwise. 'Shall I start in here today, and see how far we get?'

Two hours later, thanks to me being on my hands and knees with an old toothbrush and abrasive cleaner, Jonathan's entire downstairs woodwork was grot-free. His joy seemed disproportionate to the result, if you asked me – but then I'd never been a domestic goddess, so I was hardly the right person to appreciate the improvement. Still, as long as he was happy.

'Tea, lovey?'

'Please.' I was parched.

When it was made, he opened the back door onto a little yard. Crazy-paved and enclosed by ivy-topped walls, there was a small table with two chairs, and ceramic pots containing every colour of flower imaginable.

'Oh, Jonathan, it's gorgeous out here!'

'It's quite a little sun-trap. I spend a lot of time here, reading and dozing.'

'I would, too. Did you do all these pots?'

'I tend to them, but Rupert helps me plant, because I can't lift.'

Good old Rupert.

When I left, Jonathan reached for his wallet and started to take out notes, but I laid a hand on his to stop him. 'I don't want you to pay me, Jonathan.'

'But that's what we agreed. I wouldn't have asked you to do this, otherwise.'

'I know, but I'm happy to come round now and again for one-off things like this. Honest. What are friends for?'

I waited for his reaction, worried I might have offended him, but I didn't feel comfortable about him paying me for something he was too scared to ask his friends to do.

'Well, thank you, Emmy. That's good of you and I appreciate it. But you know that means I can't ask you again.'

'You don't have to, now, do you? I'll be round next week some time. Bye, Jonathan.'

I shot off before he could argue.

CHAPTER TEN

'Is the deed done?' I asked Rupert when I got back. That chicken hadn't been far from my mind all day.

'All done.'

'Isn't it hard work?'

'Certainly is. Don't go endearing yourself to Madame Dupont too often, will you?'

I made a face. 'I know she meant well, but why would she imagine I'd know what to do with it? And even if I did, why wouldn't I just buy one from the supermarket?'

'Older generation and country ways, Emmy. Fresh birds, hand-raised – why buy from the supermarket when you don't know where it's come from and what it's been fed?'

'S'pose.'

'I'm sure she guessed you might not know what to do with it, but she would expect me to show you for future reference. And she would expect you to know how to roast a chicken at your age.'

'Then she doesn't know me very well, does she?'

'But fortunately, I do. And because I knew you were going to Jonathan's, I have it all ready for you. The chicken is stuffed with lemon and tarragon, there's a dish of summer vegetables chopped and drizzled with olive oil ready to roast, and another dish with diced potatoes in herb butter. I laid off the garlic on this occasion.' He gave me a knowing look. 'All you have to do is put them in at the right time.' He handed me a piece of paper with instructions scribbled down.

'You're a star. Thank you.'

Jittery about my 'proper' date with Alain, I showered and chose a sundress, swapped it for linen trousers and shirt, then swapped back to the dress again.

Looking for something to distract me, I checked my e-mails – two of the bands Alain had e-mailed last night had declined my offer. Great. I made another paranoid review check, and finally saw something that pleased me. After all the comments on Geoffrey Turner's blog along the lines of *Sounds dreadful!* and *Thanks for the heads-up, mate*, there was now a lengthy comment from a Mrs S Baxter. I took it through to Rupert in his lounge and read it out.

'"My husband and I had a thoroughly enjoyable stay at this establishment only a few short weeks ago. I find it hard to reconcile the descriptions in this review with our own experience, which was nothing short of idyllic. I can only assume the Silver Fox has taken an unfortunate experience there and deliberately twisted it to entertain his readers. I can and do wholeheartedly recommend *La Cour des Roses* to anyone."'

Rupert applauded. 'Good old Sheila. She was here after you left. Lovely woman.'

'Indeed. Now let's hope he doesn't remove the comment.'

'Can he do that?'

'It's his blog. If he has any shred of decency, he won't.'

Rupert grunted. 'Shame he didn't have the decency to wear something in bed, then none of this would have happened in the first place. By the way, you're not going to like this. Apparently there are going to be major roadworks nearby, starting some time next week.'

'Next week?' My face fell. 'Will it clash with the Thomson thing?'

'It will, if they get started when they say.'

'Parking's going to be impossible as it is. We could do without any access issues to add to it.'

'Not much we can do, other than hope they're delayed for some reason.'

'Did you get anywhere with decorators?'

He sighed. 'Yes. I found someone willing to start on the Saturday afternoon after the *gîte*'s vacated and work through the weekend and beyond. Charging me extra, of course, but there's two of them and they'll work as fast as they can. I told them to do the whole place while they were at it. No point in doing half a job. Besides, there's still that black smudge in the bedroom where some idiot had a candle too near the wall. They'll move as much furniture as they can into the *gîte* next door on the Saturday, and start decorating on the Sunday.' He narrowed his eyes at me. 'But if Julia Cooper complains about paint fumes, Emmy, *you* can be the one to deal with it.'

There was a knock at the door. Alain. My jitters came back in full force.

'For goodness' sake, Emmy, put a smile on your face,' Rupert growled. 'You'll put the poor bloke off, looking like that! Besides, this date had better go well – I've spent half the day plucking and degutting a ruddy chicken for it.'

I popped a kiss on his cheek. 'Thanks, Rupert.'

Wiping my damp palms on my dress, I went into the hall and opened the door.

'Hi.' Alain was freshly showered, and the contrast of his faded shirt against his tan made me want to lick my lips.

A proper kiss this time. Mmm.

'Don't forget that chicken,' said Rupert, stepping into the hall. 'And I expect you home by ten.' I gaped. He winked.

We dutifully gathered the dishes in our arms and ferried them across to Alain's little car, laying them carefully across the back seat.

He opened the passenger door for me, went around to fold his six-foot-something frame behind the steering wheel of the tiny blue hatchback, and we set off down the lane.

'We had a couple of refusals from the bands,' I told him. 'One was a simple "No, sorry". The gist of the other seemed to be that they had to leave directly after the festival to get back to work on Monday.'

'That could be a problem, I suppose – the fact that it's a Monday night. Don't worry. We'll keep at it.'

As we reached the outskirts of town and the groupings of houses got more frequent, Alain turned off the main road, following a series of suburban streets with cream, white or yellow detached houses nicely spaced apart, until he pulled up at the kerb. I glanced at the nearest house. It was small and neat, its surrounding lawn interspersed with clumps of glorious hydrangeas.

I was surprised he lived in a house in the suburbs, but then, he had been married, so perhaps they had bought the house with a view to starting a family.

He could read me like a book already. 'Sabine and I chose this place when we moved down from Paris,' he told me as we carried the dishes up the path. 'When she left, I decided I liked it and it was convenient for work. We hadn't had time to do much with it, so I did it up the way I wanted it, to make it mine and mine alone.'

'No bitterness there, then.'

His lips twitched. 'Not a jot.'

He kicked open the door and we lined up our cargo on the worktops. He peered appreciatively under the foil, with no clue that he might soon be poisoned by roast chicken *à la Emie*. (Well, *à la Rupert* – but since I was the one in charge of timing it all, there was still room for manoeuvre in the salmonella department.)

Turning, he looked at me for a long moment, and then he bent his head and his lips were on mine. It felt good – more than good – but I got the impression he was holding back, being too polite. A little devil on my shoulder told me to push. I applied more pressure and got what I wanted. He cupped his hand around my neck and deepened the kiss, backing me against the counter until I had nowhere to go. Not that I wanted to go anywhere.

'Wow!' he said when we came up for air.

'Yeah. Wow.'

He came back down for a second helping, his hand straying to my hips, gripping me possessively, kissing me senseless, until we were both breathing too rapidly for our own good.

'Okay. So.' He shook his head as though to clear it. 'Wine? I was going to suggest an afternoon walk, but I've lost interest in that idea.'

'Wine would be nice, thanks.'

He poured us both a glass.

'Maybe you should put the oven on so it can warm up,' I told him.

He turned it on. 'Why did Madame Dupont insist you cook for me?'

'She reliably informed me that the best way to win you over is by pleasing your stomach.'

Tasting his wine, he caught me in a long stare over the top of his glass. 'My stomach isn't the only part of me you could please to win me over.'

As he put the glass down carefully, his smile was wicked. My stomach did a triple somersault that would have won awards in a gymnastic tournament.

I gave him an innocent look. 'Oh? And what part would that be?'

He moved in close, pinning me hard against the counter as he brought his lips back to mine, and leaving me in no doubt as to which part of him might require pleasing. His kiss was urgent, heated. I responded in kind, allowing my hands to roam beneath his shirt, splaying my fingers across the firm muscles of his back.

'How long will that chicken take?' he murmured against my lips.

'Not long enough,' I warned him.

'God, Emmy, how long do you think it would take us?'

'It's not that.' I waved my hand at the row of dishes on the counter. 'But I won't be able to concentrate if I'm worrying about what has to go in when.'

Alain nuzzled my neck. 'I'm experienced in these matters. I can tell you what needs to go in when.'

I slapped him and gently pushed him away. 'You know I'm talking about the food. I have it all timed out.'

'It'll take fifteen minutes for the oven to warm up.'

'Alain Granger! I have no intention of a quick shag with half an eye on the clock . . .'

He shook his head and moved his hands from my hips, slowly up the side of my ribs, resting at the sides of my breasts so that his thumbs brushed lightly against them.

My breath caught in my throat.

'How about a quick bout of necking on the sofa?'

'Oh. Well. I think I could countenance that.'

He took my hand and led me through to the lounge, pulling me onto his lap. Teasing me with tiny kisses at my ear, my neck, my collarbone, he murmured endearments in French as his mouth travelled. '*Ma colombe . . . Mon chou . . .*' I had no idea what they meant but, oh my God, if my pulse beat any faster, I was going to have a heart attack.

He moved back to my mouth and whispered against my lips. 'Once that chicken is in, it's going on a *very* slow cook. I intend to savour every last millimetre of you.'

Every last millimetre of me melted as I moulded against him, my mouth to his, my breasts against his chest, my . . .

'Wait.' I pushed against his chest. 'Will the oven be ready yet?'

Groaning, Alain cursed. 'Sod it. That chicken is going in *now*.'

He pulled away, bounced to his feet and strode purposefully into the kitchen. I heard the oven door slam. He was back before

I'd even had time to get to my feet. He held out his hand and I allowed him to lead me upstairs. We stood at the foot of his bed as he took me back into his arms and kissed me thoroughly. When he pulled away, he studied me for a moment.

'I could spend all day kissing you, Emmy.'

That caramel gaze of his was spellbinding, when I knew it was for me and me alone.

Alain made short work of my dress. It pooled on the floor at my feet as I tugged at his shirt to make things fair. Impatient, he pulled it over his head, dragged off his jeans, then pulled me down next to him on the bed.

I ran my hands across the firm plane of his chest and stomach, wondering how he kept so toned, looking after people's accounts all day. He had a small birthmark just under his ribcage, and with delight, I traced it with my finger, thinking it looked just like a little heart.

His arm snaked round my shoulders to pull me close. I breathed in the scent of him, lemon and mint. The feel of his skin next to mine was so good.

'Just so you know,' he murmured into my hair. 'Knowing you were here in France and not being able to see you? To touch you? It was killing me slowly.'

I let out a delighted laugh. 'Really?'

'Really.'

And then his mouth was on mine – no more preliminaries, no messing about. He meant business with that kiss. My hands moved to his face to feel the light stubble there, then down to his shoulders and around to the smooth skin of his back.

Alain dispensed with the remaining fabric barriers between us. 'You're so lovely.'

I decided to take the compliment graciously as his hands smoothed down my arms, over my back, down my sides to brush my breasts, one hand lingering there while the other moved downwards.

I gasped. 'Alain, please . . .'

'I promised to explore every millimetre, remember?'

Oh, I remembered, all right. 'I think that would kill me. My heart's beating too fast as it is.'

He smiled and nuzzled my neck. Other parts of him nuzzled elsewhere. Slow lovemaking was no longer an option, as far as I was concerned.

'How about we do all that later?' I murmured.

I took his desperate groan as acquiescence, and all talking ceased.

As we lay together afterwards, our bodies slicked with a light sheen of sweat from the day's heat and our own, I curled into the crook of Alain's arm, my hand splayed across his chest, in no doubt whatsoever that I belonged there and always had.

Being a natural cynic, I'd always thought that people who said stuff like that were hopeless romantics or deluded, or both, but experiencing it for myself was eye opening. It made me realise that I should have always known that Nathan and I weren't right for each other. We'd never had this feeling of . . . oneness. And other lovers had simply been a stepping stone along the way to this.

I mentally rolled my eyes. Any minute now, I would be saying that Alain and I were destined for each other in some grand universal scheme, or something equally demented. I snuggled in closer.

'Are you okay?' he murmured, kissing the top of my head.

'Mmm.'

I could feel his lips curve into a smile. 'I'll take that as a yes.'

He turned to face me and we lay side by side, almost nose to nose. His hand came up to brush the hair from my face and caress my cheek.

'I'm glad I came back early.'

'Me, too.'

We dozed and kissed and dozed again until I realised something was bothering my senses. My mind struggled through a mist of sleepy post-sex euphoria, trying to get to grips with what it might be.

'The chicken!' I shot out of Alain's arms and out of bed, tugging on my sundress as I made for the stairs.

In the kitchen, there was a distinct smell of burning. I yanked open the oven door to a billow of smoke, grabbed oven gloves and pulled it out.

The smoke alarm went off. Alain, tugging on jeans as he followed me into the room, unlocked the back door and opened it wide as I stared at the blackened object in front of me, and my chin wobbled.

'Don't get upset, Emmy. It's just a chicken.'

'But it's not just *any* chicken! It's Madame Dupont's chicken! And now it's died for nothing!'

Alain paled a little, but he was highly impressed that I'd been gifted one. 'That old lady must be fond of you.'

'Yes, well, you'd better tell her how delicious it was if you bump into her, or my life won't be worth living,' I mumbled.

He kissed away my misery. 'I'm sorry we got so distracted that we forgot about it.'

'Are you?'

He burst out laughing. 'What do you think?'

Velvet soft, his laughter was infectious, and I had to join in. He took the bird outside, where it could finish smoking before being binned, then came back in and took the foil off the other dishes.

'Roasted veg and potatoes? Gives us time for a glass of wine outside first.' He picked up the oven gloves. 'Take a proper look around while I sort it out, if you like.' When I hesitated, his lips twitched. 'You know you want to.'

He was right. I'd been too distracted earlier to take much notice of my surroundings, but now my curiosity was niggling at me, so I went off to inspect his lounge. Perhaps because he was an accountant, I'd anticipated an element of the clinical, but there was nothing of the kind. His space was inviting and comfortable – cream walls, slouchy sofa and armchair with cream covers and coffee-coloured cushions, warm wood bookshelves, a large lamp with a driftwood base, a wooden coffee table scattered with newspapers and books.

The dining area held a small square table and chairs, currently playing host to the entire contents of his briefcase by the looks of it. I was touched that he hadn't over-tidied before I arrived. I took that to mean that he was comfortable with me and didn't feel the need to impress. I liked that.

A glass-fronted shelf unit held a few knick-knacks, including a photo of a couple around my parents' age – presumably Alain's parents – and another of a young boy and girl smiling at the camera, who I guessed must be Alain's niece and nephew. No photo of the children's parents – hardly surprising, under the circumstances.

I went back through to the kitchen, a soothing space with sage green and pale blue tiles, white units and grey worktops, and he handed me my wine.

'So. Do you like what you see?' There was a twinkle in his eye.

I had a twinkle in *my* eye. 'You know I do.'

We sat at the back of the house amidst the hydrangeas, with a glorious view across farmland. To the right, there was a profusion of colour in the distance.

'What's that?'

Alain lapsed into French. 'Roses. They grow a lot of them around here. The region's well known for them.'

'Crikey. It's a hell of a view.'

'In French.'

I made a face, but I did it anyway, after a fashion. He asked what else I could see, and I managed to describe the fields and the trees. The road in the distance. What the guests had been up to.

After a quarter of an hour, he smiled. 'You did really well this evening.'

'Thanks.' He had no idea *how* well. Concentrating on speaking a foreign language was hard enough, but it was twice as hard when all you wanted to do was kiss the guy teaching it to you. 'Do I get a reward?'

'You had your reward in advance. Anyway, I'm hungry. A man can't perform on an empty stomach.'

We ate outside. 'That was delicious, even without the chicken,' Alain said as he finished. 'Thank Rupert for me, will you?'

'What makes you think Rupert made it?' I asked him, indignant.

He laughed. 'Emmy, I've known Rupert a long time. I know his cooking when I taste it.'

'And how do you know he didn't just tell me how to do it?'

'Did he?'

'It was my chicken,' I said sulkily.

'"Was" being the operative word.' He glanced across at the blackened remains next to the dustbin. 'Can you stay tonight?'

'I . . .' I remembered that I didn't have my car. Or any toiletries. Or a change of clothes.

'I can lend you a toothbrush. Anything you need. We'll get up at the crack of dawn and I'll get you back to *La Cour des Roses* in time for you to change.' When I didn't answer, he asked, 'Worried what Rupert might say? That man has made it his life's mission to get us together. He'll be thrilled.'

'Okay. I'll stay.'

'Good.' He relaxed a noticeable fraction. 'If we have to get up early, we ought to get to bed early, don't you think?' He gave me a top-to-toe appraisal. 'And I seem to recall that you shot out of bed so quickly, you forgot to put any underwear on under there.'

I let out a long, slow breath as he led me upstairs. And then my mind turned to mush as Alain slowly made a start on fulfilling his earlier promise, using his hands and his mouth, until my body hummed with desire.

He'd said every millimetre – and he'd meant it.

The alarm on my phone went off at the godforsaken hour I'd set it for, but I was already waking with the light coming through the window. We'd left the shutters open during the night to allow some air in.

Alain grunted and rolled over, but he wasn't getting off that lightly. I rolled over too, my arms around his waist, my breasts against his back.

'You're playing a dangerous game, Emmy,' he murmured sleepily.

I trailed kisses across his shoulders. 'I like a little danger sometimes.'

'Oh, you do?'

In a split second, he'd spun around and pinned me against the mattress. 'I thought you needed to get back early.'

'Early's a flexible term.'

'I'm a flexible kind of guy . . .'

Afterwards, I looked at the clock in a panic, leapt out of bed and began to dress.

Alain dutifully dragged on shorts and a T-shirt.

'You're not going to work like that?'

'Hardly. I'll have a run after I've dropped you off, then shower and change for work. God knows, it's early enough.'

'Is that how you stay so fit?'

'Yup. I run every morning, cycle at weekends sometimes. And I do my own garden. It keeps me fit enough.'

'It certainly does,' I agreed, openly admiring his physique as we went to the car.

'When can I see you next?' Alain asked me as we drove. 'Are you free Friday?'

'Yes. But I don't think I can come to yours again, or stay over. I don't want Rupert to think I'm deserting him because you're back. Does that make sense?'

Alain gave me an easy smile. 'It's okay. I understand. How about if I come over to *La Cour des Roses?* I ought to spend some time with Rupert anyway.'

I sent him a grateful smile. I loved that he wasn't complaining. 'Thanks.'

Back at the guesthouse, our kiss was easy, relaxed, his lips soft on mine. I let myself into my room, threw myself in the shower and quickly dressed. By the time I got to the kitchen, I was a little flustered and Rupert had started on breakfast. Several guests were already at the table.

'Sorry I'm late,' I said as he made me an espresso. 'The . . . alarm didn't go off.'

'No worries.' He lowered his voice. 'Alarm, my arse, Emmeline Jamieson. Did you have a good time at Alain's?' His eyebrows wiggled.

I opened my mouth to deny, but I was so filled with euphoria at the way things had gone with Alain that no words would come out. I closed it again and simply smiled and nodded. Rupert was a good friend, and at that moment I could have told him anything, but even I realised that telling a bloke thirty years older than me about a long evening of glorious sex with his accountant was possibly over-sharing.

I didn't need to say anything. My face must have said it all.

'I'm glad. It's about time you two got it together. Your eyes are shining, Emmy. If I didn't know better, I'd have said you'd been at the dog's vitamins.'

But despite his light tone, I thought I detected a sadness in his eyes. I was moving on from Nathan and Gloria's actions, and I'd thought Rupert was too, but perhaps he was still somewhere in limbo.

* * *

It was surprising what a bout of spectacular sex could do. The fact that it had been with someone I felt could become someone very special was just the icing on the cake.

I was on a roll. Not one but two bookings came in to fill last-minute vacancies, both from the e-mail I'd sent to Rupert's loyal customers and one of them for the coming weekend.

And I had an e-mail from Ellie. I told Rupert about her offer to help and showed him her proposed e-mail to clients, to which she would attach my leaflet.

'That's good of her. I always knew she had a soft side underneath that intimidating front she puts on.'

'I know. I've seen a different side to her lately.' I fired off a reply, telling her it looked great and thanking her profusely, then brought up the reservations. 'I've filled two vacancies already,' I told him, showing him the spreadsheet.

'Really? Well done!'

'Don't you ever get any French people staying here? These are nearly all British names.'

'Mainly British. Some Dutch – who always speak perfect English – and a smattering of other nationalities. But no, I rarely get any French.' He laughed. 'Think about it, Emmy. A Frenchman allowing himself to be cooked for by a Brit? He'd rather starve!'

I'd had another no from another band, but since I was on a high, I decided that was a positive, in that it was narrowing down our field.

I phoned the letting agents to harangue them again. They said they had one couple who might be interested. I told them to make them more interested.

And then – the moment I'd been waiting for – a yes from a band. I asked Rupert to make sure my French comprehension skills weren't playing tricks on me.

He replied with a hug. 'You did it!'

'Ha! With a little help from my jazz-loving friend.'

'Did you get him to play for you?' he asked curiously.

'I . . . er . . . forgot all about it. There was the chicken to worry about and then . . .'

Rupert snorted with laughter. 'No need to explain. I get the picture.'

I cleared my throat. 'Right. One victorious e-mail to Julia Cooper coming up!'

'Er. Before you do that, Emmy . . .'

His sheepish expression made me nervous. 'What have you done?'

'I agreed to do a barbeque for them on the Thursday night.'

'You *what?* When was this? Why didn't I know about it?'

'She phoned yesterday when you were otherwise occupied at Alain's, and asked if it would be possible. She's worried that they'll be tired and emotional and it would be a shame to all eat separately on the first night that everyone's together. I agreed to it.'

I shook my head in despair. 'You're soft and daft. Are you expecting *any* profit? We might as well just write Julia Cooper a cheque and be done with it!'

'Don't worry, Emmy. Julia will pay the food bill. We're only doing the shopping, the cooking and the clearing up afterwards.'

'Oh, is that all?'

'And we've agreed to keep it simple. Meat, bread, salad. Bought desserts. That's it.'

'For thirty-four people.'

He ruffled my hair. 'Cheer up, Emmy. It'll be fun.'

I didn't bother to argue. What would be the point? It was a done deal.

I sent my e-mail about the band to Julia, and got a highly con-gratulatory one back. Along with notification of three vegetarians and a vegan. And since we were now providing breakfast for all the guests, could we also extend the buffet lunches for the three days of the festival to all the guests? (At an extra charge, of course.)

Rupert's head was back in his hands. 'I may retire. Preferably *before* the Thomson weekend.'

I punched his arm. 'Don't you dare desert me now, Rupert Hunter. Right. We need to do a little planning. I can feel a sizeable internet supermarket order coming on . . .'

My phone rang. It was Sophie.

'Emmy! Wine, pizza, my place with Ellie tonight? *Please* say you can come.'

'Oh, Sophie, I'd love to, but I can't. We have a guest meal and . . .'

Rupert frowned and indicated that I should hand him the phone. Startled, I did.

'Sophie? Rupert here. Yes, she can come. No, I'll manage, but she can't be there till at least half seven, if that's okay? And she'll need to be back by eleven or so. Okay. Bye.'

I gaped. 'What did you say that for?'

'You can help me prep and get the guests settled. I will entertain them. And you can help clear up when you get back. Now, do you want to discuss this feeding of the five thousand or not?'

CHAPTER ELEVEN

Before I got started in the kitchen that evening, I squeezed in a quick chat with Kate. My chin wobbled when her face appeared on my screen, but I was grateful for the modern technology that allowed us to do this.

I filled her in on my just-over-a-week in hotel management, about which she managed to sympathise whilst laughing her socks off.

'Oh my God, Emmy, what *have* you got yourself into?'

'I can honestly say that every day is different.'

'Don't you miss your job here?'

'Haven't had time to. Plus, I work flexible hours, eat fresh food, take breaks in a magnificent garden in bright sunshine, have a vested interest in what I'm doing, and my only colleagues are a man and his dog. Do I miss my stressful job and characterless apartment? Do I heck!'

I'd saved the juiciest morsel till last – Alain's early return.

'How did it go?' she asked, bouncing up and down in her chair. 'Have you done the deed yet?'

My smile was the widest it had ever been.

She clapped her hands like a two–year-old. She was as bad as Rupert. Honestly, why everyone was so thrilled that I was getting laid, I had no idea.

'I take it that it was satisfactory, then?' she enquired.

'More than satisfactory! It's . . . Well, I shouldn't say.'

'Yes, you should say! It's *what*?'

'It was incredible. Honestly, Kate. Best sex *ever*. But it's more than that. We fit together perfectly, you know? Like we were meant to be.' I rolled my eyes to mitigate the soppy nature of the statement.

Kate sighed dreamily. 'I'm glad. He isn't a boring accountant in bed, then?'

'Absolutely not.'

'Hmmph. Wish I could say the same about me and Jamie.'

'I thought you and he were okay in that department? You did nothing but have sex on your holiday, you said.'

'I think we were influenced by the exotic surroundings. Now we're back in boring old Brum, the fire's gone out.'

'Oh, Kate. I'm sorry.'

'No worries. It might just be a post-holiday slump.'

I thought back to the way my relationship with Nathan had slowly declined, both in and out of the bedroom, and I knew the fact that we hadn't discussed it had made things worse. 'Have you talked to him about it?'

She made a face. 'Not yet. I'll see if I can pep it up a bit first. I might go into town to that shop in the mall . . .'

I waved my hands in the air to stop her. 'No mental images that I'll struggle to erase, Kate, thank you!'

When Rupert was sorted with the guest meal, I set off to Sophie's. She lived in a flat above her hairdressing salon; it was bijou but very Sophie-like, with flower motifs on the cushions, fairy lights draped here and there, candles dotted around every surface. I loved it.

We settled in with wine – mine diluted with sparkling water, as I was driving – to wait for Ellie, who arrived ten minutes late, looking flustered.

'*So* sorry I'm late.' She kicked off her shoes, dropped onto the sofa, snatched Sophie's wine glass out of her hand and took a large gulp. 'That's better. Men! Drive you mad.'

Raising a perfectly arched eyebrow, Sophie asked, 'Shall I get you your own glass?'

'Yes, please. But could you add a load of ice? I'm feeling hot and bothered, and it's *not* just my age.'

When she was suitably medicated and the pizza was in the oven, we waited, agog.

Ellie frowned. 'What? Why are you both staring at me?'

'We are waiting for you to tell us what is wrong,' Sophie pointed out.

'Oh.' She shook her head. 'No. I don't go in for that sort of thing. Girly group confessions. Sorry.'

That didn't surprise me, but Sophie winked at me and we waited like vultures until, after what seemed like an age, Ellie buckled.

'Okay. Fine. What the heck? So, I met this man two months ago. We were attracted. I ascertained he wasn't married – been burned *there* before – and I told him in no uncertain terms at the start that I don't do romance. We had sex. He sent me flowers. I told him off. He was contrite. I forgave him. The sex was good, so I figured he deserved another chance. It's been fine for weeks. No flowers, no proclamations of undying love. Just how I like it.'

'So what went wrong?' I asked her, amazed at this new side to Ellie. So far, I'd got the impression that she was decidedly single and disapproved of men altogether.

'It turns out he'd been holding it all in.' When Sophie giggled, Ellie clarified. 'The undying love, that is. He's madly in love with me for some reason, and he wants us to have a proper relationship involving candlelit meals and holding hands and all that crap.' She shuddered.

Practically helpless with laughter, it was made worse when Sophie tried to drink her wine and was shaking so much that she missed her mouth.

'Well, I'm glad to be able to provide the evening's entertainment,' Ellie said wryly.

'So what happens next?' I asked.

She looked at me, puzzled. 'Nothing happens next. I broke up with him.'

'But why?' This from Sophie. 'Most women would love a man to offer that kind of affection.'

'Not me. I told him the score when we got started.'

'But why *not* you?' Sophie bit her lip. 'Or shouldn't I ask? Sorry.'

'There's no deep, dark secret,' Ellie told her. 'No abusive ex-husband, nothing like that. I just learned through trial and error that I haven't got the patience to be in a stable relationship. I'm selfish, I want to live my life exactly to suit me, and that's only got worse over the years.'

Her words reminded me of how Rupert had once described himself when he told me he probably wasn't suited to married life.

'Don't mind decent sex now and again though,' Ellie added, much to our amusement. 'Anyway, enough about me. Where's the pizza? I'm starved!'

During pizza, it was my turn to be interrogated.

'We want to hear all about you and Alain.' Sophie got straight in there. 'I saw him in town yesterday and he said he'd decided to come back early. Was that because he wanted to see you? Are you getting on okay? Have you had a proper date yet?'

I told them about Madame Dupont's gift for our date, and its fate.

Ellie laughed loudly. 'Well, I bet *that* was romantic – you cinderising that poor bird for your new beau.'

Sophie gave me a sly smile. 'I don't think you need to impress Alain with your cooking, Emmy. He has already fallen for you.'

Ellie tutted at her. 'Hopeless romantic.' When my face broke into a sappy smile, she rolled her eyes. 'God, it's catching.'

Sophie gave a delighted squeal. 'So are you *with* Alain?' she asked, leaning conspiratorially across the coffee table.

Ellie shook her head in despair. 'For heaven's sake, what are we? Fifteen again? Emmy, please inform us as to whether you are having sexual intercourse with our accountant before Mademoiselle Romance here explodes.'

I spluttered wine.

Ellie turned to Sophie. 'I would say that's a yes.'

Sophie's eyes shone. 'And is he . . . is it . . .?'

I gave her an indulgent smile. 'Yes, Sophie. He is. It is.'

Even Ellie grinned.

'Do you mind if I pop out for a couple of hours this afternoon?' I asked Rupert the next day. 'Ellie's visiting a couple of properties and taking Bob with her to do the photographs. She suggested I go with them. I haven't seen him yet, and it would give me a chance to talk to him about photos for my website.'

'No problem.'

When Ellie called for me, Bob jumped out of the car and greeted me warmly. 'Welcome back, Emmy. Sorry I haven't caught up with you yet. Been busy running around after Jonathan.'

'I can imagine.'

'Although I gather you've been roped in, too.' He gave me a sympathetic smile. 'I'm sorry if you're getting embroiled and didn't want to be.'

'I don't mind. What he's asked me to do is one-off stuff, and I can live with it.'

'I was round there yesterday. You're doing a grand job. That house has been getting in a state for a while. I thought about offering – I knew he couldn't afford to have it professionally cleaned – but the one time I hinted, he got quite offended. Said he appreciated the errands and driving him about, but he didn't expect me to skivvy. Only now you're having to skivvy. Doesn't seem fair.'

'The only reason he asked me is because he thought he would pay me. He wouldn't have asked as a favour.'

Bob gave me a warm smile. 'He told me you wouldn't accept payment.'

'No. He needs his friends. Everybody has to chip in.'

'You're a soft touch, Emmy.'

'That's what Rupert says.'

'And no doubt why he's so fond of you.'

Ellie drove an open-top saloon – *very* classy – and I enjoyed the fresh air as we raced along the country roads at a rather alarming speed, the fields passing by in a blur.

'I thought you could shadow Bob today,' she said. 'See what he gets up to and why his photos do the trick for us.'

Bob turned to me. 'Don't be fooled into thinking it's my expertise that sells those houses of hers. Once she gets her teeth into a buyer, she doesn't let go. They don't stand a chance.'

I laughed.

'That's very true,' Ellie conceded. 'But it's the pictures that bring them across the threshold in the first place.'

'That's what I need to do, figuratively speaking,' I said.

Bob frowned. 'Most agencies would use the owners' photos.'

'I know, but I need to stand out. I don't want rubbish photos that someone's taken on their phone in the drizzle at the worst angle they could have picked. A good photo goes a long way in marketing.' I gave him a sheepish smile. 'But I'm sure I don't need to tell you that.'

The two houses we visited couldn't have been more different – one a modern villa with a pool, the other a ramshackle rustic property in need of renovation. I enjoyed Bob's gentle company and found it interesting to observe the way he worked, how he chose his angles, his patience.

On the drive home, Ellie said, 'So, are you going to avail yourself of Bob's services?'

'I might *like* his services. I won't necessarily be able to afford them.'

Bob gestured at his faded shirt and even more faded jeans. 'I come pretty cheap, Emmy, if you hadn't already guessed. I don't set much store in monetary things. I need enough to live, to run the bike. That's all.'

'I know, but . . .' I told him how, in order to bring lets on board, I wouldn't earn anything other than by commission, so was unlikely to see any income before next year.

'So if you pay me an up-front fee, you'll be a long way out of pocket?' He stroked his scruffy beard. 'How about this? Pay me once commission comes in for each property I take photos for.'

'You'd be willing to work on that basis?'

'Why not? The better the job I do, the quicker I get paid.' He held out his hand. 'Deal?'

I shook it. 'Deal.'

'Are you going to the fête in Pierre-la-Fontaine tonight, Emmy?' Ellie asked.

I jolted. 'I'd forgotten all about that! Alain's coming round to *La Cour des Roses* for the evening.'

'It's on tomorrow as well.'

'But I'll be up to my eyes in *gîte* cleaning and guest meals tomorrow.'

'Why don't you ask Alain to meet earlier tonight then? You could go into town for a couple of hours first, then go back to *La Cour des Roses*. It would be a shame for you to miss it. And it would be something local to write up for your website.'

'That's true.' I took out my phone to text Alain.

The square and side streets were crammed. We wandered slowly – it wasn't possible to hurry – past craft stalls and food stalls, buskers and jugglers. Alain was patient as I took photos and examined tens of pairs of earrings, buying me the pair I hovered over longest. He also bought gifts for his niece and nephew – their names twisted out of thick wire and embellished with beads that could stand on a shelf in their rooms.

The food smells were conflicting, sweet and savoury, but all tantalising. Sugar, salt, melted butter, spicy meat, chocolate . . . A child passed us with a stick of candy floss bigger than she was, and I laughed as Alain dodged sideways before his jeans got covered in jammy sugar strands.

'Time for a *crêpe*, I think, don't you?' he asked.

As we queued, I watched, fascinated, as the woman behind the stall poured a ladle of runny batter onto a large, round, smooth hotplate, used a flat palette knife to spread it evenly to the edge, then deftly flipped it at just the right moment. When it was a perfect golden brown, she sprinkled it with sugar or drizzled it with chocolate or honey or whatever had been requested, folded it into a quarter and handed it across to the customer in a paper napkin. She must have made half a dozen as we waited, and I marvelled that not one of them burned or stuck. If I'd tried, it would be a mangled, sticky mess.

'Have you had a proper French *crêpe* yet?' Alain asked as we reached the front of the queue.

'No.'

'We'll keep it simple, then.'

When the hot, sugary, buttery package was placed in my hand, I savoured the smell before sinking my teeth in. It was heavenly. Alain smiled and gave me a light, buttery kiss. Mmm.

The cafés were doing a roaring trade and the atmosphere was friendly, with locals and tourists both young and old enjoying themselves. A crowd was gathering outside the *Mairie*, so we went over to see what was going on, drawn by the sound of laughter.

Two men were beginning their act, making a comical show of setting up. Dressed in old-fashioned one-piece striped bathing suits, with handlebar moustaches and straw hats, they spoke to each other and the audience in strong accents I struggled to understand, but I guessed it was all part of the act.

Besides, language wasn't really needed – they were hilarious. Acrobatics, juggling, playing practical jokes on each other. One stood on the other's shoulders, deliberately teetering dangerously, juggling unlikely objects suggested by the crowd.

In an unspoken consensus, the adults all moved back to allow the children to sit cross-legged at the front, some sucking on sweets and lollipops, and one little boy so engrossed in the show that he forgot his *crêpe*, dripping chocolate sauce onto his bare knees. Every single person there had a huge smile on their face, no matter what their age. Old-fashioned entertainment at its best.

For the finale, one of the performers held a huge sheet of paper while the other cracked a whip to tear it in two. Then he held up a half . . . and so on and so on, the paper getting smaller each time and the one holding it hopping anxiously about, his face more and more comically terrified as the whip cracked in his direction.

I was as gullible as the kids in the audience, my mouth wide open, marvelling at the skill of the bloke with the whip, until the paper got so small that I realised it was impossible and the man with the paper was cleverly tearing it in two with a swift action that made it look real. Duh. I hadn't laughed so much in a long time. I felt carefree, with Alain's arm comfortably draped around my waist.

'Can I help you with that?' Alain murmured, indicating the finger I was busy licking sugar from. Not waiting for an answer, he leaned in for a quick kiss, chaste enough to onlookers but in reality whisking a grain or two from my lips with his tongue.

Embarrassed, I turned back to watch the performers take a bow, the audience unwilling to let them go without showing their appreciation, cheering and whistling. Across the crowd, I caught a glimpse of Sophie with Ellie, and Philippe with his wife, Martine. I sent a little wave across and got one back from Sophie, but Ellie was too busy to notice, doubled over with laughter. Those boys must be good, if they had cynical estate agent Ellie Fielding guffawing like a five–year-old.

Back at *La Cour des Roses*, we sat out on the patio with Rupert. It was a perfect temperature. I lit a citronella candle to keep the insects at bay, and we opened a bottle of local white, the dog enjoying the cooling evening air at our feet.

Alain demanded I brought out the laptop, and he replied to the accepting band, confirming details.

'Thanks for that,' Rupert said with sincerity.

'Happy to help. I know these guys a little. I played with them a couple of times, but it was maybe three years ago now. I think they'll be a good choice.'

I tried to picture Alain playing at the jazz festival and couldn't, so I made a mental note to cajole him into playing his sax for me some time.

'If this goes well, maybe we could use the jazz festival next year,' I told Rupert. 'We could advertise as a convenient place to stay.'

'You want to *repeat* the experience?' Rupert's horrified expression made us both laugh.

'I only meant using it as a plus point to make sure we're full in September. I wasn't suggesting we encourage every man, his dog and a caravan for anniversary parties.'

'I don't see any harm then. Talking of being full, the couple in the end *gîte* asked if they could stay on a couple of days, Emmy, since nobody's due to replace them on Saturday. I said they could.'

I glared at him. 'As long as they're out by Monday. We have the Australians due, and the other two *gîtes* won't be useable.'

'That's what I told them. They're happy with it.'

'Got a decent set of guests at the moment?' Alain asked Rupert, sensing my irritation and circumspectly changing the subject.

Rupert lowered his voice so we wouldn't be overheard. 'Depends what you mean by "decent".' He made quote marks in the air. 'Our fun foursome left yesterday, but we now know everything about their dubious youth. And our "late risers" leave tomorrow. I'm not kidding, Alain. Every. Single. Morning. They're getting embarrassing, frankly.'

Alain laughed. 'Are your other guests showing a bit more decorum?'

'Violet and Betty couldn't do anything but,' I told him. 'Rupert's having to watch his language. Marcus and James Morgan arrived yesterday, and they're lovely.'

'Same surname? A couple, or brothers?'

'They didn't ask for the twin room – not that they could have had it, since Violet and Betty are in there – so I'm assuming a couple. I was worried about how Violet and Betty would react, but I think they're oblivious, bless them.'

Alain laughed. 'How do you know Violet and Betty aren't a couple?'

I gave a cynical grunt. 'They don't argue enough.'

'Don't forget our other new arrivals, Jess and Steve,' Rupert said. 'She can't be more than early twenties, and he must be late thirties, I reckon.'

'Rupert, you're ten years older than Gloria. Alain is five years older than me.'

'I know, but we're all settled in our skin. Theirs comes across as such a big gap because Jess is almost childlike. You weren't there at dinner on Thursday, Emmy, but she was hanging on his every word, as though she idolises him.'

'Maybe she does. Plenty of men would love that.'

'Oh, I bet he does. Steve spent half the meal whispering in her ear, if not nibbling on it, and the other half glancing at his phone and jabbing at it as though he was rejecting calls. *Numerous* calls. He's hiding something, you mark my words. You get a nose for these things, running a place like this.'

I smiled as Rupert and Alain laughed together – the laughter of two very good friends – and it made my heart melt that little bit more for both of them, their faces lit by the light shining out from the kitchen and casting shadows at the edges of the patio.

'So how was the family ordeal?' Rupert asked Alain.

'The usual,' Alain told him. 'I've got quite devious, nowadays. I offer to take Mum and Dad out to lunch on the pretext of allowing Adrien and Sabine some family time with the kids. Or I offer to spend time with the kids to give Sabine and Adrien a break. The only time it doesn't work is when Mum and Dad want grandparent time with the kids, leaving me and Adrien and Sabine as an awkward threesome. Although it's surprising how much work I have to take on holiday with me. How many phone calls I have to make with clients. You were particularly aggravating this time, Rupert. In fact, it's your fault I had to come dashing back.'

Rupert laughed. 'Happy to be of use. How are your niece and nephew?'

'Gabriel's into cars and planes. Chloe's on the bossy side. Takes after her mother. And the tantrums are a sight to behold.'

He smiled broadly, and my heart gave a little kick as I pictured him playing with them. I imagined he would be kind and patient and indulgent, and I reckoned it was all credit to him that he didn't hold their parentage against them. I felt a little light-headed, and wondered if I'd drunk my wine too fast.

Warm evening, beautiful surroundings, delicious chilled wine and a handsome half-Frenchman. What more could I ask for?

When Rupert went back into the house to chat to a couple of guests returning from the fête, Alain asked me, 'Are you okay? You seem a little vague.'

'Just tired, and a bit woozy from the wine.' I linked my fingers in his. 'It must be so hard for you, Adrien and Sabine having a family.'

He shrugged it off. 'It was at first. Like I said, when Sabine and I moved down here, we were thinking about starting a family. When she left me, for a while I felt like I'd lost that possibility along with her. But imagine if we *had* started a family, and then she'd left. It would have been so much worse. Anyway, now I get to play and read stories and act the jolly uncle and wind them into a giddy frenzy, then hand them back to their frazzled parents afterwards.'

I smiled at the image of small children running rings around him and closed my eyes, allowing myself to drift, the wine humming in my bloodstream, the distant murmur of the guests fading . . .

A feather-light touch of lips on mine. Mmm. I responded dozily but enthusiastically . . . until it occurred to me that I had no idea who I was kissing.

My eyes shot open. 'Hmm – what – huh?'

Alain's face was inches from mine. 'You're falling asleep. Rupert's thinking of turning the hose on you.'

I looked around to see the threat was real, and wrinkled my nose.

'C'mon, sleepyhead.'

He hoisted me out of my chair and we walked back up the garden, his arm around my waist.

The next day at breakfast, everyone around the table was talking about the fête and what they'd seen and bought and eaten. It turned out that Marcus and James had driven Violet and Betty into town, knowing they wouldn't brave it themselves, which I thought was a very thoughtful thing to do.

As I soaked up the happy chatter and camaraderie, listening to the great memories these guests held of their evening, I wished I could bottle it and send it out as a taster of what a stay at *La Cour des Roses* could be at its best. Instead, photos and my 'report' on Rupert's website would have to do, and I would add it to my own website as an event recommendation, too.

'Emmy?' Marcus broke into my thoughts. 'We'd like to come again next year and try to make sure we're here for the fête. Could you let us know as soon as next year's dates are advertised?'

'Of course!'

'Gold star for you this week,' Rupert whispered as he passed.

During my tea break with Madame Dupont halfway through her shift, I ventured a question I'd been wondering about for a while. I could have asked Rupert, but since I was supposed to be speaking French whenever I could and my cleaning companion was always delighted with my attempts, I decided to give it a go.

'What happened to your husband, Madame Dupont?'

'Ah, *Emie*, he died six years ago. A heart attack.' She punched at her chest to help me understand the cause of death.

'I'm sorry.'

'It was quick. That's always best.' She smiled. 'He was a good man for many years. We never had much, but he worked hard and so did I. But as he got older, he changed. He had aches and pains and they made him bad tempered. He had no patience with the grandchildren when they came.'

'That must have been difficult for you.'

'Yes.' She smiled sadly. 'But I still miss him.'

'I'm sure.'

She straightened her spine. 'I may not have much money, but I have my children and grandchildren and even great-grandchildren. And I have my house – such as it is – and my chickens. Minus one.' She winked at me. 'And my job here. I can't complain.' She hoisted herself to her feet. 'Come on. We have work to do!'

Rupert's decorators arrived as we were finishing, ready to begin moving what furniture they could from the *gîte* to be decorated into the one next door and set up ready to start the next day. They hauled the longest ladder I'd ever seen out of the back of a van that seemed too short for it, shouting at each other in guttural French. I could only keep my fingers crossed that they would be done in time – if this went wrong, Rupert would kill me.

As we walked to my car so I could drive her home, Ryan waved from the garden, then ambled over.

'Hello, ladies. Been a long day?' he asked, in French for Madame Dupont's benefit.

We groaned in unison, making him laugh.

'I hear Alain's back in town.' He winked conspiratorially at Madame Dupont, making her cackle.

'*Emie* cooked for him,' Madame Dupont confided. 'I gave her a chicken.'

He grinned broadly, merriment in his eyes at the thought of what my reaction must have been. 'You did? How very kind of you, Madame Dupont. So how are things going, Emmy?'

With an apologetic glance at Madame Dupont, I answered in English, since I didn't know the French for 'Manic. Naked sleepwalkers. Caravans with dogs. Cakes. Jazz bands in the garden.' As his eyes grew wider, I grinned. 'Sorry you asked yet?'

'Er, yeah.' He glanced at Madame Dupont. 'I'd ask for details, but I'd better let you get the old dear home before she falls over.' He moved off, then turned back again, and in an overly casual tone, asked, 'Emmy, that friend of yours – the hairdresser? Will she . . . be around at *La Cour des Roses* often?'

I smirked. 'On and off, I should think. Whether those visits will coincide with yours, I have no idea. Want me to take some lessons from Rupert and engineer something?'

'Ha! Er, no, I wouldn't go that far. We'll see how it goes.'

My lips twitched. 'She's older than you, Ryan.'

'Never stopped me before.' With a cheeky smile, he went off back to his hedge.

The Jacksons had left, to embarrass guests at a place further south with their morning routine, and they had been replaced by Debs and Phil Holland, a pleasant pair with several hundred pounds' worth of bikes on their roof rack.

As I helped Rupert prepare for dinner, I felt sickly and headachy – probably a combination of the heat, hard work and not drinking enough during the course of the day. I poured a large glass of water and added ice from the fridge.

'Are you all right?' Rupert asked. 'You don't look so good.'

I blew hair out of my eyes, but it stuck damply to my forehead. 'Just a headache. I'll probably feel better when I've eaten. I'm too hot. I feel like a beetroot. And I thought Madame Dupont's varicose veins would burst in those support tights of hers!'

'Thirty-five degrees today. Go easy on the wine if you're dehydrated.'

'I might have a night off from it, actually.' The sound of tyres on gravel made me frown. 'Everyone's here already, aren't they?'

Footsteps crunched. I heard them go round the side of the house, clicking onto the patio.

Our heads swivelled in unison to the patio doors.

Oh. Dear. God.

Gloria.

CHAPTER TWELVE

'You can close your mouths now. You're catching flies.' Gloria crossed the kitchen to her husband and pecked him on the cheek. 'Hello, Rupert. You're looking well. Not sure about that beard though.'

She turned to me. 'Emmy.' It was less a greeting, more a tight-lipped acknowledgement of my existence.

Rupert found speech. 'Gloria. What the hell are you doing here?'

At the sound of her name, the dog came shooting out of her basket in the hall, but stopped short in the kitchen doorway. Her usual ebullience when greeting people was absent as she stood warily eying her namesake, unwilling to get too close. She was a wise judge of character, that dog.

Gloria almost dropped her handbag, but then recovered herself. 'I noticed on the website that you'd acquired an animal.' There was a note of disgust in her voice.

Rupert walked over to the dog and stroked her protectively. 'This is . . . Gloria.'

I watched as human Gloria fought her distaste, managing a mask of brittle sweetness and a smile that didn't reach her eyes.

'And you called her after me. How touching, darling. You must have missed me, to do something as sentimental as that.'

Despite trying to keep his cool, Rupert looked pretty shaken up. He wasn't the only one. The seconds stretched out, but he made no further remark.

Looked like it was down to me, then. 'Gloria. To what do we owe the pleasure?'

The dog barked at her name again.

'Gloria! Hall! Basket!' Rupert said sternly. For a change, she didn't need to be told twice. She slunk to her basket, well away from this dislikeable stranger.

'I came back,' she declared in answer to my question. Bold as brass.

I thought Rupert might faint. Someone had to take charge here, and quick. The guests would start assembling for dinner soon.

'It's quite late, Gloria. We're about to serve dinner. Where are you staying?'

'Here, of course.'

I almost choked. 'I'm sorry, but all the rooms are occupied.' I thought about the *gîtes* – one still occupied, one stacked high with furniture and the other bare and ready to be painted. 'As are the *gîtes*. We have nowhere to put you up for the night.'

Her lips stretched into an arrogant smile. 'No need to apologise, Emmy – or to worry about where I'll sleep. I do have my own quarters here, after all. I'll get my bags from the car.' She turned to Rupert. 'No need to help. I know you have guests to see to.'

She left through the main door in the hall and began ferrying her bags and cases from her car to their private rooms.

Rupert's eyes were glazed.

'For God's sake, Rupert, snap out of it!' I thought I might have to slap his face like they do in the movies, but I tried a shake of his arm first. 'Rupert!'

'Shit!' he muttered. 'Shit, shit, shit.'

Not eloquent, but I couldn't have put it better myself.

'Go talk to her. Sort it out!' I hissed.

He finally focused on me. 'Sort what out? I don't know what I'm sorting out, do I? I have no idea why . . .'

But it was too late. Guests began to appear and settle themselves at the table. Rupert took a deep breath, gave me a firm glare and immediately moved into welcoming host mode.

Gloria came through as they took their places. 'Hello, everyone,' she said brightly. 'Nice to meet you all. I'm Gloria, Rupert's wife. I just got back from a trip to the UK.'

This was greeted by puzzled expressions.

'Is that a coincidence or deliberate?' James asked. 'Two Glorias?'

'My husband's mind works in mysterious ways.' Gloria gave an exaggerated wink. 'Sorry to rearrange everyone, but would you mind if we set an extra place at the table? I'm starved!'

Everyone politely shuffled around as Rupert brought an extra set of cutlery, a napkin and a chair. At the last minute, he remembered that the dog should be away in his lounge during the meal and went to shut her in.

'Were you visiting family in the UK, Gloria?' Betty asked politely as Rupert ferried individual Greek salads to the table.

'No, I was staying with a friend,' Gloria replied smoothly.

Not one iota of discomfort! That woman had the gall of . . . I don't know what. I wasn't sure there was a living creature on the planet with the nerve that she had.

As the meal proceeded, I felt more and more distanced from the conversation, as though it were taking place underwater. The sick feeling I'd had earlier was getting worse, and my head was pounding. I forced myself to eat something, but I had no idea what it was. I took little notice of who said what. I remember glancing across at Rupert every so often, an inner voice reaching through the murk and telling me to check that he was okay. He seemed it – or at least he was putting on a good front.

By the time dessert was over, my headache had improved a little, but as the pain slowly receded, my indignation and panic at Gloria's return came back to the fore.

When he'd made coffees, Rupert excused himself and went off to his room, ostensibly for the loo. Two minutes later, I used the same excuse, half closing the kitchen door behind me and letting myself into his private lounge, where I petted the dog, waiting until Rupert came out of the bathroom.

He jumped a mile. 'Emmy! Don't do that! I have heart problems, remember?'

'Sorry. Needs must.'

'What's up?'

'What's *up*? You really need to ask?'

'Besides the fact that my supposed soon-to-be-ex-wife has made an unexpected return.'

'And is brazenly passing herself off as your *happily married* wife. How dare she?'

'Emmy, you and I both know that Gloria may be many things, but short of brazenness is not one of them. Did you honestly expect me to put the record straight with all my guests? Tell them she ran off with someone weeks ago and I haven't seen hide nor hair of her since? I'm sure that would have made everyone feel *most* comfortable and relaxed.' He gave me a glare. 'My guests come first.'

'And what about you? What about *your* comfort and stress levels?'

'They might have to take a back seat while I find out why she's here and what she wants. But this evening is not the appropriate time for that.'

'But where will she sleep?'

'I've offered to book her into a hotel, Emmy, but she won't have it.' He gestured to the open bedroom doorway. 'She's already dumped her bags in there. And since, as you bravely pointed out to her, every single room and *gîte* is either occupied or unusable, I don't see where else she can go.'

'You know she probably timed all this deliberately, don't you? Arriving on a Saturday evening, when there's always a guest meal, knowing you'd be up to your eyes cooking and entertaining with a houseful of people, so you couldn't make a fuss. She also knew there was every likelihood we'd be full.'

'I'm sure you're right. It doesn't alter the facts, though, does it?

'You could make her sleep on the sofa.'

'I'm sure *that* would work. About as well as trying to get a tiger to roll over so you can tickle its belly.' He scratched his neck. 'But I suppose *I* could sleep on the sofa. I'd use one of the *gîtes* if we had one that was habitable.' He glared at me.

I opened my mouth to object, then closed it again. We were looking at a stark choice here. Better that Rupert should spend an uncomfortable night on the sofa than in bed with that viperous wife of his, using her wiles for goodness knew what. I shuddered at the thought of what she might resort to.

'Yes. Definitely. I think you should.' I gave him a firm look. 'Promise me?'

He squeezed my hand. 'I promise, Emmy. And I appreciate your concern.'

'What's going on?' Gloria appeared in the doorway. 'You've been gone ages, Rupert. I thought you must have drowned yourself in the toilet.' Her eyes narrowed as Rupert dropped my hand. 'Getting a little friendly nowadays, you two, aren't you?'

My hand itched *so* hard to slap her. Instead, I walked away . . . with my open palms clamped hard against my thighs as I passed.

I couldn't say I slept well that night. Thoughts of Gloria trying to wheedle her way back into Rupert's affections after all she'd put him through tormented me, making my blood boil.

I'd always been a firm believer in not meddling in other people's affairs, but I thought I might make an exception in this case. I felt as protective of Rupert as I would my own father, and I would *not* stand by and watch that woman stomp all over his heart the way she had last time. I'd so desperately wanted to phone Alain, but it was after midnight before I got the chance, and I didn't see the point of us both losing sleep.

Gloria came into the kitchen as I was getting breakfast together. 'Where's Rupert?'

'Good morning to you, too.'

The way she narrowed her eyes made her look like a cobra ready to strike, and it occurred to me that if she *was* back for good, I ought to be a tad more polite . . . although in that case, it wouldn't matter, because my employment would rapidly be terminated – if not through Gloria's insistence, then because I wouldn't be able to stomach it.

For now, I hedged my bets and gave her a small smile. 'He's walking the dog.'

She wrinkled her nose as she set to at the coffee machine. 'I can't imagine why he thought it was a good idea to get a dog.'

Because he needs companionship. Because he needs someone to love him the way he deserves to be loved.

'He said he's always wanted one.' *But you would never let him.*

'Yes, well, we don't always get what we want, do we?' Sipping at her coffee – she hadn't offered me one – she stared me down. She was good at that, but I'd learned not to be intimidated by it. 'You got your feet under the table pretty quickly, didn't you, Emmy? And I noticed I've been removed from the website.'

She'd spotted that, had she? Good. 'Rupert didn't want to mislead the guests.'

'But you're on there now. Described as a *manager*, no less.'

'That's my role.'

'Manager? Is that what you call it, helping that old witch Dupont to clean? Feeding the chickens? You're getting ideas above your station, aren't you?'

'There's far more than that to running this place, as you'd well know if you'd ever bothered. Rupert wants to move forward and make changes. I'm here to do whatever I can to help him.'

'Hmm. Talking of which, my husband assures me that you haven't been . . . *helpful* in other departments. I presume your story's the same?'

Part of me longed to tell her that Rupert and I had been swinging from the chandeliers for weeks. That we'd enjoyed wild sex in every corner of the house and garden. But I would tell her the truth, for Rupert's sake.

'Yes, my story's the same.' This conversation – or battle of wills – was exhausting after so little sleep. 'If you'll excuse me, I have things to do.'

Whatever poisonous retort she'd been dreaming up thankfully remained unspoken, as guests appeared for breakfast. Gloria joined them, making polite conversation, while I took requests for anything cooked and prayed that Rupert would be back soon to deal with them. Where the hell had he got to?

When he arrived, the dog slunk straight to her basket without having to be told, and he hobbled over to the oven.

'Is your leg playing up again?'

'Not my leg. My back,' he hissed. 'Bloody sofa. Bloody uncomfortable.'

After breakfast, Gloria insisted that Rupert join her for a drive and a coffee in a nearby village. 'Away from this place. A bit of *privacy* wouldn't go amiss.' They set off in her sports car, and I did my best not to think about what ploys and wiles and arguments she might try out on the poor bastard.

Taking my coffee outside, with the dog trotting along, I smiled at Jess and Steve on the patio, then heard the whine of a motor. Glancing back to the courtyard, I saw Ryan's car was there, so I made another espresso for him and followed the noise, the dog at my heels.

He was trimming the tall hedge right around the side of the house that separated the orchard from the road. My companion immediately flopped in a shady corner to watch him work.

Not wanting to make him jump and chop his own arm off, I waited until he spotted me and turned it off.

'Emmy. Hi. Is that for me?' He took the coffee and smiled his thanks, then registered my expression. 'What's up?'

'I'd drink your coffee first, if I were you. You're going to need it.'

'What is it?' But he took me at my word and had a sip.

'Gloria's back. She turned up last night.'

'She *what?*' His face was a picture. 'What the . . . ?'

'Yeah, yeah. Been there, done that.'

'But when you say she's back, do you mean she's *back* back? As in, back for good?'

'She'd like to be. But ultimately it's down to Rupert, isn't it?'

Ryan wiped his forehead with the back of his hand. 'I hope he's not stupid enough to be persuaded.'

'Me too.'

There was nothing more to be said. I turned and called for the dog to follow, but she seemed reluctant to move from her shady spot.

'Leave her with me,' Ryan suggested.

Back at the house, I took the bedlinen that Rupert had washed down to the bottom of the garden to peg it out, then stuffed another load in the machine. That done, I pulled my phone out of my pocket to put Alain in the picture.

'Hi. Am I still seeing you this afternoon?' he asked.

'Yes, but I need to tell you something. Gloria's back.'

I heard a sharp intake of breath. 'When?'

'Last night. It's a long story. I'll fill you in when I come round.'

'Where is she staying?'

'She's installed with Rupert. He slept on the sofa. Nowhere else he could go.'

There was a silence as he absorbed the news. 'You need to get away from there sooner, if you ask me. I had an idea for today, so wear shorts and trainers, okay?'

I didn't need telling twice. 'Okay. But I need to catch Rupert on his own first. I want to talk to him.'

'I bet you do.'

Rupert found me before I could look for him. I was sitting on a bench halfway down the garden, nervously twiddling my thumbs. The dog had deserted Ryan and come to keep me company, after all.

'Hi. I'm going to Alain's soon, if that's okay?'

'Of course. It is Sunday.'

I eyed him carefully, trying to gauge his mood. 'Where's your coffee companion?' The last thing I needed was the enemy bursting in on us.

'Unpacking. Why?'

'I was hoping to talk to you.'

He let out a resigned sigh, lowered himself onto the grass and stretched his legs out in front of him, leaning back on his elbows with the dog's head in his lap. His leaner frame suited him. Not that he'd looked seriously overweight before, being broad with it, but it made a difference. And his experimental beard had settled into a close-cut, grizzled grey that lent him a charismatic quality, with his silver hair slightly overlong and wavy.

'You're looking good, Rupert, now you've lost weight. Much healthier. And I like the beard.'

'Thanks.'

'Has your wife said any more about it?'

'Not yet. I'm sure she will. She thinks I should get my hair cut.'

'Don't. It goes with the beard. Kind of bohemian.'

He smiled, then shot me a warning glare. 'If you're planning on interrogating me about Gloria's return, Emmy, I'd rather you didn't.'

Upon hearing her name, the dog's ears pricked up and she gave a little yap.

'*Why* did you have to call her Gloria?' I lamented. 'That poor animal is going to get *so* confused, now the original Gloria's here.'

I refrained from adding that if Rupert did resurrect his marriage, he would have to rename either his dog or his wife, and I wasn't sure which would be more easily trained.

He stroked the dog's ears. 'Then she'll have to be confused for a while. She won't be the only one.'

'Rupert, I'm worried about you.'

'Well, then, that makes two of us.'

We sat in silence for a moment or two. I wanted to respect his wish not to be interrogated, but surely it was better for him to talk.

'How did Gloria take you sleeping on the sofa?'

He swatted at an overly friendly wasp. 'Badly. She tried to . . . persuade me to change my mind. But you'll be pleased to know that I resisted.'

'Good for you.'

He shrugged. 'It wasn't difficult. I only had to think about her rolling around with Nathan and the two of them running off together. Hardly an aphrodisiac.'

'She hasn't said what went wrong between them, then?'

'Hasn't said, and I haven't asked.'

I nodded, studying his face for any sign of how much I should ask and how much he might want to talk. 'How do you feel about her coming back? Were you . . . pleased to see her?'

He became quite animated. 'Pleased? No. I'm angry that she turned up out of the blue like that. But I understand why. If she'd got in touch – if she'd asked – I'd have told her where to go.'

Sensing his change of mood, the dog transferred her allegiance – or her chin, anyway – to my lap.

'Do you know how long she intends to stay?' I ventured.

'Until we've discussed everything, I suppose.'

Well. *That* told me far more than he intended. The fact that he was willing to discuss things with Gloria for as long as it took to come to a decision . . . It meant he wasn't ruling out the idea of them getting back together. I couldn't deny that I was shocked by that, but I kept my expression neutral.

'Can you . . . Can you envisage a future together?'

'I don't know.' He scrubbed a hand across his face, then looked away, fixing his gaze on a bee buzzing busily around a bright yellow bloom. 'Dare I ask if you have any thoughts on this?'

'Ha! I have a great many thoughts, and you know full well that most of them are unrepeatable, but I have no intention of voicing them. What I think, what your friends might think, none of that matters. What matters is how *you* feel about Gloria. What *you* want. Everyone else will fall in with it.'

He pulled at the grass by his side. 'I'm scared,' he murmured.

I tried hard to hide my shock. 'Scared? Why?'

'By wanting to reconcile, Gloria's asking me to make a far bigger choice than she realises. It's not all about whether I take her back or not.' He gave a wry shake of his head. 'Although there's the unspoken suggestion that if I don't, she'll take me for every penny she can squeeze out of me. But she's asking so much more of me than that.'

'In what way?'

He looked me in the eye. 'I know my friends believe I'd be better off without her. So what she's asking me to do, effectively, is to distance myself from people I'm close to, people whose company I enjoy.'

I frowned. 'I guess you're probably right. I don't see what would be in it for her, to come back to a bunch of people she doesn't like and who don't like her.'

Rupert smiled sadly, glancing around the garden at his hard-won domain. 'No doubt things would get so awkward that she would persuade me to sell up and move on. Start afresh, with a new set of friends that suit her better.'

The idea that Rupert might give up this place that he loved so much shocked me far more than the idea of him taking Gloria back. 'Would you do that?'

'I think I'd have to accept that if I decide to make a go of it with Gloria, it would be the likely outcome.' He gave me a direct look. 'It would leave you high and dry, Emmy, which would be a disgrace, after I persuaded you to come out here.'

I swallowed down panic. 'Your happiness matters more to me than that. I do *not* want you basing your decision on my job. It might take months before you decide to sell, and months again to actually do it.' I didn't add that I knew damned well that Gloria would have me out on my ear the minute Rupert agreed to take her back.

Sensing our melancholy, the dog shifted and whined. We both looked at her, and a new horror dawned on me.

'What about . . .'

Rupert reached out to stroke her with sad affection. 'She would have to go. Gloria hates her.'

I took a long minute to decide how much to say. 'It seems to me that Gloria's asking you to give up an awfully long list of things you love, for just the one thing – her – in return.'

'But she's not asking me to give *anything* up, is she? Not yet. All this is just me jumping ahead to the inevitable outcome.'

'Then I suppose you need to decide if you still love her, and if so, how *much* you love her and how much you're willing to give up to be with her. Whether you can forgive her for what she did with Nathan. Whether you'll be able to forgive her in the future for all the compromises she'll expect you to make, or whether you'll end up holding it all against her.'

'Is that all? My head may explode!'

Good job I hadn't asked him the thing that was at the forefront of my mind then: did he trust her not to run off again, once she'd made him give everything up to be with her?

I shifted the dog's head from my lap, stood, and popped a kiss on his cheek. 'There's no rush, Rupert. Gloria's not going anywhere, more's the pity. Take as long as you need.'

CHAPTER THIRTEEN

When I arrived at Alain's, I found him sitting at the dining table, working.

'What are you doing that for, on a glorious day like this?'

'I needed to do something complicated to take my mind off Gloria.'

'Has it succeeded?'

'No. Come here and help me out.'

I gave him an innocent look. 'I don't think my maths is up to it, Alain, to be honest.'

'Not interested in your brains.'

'Charming!' I went over and sat across his lap, snaking my arms around his neck. The kiss was long and much needed by both of us.

'Better?' I asked him.

'Mmm. Better.' He leaned in for another. 'Ouch. I'm getting cramp.'

I slapped at him. 'I'm not *that* heavy.'

He stood and moved past me to the kitchen, patting my backside on the way. 'No. You're just right. Lunch?'

'Please.'

He put together a tray of cold meats, tomatoes, olives and bread, and we took it outside.

'You'd better tell me the whole story,' he said in a resigned tone as we helped ourselves.

So I did. Alain needed to know what was going on, and I needed an outlet for the numerous emotions that Gloria's return and her attitude had provoked in me.

When I'd brought him up to speed, he was as wound up as I was. 'Are we presuming that Nathan left her?'

'I can't imagine she left him only to come back to somewhere she hated enough to run away from in the first place. But the whys and wherefores don't matter. What matters is that she's back, and she thinks all she has to do is to snap her fingers for Rupert to welcome her with open arms.'

'Surely he won't?'

'I don't know, Alain. When she left him, he admitted their marriage was already on shaky ground, but even so, he was really shocked by her desertion. What bugs me is that he's been going through a kind of healing process since, in his own way, and I didn't think he was too unhappy.'

'But?'

'Well, it's possible that he's lonely, isn't it? I don't *get* that impression – he once told me he wasn't designed for marriage. And even if he is lonely, taking Gloria back won't solve that. I don't see how their relationship would be any different from before.'

Alain stood and began to pace.

'We could do some French,' I suggested. 'It might take our minds off Gloria.'

'How many swear words would you like to learn? Because I have a fair few at the tip of my tongue right now. Anyway, I have a better idea.'

He took my hand and led me to the large shed at the bottom of the garden, where he dragged out two bikes. His and . . .

'Yours, temporarily. If you like it, yours to buy for fifty euros.'

I stared at the foreign object with panic and dismay. 'What?'

'One of the neighbours is selling it, so I said you might like to try it. This is the perfect opportunity, don't you think? We need a distraction, and we need physical exercise to get rid of tension.' Seeing my expression, he laughed. 'Not that kind. Not yet, anyway. You can come closer. It won't bite. Climb aboard so I can adjust the saddle.'

Gingerly, I straddled the bike. I hadn't been on one since I was ten, when my friend fell off hers and knocked a front tooth out, pouring copious amounts of blood onto the pavement in the process. I pointed this out to Alain, to no avail.

'You'll be fine, I promise.'

He fiddled with spanners, adjusting various parts of the bike until he was satisfied that it was suitable for me, but I remained unconvinced, thinking wistfully about the day I'd originally imagined us having. I'd assumed he'd asked me to wear shorts and trainers for a country stroll, then there would have been more lounging in the garden, an afternoon 'nap' . . . Instead, I was going to get all sweaty and permanently damage all the muscles you use for cycling, which in my case hadn't been used in years.

We set off, Alain in the lead. I was a bit wobbly at first – a lot wobbly, in fact – but the residential streets were Sunday-quiet as we cycled past neat family houses surrounded by lawns parched yellow from the sun, and by the time we were on a proper road out of town, I was confident enough – unless a car went past at speed, when I had a habit of closing my eyes and praying, something that did nothing for my steering.

Alain turned off onto a country road with less traffic, and I began to relax and almost enjoy myself, daring to take my eyes off Alain in front to take note of what we were cycling past. It was obvious, of course, but it was a much better view cycling than driving. My walks from *La Cour des Roses* had only passed farms and fields, but now we cycled past vineyards and I could see how perfectly straight the rows of vines were, a deep summer green. Beyond them, on a slope, stood a huge cream-coloured house with a grey roof, several round turrets lending it a castle-like appearance, honey-toned wood shutters at the tall arched windows and doors and large weeping willows standing guard at every corner – presumably the vineyard owner's residence. Very formal and fancy.

Alain turned to check that I was okay every few hundred yards, and stopped now and again to hand me a bottle of water he had fixed to his bike. The road was reasonably flat, the weather hot, but the movement of the bike meant that a light breeze caressed my face. Eventually, he turned off onto a dirt track, which had its advantages and disadvantages – no traffic to contend with, but the rougher surface meant harder work for my legs, and the odd pothole added the extra excitement of wondering whether I might fly over the handlebars. Even so, the enjoyment of it slowly came back to me – that childhood freedom of pedalling along with no real destination in mind and no worries to plague you. The sun was hot, a gorgeous man was by my side, leaves tickled my arms and the rushing air cooled my face as I whizzed along, loving every minute.

Finally, Alain came to a stop and handed me a banana. 'For energy. Enjoying it, after all?'

I gave him a sheepish smile. 'Yes.'

'Good.'

'It might not be, if my legs collapse under me when I try to get out of bed tomorrow morning.' I grimaced. 'I am *so* unfit!'

'What makes you say that? You've kept up with me all right.'

'Yes, but I never do any of this stuff. You go running every morning and you enjoy cycling. I only have the odd stroll and chucking the occasional ball for Gloria to keep me fit.'

He laughed. 'Does she fetch them for you?'

'I meant *dog* Gloria.'

'I bet you're a lot fitter than you think. Much fitter than when you were working ten hours a day in an office. You do more than your share of physical work at *La Cour des Roses*. And you must be burning off a fair number of calories with me.'

His smile was wicked and my pulse, already racing from the cycling, pepped up the pace even more as I thought about what my reward for my exertions might be.

Alain's eyes flashed with laughter and desire, the gold flecks reflecting the sun. His smile was wide in his handsome face, his legs and arms long and strong and tanned. I'd never made love in a field before, but I wished I had a more devil-may-care attitude now.

Tearing my eyes away before I suggested something uncomfortable and possibly illegal, I turned and peered over the hedge behind me at the field beyond. This tall crop had been bothering me as we whizzed past on our bikes – I couldn't work out what it was.

'What's that?' I asked him, scrambling closer to get a better look.

'Cob corn.'

The minute he said it, it was obvious. Between the large, dark green leaves, I could see the stringy husks clinging to the tall, thick stalks.

'Come on, country girl, we'd better turn back before you get too tired.'

Back at the house, with an unspoken agreement, we climbed the stairs hand in hand – but at the door to his room, I hesitated, practicalities knocking at the small section of my brain that wasn't filled with him.

'Alain, I . . .'

He groaned. 'Don't tell me you've changed your mind. Please.'

I aimed a pointed glance at the bulge in his shorts and smirked. 'No. But can I have a quick shower first? I'm sticky and disgusting.'

'Me too. You go first and I'll follow you in.'

When my eyes widened, he laughed. 'The bathroom's not big enough for that, Emmy. I meant one at a time.'

Mindful that I didn't want Alain's . . . *enthusiasm* to wane, I was quick. When I left the bathroom wrapped in a towel, he kissed me briefly on the lips and sent an appreciative glance my way before going in there himself.

As I heard the shower running, I felt slightly awkward. Last time, things hadn't been this premeditated – we'd just fallen into bed together. Should I perch demurely on the edge of the bed? Or should I lie wantonly *across* the bed, my towel gaping enough to flash a little thigh and cleavage?

When he came in, I was standing at his bedroom window, looking out across the rose fields and catching the breeze from the open window. I turned to see him standing there, a towel anchored on his hips and an enquiring look on his face. A jolt of lust punched through every nerve ending I possessed.

His mouth twitched. 'I don't think this is going to work if you stay over on that side of the room.'

When I reached him, he took my mouth in a heated kiss, and with a flick of his fingers, the towels dropped to the floor. One light push and I was on the bed, Alain hovering above me.

'Will you be murmuring endearments in French again?' I enquired.

'Do I do that?'

'You do. And let me tell you, for a girl from Birmingham, it's *very* sexy.'

'*Alors, ma chérie.*' I shivered with pleasure as he nuzzled my neck. '*Mon petit chou-fleur.*' He moved to the pulse in my throat. '*Ma jolie artichaut.*'

'Did you just call me a cauliflower? And maybe even an artichoke?'

'You said it turns you on when I speak French. You didn't specify what kind of French.'

I laughed and slapped at him. 'Do it properly, or I won't play.' And he did. So I did.

This was one way of learning French that I had *no* objection to.

* * *

We sat outside in the cooling evening breeze with a lazy pizza and salad.

'Can you stay over?'

'Not tonight. You know, the first of the Thomson party are arriving tomorrow and I need everything to be in order. And I don't trust Gloria. I . . . I feel like I need to keep an eye on Rupert.'

He nodded his understanding. 'You should take every Sunday off. I know your hours are fluid, but it's not unreasonable to have one day a week to yourself. There's so much we can do together. *Châteaux*, all that sightseeing stuff. It's busy at this time of year, but it would all be good to put on your website.'

I smiled at his tactic of appealing to my business goals as a way of getting some downtime with me, but it wasn't as simple as that. 'Sounds great, but making plans like that at the moment . . .'

He rolled his eyes. 'You're back to worrying about Gloria.'

'Yeah. It's unsettling enough moving to a new country and starting a new job and a new relationship without it all turning upside-down just a few weeks in.'

'I can't believe he'd give it all up for her.'

'She's his wife. He chose to marry her, to spend his life with her. In the long run, that might mean more to him than bricks and mortar.'

'*La Cour des Roses* is more than bricks and mortar. It's what defines Rupert, almost.'

'I know. But maybe Gloria means more to him.'

Alain curled his lip. 'If she finds a better option, she'll be off again, and then where will he be?'

'But that's his decision to make.'

'What will you do if Gloria stays?'

I would have the rug swept out from under me. No job. Nowhere to live. The thoughts I'd managed to push to the back of my mind ever since I'd spoken to Rupert that morning poured out in a torrent.

'I'd have no salary, Alain. We have no tenants in Birmingham. My business is making progress, but it's not live yet, and there won't be any income for a while.' I sighed. 'I'm wondering whether I should put it on hold for now. There's no point in getting people on board for something that might never happen.'

His expression was one of shock. 'Are you . . . Are you saying you might go back to England if Gloria stays?'

'I'm saying I don't know.'

He looked at me for a long time. 'But I only just found you.' A frown. 'I thought you had savings?'

'I do, but my grandmother left me the money, and I *really* hadn't wanted to use it for something like this.'

'May I ask why?'

'Because she didn't leave me it to squander on a flat I'm not even living in!'

'Are you sure about that?' He looked at me in a considered way. 'Tell me about your grandmother.'

I smiled and remembered Gran: reading to me sitting on her lap; striding through mud in wellies ahead of us all; bringing me a hot water bottle and talking me through my first heartbreak. 'My dad's mum. I loved her to bits, and the feeling was mutual. She was unfailingly encouraging – never put me down or laughed at my ideas, even if it was something daft like wanting to be a model or a surgeon. She would just listen quietly and give a considered opinion.' My voice hitched. 'She told me all she wanted was for me to be healthy and happy; that money was all very well, but it was nothing compared to those things. She wanted me to find a nice man who would care for me. Thank God she never met Nathan. But I think she would have liked you.'

Alain squeezed my hand. 'How old were you when she died?'

'Twenty-two. It was awful, Alain. She just withered away from cancer. I remember her lying there, so thin and frail, saying she would rather have had a quick heart attack and be done with it.'

A tear rolled down my face. 'A couple of weeks before she died, she told me she was leaving me a little money for a rainy day.'

'Do you think she would class this as a rainy day?'

'I don't know.'

'What would she have said about you coming to France?'

'She would have told me to go for it.'

'And if you could ask her whether she would rather you went home with your tail between your legs, job hunting and living with your parents like a twenty-year-old, or persevered with your dreams by using some of the money she left you, what do you think she would say to that?'

'I . . . I think she would want me to use it.'

Alain's face was still tense. I liked it so much better when he was relaxed, his lips curved, the smile lines fanning out from the corners of his eyes. He stood and ran his hands across my back, finding the knots and kneading gently at them with his thumbs, then smoothing over the sore spots. 'Don't go, Emmy. If Gloria gets her way? Don't go.'

'Did you have a good afternoon off?' Rupert asked me the next morning as he scrubbed burnt eggs from a pan at the sink. That worried me. Rupert never burned eggs.

'Yes, thanks.'

'Then you should do it more often. It's put a bit of colour in your cheeks.' He waggled his eyebrows suggestively.

'That would be the cycling.'

'Cycling? Are you into that kind of thing?'

'Not since I was ten,' I admitted. 'But I enjoyed it. Are you okay?'

'Hmmph.' He lowered his voice. 'My back's getting worse. That sofa is not comfortable, Emmy.'

'I know. But I'm proud of you.'

He looked away.

'Rupert, I know you've had bigger things to worry about, but you do know the first of the Thomsons are arriving tonight?'

He nodded. 'We've covered everything we can, Emmy.'

'What's all this whispering, you two?' Gloria came over, having driven Marcus and James away with her expertise on the possibilities for retail therapy in the area.

'Nothing important.' Rupert scuttled outside to feed leftovers to the birds.

'Take a lot of time off, do you, Emmy?'

I took a deep breath. 'Firstly, Gloria, my hours are fluid. Nobody complains when I'm washing dishes at midnight or doing laundry at weekends, so the occasional late start is hardly an issue. Secondly, and more importantly, *you* are not my employer. I take orders from Rupert, not you.'

'Not for much longer. If you haven't noticed, I'm back.'

'Yes, you are. And if you ask me, you're also counting your chickens. Excuse me. I have work to do.'

But Gloria didn't take the hint. 'I see you altered the lounge.'

'Yes. It was unwelcoming. Nobody ever went in it.'

'And you think a few cushions and throws will make a difference?'

'They already have. Several people have actually set foot in there this week.' This was true, and I couldn't be more pleased. 'I have further plans, but it'll do for now.'

'Why on earth have you got decorators in at this time of year?' She gestured at the van out in the courtyard.

'There was some damage. It wouldn't wait, and we had a few days' leeway.' I certainly didn't want to get into the Thomson booking with her at this stage.

'Hmm. Enjoy your evening at your boring accountant's, did you?'

'Yes, I did. *Very* much. Thank you.'

Gloria lounged against the patio doors, watching me up to my elbows in the sink with eggy skillets and grill pans.

'Feel free to muck in any time, Gloria, if you're at a loose end,' I snapped before I could stop myself.

'You're paid. I'm not,' she said. 'I'm not here to work. I'm here to spend time with my husband. I don't see how scrubbing pans will assist a reconciliation, do you?'

Luckily, she flounced off before I could open my mouth.

As I went around the outside of the house to my room to fetch my bag for going into town, I found Ryan dragging his stuff from the boot of his estate car.

'Hi. Is the wicked witch still . . .?'

'Yes. She is still, I'm afraid.'

Alain's blue hatchback pulled into the courtyard, making me frown.

He climbed out. 'Emmy. You left your mobile last night.'

'Did I? I hadn't even noticed!' I took it from him. 'I think I'm going senile with everything that's going on around here. Thanks.'

Ryan came over to shake hands with him. 'Gloria tends to have that effect on people. Morning, Alain. How was your trip?'

They chatted for a few minutes, while a growing sense of unease crept over me. I hadn't thought about my ex-lover and my current lover being on such friendly terms before – or how that would make me feel. I had no regrets about my fling with Ryan . . . but Alain didn't know about it, and the whole thing made me a little antsy. When Alain set off back to work, I breathed a quiet sigh of relief.

Madame Dupont arrived as Rupert and I were about to leave for Pierre-la-Fontaine. She must have spotted Gloria's car in the courtyard, because she looked at me askance when she walked in, and made no bones about how she felt. Greeting Gloria with a minimum of politeness, she wished her a pleasant *stay*, then crooked her finger, beckoning me to follow her upstairs.

In the first room she found empty, she shut the door and rounded on me, her wiry little body stiff with outrage.

'What is that terrible woman doing here? She isn't staying, is she? Rupert won't permit her to come back, will he?'

'I don't know,' I admitted.

'*Mon Dieu!*' She sank down on the edge of the bed. Gloria's reappearance seemed to have the same unfortunate effect on everyone.

I battled through a fairly appalling French version of Gloria's arrival on Saturday, then took her hand and gently squeezed. 'Don't worry, Madame Dupont. Rupert isn't stupid.'

'Ha! He is stupid when it comes to *that* woman!'

CHAPTER FOURTEEN

Jonathan seemed to be of the same opinion as Madame Dupont when we met him at the café. The market had been hard going: Rupert was distracted and we were hampered by the dog. We'd never brought her with us before, but I assumed he hadn't wanted to leave her at *La Cour des Roses* with a wicked animal hater.

Bob was with Jonathan, and when she'd greeted them both, Jonathan held her close to his leg, fondling her head and ears whenever she nudged at his hand. We sat out on the terrace with her, lucky enough to grab a table under the awning, and my mind wandered back to Ryan and Alain. Would Alain be upset if he knew about Ryan? Should I tell him? I wished he'd known from the start, so I didn't have to worry about it or make a decision.

The café owner brought the dog a bowl of water along with our coffees, and I shook myself out of it.

When Rupert told them about Gloria's return, Jonathan didn't mince his words. 'I can't believe she came back! Of all the cheek! She just waltzed in and expects you to take her back?' His onslaught turned into a coughing fit.

'In a nutshell.'

'And will you?' It was obvious from Jonathan's tone of voice that he hoped for better from his friend.

'Don't know yet.'

Bob studied Rupert in his understated way. 'And what does she think of *this* beauty?' He indicated the dog.

Rupert's expression was downcast. 'She hates her.'

The dog gave a pitiful whine and pushed closer into Jonathan's hand.

I decided it was best to change the subject. 'Bob, did you take those photos of *La Cour des Roses* that Rupert sent me when I was updating his website?'

Rupert laughed. 'He did indeed. I tried myself, but then Bob brought Jonathan round for a beer and I thought what the hell am I playing at? I'm friends with a freelance photographer. Might as well get the job done properly. Bob wouldn't charge me for them, silly sod. Said he'd drunk me out of house and home over the years and intended to continue doing so.'

Bob grinned. No wonder he appeared to be wearing the same jeans he must've been wearing twenty years ago. The only thing new and shiny about him was his motorbike.

'Do you take other photos, besides those for Ellie and Philippe?'

'I do some landscape photography. I have a website, but I can't say I sell much from it. Sometimes I take a stall in market towns in the summer, selling mounted photos to tourists.'

'Hmm.'

'And there it goes again,' Rupert muttered. 'I can hear the whirring when your brain takes off on a spin cycle, Emmy. What are you thinking?'

'How to fix the Silver Fox's criticism of dreary pictures on the walls. Why not get Bob to do you some framed photos for the hall and lounge, instead of those boring prints?' I turned to Bob. 'We'd pay, of course.'

Bob raised an eyebrow at Rupert. 'Spending your money freely, isn't she?'

'*But,*' I went on, 'I was wondering if you'd be willing to provide some for free – one for each bedroom and *gîte.*'

'And why would he do that?' Rupert demanded to know.

'We could tuck his business card in the corner of each. We get a professional regional photo in each room, and Bob gets to show off his wares to a targeted audience without lifting a finger.' I turned to Bob. 'You could leave a portfolio in the guest lounge, too, with a price list in the back. Holidaymakers falling in love with the region might want to purchase a memento.'

Bob exchanged a look with Rupert. 'Is she always this bossy?'

'Always,' Rupert said with a resigned expression, making everyone laugh – although Jonathan's turned into a cough again.

'Where has that cough come from?' I asked him.

'Had it a couple of days,' Jonathan mumbled. 'Nothing to worry about. It'll go.'

Bob gave me an encouraging smile and jerked a thumb at Jonathan, who had been looking fit to bust throughout the change of subject. 'Perhaps we can discuss landscapes between us, and leave those two to battle it out over Gloria's merits or otherwise.'

Ten minutes later, Rupert looked a little shaken. No doubt Jonathan had given him some not-so-tactful advice regarding Gloria. He stood, ready to go.

'Emmy, there's a Scottish couple with a holiday home a couple of miles from me,' Bob said as I finished my coffee. 'I bump into them sometimes in the next village. I told them about your agency and they said they'd love to try it. They're not getting enough business through the one they use.'

'That sounds promising. Do I need to contact them?'

'They're going to Scotland for a couple of weeks, but they'll let me know when they get back.'

'Thanks. Oh!' I delved into one of the bags for the bunch of leaflets I'd collected from the printer. 'Could you give them one of these when you see them?'

'Give me a few. You never know.'

'Can you still come round later this week?' Jonathan asked me. 'Or have you got too much on?'

'You mean would I rather scrub every inch of your bathroom and toilet with a toothbrush or would I rather spend quality time with Gloria?'

Jonathan smiled. 'Does tomorrow suit?'

As we headed back down to the main square, Rupert kept glancing around in a furtive manner.

'What are you looking for?' I asked him, trying not to trip over Gloria as she wound between our legs, sniffing at the sausages in the bags, undeterred by Rupert's admonishments.

'Nothing, Emmy. Nothing at all . . . Oh, now, look there.' He lifted a hand in greeting and went over to the café by the fountain.

'*Monsieur le Maire! Vous allez bien?*' he asked, greeting a man, forty-something and definitely on the handsome side, vacating a table. 'Emmy, I'd like you to meet the mayor of Pierre-la-Fontaine, Patrice Renaud. Patrice, this is Emmy Jamieson, my manager.'

'*Enchanté.* How do you like your new home and our town?'

All this in French, of course.

I took a deep breath and did my best. 'I love Pierre-la-Fontaine and *La Cour des Roses*, thank you.'

'I hope Monsieur Hunter is not making you work too hard?'

I smiled, lifting my bags to illustrate. 'Monsieur Hunter has no choice, but that means business is good.'

'Emmy has plans to set up her own business,' Rupert chipped in, much to my annoyance.

'Oh? What kind of business?'

Oh dear. My French wasn't up to that kind of discussion. But Rupert came to my rescue, giving a brief outline that I could follow, even if I couldn't have said it myself.

'I would be happy to see you succeed in something that brings visitors and business to the town,' Monsieur Renaud declared. 'If you need any help or information about how to proceed, please let me know. I spend half my life in there.' He jerked a thumb at the town hall behind us. 'Do you know Alain Granger, the accountant?'

Rupert smothered a smirk.

'Yes, I do.'

'That's good. He will look after you with all the forms you need. I have a couple of *gîtes* on the outskirts of town myself. Perhaps when you are properly set up, you could get in touch?'

I smiled. 'Of course. It's nice to meet you.'

'You, too.'

'What was all that about?' I demanded of Rupert as we went to the car.

'What was all what about? We bumped into the mayor, that's all.'

'We did not bump into him. You engineered it. You were looking out for him.'

'Yes, well, that's true. It's time you met him on an informal basis. You need to get to know who's who in the town, Emmy. And you definitely want to be on the right side of Patrice Renaud in particular, and the *Mairie* in general. He'll be happy to know that Alain is your accountant. He knows Alain won't cut corners, so you're in his good books already.' He cast me an annoyingly smug smile. 'No need to thank me, Emmy.'

'Are you okay?' I asked him as we drove back. 'Was Jonathan a bit too . . . honest with you?'

'He didn't say anything I didn't expect. And as a good friend, he's entitled to express an opinion, after all.'

'Not if it upsets you so much.'

'I'm already upset, Emmy. I hadn't expected to see Gloria again, other than within some kind of legal setting, and now she wants me to take her back. It's a bit of a turnaround in one weekend.' He paused as he negotiated a busy junction. 'I just don't know what to do.'

Staring out at the tree-lined street, I tried to think of something to say that didn't come out of my obvious bias. 'What about that good old standby, gut instinct? Does it feel right, having her back?'

He puffed out a breath. 'The honest answer is "not really" – but that's understandable after what happened with Nathan.' He glanced across at me. 'I'm no spring chicken, Emmy. And Gloria is the only woman I loved enough to marry. If I turn her down now, I figure that's me done in the relationship department for good.'

I frowned. 'I don't think that's necessarily true. But if you take her back, it should be because you want to be with her, not because you're scared of the future.'

We fell into silence as I consulted my own gut instinct, which was currently screaming at me that there was a very real danger that Rupert would indeed take Gloria back. And as much as I didn't want to bring my own situation into the equation, I couldn't ignore the knowledge that if he did, I would be out in the cold.

I thought about my hostile exchange with her this morning, and it occurred to me that it was a good thing Rupert hadn't been around to hear it. Gloria's attitude to me was crystal clear, but I was descending to her level with my side of the conversations – if you could call them that. Not only did I not want to be that person, I didn't think Gloria and I sniping at each other like fishwives would help Rupert in making his decision. And it was stretching my already-stretched nerves to breaking point.

And if I wanted to be really grown-up about all of this, Gloria may have done some pretty shitty things, but if it hadn't been *my* boyfriend she'd run off with, and *my* job in jeopardy, would I be this set against her? Yes, she could be poisonous, but Rupert had shown me a different side to her. It wasn't her fault the man she married swapped their swanky, jet-setting lifestyle for a place she didn't like, in the middle of nowhere. It was hard to understand her perspective, because her hell was my heaven, but the truth was *La Cour des Roses* was not what she signed up for. I let out a big sigh. I was never going to like Gloria, but maybe I was letting my bias blind me to the complexities of the situation.

When we got back, Madame Dupont had left a note explaining that she'd only had time to press the bedlinen and hadn't got to the rooms. Whether this was because she'd cut short her stint due to Gloria's presence was unclear.

'I need to do the rooms straight after lunch,' I told Rupert, flapping the note at him.

'Ah. I meant to speak to you about that. You need to be careful with Jess and Steve's.'

'Why?'

'I think they're "afternoon" people.'

'Afternoon people?'

'Yesterday, when you were out at Alain's, and Saturday when you were busy with the *gîtes*, they were enjoying a . . . siesta.'

'Maybe they were tired?'

'If I was his age, with a girlfriend her age, I'd be exhausted! But I don't think they were getting much sleep.'

'Urgh. It's like the Jacksons all over again, except at a different time of day.'

'We're here to provide a service, Emmy, and if that means guests accessing their room at any of time of the day for sex, then so be it. People bonk more on holiday. It's a natural phenomenon. Surely you're not embarrassed because we have frisky guests? Anyway, it's your fault.'

'*My* fault?'

'If you didn't make the rooms so welcoming, people might be inclined to spend less time in them. Just make sure you let Madame Dupont know, in case she goes blundering in there, will you?'

'Okay.'

As I headed for the den, I bumped into Gloria.

'Emmy. Fun day at the market?' Sarcasm dripped from every word.

Here we go again. 'Yes, thanks. Er – could I have a quick word, Gloria?'

She raised an eyebrow. 'If you must.'

We went into the den, where she stood waiting for whatever diatribe I was about to spew. The startled look on her face almost made me laugh when I said, 'I'd like to call a truce.'

'*What?*'

'Gloria, you and I are both harbouring a lot of resentment towards each other. I'm not going to forget what you did to me in a hurry, and I know you see me as a threat here at *La Cour des Roses*. But I need you to understand that I'm not.'

At that, she snorted with derision. 'Oh, really?'

I reined in my temper. 'All I've done is to provide an understanding ear if Rupert needs one, and I won't stop doing that, but I'm *not* trying to influence him. And I don't think you and I being at each other's throats is helping him. Can we try and be civil?'

A stunned silence. She finally opened her mouth to say something, then seemed to think better of it. A simple nod.

Well, wonders never ceased.

When she'd gone, I took out my phone to get on to the letting agents again. I wanted to know if the couple who had been 'interested' had been suitably persuaded yet. But when I saw a missed call from Sophie, I called her first.

'Hi, Sophie. Did I miss a call?'

'Yes. I promised Ellie I would phone you. Are the rumours true? That Gloria's back? Ellie heard from Philippe who heard from Martine who heard from the owner of Rupert's café who heard from Jonathan.'

I couldn't help but smile. Half of Pierre-la-Fontaine was in on the act. 'Yes, it's true.' I filled her in on Gloria's reappearance.

She tutted sympathetically. 'Is it awful for you? Having her back, after what she did to you?'

'I've called a truce, but I doubt it'll last.'

'Do you fancy a coffee on Wednesday lunchtime with Ellie? We could drive to Saint-Martin for a change?'

'I'd *love* to.'

My conversation with the letting agents did not go quite so well.

'No, I'm sorry, Ms Jamieson, but of course, there's no point in showing any prospective tenants around the flat at the moment anyway.'

'Not showing? What do you mean?'

'Due to the damage. That will all need to be fixed before we could even consider—'

'What damage?'

'Well, I – er – I assumed you knew about it. Your partner told us he would e-mail you. We would have done so ourselves otherwise. Although I would add, Ms Jamieson, that we don't appreciate acting as go-betweens between two . . . differing parties.'

'That's fine,' I snapped. 'Thank you. I'll deal with it.'

I clicked off the phone and checked my e-mails. One from Nathan, sent mid-morning while I was out in town.

Emmy.

I thought it best to stick to e-mails, as our phone calls inevitably end acrimoniously. I'm writing to let you know that there is no prospect of tenants in the flat for the next few weeks. The flat above has had a slow leak in the bathroom for weeks, which has flooded under their floorboards and now down into our ceiling, causing serious damage. The good news is that their insurance will pay for all repairs, replastering, redecorating etc.

The bad news is they won't compensate us for lost income, as we had no tenants signed.

I'm not happy about taking sole responsibility for this. I've had to take time off work to go up to Birmingham and deal with it, aside from the many phone calls and e-mails. I will follow this through,

Emmy, but if anything else major happens, it will have to be you who deals with it, whether you're across the Channel or not. There is a limit to what you can expect.
Nathan

I sat staring silently at the screen for a few long minutes while my stomach slowly relocated itself somewhere higher than my feet.

Nathan had made no mention of Gloria leaving. No mention of where he was staying now. Was he still at Rupert's flat? Surely not! But my curiosity was dampened somewhat by my panic over the mortgage.

I thought about my small inheritance, and what Alain had said about it. That my grandmother may well have approved of me using it this way. I hoped she did. Because that's what I was going to do. There was no point going at this whole life-in-France thing half-cocked. I wanted it, and I would do what I had to do to keep it. I had to avoiding wallowing and do something constructive.

Checking the rest of my e-mails, I saw one from Ellie, forwarded from one of her former clients who had replied to her round-robin e-mail about my agency. He had converted his property into a complex of *gîtes* and was interested in listing with me. Could I phone him to make an appointment?

I did. Jerry Barnes sounded most keen – so keen, in fact, that I arranged to go round the next day.

I texted Nick. *Could we chat about the website some time?*

He phoned back five minutes later. 'Hi, sis. Taking a break. What can I do for you?'

'I don't want to hassle you, but I'm starting to get some genuine interest.'

'That's great!'

'Yes, it is. And I know we won't be ready to go live for quite a while, but I wondered if there was any chance of some sort of prototype – you know, sample pages so I can show people how it might look when I go to see them?'

'That's what I was hoping to do for you. I can probably send you the page with *La Cour des Roses* on it, although I'm still working on an availability facility. And maybe that page with the *château*? And your home page. Would that do for now?'

'That would be brilliant. Thanks, Nick. Er . . . any chance of that by tomorrow?'

I smiled at his good-natured but unrepeatable response. It was good to know that I was making progress with *something*, and it reminded me that I needed to put the things that I couldn't do anything about to the back of my mind and focus instead on the things I *could* do something about.

Early evening saw the first arrivals of the Thomson brigade. Obliged to fly halfway across the world, Chris Thomson was Julia Cooper's younger brother. He had in tow his wife Michelle and three teenagers. Chris's English accent stood out like a sore thumb compared with his very Australian family, making me smile. All were tall and tanned and excited about their holiday. Chris hadn't been to France since he was a kid, and Europe was a complete novelty to the rest of them. I hoped they would have a wonderful time.

Lacking an airbed until it was brought over by someone driving, they had planned for the two girls to share a single bed for the first night, but Rupert wouldn't have it, so he and Chris carried one of the single mattresses from the twin room in the guesthouse to use temporarily.

They'd only been there an hour when Julia phoned to double-check that everything had been okay for their arrival, and to triple-check all the arrangements we'd already double-checked.

I held my irritation in check. This woman had gathered together ten separate family groups and put together an event to remember, all whilst doing a full-time job. She obviously cared about her parents very much, and was willing to make a huge effort to get this right. Patiently, I went through her concerns. Again.

'Well, Emmy, I know I've not been entirely happy at times, but I must say that you and Mr Hunter have done your best to ensure that everything goes as smoothly as possible. I do appreciate it.'

'You're more than welcome.'

Once I'd put the phone down, it belatedly occurred to me that Gloria could have answered that phone call just as easily as me – and then heaven knew what havoc she might have wreaked. As Rupert walked past me, I grabbed his arm.

'Have you spoken to Gloria about this Thomson thing?' I whispered, not knowing whether she was in earshot.

'No. I thought it was best left alone. We have enough stuff to argue over, without bringing up her total lack of interest in our livelihood.'

He had a point. 'That's fine by me.'

I hadn't been off the phone two minutes when Alain rang to ask if I'd like to go round that evening.

I was torn with indecision. Truth be told, I was still feeling out of sorts after his encounter with Ryan that morning. Should I tell him? Shouldn't I? Why should I? Why shouldn't I? *Urgh.*

I took the coward's way out for now. 'Alain, I'm sorry, but I'm feeling a bit under the weather. I could do with a quiet night.' And that wasn't an outright lie.

He took it at face value. 'Is there anything I can do?'

Feeling guilty at my pathetic avoidance tactic, I laid it on a bit thicker than I might have done about the latest developments with the flat in Birmingham.

'Damn, Emmy. That place is jinxed!'

'I know.'

'Don't worry. It might not take too long to fix. And the agents could still be lining up interested parties, I reckon. It sounds like Nathan's on top of it, anyway.'

'Yeah.'

'Get some sleep.'

'I will.'

As the evening wore on, I worried more and more about my reasons for avoiding him. It was ridiculous. I needed to make a decision and stick to it.

I needed Kate.

But when I texted her to ask if she could chat, she texted back to say she was out with friends – could it wait till tomorrow?

Ah, well. What was one more night of panic and introspection to the queen of these things?

CHAPTER FIFTEEN

Violet and Betty were tearful as Marcus and James packed their car the next morning. They went outside to see them off, kissing their cheeks and wishing them a safe journey.

'Such nice boys,' Betty announced as they came back in to the fresh pot of tea that Rupert had solicitously brewed for them.

'Oh, yes,' Violet chipped in. 'It's *so* nice to see brothers getting on so well together, isn't it?'

Rupert snorted, and several guests around the table turned their laughter into coughs and sneezes.

Bless the old souls.

'I think you should leave as soon as you've helped Rupert prep for dinner tonight,' Gloria told me as I cleared up. 'Now I'm back, there's no need for you to stay for the meal.'

I tried very hard to count to ten. So she was perfectly happy for me to slave in the kitchen then be sent away without enjoying the end result? And yet *her* only contribution was to grace the table with her presence, playing hostess? The cheek!

But I supposed I *had* called a truce with her yesterday, and there *was* a remote chance she was trying to be considerate. Hmm.

I glanced across at Rupert.

'You're welcome to stay, Emmy, but you're equally welcome to the night off. Gloria can help me clear up afterwards.'

Yeah. Right.

When Madame Dupont arrived, I had the embarrassing task of explaining *en français* about Jess and Steve's daytime *liaisons sexuelles* – something she told me she was quite used to at *La Cour des Roses* but made her cackle anyway.

While she went off to see whose rooms she *could* do, I went to find Rupert. That e-mail from Nathan yesterday had me seriously worried. I didn't want to push Rupert into a decision, but a little prodding each day to see which way the land lay wouldn't go amiss.

He was faffing in the chicken run, most likely hiding from the new – or rather, old – thorn in his side. He did have a Gloria in tow, but since it was dog Gloria rather than wife Gloria, I could live with it.

When he came out, he praised her for waiting patiently outside for him – as opposed to following him in and decimating the fowl population – and we walked up the garden together.

'Can we walk the dog?' I asked him.

The poor thing was being referred to as 'the dog' more and more to avoid confusion, which I felt was a bit ignominious for her, even though I never used her name myself.

'Why? I only walked her a couple of hours ago.'

'I thought we could have a chat.'

'And what am I supposed to tell Gloria?'

'Tell her you feel like going for a stroll. She's not your keeper. She doesn't have to know I'm going with you.'

'Fine.'

I shoved my trainers on, met him in the courtyard, and we set off down the lane, Gloria sniffing at every interesting clump of grass until she decided which to pee over. This palaver over, we veered onto a path between farms, some of the harvested fields looking a little barren without their crops.

'The decorators are moving the furniture back as we speak,' Rupert told me. 'So if you do a quick clean of that *gîte* and put on bedding before this evening's arrivals, and the same with the decorated one first thing tomorrow, we should be all set.'

'Does it smell of paint?' I asked worriedly.

'Not too badly. And the windows can stay wide open for now.'

There was an air of melancholy about Rupert that I could almost touch. We walked in silence for a while at Gloria's speed, which was impressive. She stormed along the narrow path like a racehorse nearing the finishing straight, and my lungs were complaining. No wonder Rupert was getting so fit. He reined her in a little so I could catch my breath, and stretched out his back.

'How are you doing?' I asked him.

'Not good. My spine will be permanently bent from that sodding sofa at this rate.'

'I didn't mean physically.'

'I know you didn't.'

I decided to be more specific. 'The other day, you said that Gloria might expect you to sell up and move on.'

'That has now been clarified. She's willing to put up with it for a few months, a year at most, while we get back on an even keel and look for a buyer. But *La Cour des Roses* will have to go.'

My hackles rose. 'Are you happy for her to dictate to you like that?'

'You would think not,' he answered mildly. 'But as she pointed out, it's not only about what I want. A marriage involves two people, and Gloria has put forward a case that makes a surprising amount of sense.'

'Really?' The disbelief in my tone was clear as a bell.

He chuckled half-heartedly. 'Yes, really.' He sighed. 'She kindly pointed out that I'm getting older.'

I winced. 'What's that got to do with anything?'

'I only have so many years left in me with regard to *La Cour des Roses*. Would I still be up to it at sixty-five? At seventy? Eventually, it would become too much and I would have to sell. And so, selling sooner wouldn't make much difference, according to Gloria.'

I was tempted to point out that the world according to Gloria was very different to the world according to normal people, but

I refrained. Instead, I asked him, 'How do you feel about being forced into your dotage so soon?'

'I don't like to think of it that way, Emmy, but she does have a point. *La Cour des Roses* can be tiring – as you well know. And, as Gloria reminded me, my health has not exactly been sparkling lately.'

'That's ridiculous! You had a scare, that's all. Your angina is under control now, and you're miles fitter than you were before. How much weight have you lost?'

'Over a stone,' Rupert admitted, running a hand over his stomach.

'Well, then. Look at me, Rupert. I'm nearly thirty years younger than you, but I'm as red as a beetroot following that ruddy dog of yours and I can barely breathe. You're doing fine. I think it's more a question of whether you've had enough of the rest of it. The cooking. The guests. The company. Your downtime in the place you built from nothing.'

He was quiet for a moment, staring off across the fields. 'No. I still enjoy those things. And now that you're here, the tiredness has improved no end. You do a darned sight more than Gloria ever did.'

'That wouldn't be hard.'

'I know. But it's made my life so much easier, having someone I can trust who'll get on with things. I don't know how long you'd be with me, but while you were, I could manage. I don't see why a few extra years on my clock would make any difference.' He tugged at the dog's lead and we turned to retrace our steps. 'What do you think?'

'I think you've told me very clearly what Gloria wants, but not really what *you* want.'

He sighed. 'I like my life here, Emmy. I have friends. The dog. You. I enjoy the guests' company, mostly – meeting new people. But if I want to stay here, it would be without my wife. The only woman I really loved.'

And now for the million-dollar question. 'Do you . . . Do you still love her?'

'I used to. Very much. But she's changed, and maybe that's my fault and the fault of *La Cour des Roses*. Perhaps she's right – perhaps we *could* get all that back, if we do things the way she wants.'

'Perhaps.'

'You don't sound convinced.'

That's because I'm not. 'Have you . . .' I wondered if I was going too far, then thought *what the hell*. 'Have you slept with her?'

Rupert suddenly became very interested in his shoes. 'She tried a few times, but I held out. Gloria can be very persuasive.'

'I bet.'

'Don't read anything into it, Emmy. If it happens, it's only sex.'

I let out a strangled laugh. 'Well, it shouldn't be! You're man and wife! You're considering giving everything up to spend the rest of your life with her. It shouldn't be "only sex". It should *mean* something.'

'That's . . . interesting.' He straightened his shoulders, which had been sagging throughout the walk, as though he had the weight of the world on them. 'This is putting a strain on everybody, not just me. I feel like it's my duty to make my mind up sooner rather than later. Put everyone out their misery.'

'Your only duty is to yourself, Rupert, and if you don't know how you feel yet, then you don't. But if, deep down, you *do* know, and you're only delaying the inevitable, then you might as well get it over with – whatever "it" might be.'

As we turned onto the lane, he asked me, 'No final words of wisdom?'

I dredged my brain for something helpful. The lines on his forehead were etched deep. 'Do you remember what you said to me when you were trying to persuade me to give everything up to come here?'

'No.'

'You told me that it was my life, and to follow my heart.'

'And what did you say?'

'I asked if you thought my heart belonged here at *La Cour des Roses*.'

'Did I have an answer to that?'

'You told me it wasn't for you to say.'

I went to my room, leaving him standing in the courtyard with the dog at his side.

My daily check of review sites revealed another couple of short but positive reviews from previous guests, and an absolute cracker from the Stewarts, a couple who had stayed at the guesthouse when I was there last time.

We spent a wonderful few days at La Cour des Roses in June this year. Rupert Hunter is the perfect host – helpful and good-natured, and knowledgeable about the local area. Breakfast was ample and varied, and the evening meals were out of this world – certainly comparable to the meals we ate at local restaurants. Our room was large, comfortable, spotlessly clean and tastefully decorated, and we could not fault the garden with its many beautiful sitting nooks. We would give La Cour des Roses six stars if we could, and we will definitely be back!

I beamed with contentment. *This* was more like it!

But when I trotted along the hall to show Rupert, I could hear his and Gloria's voices coming from his lounge, so I bid a hasty retreat.

Back in my room, the momentary victory and pride in *La Cour des Roses* that I'd felt from reading the review rapidly faded as I thought about our conversation that morning. The fact was, there were no guarantees that *La Cour des Roses* would be a going concern much longer if Gloria had her way . . . and after speaking to Rupert, I wasn't convinced that she wouldn't get just that.

By lunchtime, Nick had sent me a link, as promised, for the sample pages of the website. They looked brilliant – and they were timely. After a quick lunch, I drove out to meet Jerry Barnes at his *gîte* complex. He was a lively and jovial man who was rightly proud of what he'd done with the ramshackle set of barns and outbuildings he'd got dirt cheap. They were now a series of half a dozen self-catering units, each with private seating and barbeque areas, and a communal pool. It would take a couple of years for the grounds to look a little more lived in, but other than that, I couldn't fault them.

I showed him the pages on my laptop and explained that the business would not go live until I'd gathered together a small number of clients and the website was finished. He said he would be happy to list with me, since it would be at no cost to him. In a cheeky bit of experimentation, I told him that I would be willing to accept his own photos but strongly recommended we use a professional photographer for a minimal flat fee – the only thing he would pay up front. He was willing, and I left happily smug.

I went on to pay my promised visit to Jonathan. As I emptied and scrubbed his food cupboards, I gave him an abridged version of recent events, omitting anything Rupert had told me in confidence.

'So your working life is being made a misery by Gloria, a horror that is only mitigated by the fact that you're having sex with a tall, handsome half Frenchman?'

'That about sums it up. These lentils are three years out of date.'

'Chuck 'em.' He coughed.

I lobbed the packet in the direction of the large bin bag I had out. Unfortunately, the seam burst on the way, and a sea of tiny dried lentils washed across the floor. I climbed down from the stepladder and picked up the dustpan and brush, then got down on my hands and knees.

'Your cough doesn't sound any better, Jonathan.'

'It's fine.'

'Have you been to the doctor?'

'They don't like to give you anything nowadays, do they? It'll go in its own sweet time.'

With the lentils swept up – although I had a nasty feeling we'd be discovering them everywhere for weeks – I clambered back onto the stepladder. 'Do you ever eat anchovies?'

'Not unless Rupert cleverly hides them in something. Why?'

'You have three jars at the back here.'

'Can't think why. Could you take them to Rupert's?'

I searched for the faded dates on the jars. 'Not unless he wants to poison the guests.'

'Chuck 'em. Will you speak to Rupert again?'

'I think he's told me all he's willing to. I don't want to pry any more.'

'You two have been to hell and back together, Emmy. I don't think he'd see it as prying, but perhaps there's nothing more to be said. All you can do now is pray he makes the right decision.' Yet another cough.

'Do you have any cough medicine?'

'In the bathroom cabinet.'

'How out of date will *that* be?' I trooped upstairs to fetch it. 'What's all this?'

'Oh. Washing. Sorry. Could you bring it down and shove it in?'

I did that, made him take some medicine, then looked at the clock on the kitchen wall. 'Right. What next?'

'Can we make a start on the junk in the spare room? I can never find anything in there.'

We trudged upstairs, and Jonathan perched on a stool while I clambered amongst boxes and discarded lamp shades and teetering piles of books, showing him stuff so he could decide whether to keep or bin.

Feeling hot and grubby, I was about to call it quits when a heavy book fell on my toes, making me yelp. It was an old photograph album, and dust whooshed from between its pages when I opened it.

'You ought to take better care of this,' I told him, blowing ineffectually at it before handing it across.

He silently took it and, without even looking at it, placed it on the bin pile.

'Wrong pile, Jonathan.'

'Right pile. I'm not senile.'

'But that looks like an old family album. You must want to keep it.'

His face was hard. 'No. I haven't looked at it in the last twenty-five years, and I'm not going to start now.'

I suddenly realised that there were no family photos in the lounge. 'But Jonathan . . .' I picked up the album and flicked through it, making myself sneeze as I glanced at black-and-white photos, some so faded you could hardly see the people. 'What family do you have back in the UK?'

'Brother. Sister. Nieces and nephews.'

'Do you see them very often?'

'Never.'

I couldn't hide my shock. 'Never? Why?'

'Because they disowned me, Emmy.'

'They *what*?'

'When I told them I was gay. I waited until my parents died, because I knew the truth would kill them. They would have been so disappointed in me. Once they were gone, I couldn't live a lie any longer. I had to tell people or go mad. My brother and sister said they never wanted to see me or speak to me again.' His hands twisted together in his lap.

'But why would they do that?' I spluttered. '*How* could they do that?'

'Different generation, Emmy. A very strict upbringing. It went against the grain of everything they'd known and been brought up to believe. That was why I kept it hidden for so long. But eventually, I had to be true to myself.' He let out a heavy sigh. 'I paid a very high price.'

'Is that why you came to France?'

'Yes. I was in my mid-fifties so I took a reduced pension and made a new start. Not too long after, I found Matthew and some happiness. Even though Matthew's gone, I have those memories to cherish, and I'm grateful for the time we had together.'

'Oh, Jonathan, that's awful. I had no idea!' I couldn't imagine not having any family to turn to. Not knowing that Mum and Dad and Nick and Aunt Jeanie were all there for me if I needed them.

'It's over and done with, Emmy, and it has been for a long time.' He reached out and patted my hand. 'I think we've done enough up here for today. I need a cup of tea.' He hoisted himself from the stool and set off downstairs.

Placing the album carefully on a shelf, I followed him down, but as we went through the lounge towards the kitchen end, we stopped in dismay. There was water all over the floor. Slipping off my sandals, I sloshed through it to turn the washing machine off. The door was sealed tight, so I could only presume it was the hose around the back – and there was no way of getting to that without pulling the machine out. I tried, but it was tightly fitted and I couldn't get a purchase on it – and I suspected I wouldn't be strong enough anyway.

I turned to Jonathan. 'Don't you dare come any nearer!' I warned him. 'That's all I need, you going flying and me trying to get you up again! Do you have a plumber?'

'Someone came to do something with the bathroom once.'

He went off to make the call, while I hunted for a mop and bucket.

'Monsieur Bonnet agreed to come, but he'll be a while yet. His wife spent all morning cooking a beef-and-wine casserole and they're having a late lunch because he was out on a long job this morning.'

'Damn.' This everything-stops-for-lunch malarkey was going to take some getting used to.

'Is it really that urgent?' he asked, frowning.

'A load of water has gone round the back and I'm worried about the electrical sockets. They're all really low down the walls everywhere else. Do you know where they are at the back here?'

'Can't remember.'

'Then I'd rather get this machine out sooner rather than later, so we can see if the water's gone anywhere it shouldn't. What's through there?' I pointed to a narrow door in the corner of the kitchen.

'Cellar. I don't want you going down there. It's not very safe.'

'Are there electrics?'

He winced. 'Lighting. But I could do without you turning off all the electrics for no good reason, Emmy. It's an old house, and everything's temperamental.'

I took out my phone. Rupert was out at a hospital check-up for his angina. I knew Alain had several appointments, but I tried anyway. It went straight to voicemail, so all I could do was leave a message. That done, the only option left was Ryan.

'I'll be there in half an hour,' he said.

'Are you sure you don't mind?'

'Friends help each other.'

I texted Alain to tell him not to worry, and while Jonathan looked helplessly on from a chair, I began the dreary job of mopping up. It struck me that this could well be a case of karma coming back to bite me on the arse – since I'd avoided the flood in Birmingham and left Nathan to deal with it all, the gods must have decided to even things up at the French end.

By the time Ryan arrived, I was tired and sweaty and grumpy, with the potential for weepiness. He studied the washing machine wedged in its tight spot and, to my amazement, proceeded to slosh washing-up liquid all over the floor. Getting the best grip he could on the machine, slowly but surely he prised it out just a little. Once he'd got it moving, the slippery liquid eased its way until he could pull it fully out.

I raised an eyebrow at Jonathan. These handy people with their clever tricks.

Ryan grovelled around the back. 'The joint on the hose has come loose, but it's old and knackered and needs replacing.'

'Hmmph. Takes after its owner, then,' Jonathan muttered.

'The sockets are high up, presumably because the kitchen was fitted more recently, so that's fine. Have you got a torch, Jonathan?'

'In the drawer next to the cooker. But I don't want you in that cellar, young Ryan. Haven't been down there in years.'

'All the more reason for me to check it, then, don't you think?' And without waiting for an answer, he was gingerly making his way down there. 'Try the light switch, Emmy.'

I did. No fizzing or sparks.

He came back up. 'It's fine. It'll all dry out. You're good.'

We heard a van pull up, and Ryan and I went out into the street to greet Monsieur Bonnet, now replete with beef casserole. From the size of his stomach, it looked as though he enjoyed beef casserole on a regular basis.

Ryan took him inside while I leaned against the wall, trying to catch a little breeze and thinking that none of this was quite what I'd had in mind when I embarked on a new life in France.

'Will you be okay if I leave you both with him?' Ryan broke into my thoughts.

'If he fixes it and doesn't expect me to take part in a technical discussion on the wonders, or otherwise, of French plumbing systems in his native language, then yes.' But I was sniffling a little. 'Sorry. I'm *so* pathetic.'

'No, you're not, Emmy. You're tired and overwhelmed. You've had a lot going on lately.'

His sympathy only made me sniffle more. 'You're telling me!'

'I presume Gloria's still in situ?'

'Yes. And if she stays, I'll have no job and my business isn't ready to roll yet and I still have no tenants in Birmingham, and I wouldn't be able to persuade myself that Rupert had made the right decision or could ever be really happy with her, and I'm worried about Jonathan because I don't think he's coping, and this Thomson thing is driving me mad!'

Ryan gently took hold of my arms. He probably thought hysteria was about to set in. He wouldn't be far wrong.

'Listen to me. The Thomson thing? You and Rupert will do your best because you always do, but it will be what it will be. The flat? If you don't get tenants soon, talk to Nathan about selling. Jonathan is fine, and all the better for you helping him. As for Gloria – we can only wait and see, but it *is* Rupert's decision. And if he takes her back, you'll find your own way here in France, Emmy, if it's what you really want.'

Tears rolled down my face. Hesitantly, he wrapped his arms around me.

I leaned in. 'Thank you for coming to help,' I mumbled.

'You're welcome.'

'Maybe I could pay you back some time? Help you in the garden?'

Ryan laughed. 'What? And have you pull up swathes of perfectly healthy plants, thinking they're weeds? No, thanks.'

I joined in his laughter – the perfect release of tension. I was about to pull out of his arms when I heard a car door slam.

'Emmy!' Alain was striding towards us.

CHAPTER SIXTEEN

'Everything okay?' Alain asked as he reached us, by which time Ryan and I had jumped apart like guilty bunnies.

'Hi. Er, yes. The plumber was delayed, so Ryan came till he got here. Didn't you get my second message?' I asked, dismayed that he'd dropped everything to come to my rescue.

'Yes, but it just said a plumber was on the way. I didn't know you had a helper. I thought I'd come over to check you were okay.'

'I'd better get going,' Ryan said awkwardly. 'See you around.'

'Thanks, Ryan. I really appreciate your help,' I told him.

He smiled and hurried off to his car.

'Is Jonathan okay?' Alain asked.

'Tired, that's all.'

'Well, if everything's under control, I should go.' He hesitated and his gaze flicked between Ryan and me.

'Alain . . .' I started.

'I have a late appointment.'

'Okay. Thank you for coming.'

'No problem.'

I watched him walk back to his car. Did he think something might be going on between me and Ryan? It must have looked pretty compromising. *Why* did he have to turn up at that exact point in time?

When I went inside, Jonathan and Monsieur Bonnet seemed to have everything under control, so I decided there was no point in hanging around and took my leave. But as I drove home, I had

Alain's arrival playing on perpetual rewind in my head, making myself ill with worry. What had happened had only solidified the feeling that I ought to fess up to my fling with Ryan so it was all out in the open. But I wasn't sure if that was a dangerous thing to do.

I texted Kate to ask if we could chat as soon as she got in from work. Bless her, she was looking out at me from my screen less than half an hour later.

'Hey! How's it going?'

I took a shaky breath and recounted the events of the day. She laughed and grimaced and winced in all the right places, and at the end of it all, she shook her head and sighed.

'So you're worried about what Alain might think?'

'Yes.'

'But he didn't say anything?'

'No.'

'It's not as though you have anything to hide, Emmy.'

'But I *have* got something to hide, haven't I? There may be nothing going on with Ryan now, but there was once. It feels . . . dishonest.'

Kate's voice was stern. 'You were a free agent at the time and it had nothing to do with him. I'm sure *he's* got a past. But if you don't tell him, it'll only eat away at you. If you do tell, and Alain doesn't like it, then he's not the right bloke for you anyway.' She looked at her watch. 'Emmy, I'm sorry, but I'm going out tonight. I need to go change.' She gave an apologetic look.

I glanced at the time and jumped. 'I have to go, too. How are things going with Jamie?'

'Not so good. I'm thinking of jacking it in. I'll see what happens for another week or so. Good luck with Alain.' She blew me a sympathetic kiss, and her face was gone from the screen.

Oh, I missed her.

My phone pinged. A text from Ryan. *Everything okay with Alain?* I took a deep breath and texted back *Not sure.*

A couple of minutes went by before his reply. *If you need to tell him, Emmy, it's fine with me. Alain's a good guy. I doubt it'll be a problem. x*

As I smiled at his understanding, I knew that Kate was right. It would always eat away at me. I didn't want to feel guilty around Alain, or for things to get awkward between me and Ryan. I remembered what Alain had said about language skills, and I figured it could apply to relationships, too. If the bottom rows of bricks weren't solid, what came after would be weak at best and dangerous at worst.

My mind was made up. Didn't mean my nerves were happy about it, though.

'You were ages at Jonathan's, Emmy,' Rupert said as I went through to help him prep for the guest meal.

'Yes, well, it was all rather unfortunate . . .' *In more ways than one.* I filled him in on the flood and omitted the part about Alain.

Rupert tutted. 'I ought to pop round there more often. Or have him here, so he can sit in the garden.'

'I'm sure he'd like that. Did you . . . Did you know about his family?'

Rupert nodded sadly. 'Yes.'

'I don't understand how they could do that! Why he had to hide it all those years.'

'Hell, Emmy, it wasn't just that his sexual orientation was *disapproved* of. It was still *illegal* when he was younger. It's all very sad, isn't it? That he finally met someone in middle age, and they only had ten years together.'

'He didn't have anyone before Matthew?'

'No. Nothing serious, anyway.'

Some people never found love, I supposed. At least Jonathan had had Matthew in his life, for however short a time.

Julia's daughter, Wendy, and her husband, Aaron, arrived in the middle of our kitchen endeavours, with a feisty toddler and a very colicky baby in tow. Wendy looked permanently harassed, while Aaron had a kind of resigned air about him that would have better suited someone middle-aged, the poor bloke. As the first lot to arrive by land, they had been designated the task of bringing the promised airbeds for the excess guests, which we pumped up and doled out, along with bedding, taking our single mattress away from the Australians and back to the guesthouse.

When I'd got them settled, I peeped into the newly-decorated *gîte* with trepidation. It looked so new and clean, and there was barely any paint smell at all. I sighed with relief. My gamble had paid off.

When I went back to the kitchen to help Rupert finish off, I said, 'Thank you. The *gîte* looks lovely.'

I got a weary grunt in reply. 'Nice to know my guests are sleeping in the lap of luxury while I'm sleeping on my own bloody sofa.'

Gloria timed her appearance, as usual, for when the meal prep was done and the guests came downstairs. She was pouring wine and I was entangled in trying to remove my apron, ready to be banished for the evening, when the phone rang.

Rupert answered it in the kitchen. 'Steve? Yes, he's here.'

He waggled the phone at Steve. 'Someone who couldn't get you on your mobile.'

For a man who had developed a nice tan over the past week, Steve blanched considerably. 'It can't be for me. Nobody knows I'm here,' he hissed.

In contrast to Steve's pale complexion, young Jess's was now turning an interesting shade of bright pink.

'Well, someone does. It's a woman.'

'Tell her I'm not here.'

The table had gone deadly quiet, initially waiting for the phone call to be dealt with but now avidly listening for the next instalment.

Rupert belatedly pressed the mouthpiece against his chest. 'But I already told her you're here.'

'Then tell her you were mistaken! Tell her . . . Tell her I've already left!'

'I'm so sorry, madam, but my wife tells me I was mistaken. Steve *was* staying here, but they . . . he . . . left earlier today.'

The caller's response was loud and clear, even with the phone against Rupert's ear. 'Then why did I just hear his voice in the background? You tell that cheating, Lolita-chasing bastard of a husband of mine to get his arse back here to his three kids, or else I'll . . .'

Rupert scuttled into the hall with the phone, but it was too late. Steve's face now matched Jess's, except the poor girl also had tears rolling down her cheeks. I handed her a napkin.

'Excuse me. I'm not hungry.' She fled upstairs.

An uncomfortable silence filled the kitchen – hardly the convivial atmosphere promised on our website.

Steve pushed his chair back. 'Would you go ahead without us, please?' He hared after her.

'Do dig in,' Rupert said to the others, hurriedly bringing plates of mini quiches with salad to the table. He'd obviously decided that the least said, the soonest mended.

But Gloria had the opposite view. 'I do wish that people wouldn't bring their personal problems to *La Cour des Roses*. It makes everyone *so* uncomfortable.'

It was a good job I wasn't eating with the others. I would have choked on my food.

'Would you care to join us, Emmy?' Rupert asked, his eyes pleading for me to stay, as he indicated the vacant spaces at the table.

'No, thanks. I have somewhere I need to go.'

I drove to Alain's house like a condemned woman, where he answered the door with a puzzled look and a warm smile.

'Hi. I wasn't expecting you. I thought you had a guest meal.'

'Gloria ousted me. Do you mind?'

'Of course not. Come on in. Tea or wine? Or do you need something to eat?'

'Tea, please. I . . . I'm not hungry.'

'Everything all right at Jonathan's now?'

'Yes. Thanks.'

He didn't seem tense. He hadn't asked about what he'd seen. But even so . . . He turned and handed me a mug.

'Can we go for a walk instead?' I blurted.

His brows drew together. 'Are you okay?'

'Yes, but I need some air.'

'Okay.'

We stepped outside. Taking me by the hand, he led me along the quiet suburban streets. 'Is everything all right?'

Oblivious to the trim gardens we were passing, I took a deep breath. 'I want to speak to you about something.'

He gave me a sideways look. 'Sounds ominous. What's wrong?'

'Today, when you arrived at Jonathan's, I . . . I wondered if you were upset.'

'Not particularly. I wished I'd known you had a helper so I hadn't driven round when you didn't need me, but it didn't matter. Why?'

'When you got there, Ryan and I . . . I was worried about how it might have looked to you.'

He slowed his pace. 'It . . . looked as though you'd got the help you needed. That you were upset and Ryan was there to deal with it.' From the corner of my eye, I saw his chest rise as he took a breath. '*Should* I be worried?'

'No! But I can imagine how it might have seemed and I . . . I wanted you to know that there's nothing going on between us.'

An ominous silence filled the space around us.

'I can sense a "but",' he said, so quietly that I barely heard him.

God, I hoped I was doing the right thing.

'*But*. Ryan and I had a brief affair after Nathan left me.' I kept on walking, not daring to look at his face, but when he stopped, I had no choice.

Open shock. Shit.

I started to babble. 'I'm talking a few days, that's all. We agreed to be friends and it ended before I got to know you properly. Before you and I went on any dates together. I just want to be honest with you. This afternoon, when you saw him hugging me, he was only being a good friend . . . Anyway, he said it was okay for me to tell you if I needed to and I thought that was best but . . .'

Now it was my turn to be shocked. Because Alain threw back his head and laughed. 'Oh my God, Emmy!'

'What? *What?*'

He shook his head, still laughing.

I batted him, trying to figure out what was going on. 'Why are you laughing?'

'You cradle-snatcher! That boy is just a teenager!'

'He is not!' I said hotly, still bewildered by his reaction. 'He's twenty-four!'

He squeezed my hand. 'Well, when I moved down here, Ryan was only eighteen and still coming here with his parents for holidays, so I still think of him that way.' He frowned. 'Makes me feel a bit middle-aged, actually. *And* he has all those muscles. I'm afraid I lag behind him in both attributes.'

I glanced sideways at him. He was so tall, his strides were long, and he was lean and fit. I gave him a light nudge. 'You have your own attributes.'

'Ha! Well. Maybe.' He cocked his head to one side. 'So if I thought about it, I *could* feel pretty good about the fact that I've enticed you away from a virile, muscle-bound youth, I suppose.'

'You're not . . . upset?'

He gave me a puzzled look. 'Why should I be? You had a crap time, and you had some fun, blew off steam. I don't get a say in what you did before me.' He caught my gaze and held it. 'I do have one question for you, though.'

'What?'

'You were hurt and vulnerable. Did Ryan take advantage of you?'

'No! Not at all.'

His expression was one of pure relief. 'Thank God for that! I might have felt obliged to go and beat him to a pulp or something equally macho, and I suspect I would have come off the worse.'

I gaped at him. 'Would you have done that?'

'Well, I don't know about the beating-to-a-pulp part. But there might have been heated words.'

I felt a little warmer inside. It was nice to have someone looking out for my interests.

As we turned to retrace our steps, he gave me a sympathetic smile.

'Maybe you should know that Rupert knew,' I admitted. 'I didn't tell him. He guessed at the time.'

I thought *that* might make Alain uncomfortable, but he only chuckled. 'That man is unbelievable! He knew you were . . . liaising with his gardener, and yet he spent every spare minute trying to set you up with me?'

'Yes, well, he's not as daft as he looks, is he? He knew the Ryan thing was only temporary. He wanted to find me something more . . .' I stopped, embarrassed.

'More permanent?'

'More likely, anyway.'

'And are we? More likely?'

'I should say so.' I moved in closer to his side and stopped walking. 'Do I need to prove it?'

Alain turned, his eyes dancing with flecks of gold. 'I'm feeling a little delicate after your confession. I may need plenty of reassurance.'

Our lips met, and the kiss was sweet and long. I gave an inward sigh of relief. I had good things to report to Kate tonight.

When we got back, Alain asked me if I'd eaten yet, then smiled when I had to think about it before shaking my head. He threw together a salad for me, and I accepted a much-needed glass of wine on the basis that it would have wended its way through my system by the time I drove home – if I bothered driving home.

'Do I gather you've had a hard couple of days?' he asked as I ate.

'Could have been better, could have been worse.' I filled him in on Gloria and Rupert, and told him about my attempted truce, at which he made a face. 'I couldn't let it descend into open warfare, for Rupert's sake,' I explained. 'He has a big decision to make, and I don't want him to be influenced by anything that's not relevant.'

He kissed me. 'Martyr.'

'Yeah, that's me.'

'Talking of martyrs, is Rupert still sleeping on the sofa?'

'As far as I know. He complains about his back every morning.'

'I'm surprised Gloria's allowing that.'

'She can't do anything about it, if Rupert sticks to his guns. She can hardly force herself on him, can she?'

'I wouldn't put it past her,' Alain said quietly.

Realising I was only spewing out a litany of woes, I politely asked, 'How was your day?'

Laughing, he asked, 'Are you really interested in the ironmonger's tax returns?'

'No.'

'Then I'll say "better than yours" and leave it at that.'

I took my plate through to the kitchen and added it to the dishwasher. When I turned, he was standing there, watching me.

Reaching to wind my arms around his neck, I had to stand on tiptoes to get anywhere near his mouth, but he bent his head to meet me halfway. We let ourselves go a little, deepening the kiss, our bodies pressed close, until Alain placed his hands on my hips and prised us apart.

'That was quite a kiss, Emmy. Dangerous ground.'

'Are you saying you can't resist me?'

He held my gaze, his own soft brown and deadly serious. 'That's exactly what I'm saying. But we have work to do. One hour each date, remember? We haven't been keeping to it very well so far.'

I trailed after him like a sulky schoolchild as he went through to the dining table, where he took an A4 pad and pens from his briefcase. He found his reading glasses and put them on.

'Do you *have* to wear those?'

'Well, I could take them off, but then I'll only get a headache.'

'Oh, don't take them off for me.' I reached for my wine. 'Okay. I'm concentrating.'

His lips twitched. 'Good. So, present tense of verbs ending in *–er . . .*'

It wasn't the post-dinner activity I would have chosen, but I couldn't deny it was useful, and Alain was tailoring it to my specific needs. But inevitably, there was only so long I could concentrate before I inveigled my way onto his lap and wound my arms around his neck.

'Forty-seven minutes,' he remarked when I planted my lips on his. 'You lasted well.'

'You have no idea how well.' I touched the bridge of his glasses with my finger. 'They do add an extra something.'

'I'll bear that in mind if I ever feel your interest is flagging.'

'I don't think there's much danger of that.'

'Your French is improving.'

'I have other skills that are improving, too.'

'Oh, really? Maybe I could test that out later.'

He put on a CD, and we moved across to the sofa to curl up together as mellow notes filled the lounge.

I stroked a finger along the laugh lines at the corner of his eye. 'This music's nice.' I reached for my wine.

'I thought it was time I educated you in the ways of jazz before the Thomsons arrive.'

I placed small kisses at the corner of his mouth. 'Where's your saxophone?'

'Up in the spare bedroom.' His eyes narrowed with suspicion. 'Why?'

'I thought you might play it for me.'

'Ha. Ah. No, I don't think so.'

'Why not?'

'I . . . It would be weird. Playing for one person.'

'But you said you wanted to educate me in the ways of jazz.'

'You can listen to the CD.'

Shaking my head at his reticence, I did my best, but I only had half an ear on it. My attention was too quick to stray. I began to unbutton his shirt, sliding my hands across his chest, around to his back, pressing my body against his. His reaction was instant and gratifying. I smiled smugly.

Alain kissed the smile away. 'I think that gives you a power kick, being able to do that to me.'

'Are you complaining?'

'No. Upstairs. Now.'

We were naked on the bed in less than three minutes.

The next morning, I made sure I was up early enough to seduce my boyfriend *and* get to *La Cour des Roses* in time for breakfast.

When the phone rang, Gloria immediately took it into the hall as a shrill voice sounded across the airwaves.

'I would request that you stop phoning this number,' I heard her say tartly into the phone. More shrill noises in return. 'I cannot force someone to take a phone call, madam, and your personal issues are none of my concern. I would thank you not to call again.'

It wasn't hard to see that poor Violet and Betty and the Hollands were not happy. I couldn't blame them. They were on holiday to get away from their troubles, not to spend mealtimes embroiled in other people's.

I glanced across at Rupert. He'd been eerily quiet all morning and wouldn't catch my eye . . . and he looked appalling. His hair was a mess, as though he hadn't bothered to run a comb through it, and his beard was beginning to straggle. The bags under his eyes were noticeable.

'You look bloody awful, Rupert,' I whispered.

'That's probably because I feel bloody awful. Didn't sleep a wink last night.'

I never got the chance to find out why.

Gloria's head appeared round the doorway. 'Rupert. Emmy. A word.'

Meekly, we followed her into Rupert's lounge, where she closed the door.

'I'm not having it,' she declared.

'Having what?' Rupert asked her.

'You should have heard that woman! Steve's wife. She knows they're here because she hacked into his e-mails, would you believe. Shrieking at me, calling me every name under the sun.'

Rupert trod cautiously. 'I know it must have been unpleasant, Gloria, but I don't see what we can do about it, other than screen calls.'

'Well, now, that's not my problem, is it? You're the manager, Emmy, according to the website, so it's your job to sort this mess out.'

'Gloria . . .' Rupert would have jumped to my defence, but I laid a hand on his arm to stop him as she flounced off.

'It's not worth it, Rupert.'

He nodded and followed me back out to the kitchen. Jess and Steve had disappeared in mortification – again. The Hollands thanked us for a lovely stay and went upstairs to pack, promising to leave a review. Rupert accompanied Violet and Betty upstairs to fetch their bags and pack them into their little hired car. The guesthouse was emptying, ready for the Thomson invasion, although Jess and Steve weren't due to leave till the next day.

'Does that mean I can swear again now?' Rupert asked as we waved Betty and Violet on their way, his wife at his side to add to the farewell committee. 'Twelve days of watching my sodding tongue!'

'Well, you worked your magic on those two,' I told him. 'They've already provisionally booked for next year.'

'Really? Oh, well, that's good, I suppose.'

'You certainly get a mixed bag here.'

'I like it that way. Keeps me on my toes.'

Gloria's expression was sour. 'That's one way of putting it.'

Back inside, Rupert asked me if I was okay to clear up by myself. If it meant he might spruce himself up so he looked less like the living dead, I was happy to oblige.

Ten minutes later, the dog pushed her way into the kitchen from the hall.

'What's up, sweetie?' I stroked her head. 'You know you're not allowed in here.'

She whined pitifully. I crouched down and nuzzled her face. 'What's up?' But there was no comforting her. Thinking Rupert would have the magic touch, I went into the hall to knock on his door.

My hand stopped in mid-air. Raised voices. Gloria's, shrill and weepy. Rupert's, clearly shaken. Had the dog picked up on her master's distress?

I patted my thigh. 'C'mon, then. Let's sit outside for a while.' I took her out to the patio, where she rested her chin dolefully on my knee. 'Everything'll be all right,' I told her – although I was far from sure of that.

Five minutes later, I heard Rupert's door open.

'Ten years, Rupert! I can't believe you're willing to throw it all away!'

Despite her dislike of Gloria, the dog rushed through to her master. I started to follow, if nothing else but to pull her away from where she wouldn't be wanted right now, but I stopped short in the kitchen.

Gloria was in floods of tears. They were streaking down her face, mingling with mascara to make smudged stripes – but for once she didn't care. She turned to him. 'I thought if I came back . . .'

'Gloria. I've explained. Don't make me do it all again. Please.' Rupert's voice was raw with emotion.

Gloria's hands were shaking as she took her car keys from her handbag. 'I . . . I'll be back for my stuff some time.' Through a curtain of tears, she stumbled through the front door.

I ran after her, putting out a hand to stop her before she could climb into her car. 'Gloria. Will you be all right?'

She lifted her chin a little in defiance. 'Do I look all right? And anyway, why should you care?'

I tried to hold her gaze, but she was looking everywhere but at me. 'I'm sorry it didn't work out for you.'

'I bet. Well, you got what you wanted, Emmy. Your precious *Cour des Roses*. Enjoy.'

And she was gone.

CHAPTER SEVENTEEN

Rupert was slumped in his doorway, his face ashen.

'Do you want to talk about it?' I asked him doubtfully.

'Will you be mortally offended if I say no?'

'Of course not.'

'I appreciate that. If you need me, I'll be in here.'

'Okay. I . . . I'm supposed to be meeting Sophie and Ellie for coffee at lunchtime, before I go to the supermarket. Is that still okay?'

'Yes. Don't worry, I'll keep an eye out for the arrivals.' He hesitated. 'Perhaps you could set off the village grapevine for me, Emmy? If you start with Madame Dupont, it shouldn't take long.' He took the dog in with him, closing the door, so I left her to comfort her master as only a faithful hound could and set off to find Madame Dupont.

'*Bonjour, Emie. Ça va?*'

'*Bonjour*, Madame Dupont. I . . .'

She frowned. 'Are you all right?'

'I'm fine. Madame Hunter . . . She's gone.'

The old woman's eyes lit up like a Christmas tree. 'Gone? For good?'

'Yes.'

'But that is marvellous news!' She clasped my hand in hers. 'Why aren't you happy?'

I managed a wan smile. 'Because . . .' My French really didn't stretch to this kind of thing. I placed my hand across my heart. 'For Rupert.'

'He will be fine. You will see. Where is he?'

'In his room. Please don't disturb him.'

'I wouldn't think of it! And the dog?'

'With Rupert.'

'Then we shall get to work!'

I think that was her answer to every problem in life. I'd expected her to gloat about Gloria's departure as we set about our business, but she didn't, and I was grateful.

I took five minutes out to phone Alain, but it went straight to voicemail, so I left him a message, knowing he would be immensely cheered by the news.

'Do you mind if I leave you to finish off?' I asked Madame Dupont soon after midday. 'I'm meeting friends for coffee.'

'No problem, *Emie*. That is good. You work too hard. You should slow down. Make time for yourself and your friends. Time to sit and enjoy the sun and the flowers and each other. I will see you next time.'

As I drove into town to pick up Ellie and Sophie, I was dismayed to see that the roadworks had been set up a quarter of a mile from the turning onto our lane. I couldn't tell yet how much disruption they would cause, but I did know we could have done without them.

With Sophie and Ellie in the car, they directed me towards Saint-Martin. Along the road leading into the town, posters were tacked up on every available pole and surface. I slowed the car as we approached the town centre and pointed to a large field where a covered bandstand was half erected. 'What's that?'

'I believe the ticketed events are held in there,' Ellie told me. 'People sit on rugs or bring folding chairs.'

'And pray it doesn't rain?'

She laughed. 'I imagine so. And there are free little gigs in town, too – bands set up in the main square and take slots playing to whoever's passing or wants to listen.'

We chose a café in the square, with a covered terrace where we could sit looking out at more posters and the platform to be used by the performers. I could imagine relaxing over a coffee, listening to the music.

Ellie and Sophie were both predictably ecstatic at the news that Gloria had left – and especially that Rupert had been the one to make the decision.

'Well, thank heavens for that!' Ellie announced. 'Rupert did the right thing.'

'Yes, he did.'

'Cheers!' Sophie chinked coffee cups with us. 'To Rupert!'

Ellie and I echoed the sentiment.

'I wonder what Gloria will do now,' Ellie mused.

Sophie frowned. 'She has . . . What is that expression? Something about a mattress?'

'You mean she's made her own bed and now she has to lie in it?'

'Yes! That's it!'

'You know, I *could* almost feel sorry for her,' Ellie said quietly. When Sophie and I gaped at her, she explained. 'I don't like the woman. Never have. And God knows she goes about everything in the worst way possible. But as we've said before, *La Cour des Roses* was never what she wanted. It was a recipe for disaster from the minute Rupert bought it.'

'Rupert does feel responsible for the way things went sour,' I admitted. 'When she left, she was so upset, it made me think she really did care. But maybe she just doesn't know how she's going to survive without him. And I can't say I'm going to miss all the barbed comments.'

'You shouldn't have put up with that,' said Ellie.

'I could hardly fight back with full guns blazing, could I? Rupert had enough on his plate.'

'You are very good, when *she* is the one who wronged *you*,' Sophie said kindly. At that, her perfect brows knitted together.

'Although I don't understand why she dislikes you so much. You've done nothing to her. It's the other way around.'

'Jealousy,' Ellie supplied, drumming her mint-green nails on the table. 'She's jealous of Emmy because of her friendship with Rupert – a natural friendship that I'm not sure Gloria and Rupert had as a couple. And she felt threatened. She didn't want Emmy taking over at *La Cour des Roses*. Taking her place. Influencing Rupert's decision.'

'Well, I am glad I never met her,' Sophie declared. 'She must have used a different salon in town, but for once I am not sad at this loss of business.'

Ellie and I both laughed, and I decided it was time for a change of subject.

I turned to Sophie. 'A certain hunky gardener was asking about you the other day,' I told her mischievously.

Her cheeks turned pink. 'Really?'

'Really.'

Sophie's dimples flashed, even though she shrugged her shoulders. 'Well, that's nice.'

'I'm going to be the old maiden aunt at this rate,' Ellie murmured.

Sophie gave her a stern look. 'Then you shouldn't be so unromantic. It's your choice.'

'Yes, it is.' Ellie smiled, stretching back in her seat. 'And it's a choice I'm perfectly happy with, thank you.'

I wasn't sure that Rupert felt the same way about his own choices. I thought he'd made the right one, and I was sure most people would agree with me, but that didn't mean it had been an easy one for him to make.

But as I sipped my coffee, looking out across the square and listening to Ellie and Sophie joking with each other, I reckoned that if I could see Rupert through this, life was looking pretty good.

Alain and I had something special, I was sure of it, and with the weight of coming clean about Ryan off my mind it was looking even better.

And with Gloria gone, my future at *La Cour des Roses* was now secure. I felt a burst of enthusiasm at the thought of how I could make it work, getting stuck into the things I wanted to change. I needed to make sure that *La Cour des Roses* was an ongoing success, able to financially support us both (and Gloria's divorce settlement, no doubt) in a way that kept Rupert happy and healthy . . . Although with the Thomson weekend looming, it would have to be a case of first things first. Once they were out of the way, I would also renew my efforts at chipping away at my agency until it was up and running.

The only cloud on the horizon was the flat in Birmingham, but for now that was out of my hands. All I could do was try my best to make things work here in France, hope my savings lasted with regard to mortgage payments, and that I could make the money back somewhere down the line. I would be using my grandmother's money for the right reasons – to enable my dreams.

I dropped the girls back in town, and as I pushed a trolley around the supermarket I thanked the heavens that I'd galvanised Rupert into placing several online orders to cover us for the next few days. Still, he'd forgotten to order a few bits and pieces, and there were some things he didn't trust the supermarket staff to pick out for him.

Five days' worth of breakfasts for over thirty people, and three days' worth of lunches . . . and the barbeque. Urgh. He'd wanted to place the meat order with the local butcher and get the breakfast pastries from the bakery who usually delivered, but the simple fact was that half of this food wasn't even being paid for by the booking. I'd persuaded him that we couldn't afford loyalty this time, but I felt pretty bad about it.

I was so preoccupied, I was already halfway around before I remembered to phone Jonathan to see if there was anything he needed.

'Hi, Emmy. I haven't got out yet this week. Can I give you a little list?'

'No problem.' I scrabbled in my bag for pen and paper. 'What do you need?'

Jonathan's 'little list' wasn't so little, but he was grateful for the errand.

'Thanks, lovey,' he said when I got there, helping me in his limited way – getting under my feet – to bring it from the car to the kitchen.

'Have you been to see the doctor about that cough?'

'No. It seems to be getting better.'

'You sound awfully wheezy.'

'I get mild asthma, on and off.'

I let it go for now. 'Any chance of a quick cup of tea?' That should give me long enough to assess this so-called asthma of his.

When I told him about Gloria's departure, he looked over the moon and terribly sad for Rupert at the same time.

'You will look after him for me, Emmy, won't you?'

'You know I will.' As for his asthma, I wasn't happy. 'Have you got your mobile on you?'

'Yes. Why?' He dug it out of his pocket.

'Phone your doctor to make an appointment.'

'I'm fine.'

'No, you're not. You've had that cough for days, and now you're wheezing. I'm not going until you do what you're told. I mean it.'

'Hmmph. Bossy little bag, aren't you?'

Under my glare, he gave in, made the call and managed to get an appointment for Monday morning.

I got up to go. 'That's all very well, but if that chest of yours gets any worse, I want you to call us, okay?'

'Okay.'

Stubborn old sod. I'd get him sorted if it killed me.

When I got back to *La Cour des Roses*, I noticed the delightful addition of a portable toilet in the corner of the courtyard.

Rupert came out to help with the bags, and I gestured towards it. 'That adds a certain *je ne sais quoi*, don't you think?'

He shook his head in despair at the eyesore. 'You've been gone a while.'

'Sorry. I got caught up with Jonathan.' I explained about the shopping and the doctor.

'Good girl. It's about time he got that chest seen to. Probably something and nothing, but he is getting on a bit.'

'Are you okay? After this morning?'

He grunted. 'I'll live.'

My phone rang and I dug it out of my bag. It was Alain. 'Hi. I got your voicemail. I can't believe it! What happened?'

'I can't talk about it right now.'

'Ah. I assume Rupert's there. Do you still want to come round tonight?'

'I don't think I should. I . . . have a lot to do here.'

'Don't worry, Emmy. I'd rather you looked after Rupert.'

But the subject of our discussion butted in. 'Is that Alain?'

I nodded, and he gestured for me to hand him the phone.

'Alain? Do you remember when your wife left you and you came here and I got you horribly drunk? It's time for you to repay the favour. We'll see you here at seven. Don't eat. I'll shove some supper together.'

I took the phone back. Alain was chuckling. 'I'll see you at seven, then, Emmy, by the sounds of it.'

'Are you sure, Rupert?' I asked him as I ended the call.

'I'm sure I need to drink, and I can't think of two better people to do it with. Now then. Down to business. Jess and Steve have left a day early, I'm afraid.'

'Damn.'

He shrugged. 'Didn't surprise me. I'm not refunding him the night lost. I'm not in the mood. And the first of the Thomson guesthouse lot are here. Donald and Patricia. Donald is Frank's brother.' He smiled. 'Delightful old chap, but he has dementia. When they arrived, his wife explained to him in great detail what was planned for the week ahead, but he asked her again when I took them up to their room, and again when I took them a pot of tea out to the garden. That poor woman is going to be exhausted by the end of the stay! She told me they'd deliberately come a day earlier than Frank and Sylvia, so he could get acclimatised to his surroundings before all the excitement starts. And then . . .'

We were interrupted by the arrival of the first of the caravans, a dinky thing containing an amiable, retired couple – Annie, a younger cousin of Sylvia's, and her husband, Fred. We let them get on with setting up in their corner of the courtyard, took them a welcome pot of tea, and settled down at the kitchen table for our final planning session.

'Right.' I dragged the lists towards me. 'Another caravan arriving tomorrow.' I rolled my eyes. 'Those roadworks are underway. I hope they leave enough access. Then the tent. And the rest of the house guests, too. It's going to be quite a day.' We looked at each other in trepidation. 'Food all sorted?'

'Yep.'

'When's the marquee due?'

'Just after lunch on Sunday.'

'I assumed you'd have it delivered on Monday.'

'There'll be plenty of other things to worry about on Monday, what with the caterer and the band. Is that all in hand, still?'

'Yes, thanks to Alain.' I sat back, smiling. 'We're going to do this, Rupert. Despite all the hassle. It's going to work.'

'Hmmph. Yes, well, don't jinx it by saying something like that.'

I hesitated, wondering if I should use the moment to ask him about Gloria. But he'd seemed calm since I got back from Jonathan's. Settled. He had colour back in his cheeks, and he'd showered and shaved. If he'd found some equilibrium, I didn't want to jeopardise that. And in the time I'd known him, I'd learned that he preferred to talk about things when *he* was ready. I let it be.

Instead, I quickly checked reviews in the hope of cheering us both up, but unfortunately it had the opposite effect.

Four stars: *Loved our stay. All our needs catered to. One star knocked off as the resident dog can be bouncier than we would have liked.*

'You're going to have to have words with that dog of yours,' I told Rupert sternly.

And a one star: *A disgraceful establishment that allows adulterous couples to flaunt their relationship in front of all and sundry with no respect for the sanctity of marriage.*

Rupert and I looked at each other and said in unison, 'Steve's wife.'

By the time Alain arrived, the newly-decorated middle *gîte* had been appropriated by a family with four children ranging from three to ten. As the *gîtes* were only designed to sleep four, this meant a couple of airbeds in the lounge, but they all seemed determined to treat it as some kind of indoor camping exercise, and the two older kids were happy to be taking an illicit few days off school, for which their parents would no doubt be lambasted – unless they'd inventively phoned in a sudden outbreak of chicken pox or impetigo and were making sure the kids didn't get too much of an obvious tan during their stay.

Alain shook hands with Rupert, as he always did, but then drew him into a brief hug. 'I'm sorry, Rupert. About Gloria.'

Rupert patted his back, then pulled away. 'A valiant attempt at sincerity, Alain, but unconvincing.'

Alain smiled. 'But I *am* sorry you had to go through it.'

'Me too.'

We settled out on the patio with large glasses of wine and a tray of whatever Rupert had lurking in the fridge that he needed to clear out before the full Thomson invasion, the dog lying proprietorially across Rupert's feet and no doubt hoping for scraps.

'All set for your big weekend?' Alain asked politely.

We both groaned and took large gulps of wine, making him laugh.

'My private lounge looks like the headquarters of some kind of humanitarian food bank,' Rupert told him. 'The delivery of a rather sizeable online grocery order proved to us that the kitchen at *La Cour des Roses* is not as large as we thought, despite the commercial-sized fridge and freezer.'

'That sounds like a lot of catering over the next few days.'

'At least we're not catering for the party as well,' Rupert told him. 'I think that *would* kill me. Talking of catering, when we've finished eating, could you help me with the barbeques for tomorrow, before we get too pissed?'

I continued to nibble and sip, watching the boys with their toys as they wheeled them out of the shed, set them up on the patio, decided which bits belonged where, and cleaned them off. They seemed happy enough, as was I. My two favourite blokes in France, working side by side, laughing and joking together. You wouldn't have guessed that Rupert had irrevocably split up with his wife that same day.

But as the level of the wine went down and another bottle was opened, Rupert slumped a little more in his chair – and it wasn't only due to the alcohol. He'd been putting on a front all day, and now he was allowing it to drop by degrees. I sensed it, and I knew Alain did, too.

'I know everyone will be saying good riddance to bad rubbish,' Rupert finally muttered, staring out across the darkening garden.

'That's not true,' Alain told him sternly. 'Everyone has an opinion, but they all want what's best for you.' He tried a wry smile. 'It just so happens that Gloria leaving *is* what they think is best for you.'

Rupert took another large gulp of wine. 'It was so hard. To decide.'

Alain topped his glass up and winked at me. We would deal with the hangover in the morning. Rupert needed to do this.

'When she left me for Nathan, that was *her* decision. I didn't have to do anything, make any choices. Her coming back here, wanting another chance . . . For the past few days, it's like someone was holding a balancing scale, but they kept taking weights off one side and piling them on the other and then changing it back again. Every two minutes.'

'So what was it that tipped the scale?' I asked him quietly.

'Steve's wife, and Violet and Betty.'

'*What?*' I was a little sozzled myself, and that didn't sound like much of a basis to give up on ten years of marriage to me.

'I'd been up all night agonising. On the verge of calling it quits. This morning was the final nail in the coffin. It's funny how it's the smallest things, sometimes, isn't it? After Steve's wife called again this morning, I didn't blame Gloria for being upset. But she's never learned to take the rough with the smooth here. Or to try to see the funny side. That's what I like about you, Emmy. You get stressed, but you'll always laugh about it if you can. And the way she rounded on you, telling you to sort it out when it was clear there was nothing to be done . . . And then she was so unfeeling when we were waving Violet and Betty off. She'd made no effort to find any rapport with them, or to see them for the sweet souls they are. To her, they were just another mild inconvenience to be got rid of.'

'But you would sell up anyway, if Gloria stayed. So none of that would matter.'

'It would matter to me. The rough with the smooth. Interesting people. Boring people. I enjoy that. Fun times. Problems. I would be *so* bored, Emmy. I wouldn't be . . .' His voice hitched.

'You wouldn't be you,' Alain supplied quietly.

Rupert nodded. 'I like the me that goes with *La Cour des Roses*. I finally found my niche in life. And what was left of my love for Gloria wasn't enough for me to walk away from it.'

We sat in silence for a long moment.

'Gloria seemed so upset,' I finally ventured. 'I thought she'd be angrier.'

'I think she was too shocked to be angry, Emmy. She'd honestly expected me to roll over.'

'Did she say where she was going?'

'No. We have friends further south. Maybe she's gone there for a few days. I've packed up her things, so they're waiting for her when she decides to come for them.'

Alain reached out a hand, laying it over the top of Rupert's in a gesture I found touching. 'Will you be okay?'

'I will. With the help of my friends. And now I want to stop being maudlin and tell you about the time my best friend set me up on a blind date in London. You wouldn't *believe* how horrendous this girl was . . .'

It was midnight by the time we staggered back to my room. Donald Thomson had come outside three times to introduce himself to us, and at one point asked us why he was in Italy. The Australians had come over to tell us what a brilliant meal they'd had out in town and to thank Rupert for the restaurant recommendation.

As Alain and I staggered – literally, because we'd been trying to keep up with Rupert on the wine front before we realised we couldn't – into my room, I started to giggle.

'What's funny?' He was slurring slightly, and it made his accent that bit more pronounced.

'It's a bit . . . clandestine, you sleeping here. Sort of naughty.'

'Naughty, as in, it turns you on, naughty?'

'Yeah. And by the way. You sound Frencher when you're drunk.'

'Frencher? That's not a word, Emmy.'

I started to undress, although I needed help with the buttons. Alain was happy to oblige. Maybe the alcohol hadn't reached his fingers yet.

'I'm *never* going to sound Frencher at this rate,' I whined. 'We've hardly done any French lessons.'

'I'll give you a French lesson now, if you like.' His mouth travelled slowly down the length of my neck.

'Will it involve grammar?'

'No. I thought I'd concentrate on technique. I think you require practice on quite a few fronts.'

'Oh, you do?' I tried and failed to unbutton his shirt.

'Lots of practice. Might as well start now.'

'Mmm-hmm. Where would you like me to start?'

Afterwards, with the light breeze from the window cooling our heated skin, I stretched like a cat, luxuriating as Alain ran his hands lightly across my body. Tracing the heart-shaped birthmark under his ribcage, I'd never felt so easy with anyone, never felt so cherished. And if that was an old-fashioned word, then so be it. When I was with him, everything else melted away until it was only the two of us.

I fit my body against his, his arms tight around me, holding me close, and drifted to sleep.

CHAPTER EIGHTEEN

A nightmare hangover wasn't the best idea when you had to get up at the kind of hour we did at *La Cour des Roses*.

Rupert and Alain were obviously of the same opinion. Alain was monosyllabic until the shower had woken him up, and Rupert's idea of walking the dog was to let her out into the orchard and then pick up after her.

We huddled around the coffee machine as though our lives depended on it, and when Rupert had created the life-saving brew we needed, we sat at the kitchen table, clutching our cups or with our heads in our hands.

'Well, at least you saved time not walking the dog,' I said brightly, wincing when I realised that talking brightly hurt. 'Still, we could do with getting a head start on breakfast.'

'Urgh. Don't talk about food.'

'Never mind talking about it, we're going to have to produce it.'

None of us made a move. When the main door in the hall opened, we looked around in surprise.

Gloria.

'Well, this *is* a cosy threesome.' The tears were gone, replaced by open hostility.

'What are you doing here?' Rupert managed.

'I came for my stuff. But I would like a word.'

Rupert hoisted himself from his chair, his hands shaking slightly as he followed her.

'*Merde.*'

I gave Alain a reassuring smile. 'You heard her. She came back for her stuff, that's all.'

Alain finished his coffee and stood. 'Maybe I should go.'

As he moved to clear away his empty cup, we heard the sound of arguing voices – or one voice, in particular – getting louder and angrier.

'. . . won't even reconsider?' The sound was shrill, and coming from Rupert's room.

I stood, too, wavering.

'You have no idea how big a mistake you're making, Rupert. No *idea*!' The last word was shrieked as the row spilled out into the hall, peppered with barks from the dog. 'I have put up with this place for you for *years* – how much do you think that's worth?'

I made a move to step out there, but Alain held me back. 'It's not your fight, Emmy. There's nothing you can do that won't make it worse.'

My whole body sagged with the knowledge that he was right. The dog shot over to us, cowering at my feet.

I held her tight against my legs. 'It's all right, sweetie,' I soothed. 'Nobody's going to hurt you.' Although I wouldn't put it past Gloria to aim a kick at the poor animal.

'I'm well aware of what I'm doing.' Rupert spoke quietly, but I could hear the strain in every word. This couldn't be good for his angina. *None* of Gloria's stay can have been good for his angina. 'We went through all this yesterday. I explained why . . .'

'I don't want your pathetic explanations.' Gloria was dragging her bags and cases out. 'All I want is to get away from this *sodding* house that you've sold your soul to! And then I want every penny that's owing to me for putting up with being stuck for so long in this *godforsaken* place with your *godforsaken* guests and chickens and . . .'

'Keep your voice down!' Rupert warned. 'Or come back in here.'

'No way to either.'

'We should leave. We could go out into the garden,' I whispered to Alain, nodding my head towards the patio doors.

'Sounds like a plan to me.' He began to lead me by the hand.

'Going somewhere, you two lovebirds?' Gloria's voice stopped us in our tracks.

We turned to face her.

'Leave them alone, Gloria,' Rupert said sternly. 'This has nothing to do with them.'

The look Gloria cast my way was pure venom. I didn't know that anyone could hold so much hatred inside them, and just because something wasn't going their way. It made me feel slightly sick.

'Oh? I beg to differ. I'd say Emmy has had plenty to do with this. All those cosy little chats you two enjoy? Walking that filthy animal together?' She started to shift her bags one by one from the hall to outside the main door. 'I presume it was *her* idea that you slept on the sofa, so I couldn't even sleep in my own bed with my own husband!'

That was when Rupert snapped. I could see the shift on his face. He'd had beyond enough.

'It's not *your* bedroom any more. It's mine. I didn't want you in my bed until I was sure how I felt about you coming back. Seems I made the right decision. As for Emmy being involved, *you* involved her when you slept with her boyfriend, and don't you forget it!'

The dog whined and pressed close against me. I couldn't see what this was gaining anybody, other than giving us all ulcers.

But Gloria hadn't finished. It seemed she wasn't going without a parting shot.

'You think that was the only time that happened?' she snarled at him. It was almost feral.

'What?'

'You think I didn't need to amuse myself while you played at hotels? While you went into town to meet up with all your Brits-together ex-pat chums? Nathan wasn't the only one, Rupert. Not by a long chalk.'

I gasped. Alain's hand tightened on mine to the point where it hurt. He was so tense, I could feel the strain emanating from his body.

All the colour drained from Rupert's face. He opened his mouth to say something, but if he was trying to shut her up, he wasn't quick enough.

'Let's see . . . Remember that architect bloke? Graham somebody-or-other? His wife used to go for solitary afternoon walks. Foolish woman.'

Rupert swayed a little.

'That chap whose girlfriend went to the market on her own because he had a stomach bug? You went to your precious market, too. As you always do. There was nothing wrong with his stomach, Rupert. Nothing wrong with *any* of him, that I recall.'

Rupert was using the wall for support now. I wanted to go to him, but my feet wouldn't move. Everything had gone into some kind of slow-motion bubble. My brain felt sluggish and stupid.

'And it wasn't only the guests . . .'

I finally managed to open my mouth. 'Gloria! That's *enough*!'

Her head whipped round, and her eyes fixed on me. Then on Alain.

I heard him mutter under his breath. 'God, please, no.'

'And then there's that delectable accountant of yours. Such a good friend to you, isn't he? Poor man – he was *so* bereft when his wife left him. So *desperately* in need of comfort.'

I turned slowly to look at Alain. His eyes were closed. His Adam's apple bobbed in his throat. No, no, *no* . . .

Gloria's venomous eyes fixed on me. 'He's pretty good in the sack, Emmy, isn't he? And *such* a cute birthmark under his ribcage – almost like a little heart. I'm sorry you got him second-hand.'

The coffee roiled in my hangover-burdened stomach. I couldn't breathe.

Rupert had straightened, but he was still using the wall as a prop. 'Get out, Gloria. Get out. *Get out!*' His face was red and his chest was heaving.

'With *pleasure.*' Shooting one victorious glance my way, she was gone, the door rattling the architrave as she slammed it behind her.

Rupert turned to Alain. 'The same goes for you.'

'Rupert—'

'Get out, Alain. I don't want to see you here again. I don't want to see you, full stop. I'm terminating your services. When I find another accountant, he'll contact you to transfer the paperwork.'

'Rupert, for God's sake . . .'

'I thought you were my friend.'

'I was. I am!'

'I meant what I said. Go!'

'But it wasn't like she said! I mean, not quite . . . She's twisted it . . .'

Rupert started to move towards us, and I was suddenly afraid there could be a real bust-up. Sending Alain a plea for restraint, I took a step in front of him.

'Rupert . . .'

His fists were balled tight at his sides, the knuckles white . . . but he turned and slammed back into his lounge.

Alain laid his hand on my arm. 'Emmy.'

Bile rose fast in my throat. Blindly, I pushed past him, through the patio doors, trying to take in air. I stayed still for several moments, my face clammy, not daring to move, Gloria whining at my heels.

When I finally looked around, Alain was standing at the patio doors. He moved towards me and placed a hand on my shoulder.

I shook it away with more force than my somersaulting stomach would have liked. 'Don't *touch* me!'

He pulled his hand back, shock on his face. 'Emmy. Me and Gloria . . .'

'Don't you *dare*! I don't want to hear about you and that woman. You hypocritical *bastard*! Pretending you despised her all these years.'

'I *have* despised her all these years!'

'Then what did you sleep with her for? Your friend's wife? How could you *do* that to him?'

'It wasn't like that. Emmy, you . . .'

'It's a bit late for denial. The guilt was written all over your face.'

'But you don't understand. It . . .'

A loud scream from one of the *gîtes*.

God almighty.

'Just leave, Alain.'

He opened his mouth. Closed it again. One long look, and then he turned and went around the side of the house. I heard his engine start up, the tyres spinning on the gravel as he drove away.

Praying that Rupert would be all right for another few minutes and hadn't put himself in an early grave with high blood pressure, I charged across the courtyard, making a wild guess that the scream had come from the nearest unit, and knocked in a panic. Aaron opened it, the baby in one arm and the toddler hanging onto his hand.

'Is everything okay?'

Wendy came rushing through from the bathroom in only a bath towel, stopping short when she saw me, her head wrapped in a smaller towel.

'Emmy!' She wrapped the bath towel tighter.

'I . . . I'm sorry. I thought I heard a scream.' My stomach was still churning alarmingly. I hoped I wouldn't be sick on their doorstep.

Wendy winced. 'I'm sorry. That was me. The water went freezing cold. It was a bit of a shock. It won't go hot again. I've got a head full of shampoo under here.'

Chris came dashing along from his *gîte* to see what was going on.

'I . . . Do you want me to come in and look at the shower?' I asked dubiously.

But Chris shook his head. 'Our kettle just went off mid-boil. Looks like a power cut.'

I blew out a breath. 'Okay. Let me check up at the house. I'll be back as soon as I can.'

It didn't take long for me to work out the power cut wasn't isolated to the *gîte* building. All the digital displays in the kitchen were dead. We had nothing. I glanced in horror at the fridge and freezer, thinking about the amount of stuff we had in there. And then a picture of Alain and Gloria together entered my brain, and I couldn't think of anything else. I leaned against the kitchen wall for a moment, my eyes closed, my breathing shallow.

'Emmy?'

I swirled around. Patricia was standing there in her dressing gown. 'There's no hot water.'

'I know. I'm sorry, Patricia. I think there's been a power cut. Please bear with me while I try to sort it out for you.' My voice was remarkably steady, considering.

She nodded and went back upstairs.

What had I done to deserve this? I allowed myself a few short moments of self-pity, my stomach hollow and my mind still reeling from Gloria's revelations, then went into the hall and knocked on Rupert's door. No answer, so I let myself in. He wasn't in the lounge, so I knocked on his bedroom door. What if he'd collapsed?

I knocked louder. 'Rupert?'

'Bugger off, Emmy.'

'Are you all right?'

'What do you think? I said bugger off.'

'But are you . . .?' My voice hitched. 'Your angina . . .'

His tone softened. 'I don't need the paramedics. What I need is for you to leave me alone.'

'I can't.' My voice was small. 'We have a power cut and I don't know what to do.'

Silence. A curse. Several more. And then he appeared at the bedroom door. He looked awful. Not that I could be much of an oil painting at the moment.

'I . . . I'm sorry. But there's no hot water. No lights. The fridge is off. The freezer.' I caught a sob. He didn't need me to break down now.

'Shit.' He tried a light switch. 'The *gîtes*?'

'The same.'

'Shit.'

'Yeah.'

He closed his eyes. Squared his shoulders a little. 'There's an emergency generator in the outhouse at the back. I'll get it going. But it will only serve the house, not the *gîtes*. It's the best I can do.'

'Okay. How do we find out about the power cut?'

'We don't. It would take forever to get through, and I have a nasty suspicion it's something to do with those ruddy roadworks. I imagine they'll get it back on as soon as they can.'

For a brief moment, we looked at each other, knowing there was so much to say but with neither of us having any desire to say it. He pushed past me to go around the back of the house while I pushed my personal problems to the back of my mind and tried to force my brain onto more practical matters.

We would have electricity here soon. The *gîtes* wouldn't. They would have to come up to the house for everything they needed. Hot drinks. Phone charging. Showers. Whatever.

I went back across the courtyard to where the anxious guests awaited news. I apprised them all of the current state of affairs and got a collective murmur of dismay in return.

'I'll open up the vacant guest bedrooms for you to use this morning, and we'll hope it's fixed by the time the other guests arrive.' I tried a winning smile, but I doubted it would take home any awards. 'Give us ten minutes to get sorted before you start coming over, okay? I'm so sorry for any inconvenience.'

Back at the house, I ran upstairs to update Patricia – the less confusion Donald faced, the better – then opened the doors to the empty guest rooms. Back in the kitchen, I worked at lightning speed, grateful there were only the two for breakfast this morning and that this hadn't happened tomorrow when we had everybody to feed. It took me several minutes to realise the fridge was humming again and the microwave display was flashing. Good old Rupert.

When Patricia and Donald appeared, I had a sudden panic about my arch-nemesis, the egg, but both of them declined cooked food – whether out of consideration or lack of appetite, I wasn't sure, nor did I care. I was merely grateful.

The *gîte* guests began pottering over, toiletry bags and towels in hand, bless them – it was going to be bad enough cleaning all the bathrooms in time for new arrivals without swapping all the towels, too. Patricia offered their bathroom out as well, for which I thanked her profusely. The only bright side was that none of them were in a rush to get off anywhere, as they were all awaiting the guests of honour later.

A knock at the door revealed a man in overalls. Speaking French. With a strong accent.

I did my best, but my brain didn't want to think in French. It was barely able to think in English right now.

Gathering that I was flustered and upset, he gave me a kindly smile and threw in a bit of miming to help me out, pointing at his overalls and performing a sawing action. The best I could gather was that something had been damaged that shouldn't have been during the course of the wretched roadworks, just as Rupert had predicted, and it would be fixed as soon as possible.

When I'd got Patricia and Donald their pot of tea, I knocked on Rupert's door, then poked my head round. No sign of him. Nor was he in his bedroom. Odd. And no sign of the dog either. Maybe he'd taken her for a walk – she hadn't had a proper one yet this morning. I went to check the courtyard. His estate car had gone. Had he taken the dog for a walk farther afield? Thought of a last-minute errand?

As the guest bedrooms began to empty, I forced myself upstairs to get them pristine again, when all I really wanted was to crawl into my room and into my bed, pull the covers over my head and never come out again.

All this mayhem and activity wasn't enough to block out the sickening fact that Gloria had ruined my life so spectacularly yet again. It was bad enough that she'd slept with one of my boyfriends, but two? It was like some kind of cruel history repeating itself. I'd long since got over the business with Nathan. But I couldn't *bear* the idea that she'd slept with Alain. The thought that she might have shared what I shared with him, that she knew his body the same way I did, even down to his birthmark . . .

Feeling queasy again, I staggered down to the kitchen to make a cup of peppermint tea.

Madame Dupont was polishing the banisters in the hall. She took one look at me and her face dropped. '*Mon Dieu! Qu'est-ce qui se passe?*'

What the hell was I supposed to say? I could hardly tell her that Gloria's reappearance had led to the demise of my latest relationship – again.

She pushed me onto a kitchen chair and made the tea for me, wrinkling her nose at the strong smell. 'Are you ill?'

'Yes. My stomach.'

'You should go to bed,' she told me sternly.

'I can't.' I scalded my tongue on the hot tea. 'I have too much to do.'

She tutted. '*Emie.*'

I smiled weakly. 'You know how many people we have coming today, Madame Dupont. I'll be okay, I promise.' Whether that promise was one I could keep, I had no idea.

'Then at least let me do the kitchen today. You go sit for half an hour. You need to.'

Doing as I was told, I went to my room and lay on the chaise longue, but my room felt stuffy so I went and lay outside. The soft grass and orchard shade soothed my body, but nothing could soothe my mind.

I just couldn't understand it. Alain had made it clear to me, ever since we'd met, exactly what he thought of Gloria. How could he have slept with her? I wouldn't have believed it – heaven knew Gloria was a piece of work and might say anything to get a reaction – but she knew about the birthmark. And the look on his face had told me all I needed to know. Horror, panic, guilt. It was enough.

I hadn't had much peace before the sound of wheels on gravel forced me around the front of the house to see the arrival of the larger caravan, bearing Sylvia's niece, her husband and their student daughter, a quiet young woman who looked like she'd rather not be sharing a caravan with her parents for a week. And two labradoodles. At least they'd managed to get around the roadworks.

Next came the tent. It was larger than anticipated, so it took some doing to find a spot in the orchard that wasn't obstructed by trees. They looked like a quiet bunch – Frank's nephew, his wife and two older children, one maybe late teens and the other early twenties – and they had all the kit and appeared self-sufficient. Thank heavens, since I knew nothing about the outdoor life whatsoever.

La Cour des Roses was beginning to look like a holiday camp.

Two more airbeds went into one of the guesthouse rooms to accommodate Julia's son, Todd, his wife, Stacey, and their twin three-year-olds, who arrived just after lunch. The rooms were spacious – if you were a couple. It would be a crush with two kids in there, but needs must.

When Rupert still hadn't reappeared by early afternoon, and with the arrival of Julia Cooper and her parents imminent, I began to panic – about him, and about the fact that I was apparently running this place alone today. What if the generator failed? I didn't know the first thing about it. I tried his mobile, but it was switched off.

There were, however, several missed calls and two texts from Alain.

Emmy. We need to talk. Please.

Then: *It's not what you think. I need to explain.*

I ignored them. I couldn't cope with any more shit right now. I was exhausted, miserable and still felt ill, to the point where I was beginning to wonder what the point of all this was. I'd moved here to start a new life, but at this stage, it was in the balance whether the sunshine and surroundings could make up for the crap I seemed to be taking. As for Alain . . . I hadn't moved to France just to be with him, but I would be lying to myself if I didn't admit he was an important factor. If he and I were over, then there would have to be an awful lot of improvements in the other areas of my life to make all this worthwhile.

Besides, my primary concern right now was Rupert. Where the hell had he got to? I realised that I was as angry with him as I was worried. If he'd gone off somewhere to lick his wounds, then he was being downright selfish. We all had our wounds to lick.

But then I only had to think about what Gloria had told him this morning, and I could hardly be surprised. Not only was his marriage finished, he'd found out his wife had been sleeping with everyone from the guests to the accountant. Poor bugger. In theory, that should make my problems fade into insignificance. In practice . . . Well.

When the guests of honour finally arrived, every family was lined up in the courtyard to greet them. Julia must have texted, to warn them they were imminent.

It was a sight to behold, and unbelievably touching, as the car drove into the courtyard and we saw Frank and Sylvia's faces initially startled, then wreathed in smiles as they were helped out of the car. The reunion with Chris and family from Australia was particularly emotional, and soon everyone was laughing and crying and chattering at once.

I swallowed hard. My personal problems, Rupert's . . . they couldn't be allowed to impinge on this.

I went across to introduce myself. Frank and Sylvia were lovely, if a little frail, Frank's hair white and wispy and his shoulders stooped, and Sylvia tiny as a bird, her head bobbing as she spoke. They couldn't stop smiling, and they held hands as they spoke to me – a comfortable gesture that I found so lovely after fifty years of marriage. Frank's speech was slightly slow, and I noticed that Sylvia was finishing some of his sentences for him.

Julia, her hair peppered with grey and in a neat, short style, her frame small and delicate like her mother's, looked tired and fraught . . . Brittle. Her husband, Robert, just looked tired. Smiling, we greeted each other like old acquaintances.

The introductions over, I offered to make a tray of tea for the arriving party and scuttled into the kitchen.

I heard the words *power cut* and *gîtes* and *no showers* being bandied about outside, so when Julia came in a few moments later and said, 'I gather you've had a few problems today, Emmy,' I steeled myself for the complaints.

'Yes. I'm so sorry. It's completely out of our control, but all your *gîte* guests are welcome to come over to the house for whatever they need at any time. I know the bathrooms will be a problem if it's not fixed soon, now the guesthouse is full, but if necessary, I'll open up my own bathroom and Rupert's to you. Whatever it takes . . .' My voice was shaking a little, and I fought hard to control it.

Julia laid a hand on my arm. 'Please don't worry. These things happen, and you've done your best. We're lucky the house has a generator, I suppose.'

Alarmed, I saw a tear in her eye. 'Oh, Julia, I'm so sorry . . .'

She scrubbed crossly at it. 'It's not you, Emmy. It's everything. I'm so tired. When I embarked on this I had no idea how big it would grow or how much it would take out of me. I've driven poor Robert mad with it.'

'I can imagine.' I grinned. 'Not about how you've driven your husband mad! I mean about how hard it must have been. I'm sorry things haven't always been smooth sailing at our end.'

'It doesn't matter now. All that matters is that my parents have a memorable anniversary.' She hesitated. 'My dad had a mild stroke recently. Nothing major, but . . .'

'You need this to be special for them.'

'Yes.'

'Then it will be. I promise.'

If I can stay sane and find Rupert and . . .

'Where's Mr Hunter?' Julia asked.

Ah. 'He had a few errands to run,' I told her. 'I'm sure he won't be long.'

Satisfied, she took the tray of tea from me and went to revive her fellow travellers while I tried Rupert's phone once more. With no joy again. I was sure he'd simply gone walkabout and would come back in his own sweet time – but that didn't stop me worrying sick about him.

Half an hour later, Julia popped her head around the door. 'Any news on the power, Emmy?'

I kept my features composed. Did she expect me to be on to the power board every two minutes? I wouldn't know where to start.

'A workman came in person this morning to say it would be back on as soon as possible.'

She nodded, seemingly satisfied. 'And what time did you envisage starting the barbeque?'

The barbeque? Crap!

CHAPTER NINETEEN

'Er. Would seven-ish suit?' I suggested to Julia.

'Sounds great. Thank you.'

When she'd gone, I stared around the kitchen in panic. What if Rupert didn't come back in time?

At five o'clock, Chris from the Australian group came over to tell me the power was back on – and that was the final straw. I had no idea whether the house would blow up if I left the generator on now the mains power was back. I couldn't run a barbeque for thirty-plus people on my own.

I stared at my phone. I couldn't call Alain. And I didn't want to call Ryan again, not so soon after he'd come to my rescue at Jonathan's. I scanned my limited list of contacts, trying to work out who might be barbeque-minded. Sophie? Hardly, living in a flat. Ellie? She'd already done me favours, and besides, I didn't have her down as a catering type of gal. More a wine-and-takeaway-pizza woman.

'Er. Bob? This is Emmy.'

'Hi, Emmy. Everything all right?'

'Not really.' My voice wobbled. 'Are you free? For a favour?'

'When? This evening?'

'Now. And this evening. I mean, this evening from now?'

'I can be if I need to be. What's up?'

I gave him a limited version – that Rupert was 'missing', Alain was 'unavailable' and I was clueless. The generator. The barbeque.

'Rupert's *missing?*'

Since I couldn't tell him what Gloria had said, I simply said there had been quite a scene, and Rupert had taken it hard.

'I'll be there as soon as I can.'

I got drinks organised and salad stuff out of the fridge, and when Bob roared up on his motorbike, I babbled apologies. 'You are *such* a star, and I'm *so* sorry. I know you must think I'm hopeless, but . . .'

'Don't worry about it. I'll sort out the generator, then I'll take a look at the barbeques while you carry on in here.' He studied me for a moment. 'You don't look too good, Emmy.'

'It's been a mad day. I'm just tired.'

He smiled sympathetically. 'I'm not stupid. Something's going on here – more than you can tell me, and that's fine. But I'm here now and we can do this. Okay?'

'Okay. Thanks.'

And off he went around the back of the house. Ten minutes later, he was rattling around on the patio. Thank goodness Rupert and Alain had sorted out the barbeques the night before.

By seven, Rupert had a phone filled with approximately twenty missed calls from me, if he bothered to look, while I had a kitchen table groaning with drinks, salad and bread, and Bob and I, though an unlikely looking pair, were stationed side by side at the barbeques. I didn't have a clue what I was doing, but he was patient and kind, for which I was grateful, and we kept up a continuous run of marinated pork steaks and chicken breasts and plain sausages and spicy merguez sausages and sardines and kebabs and veggie stuff.

Julia was somewhat confused when I introduced Bob to her. 'Oh. Is Mr Hunter not back yet?'

'No. He . . . One of our friends isn't well, so he called in there on the way back and got held up.' I crossed my fingers over the pair of tongs I was holding.

'Oh. I'm so sorry. Well, thank you, Bob. Appreciated.' And off she went to circulate.

'Have we got a sick friend that I don't know about?' Bob asked, his lips twitching.

'Ha. Well. Jonathan has a cough, doesn't he? And asthma. Which clearly requires round-the-clock care.'

As we could only cook so much at a time, naturally we had a constant stream of customers, so it was a good hour before there was any kind of lull.

Bob turned to me. 'Okay?'

'No. I'm hot and tired and I stink of charcoal. And I may never eat meat again.'

'Is . . . Is Rupert okay?'

'I don't know, Bob. I can't get hold of him. And I don't know at what point he counts as a missing person.'

'He probably just needs time to himself, Emmy. It's been pretty crap for him lately.'

'I know. And I'm so grateful to you for stepping in at the last minute like this.'

'No problem. You're lucky it wasn't tomorrow night, or I'd have been away at a mate's for the night.'

I smiled. 'Lucky, indeed.'

We were beginning to dismantle the grills when Rupert appeared on the patio.

I swallowed back tears of relief, conscious that the party was still going strong around us.

'Emmy. I'm sorry. And Bob. I wouldn't know how to begin to thank you.'

'No need, Rupert.' They shook hands.

Rupert went through the patio doors into the kitchen.

'Go after him,' Bob instructed me. 'I'll do this.'

In the kitchen, Rupert and I stared at each other for a long moment and then he came over to wrap his arms around me in a tight bear hug. We both cried a little. Thank goodness no guests made an appearance.

He pulled away, gave me an embarrassed nod and turned back to the patio doors. And like the consummate professional he was, he squared his shoulders, took a deep breath and strode out to introduce himself to his new arrivals and charm Julia and her parents, while I wished I had half his backbone.

Later, as I got ready for bed, exhausted and *still* stinking of charcoal despite a long shower, I found another text from Alain: *Emmy, for God's sake. Ring me. Please.*

And a voicemail. 'Emmy, I appreciate that you're angry and confused, but I need to talk to you. I know you were due to be really busy today, and I'm hoping that's why you haven't called me back. Please call me tomorrow, as soon as you can.'

I collapsed in bed, exhausted and miserable. If I could just get a good night's sleep . . .

But it was not to be. It turned out that the group in the tent, rather than being jazz fans, loved folk music . . . and played it, too. Guitars – with a tambourine for good measure. And they sang along. Enthusiastically. Until midnight. And their tent was situated not too far – certainly not far enough – from my room at the back of the house. I hated folk music.

Gloria also hated folk music. I could hear her whining in Rupert's bedroom. When the music stopped, she stopped. It would have been comical if I hadn't had to sleep with my pillow jammed over my head.

Breakfast for thirty-four people. For the next five days. What on earth had possessed me to make an offer like that? At least we were lucky with the weather, as the only way to cater for every- one was to pile the kitchen table high with food, and those who couldn't grab a chair in the kitchen had to go out to the patio, which, with the sun pleasantly warm and the garden so beautiful, nobody objected to.

'I have never chopped so much fruit in my life,' Rupert grumbled. 'My fingers will be down to stubs.'

'And I'd rather not be serenaded under my window by an amateur folk group half the night, but that's life.'

Bathroom confusion still reigned – at least in Donald's mind. He wandered down in his robe, thinking it was his bathroom that was out of order and asking to use mine.

'So sorry, Emmy,' Patricia muttered stoically as she caught up with him and pushed him back out into the hall. 'He's worse when he's not in his own environment, I'm afraid.'

When breakfast was out of the way, we breathed a sigh of relief . . . but not for long. Today was also the first day of our three promised buffet lunches.

'Let's at least have coffee in the garden,' Rupert said wearily.

He made stiff espressos, and we sat with the dog splayed out at our feet. 'Emmy, I'm sorry I let you down yesterday. It was unforgivable.'

'Rupert . . .'

But he held up a hand to stop me. 'It was, and that's that. You must have had a crap day. And yet, I have a favour to ask you. I'd like to request that you not tell anyone about yesterday's revelation, for my sake. It's hard enough coming to terms with Gloria's pronouncements, but I don't want people knowing she slept with every man who crossed my doorstep ever since we bloody well got here. I'm sure people had their suspicions anyway, but I don't want their pity, and I don't want to be made to look more of a fool than I am already.'

'I won't tell anyone here, I promise. That suits me, too.'

He grunted. 'I'm sure. As far as I'm concerned, all anyone needs to know is that Gloria's gone and we will be getting a divorce. And if I come across as pissed off and grumpy for a while, everyone will understand.' He jabbed a finger at me. 'You, on the other hand, might need to up the ante with regard to those woeful acting abilities of yours.'

'What do you mean?'

'Think about it. People will expect you to be over the moon that Gloria's left and your job is secure. If you walk around with a face like a long weekend, they'll want to know why. This is a small community, you know it is. It won't take much to set tongues wagging.' His tone softened. 'I know it was as much of a shock to you as to me, Emmy. In some ways, I think it's harder on you.'

'I doubt it. Alain and I had only been seeing each other for a short while, Rupert. And this was something that happened before I knew him. It's not the same at all.'

'Well, I'm not trying to make it a competition about who's the most hard done by, but after Nathan . . .' He stopped, looking long and hard at me. 'You said "had".'

'What?'

'You said "had". That you and Alain *had* been seeing each other. Does that mean you . . . You won't be, now?'

My lip quivered. 'I don't know.'

He looked at his feet. 'How serious were you getting with him?'

My throat clogged with tears. 'Pretty serious.'

He scrubbed a hand across his face. 'Then I'm sorry for what's happened and for what you must be going through. Are you . . . ?' He looked at me in a panic. 'You will stay, won't you? Here at the guesthouse?'

I tried hard to swallow, staring down the garden at the willows swaying in the light breeze. 'I hadn't thought about it yet. I imagine I will.'

Draining my coffee, I went back to my room to check my phone again. Another voicemail from Alain.

'Okay, Emmy, you're obviously not going to phone me any time soon, but I need you to know that Gloria twisted everything yesterday. The time she was referring to . . . I was drunk, and I honestly don't know if I slept with her or not. I really need to speak to you. I thought what we had was special. That you thought the same. If you do, then surely you could give me a chance to explain?'

I played it again. He didn't even know if he'd slept with her? How drunk *was* he?

And how the hell was I supposed to respond to a message like that?

I had to speak to someone. I texted Kate to ask when she could be free.

She phoned me straight back. 'I took a coffee break. I have twenty minutes. What's up?'

I poured out my tale of woe in as concise a manner as I could.

'Oh, Emmy, that's awful. I don't know what to say. Will you sort things out with Alain?'

'Dunno.'

'He has tried to reach out to you. All those messages. He says he might not have even slept with her?'

I grunted. 'He looked pretty guilty when she announced it.'

'Are you sure you're not mixing guilt with discomfort? Besides, if he doesn't know what really happened, he would look guilty, wouldn't he?'

'Why are you trying to defend him?'

'Because my gut instinct tells me he's the right one for you.'

'You haven't even met him!'

'No. But I've heard the way you speak about him. I've seen the way you look when you speak about him. I don't want this to come between you if it doesn't have to. I think you should at least listen to what he has to say.'

'Do I *have* to?'

'No, you don't. Not if you're happy to walk away from him. Are you really willing to call it a day so soon, Emmy? Without even listening to his side of the story?' When I didn't say anything, she simply said, 'I'm sorry. I have to get back to work. Let me know what happens, will you?'

'Wait – what about you and Jamie?'

She just sighed.

'Oh, Kate. I miss you.'

'Miss you, too.'

I sat for a long moment. Should I trust my gut instinct, which had been kicked around from here till Sunday? Or should I trust my oldest and best friend, all those miles away?

Before I could stop myself, I'd sent Alain a text: *I'll be at your office at eleven thirty.*

Kate was right. We needed to talk. If nothing else, I couldn't go on seething and wondering like this. It was making me ill.

I went to tell Rupert that I needed a little time out. I figured he could hardly refuse after his period of time out the day before, and I was right. He assured me that he could cope with lunch for the masses, and I took him at his word.

As I drove into town, I remembered with a jolt that I was supposed to be meeting Sophie and Ellie for drinks after they finished work that evening. Unable to face the thought, I pulled over and texted that we were far too busy at *La Cour des Roses*, and apologies, but I would have to cancel.

Parking at the top end of town so there was no chance of Sophie or Ellie seeing me from their places of business, I made my way to Alain's office, sick with nerves. I had no idea what we were going to say to each other, but we'd shared enough together that I owed him the opportunity.

I climbed the steps, knocked and peered around the door. He was just finishing a phone call. He gestured for me to enter, and I paced until he finished. He switched on the answer phone, looked up at me, then came around the desk to take me into his arms – but I put my hands up in front of me, and he had to back off.

His expression was one of misery and disappointment, but his hands fell to his sides in acceptance. 'Emmy. Thank you for coming. Can I get you anything?'

I looked around his office at the neat desk, the filing cabinets, the shelves. The window with its view over the top end of town.

You could turn back the clock and get me a rerun of the past week, if you like. Maybe strike Gloria dumb while you're at it.

'Water would be good.' My mouth was dry.

He passed me a bottle from the mini fridge, then caught my gaze before I could transfer it to my feet, and held it.

'Emmy, I know what Gloria said yesterday was horrible for you. But I believe that if you knew what *did* happen, it would make a difference. Could you . . . Will you let me explain?'

Trepidation twisted in my stomach, but Kate was adamant that I owed him this – and it was why I came, after all. I gave him an almost imperceptible nod.

He brought his chair round the desk to face the visitor chair and indicated that I should sit, then he sat too, leaning forwards, his hands clenched between his knees. I could see the strain in every muscle of his face. A pulse beat at his temple.

'When Sabine left, I'd been here a year. Rupert had arrived around the same time as me, and he was my first-ever client. He was also my first friend here. Gloria was flirty, but I got the impression she behaved that way with any half-acceptable bloke she came across.'

That I didn't doubt.

'I didn't attach much importance to it, and it didn't matter because I rarely saw her on her own. When Sabine and I were invited round for drinks, dinner – whatever – it was a couples thing. I saw Rupert more. There was a lot to discuss and deal with as he renovated the house and set up the business. And then Sabine left me.' He gave me a direct look. 'I'm sure I don't need to tell you how traumatic it is for your other half to run off with someone. But you can imagine, with it being my brother . . .'

'Yes. I can imagine.' Alain had always given the impression it was something he'd put behind him, but as he sat across from me now, a slight tremor in his hand, I began to understand the depth of feeling he kept hidden. His wife hadn't left him for just anyone – she'd run off to England with his sibling and had children with him, and for the sake of his parents, Alain still had to be civil with them. He would never quite be free of his broken marriage.

'Rupert was the first person I thought to ring,' he went on. 'I was distraught – and I could hardly phone my parents! He dropped everything and came over. I'd had a couple of stiff drinks and he was worried about my mental state, so he drove me back to *La Cour des Roses* where he could keep an eye on me, and he and Gloria could do their best to cheer me up. That involved more drinks, and I was happy to imbibe. I was past caring, and I was only grateful that I hadn't been left alone to wallow. Unfortunately, I got far drunker than I had been in a long while, and I pretty much passed out on the sofa in the guest lounge.'

I almost smiled. 'You must have been drunk. That thing's seriously uncomfortable.'

'Yes, it is. I remember Rupert covering with me a blanket and telling me to get some sleep. That he'd drive me home in the morning. Later – I don't know what time it was, but I do know I was still drunk – I woke to find Gloria hovering over me. In my haze, I assumed she'd come to check that I was all right.'

'But that wasn't what she had in mind?' I asked him, tight-lipped, forcing the words through.

'No.'

'It . . . It didn't occur to you to try to stop her?'

'Yes. No. For God's sake, Emmy, I was blind drunk and half asleep!' He sighed. 'And that's where the problem lies. I don't *know* what happened. I don't *know* if I had sex with the wretched woman or not. I remember her being there. I remember her unbuttoning my shirt.'

'That would explain how she knew about the birthmark,' I murmured, almost to myself.

'I remember thinking it wasn't a good idea. I remember thinking I didn't even like the woman. I remember her perfume – it was overpowering. I . . . I think I might have passed out again.' He let out a long breath. 'And that's it.'

'That's all you remember?'

'Yes.' His voice toughened up. 'The next day, I tried to work it out, but it was – and still is – a blur.'

'Did you talk to Gloria about it? The day after?'

'I didn't have to. While Rupert was busy with breakfast and I was still coming round, disgustingly hungover, she came in to see me. She certainly gave the impression it *had* happened. She also made it clear that she expected a repeat performance. *Ongoing* repeat performances. I made it more than clear that that was never going to happen.'

'I bet that didn't please her.'

'No. She tried blackmail. Threatened to tell Rupert that I'd seduced her.'

I hadn't thought my opinion of Gloria could get any lower, but it just had. 'You weren't scared of that?'

He barked out a strangled laugh. 'I was more scared of the idea of a full-blown affair with Gloria.'

'Rupert showed me a photo of her at their wedding,' I blurted. 'She was stunning ten years ago. She must have still been attractive five years ago.'

Alain lifted a shoulder. 'Depends on what you mean by attractive. Physically, yes. Personality-wise, we both know the answer to that. I had no intention of sleeping with the woman again – if I even had.'

If I even had. I let that sink in. 'So you called her bluff?'

'Yes. I didn't want to lose Rupert's friendship and business, but I sure as hell wasn't going to be dragged into an affair. And I made the right call. Their marriage was okay back then, I think – as long as she got a little something on the side, it seems – and they'd only just got *La Cour des Roses* up and running. They had other properties, other investments. She wouldn't have wanted to rock the boat and risk losing it all.'

His elbows on his knees, he dropped his head onto his hands, his fingers jammed in his hair. 'Everybody makes mistakes, Emmy. God knows, I've made my share. But this . . . I don't even know if it was a mistake I *did* make. It's been hovering over my shoulder like a curse ever since.'

I nodded. 'I didn't want to hear it, but I understand now why you wanted me to.'

'Thank you for listening.'

I looked through the window at the people passing by on the street below, having a normal day. 'What about Rupert?'

He sighed. 'I don't know, Emmy. If I thought he would listen . . . But you saw the way he was when Gloria left. I've left messages on his mobile, like I did with yours. He won't respond. Maybe eventually . . .' He ran out of steam. 'So where does this leave *us*?' When I didn't answer, he added, 'Nothing has changed for me. How I feel about you.'

His forehead was etched with lines of stress, his mouth strained. I wanted to ease away the worries, to reach out and trace the laugh lines at the corners of his eyes. To smooth out the frown lines at his mouth. But I couldn't. It wouldn't be fair to give him false hope, without being certain that I could get past this.

'Then I hope you'll understand that I need time to adjust. To gauge Rupert. To gauge us. To process the fact that my friend and employer has banished my boyfriend from his house, and I'm not sure I want to play piggy-in-the-middle.'

He looked disappointed, but as I stood and walked to the door, he merely smiled sadly and let me go. As I drove home, I couldn't work out whether we'd moved forwards or backwards.

When I got back, I saw a text from Sophie: *Sorry you had to cancel. Everything okay?*

I lied through my teeth as I texted back: *Fine, thank you. Just too busy here.*

Rupert was in the kitchen surrounded by food, so I mucked in to help him. Maybe I should bide my time until after the jazz-goers were fed, but we had half an hour yet, and I couldn't hold on that long. Alain's explanation, though not entirely palatable, had given me a perspective I hadn't allowed myself before, and I wanted to see if I could do the same for Rupert. A tricky task, I knew.

'Rupert, I need to speak to you about Alain.'

He barked out a cynical laugh. 'I don't think so.'

'Why won't you let me be the judge of that? I finally spoke to him this morning, and if you knew more about what really happened . . .'

'For crying out loud, Emmy!' He stopped what he was doing. 'You think I want to know any more than I do already?'

'But you don't know anything! Not really. And it's not whether you *want* to know, it's whether you *should* know . . .'

'Don't you dare tell me what I should and shouldn't know.' His voice was low and uncompromising.

'You think *I* wanted to? I didn't! I felt just like you! But once I did, it was a whole different ball game.'

'Oh, so now your boyfriend is using you to—'

'He doesn't even *know* if he slept with her! He was blind drunk! It wasn't some torrid affair, it was one occasion that might or might not have happened. Please. You have to listen to me!'

He looked at me a long moment. 'No. I really don't, Emmy.'

I placed my knife back on my chopping board and wiped my hands on my apron. 'Then you can do this on your own, and

I'll go and make myself useful elsewhere. I'm going to check on Jonathan. As far as I know, nobody went to see him yesterday.' I walked away without a backward glance.

Luckily, I'd been parking out on the lane so I could get in and out without being blocked in by Thomsons. As I drove towards town, my hands were shaking on the wheel. I knew it had been a long shot, getting Rupert to listen to Alain's side of the story, but I hadn't considered that he might outright refuse. Maybe in time . . . I heaved a huge sigh. How much time? If ever? Even if Alain and I got through this, where would that leave me, trying to mediate between two friends who couldn't or wouldn't reconcile?

CHAPTER TWENTY

When I pulled up outside Jonathan's, the curtains were still drawn and there was no answer when I knocked. Worried, I scrabbled in my bag for Rupert's spare key and let myself in. There was no sign of him in the lounge or kitchen, so I went up to his bedroom. Tapping lightly, I poked my head around the door.

Jonathan was in bed. He turned to face me, but it set off a paroxysm of coughing. When it stopped, his breathing was laboured.

Hiding my alarm, I crouched down so that I was at eye level with him. 'Jonathan. Are you all right?'

'I'll be okay, Edith. I just need to rest.'

Edith?

'How long have you been in bed?'

'Oh, I don't know.'

'When did you last eat?'

No reply.

'What day do you think it is?'

He seemed to drift off, then said, 'Tell that ruddy dog to shut up, will you?'

I couldn't hear anything. I glanced at the empty water glass by his bed and remembered that old people could get confused when they were dehydrated. It had happened to my gran a few times, especially in the evenings.

'I'm going to make us a cup of tea, okay?'

'I don't like Bakewell tart. Never have.'

'Er – right. I'll remember that.'

Down in the kitchen, there were no used mugs or plates by the sink, suggesting he might not have eaten or drunk anything in a while. I made two mugs of tea, adding a little cold water to Jonathan's, and took them upstairs.

'Jonathan, you need to sit up. I want you to drink this.'

'That woman always made Bakewell tart. Never could stand the stuff.'

'Who always made Bakewell tart?' I tried to lift him into a sitting position, but he was a tall bloke and it wasn't easy, especially without his full cooperation.

He seemed to have forgotten what we were talking about. 'Stop *fussing*, Edith!'

When I'd got him as upright as I could, I placed the tea in his hands. His breathing was loud in the small room, and it felt stuffy.

I went across to pull back the curtains and open the window, then sat back down beside him. Now the room was lighter, I didn't like what I saw. Jonathan's skin was white, but he had a flush across his cheekbones. I felt his forehead with the back of my hand. It was burning hot.

'Have you got a thermometer?'

'Nope.'

I went to dampen a flannel with cold water, placed it on his forehead, then nudged the tea to his lips. Maybe I shouldn't be giving him a warm drink, but he needed *something*. He seemed uncoordinated, and I had to help him aim for his mouth.

'Does your chest hurt?'

'When I cough. Tight when I breathe too deep.'

'Okay. I'll be back in a minute.'

Downstairs, out of earshot, I phoned Rupert. I could hear a racket in the background. The lunch crowd must have descended.

'Emmy, I don't—'

'Jonathan's really ill, but I don't know what to do.' I tried to keep my voice steady. 'Should I get hold of a doctor, or should I take him to the hospital?'

'Tell me his symptoms.'

I did.

'Don't like the sound of that at all.' He hesitated. 'A&E, Emmy.'

I swallowed down panic. 'Do we call an ambulance, or do I take him myself? I . . . I'm not sure I could manage to get him downstairs and into the car.' My voice wobbled.

Rupert cursed. 'I'll come over. Give me half an hour.'

'Don't be ridiculous! You can't leave all your guests to fend for themselves in the middle of lunch.'

'I can in an emergency.'

'We don't know how much of an emergency it is yet, and too much has gone wrong already with that lot. Julia clearly wasn't happy that you weren't there to greet them when they arrived yesterday, or for the barbeque. You really should stay there, Rupert.'

'Okay. I'll call an ambulance for you. Keep me informed, and I'll join you as soon as I can.'

'There's no need. You've got your hands full there. I'll be fine,' I lied.

'How are you going to cope with the French? With the paramedics? With the paperwork if they want to admit him?'

'I – er.'

'Call Bob.'

'Bob's away tonight. He told me yesterday. He won't be back till tomorrow, I don't think.'

'Phone Ryan, then. That way, you get a French speaker, and I get to stay here for a while longer, okay?'

'Okay.' My throat was tight with panic.

'And Emmy? I want you to phone me if Jonathan takes a real turn for the worse. I mean it.'

'I will. Bye.' I clicked off the call, and with shaking fingers, I phoned Ryan, thinking that this was the second time in a week I'd needed his help and feeling ridiculous about it.

He answered almost immediately, sounding puzzled. 'Emmy?'

I explained.

'I'm so sorry, but I'm fifty miles away, at lunch with some friends of my parents. We only brought one car. I presume you've already tried Alain?'

'I . . . Don't worry, Ryan. I'll find someone. Thank you.'

'I'm sorry I can't help. Good luck.'

I scrolled down my phone in a panic. Sophie would probably be in the middle of tinting someone's hair. Ellie would be at work.

Before I could think twice, I dialled Alain. He, too, would be at work – but maybe, just maybe, he wouldn't have any appointments this afternoon.

He answered almost immediately. 'Emmy?'

'Alain, I . . .' *No tears, or he'll think you're crying about your crap relationship.* 'I need your help. Jonathan's really ill.' I explained as calmly as I could.

'I'll be there in ten minutes.'

I allowed myself a couple of minutes' misery, then splashed cold water on my face and went back upstairs.

'Rupert's called for an ambulance.'

'What the hell for?'

'Just do what you're told, Jonathan. *Please.*'

Sensing the desperation in my voice, he reached out and patted my hand. 'Don't worry, Edith.'

I'd love to know who this Edith was.

Pulling myself together, I thought about what he'd need if they took him to hospital – and I was in little doubt that they would. Clean pyjamas. Toiletries. I rummaged in the bedroom and bathroom while Jonathan lay placidly in the bed, occasionally directing me with an 'In that drawer over there, Edith.'

Alain arrived five minutes later. 'How is he?'

'Not good.' My lip quivered. 'Thank you for coming.'

He rested a reassuring hand on my cheek. 'You're welcome.'

We stood for a long moment as mutual understanding passed between us. This wasn't about us. It was about Jonathan.

'Emmy!' A shout from upstairs.

It was an improvement on Edith, anyway. I rushed back up, Alain hot on my heels. 'Yes?'

'There was a rat at the window.'

'*What?*' I went over, but I couldn't see anything. 'You mean on the sill?'

'On the glass. Climbing up. Can you shut the window?'

'Jonathan, surely rats can't climb on sheer glass? Or up a whole storey?' I assumed he must be hallucinating, but my knowledge of rodents' gymnastic abilities was on the inadequate side. I looked to Alain for help.

'We don't want to close the window, Jonathan,' he said calmly. 'You're too hot. We'll stay in here with you and keep an eye out.'

'Is that Alain?'

'Yes.'

Jonathan nodded, exhausted from the exchange.

We sat in silence, Jonathan breathing heavily and staring into space, Alain pale and shocked by his condition. I glanced at the window every now and again to check for glass-scaling vermin.

The paramedics, when they arrived, were young and kindly. Allowing Alain to translate, I explained about the chest infection, his fever, his confusion. I stepped out of the room while they examined him, pacing the landing until I was called back in.

'The chest infection getting worse is what's led to the fever,' Alain told me. 'And the fever's probably causing the confusion. They're worried about pneumonia. They're taking him to hospital.'

I bit back panic as Alain closed the window (the paramedics disconcerted at Jonathan's mention of rats), and we waited downstairs while they got Jonathan sorted and carried him out to the ambulance.

While Alain drove, I phoned Rupert to give him an update.

'I don't like the idea of pneumonia,' he said, shaken. 'I'll get down there as soon as I can.'

'There are two of us already.' I failed to tell him who the other party was. 'No need for you to drop everything. I'll keep you updated.' I clicked off.

'Is Rupert okay?' Alain asked awkwardly.

'He's worried. He wanted to drop everything and come, but we're doing lunches every day of the jazz festival for all the guests. Jonathan doesn't half know how to time his crises.'

'I'm glad you phoned me,' Alain said, his eyes fixed on the ambulance ahead.

By the time a muddled Jonathan had been checked in and they were running tests, the adrenalin was fading and I felt like crap.

Alain fetched plastic cups of black tea from somewhere and we sat, waiting and sipping.

'You look shattered, Emmy.'

'It's been a long week, and now this . . . I'm so worried about Jonathan.'

Alain reached out to take my hand, but stopped himself. 'He's in good hands now.'

'Do you know what they're doing to him?'

'They said something about blood tests and an X-ray.'

I couldn't deny that I was grateful for Alain's company. Solid, reassuring and French-speaking. All great qualities right now.

I thought about the admissions forms. 'I had no idea that Jonathan's nearly eighty. I know he has his health struggles, but with all that hair and his full set of marbles, it's easy to forget his age when you're with him, isn't it?'

'If you ask me, there's plenty of life in the old dog yet.'

Eventually, the doctor came out to speak to us. Well, to Alain. As I got more and more frustrated that I couldn't understand better, I heard rapid footsteps and turned.

Rupert, ignoring my advice as usual, was storming towards us. Great.

Alain turned too, and he and Rupert stared for a long moment at each other, their faces shuttered.

'Alain.'

'Rupert.'

A tense silence.

'I couldn't get anyone else,' I explained to Rupert, knowing but unable to help that Alain would be offended to find out he was the last person on the list.

'What did the doctor say?' Rupert asked him.

'Jonathan's got pneumonia,' Alain told us. 'They're worried it could lead to pleurisy.'

'Oh, God,' Rupert muttered, scrubbing his fingers through unkempt hair.

'How bad is it?' I asked.

'It's not good at his age. They're putting him on an antibiotic drip and he'll get fluids by drip, too. Oxygen as and when he needs it. They want to bring his fever down, make sure there aren't any complications. We can pop into his booth and see him for two minutes, but the doctor says there's no point in waiting after that. It will just be a question of transferring him to a room and starting treatment.'

My eyes filled, but Alain's voice was stern. 'You can't cry if you want to see him, okay?'

I took several deep breaths. We plastered smiles on our faces and shuffled into Jonathan's cubicle.

'Now then, old trouper, what are you up to, causing all this worry?' Alain said cheerily. 'I know we all want to see Emmy's French improve, but this is a drastic way to go about it. Good job I was on hand to save her.'

Jonathan smiled weakly. 'Thanks, you two.'

I popped a kiss on his cheek. 'You're welcome. Do what you're told while you're in here.' I reminded him that I'd brought him a bag and that his mobile was in it. 'Phone us if you need anything.'

He spotted Rupert hanging back, and lifted a hand weakly in greeting. 'I won't eat Bakewell tart. You'll tell them, won't you, Edith?'

'I will. Don't you worry.'

Alain and I left Rupert with Jonathan, and walked slowly along the corridor towards the exit. *Not yet, Emmy, not yet. Round the corner . . .* Safely out of earshot, I burst into tears.

Alain started to put his arms around me, then stopped. 'Yes? No?'

'Yes,' I mumbled, burying my head against his chest, feeling the comforting thud of his heart against my ear. A few minutes couldn't hurt, surely.

When I'd hiccupped away the tears, he pulled away – as soon as he could have decently done so. That only made me want to cry more.

I scrubbed my face as we continued to the exit. Rupert caught up with us in the car park, where I was in an awkward dilemma. Did I go back with Alain to fetch my car from Jonathan's, or Rupert?

Rupert came to my rescue. 'Come back in mine to the guesthouse, Emmy. We can drive back to fetch your car later. You're tired.'

I turned to Alain. 'Thank you,' I managed, my voice small.

'You're welcome.' And he was off, long strides across the car park, his tall frame slightly stooped.

I got into Rupert's car, allowing my head to fall back against the headrest. Feeling sick, I opened the window to let in some fresh air.

'Why did you call Alain?' Rupert asked.

'Because Ryan was fifty miles away,' I snapped.

'It's fine, Emmy. I'm glad you had help. And it was good of him to come.'

I closed my eyes. 'How did you get away from your guests?'

'It wasn't as hard as I thought. They're a nice bunch. Sylvia overheard me talking to you on the phone about ambulances and didn't like to interfere, but she could tell I was antsy, and after a while, she spoke to Julia and they all ganged up on me. They insisted they were perfectly capable of serving themselves dessert and hot beverages, and that I was to get off. It was good of them.'

'Did you eat anything?' I asked, concerned.

'A mouthful or two. Couldn't face much.'

'Try not to worry about Jonathan. They said he's stable.'

'They said he's stable, *considering*. He's an old man, and his health isn't fantastic in the first place. Pneumonia . . . There are no guarantees, love.'

'Stubborn old men who won't go to the doctor when they're told. It's enough to drive you mad!' I said angrily.

He grunted. 'I bet you haven't eaten anything either, have you?'

I thought about it. 'No.' That was probably why I felt so travel-sick.

'I want you to have something when we get back, Emmy. I don't need you keeling over on me.'

Back at *La Cour des Roses*, I followed him into the kitchen. He stopped dead in the middle of the room and looked around in astonishment. As did I.

The table had been cleared, the cloth neatly folded in one corner. Leftover food had been covered and put away in the fridge. And every single glass, plate, and dish had either been loaded into the dishwasher or washed, dried and neatly stacked at one end of the kitchen.

The innate kindness of strangers. That was when Rupert allowed a tear to fall.

* * *

I spent half the night worrying myself sick about Jonathan, and the other half about Rupert's distress. Finally, after opening the shutters so the morning sun could slant across the bed, I allowed myself to worry about me. Or more specifically, about me and Alain.

Our unexpected time together yesterday had been unsettling. When I thought about the gamut of emotions I'd gone through over the past few days – anger at Gloria's revelation, disappointment at Alain's presumed weakness, disdain at his betrayal of his friend, understanding and confusion over his explanation – I was surprised I hadn't had a complete nervous breakdown. But all along, I had ruthlessly pushed to the back of my mind – and my heart – how much I cared about Alain, and that you can't turn that kind of thing off like a tap.

Yesterday, he had responded to my phone call without question. He hadn't run when Rupert appeared. He hadn't comforted me without asking permission, and when given permission, he had given that comfort without expectation of more, then walked away.

And that last thing affected me more than I could say. Part of me had wanted to run after him and climb into his car and go home with him and make love with him and make the whole ugly rest of my world go away.

And the sensible part had told me that unless I could come to terms with the fact that he might have slept with Rupert's wife, and figure out my conflicting loyalties between him and Rupert, that could never happen.

'Who's Edith?' I asked Rupert over double-shot espressos on the patio. Heaven knew we needed them. The tent foursome had once more sung and strummed their guitars until nearly midnight, while Gloria whined her accompaniment. She was already banished from being in the orchard or garden unless she was properly chaperoned, partly because of the two labradoodles and partly because she couldn't be trusted not to explore the tent's interior and avail herself of any tasty morsels left lying around. The singing must be topping it off for the poor animal.

'Edith?' Rupert asked, puzzled.

'Jonathan kept calling me Edith yesterday.'

'Hmm. I'm not sure. It might be his sister.'

'Do you think we ought to try to contact his family back in England, with him being so ill?'

'I thought he told you about that? That he hasn't seen hide nor hair of them in twenty-five years?'

'He did. Are you saying that if I phone his sister or brother and tell them he's on death's door, they won't come?'

'I'm saying that his brother or sister may not even be alive. His sister was older than him by a few years, his brother by a couple of years.'

'But he has nieces and nephews.'

'Who will have been indoctrinated against him for the past quarter of a century. Besides, what are the chances that anyone lives at the same address or has the same phone number after all this time? More to the point, we would be going against Jonathan's wishes. He's had a hard life, Emmy. It's his choice how to live out what's left of it.'

Upset, I stared out across the garden. Down on the lawn, Sylvia's cousin Fred had a group of kids gathered around him, and he was trying to keep them entertained with badly performed magic tricks. In reality, he was keeping them entertained because they could see exactly how he did them, which delighted them. Both sides seemed happy with the arrangement, and his wife, Annie, looked on indulgently.

'Right then!' I said suddenly, making Rupert jump.

'Don't do that, Emmy. I'm not up to it.'

'Jonathan *does* have family. He has us and Bob and Alain.' I ignored his sour face at Alain's name. 'There are plenty of us for hospital visits, and when he's well enough to go home' – my voice quavered, since that was not necessarily a given – 'then we'll all have to chip in. What do you think?'

Rupert smiled warmly. 'I think, Emmy, as ever, that you are a very kind girl. And I'd like to apologise for that ridiculous show of emotion last night. It was pathetic. But it had been such a long day and I was worried about Jonathan . . .'

'Is this another of those stupid generational things, Rupert? Were you brought up to believe that men shouldn't cry?'

'Yes.'

'Well, it's bollocks. Everyone has feelings, and everyone's entitled to express them from time to time. I don't think anyone would have been surprised, least of all me, after what you've been through these past few weeks. You've had the worst time imagin-able. Heaven knows Gloria's delightful burst of sudden honesty would be enough to make anyone cry. But now your friend is in the hospital and you're worried he might . . . That he might not pull through. You're entitled, Rupert, and if you can't let go with me, then it's a poor do. Understand?'

Startled by my outburst, he smiled. 'Yes. Thank you. You're quite scary when you're cross, you know.'

'Hmmph. If there's one thing I've learned over the past few weeks, it's that if we didn't have an outlet for everything that's been going on around here, we'd all go stark-raving mad!'

We decided that Rupert would phone Bob to put him in the picture, I would visit Jonathan that afternoon and Rupert would visit in the evening if Bob wasn't back in time. He didn't mention Alain and I didn't dare bring it up. I'd been impressed by the way he'd put his animosity aside yesterday to put Jonathan's needs first, but I didn't want to push it.

No *gîte* changeover on a Saturday seemed like a luxury to me. And to Madame Dupont – she'd taken advantage of this unexpected treat to spend a long weekend with her sister. But Rupert and I had instead battled our way through breakfast for over thirty, and we couldn't yet contemplate lunch.

Ellie phoned just as I was thinking we should make a start on it. 'Emmy. So sorry you couldn't make it for drinks yesterday. Everything okay?'

Urgh. 'Oh. Not too bad, thanks. It's just been so busy . . .'

'It sounds like you're having quite a weekend of it. Sophie and I were wondering if you could get away for a while. Maybe have a drink tonight? It would do you good to relax a bit.'

'Ah. I . . . Er.' Oh God, this was awful. The last thing I could do was meet up with those two. The whole sorry saga would come pouring out, and I couldn't do that. For Alain's sake. For Rupert's sake. I needed to be more together before I risked it. My mind scrabbled and lit on a genuine excuse. 'I'm so sorry, Ellie, I'd love to, but you see . . .' I told her all about Jonathan and how busy I would be with hospital visits.

'Oh, Emmy, I'm so sorry to hear that,' Ellie said with genuine concern. 'If you need me to do anything, to fill in on a visit if you or Rupert can't manage it, please just let me know.'

'I will. Thank you.'

When I arrived at the hospital that afternoon, I was stopped short by the sight of Alain striding down the corridor towards me.

'Hi. I didn't know you were coming. Is Jonathan all right?' I asked him.

'I couldn't see him. They asked me to come back in a little while.'

Panic hit me. 'Why? Is everything okay?'

'They're doing some routine stuff with him and preferred privacy, that's all.'

I blew out a puff of relief. 'I'll wait, then.'

'I was going to take a walk outside. Do you want to come with me?'

I almost said no, that I would wait indoors, but that would be petty. And I disliked hospitals at the best of times. 'Okay.'

We negotiated the corridors in silence.

'Did the staff say how Jonathan is?' I asked as we began a circuit of the car park. I felt a pang that his hands were shoved in his pockets instead of holding mine.

'He's stable.'

That was good news compared with the terrible thoughts I'd had during the night.

'Was Rupert okay yesterday?' Alain asked.

'He was upset about Jonathan.'

'Understandable. It can't have helped, me being there.'

'He was grateful that you could help, Alain.'

Another silence, and then, so quiet that I could hardly hear him, 'I've lost one of my best friends. For good.'

I didn't answer. I had no answer.

'You know, when that awful night happened, I'd only known Rupert for a year. I didn't feel it was my place to jeopardise his marriage over something I wasn't even sure had happened. The irony is, the closer we became, the worse I felt about it, and the more I felt I couldn't say anything. But I think he knows what Gloria is now, and if he knew what really happened . . .'

'I tried to tell him what you told me. He didn't want to hear it.'

He nodded. 'I don't blame him. But thank you for trying.'

After a while, we turned back and made for Jonathan's room. There were two beds, but the other was empty. Jonathan lay with an oxygen mask at his side, attached to drips and looking as pale as the white pillowcase.

'Jonathan.' Hiding my upset, I went over and kissed his cheek.

Sweetly, Alain did the same, then brought two chairs over.

'How are you?' I asked.

Still wheezing, he announced, 'Feel awful.'

'I'm not surprised. You gave us quite a scare.'

'I'm sorry.'

'Don't be sorry. Just get better.'

He drifted off for a few minutes, and the next half hour was spent that way – a few words, and then Jonathan would doze. I glanced across at the empty bed and wondered if it would have been nice for him to have another patient for company, or just more distressing.

When we stood to leave, I took his hand. 'Jonathan. Is there anyone you want me to phone?'

'No!' Short and sharp.

'Okay. I . . . I needed to check.'

'Thanks, Emmy.' And his eyes were closed again.

'What was all that about?' Alain asked as we walked to the exit.

I filled him in about Jonathan's family.

Alain shook his head. 'Poor bastard. What a thing to go through.'

We reached our cars and stood for a long moment, saying nothing, until Alain dared a peck on the cheek. 'Bye, Emmy.'

When I got back, I told Rupert about Jonathan, then went to my room to update Kate, remembering to ask about Jamie first.

'I called it a day.'

'Oh, Kate. I'm so sorry.'

'I'm not. Neither of us is heartbroken. Unlike certain people I could mention.'

She fixed me with a glare and demanded to know what was happening with Alain, so I told her about his explanations and Rupert's refusal to listen.

She shook her head sadly. 'All this hurt that Rupert's carrying around, it should have been directed at Gloria, or at least shared out between all relevant parties, but it's being directed at the one person he thinks he *can* blame. I never met Gloria, but that sounds just like her, doesn't it? Alain was drunk and he was hurting.' She paused. 'Surely it must have changed the way you feel about this?'

'Yes, but . . .'

'But you're not going to forgive him?'

'I may not have anything to forgive him for, Kate. Besides, it's not really my place, is it? That's up to Rupert, and he's a stubborn bastard. He won't relent. Even if Alain and I made up, I'd be shuttling between two people who can never reconcile. I don't think I can handle that.'

'You're making yourself choose between Rupert and Alain.'

I sighed. 'I suppose so. And at the moment, as the innocent party, Rupert's ahead of the race.'

Kate considered for a long moment. 'Can I be blunt?'

I smiled. 'When were you anything but?'

'I think you're allowing Gloria to ruin your life.'

'*What?*'

'She wrecked your last relationship – not that that was a bad thing – but now you have a real chance of happiness, and you're allowing her to ruin that too, with something that may or may not have happened such a long time ago. Don't let her win, Emmy. She's not worth it.'

CHAPTER TWENTY-ONE

With Kate's words ringing in my ears, I went back through to Rupert. 'Are you still going to the hospital this evening?'

'Bob's back. He wants to go.'

'That's good. It'll give you a break. Are you going to eat?'

'Not hungry.'

'I really think you should . . .'

Ellie appeared at the patio doors, Sophie a step or two behind, making us both jump. 'Rupert. We're kidnapping Emmy for the evening. That okay with you?'

He stared at her. 'Er. Yes. Fine. No problem.'

'Oh, no, girls, thanks, but I can't . . .'

'Of course you can,' Rupert interrupted. 'God knows, I still owe you for the other day when I went AWOL. Go for it, Ellie.'

And so I was bundled into Ellie's car, with Sophie squished into the tiny backseat, as she was the most petite. 'We're going to my house. Supper and drinks,' Ellie declared.

'We are? But . . .'

'Yes, we are. No buts.'

When we got there, she led us inside and I gazed around the gorgeous interior – not at all farmhousy, as I'd expected from the exterior, but light and airy and open-plan. It reminded me a little of an artist's studio. We went through to the garden at the back, a small space with a view that seemed to stretch for miles, where I was shoved onto a chair and instructed to relax while

Ellie and Sophie fetched wine and supper on a tray. We sat and sipped and nibbled, enjoying the quiet and the view for a while.

'So, Emmy,' Sophie finally said, putting on a casual tone that was anything but, 'How's it going between you and Alain?'

'Oh. Er. Well, we've been busy with Jonathan, and I have this anniversary thing going on, and . . .'

'But you need to make time for each other. If you don't, things can go downhill so quickly . . .'

'Oh for heaven's sake, Sophie,' Ellie cut across me. 'Never mind all that softly-softly stuff. It won't work.' She gave me a direct look. 'What's going on between you and Alain? And don't say "nothing", because we know *something* is. I saw Alain in town yesterday, and he was positively suicidal. You've been avoiding us. And you look ill.'

'I'm just tired.'

'Emmy . . .' Ellie's tone was low and drawn out, a warning not to mess with her.

My hackles rose. 'I don't like this heavy mob technique, you two. *If* there was something wrong, don't you think that's my business?'

'No.' Sophie took hold of my hand and gripped it when I would have pulled away. 'It *is* our business. We are your friends and we want to help. Please let us.'

I jutted out my chin in defiance, but my lip wobbled. When Ellie, scary Ellie, took my other hand, well, that was me undone. A lone tear fell, followed by another. And another. And soon a tsunami of pent-up emotion and frustration and anger and secret-keeping poured from me, streaming down my face, making my shoulders shake and my head hurt.

I expected Ellie to tut and be uncomfortable. She didn't and she wasn't. She waited patiently, as did Sophie, until I was spent.

'Better out than in, as my mother used to say,' Ellie said matter-of-factly. 'I'll make us some tea.'

'I don't want any,' I whimpered. 'I feel sick.'

'I'm not surprised. You're a very silly woman, keeping all that inside. It's not good for you. I'll put sugar in yours.'

Sophie hugged me close, her head against mine, until Ellie came back with the tea.

I clutched my mug and took a sip. 'I'm sorry.'

'Don't be,' Sophie said. 'What do you think we brought you here for?'

'Not interested in apologies,' Ellie added. 'Explanations would be good, though.'

'I can't. It's awkward and confidential . . .'

'Don't be ridiculous,' Ellie said. 'Who would we tell? I limit my social circle to people I can stand – not very many – and Sophie here is too sweet to even dream of it.'

'Remember that day you came into my salon with your awful, overgrown hair?' Sophie asked me. 'You told me all sorts of things then. This can't be any worse.'

'But it is!' I whispered.

Even so, I told them. The part of me that said I was being disloyal – to Alain, to Rupert – was past caring and into survival mode. Ellie was right. Better out than in.

When I'd finished, Sophie said, 'You're right. It *is* worse.' She looked across at Ellie. 'Don't you think . . . Ellie? Are you all right?'

We both stared at her in concern. Always pale-complexioned, she looked ghostly white, her lips pinched.

'Crap.' She dropped her head in her hands.

'What?' Sophie asked her, alarmed.

Ellie slowly lifted her head, her hands still glued to her cheeks. 'Oh, Emmy. I wish you'd told me sooner.' She lowered her hands and puffed out a long breath. Took a gulp of tea.

'*Why* should I have told you sooner?' I demanded.

'Because I might have saved you some heartache, and I could have spared Alain a few *years'* worth. I had no idea he thought .

. . I can't *believe* Gloria! That she would say that! Emmy, Alain never slept with Gloria. It never happened.'

I stared at her. 'How do you know?'

'Because Gloria told me.'

A tidal wave of relief washed over me. 'She *told* you?'

'Remember she wanted to be friends with me when she first arrived? She wanted – needed – a close girlfriend, a confidante. She suggested she was dissatisfied with her marriage, with life at *La Cour des Roses* and . . .' Ellie shook her head. 'Perhaps she was looking for validation, I don't know, but it manifested itself in flirtation. Possibly seduction. She started to tell me who she'd flirted with. Who she planned on seducing. I didn't want to be on the receiving end of that kind of information, even though I didn't believe half of what she said. But she knew I was . . . *independent* with regard to relationships. Maybe she thought I would approve. Well, I may be independent, but I'm not free and easy. It all became so uncomfortable. I tried to steer her away from it, but she never took the hint. I hoped it was a phase, that she'd settle in. I liked and respected Rupert, and it didn't sit well with me. Though I assumed a lot of it was bluff – that she flirted a lot, but then embellished for effect. Anyway, the final straw was when she told me about Alain.'

'Tell me.'

'It was pretty much as you said. His wife left him, Rupert drove him to *La Cour des Roses*, he passed out drunk. She waited till Rupert was asleep, then went through to him. Woke him up. Tried to seduce him.'

'Tried?'

'Tried. Didn't succeed, Emmy. He turned her down flat. Wouldn't have anything to do with it. I remember her saying, "Honestly, Ellie. Men! They're offered it on a plate and they *still* don't want it! Still, he was so drunk, I doubt he'd have been *up* to it, if you know what I mean." She was so brazen about it! She didn't seem to see anything morally questionable in taking advantage of someone who was drunk and hurting. It made me sick to my stomach. I told her then and there that I didn't want to listen to her sordid stories any more. That we wouldn't be meeting for coffee or lunch. That I would be civil with her in company, but I no longer wanted *her* company.'

'That can't have been easy for you,' Sophie said softly.

Ellie curled a lip. 'She'd pushed me too far. I can't be doing with playing games. Better to do it quickly and get it over with.'

'You didn't think to tell anyone?' I asked her.

Ellie scraped bright pink fingernails through her short hair. 'I had no intention of telling Rupert what she'd told me. I didn't know him *that* well, in those days, and I didn't want to interfere in their marriage. Besides, I had no idea whether what she told me was true half the time – except for the thing with Alain. I doubted she'd make up an actual defeat on her part.'

'And Alain?' I asked. 'You didn't think to speak to him?'

'He was my accountant, Emmy. It was a professional relationship. I didn't think he'd appreciate me saying, "By the way, I gather you embarrassed yourself by getting legless but managed to turn Gloria down flat. Well done, you."'

'But he didn't *know* he turned her down!'

'And I didn't know he didn't know that!' she pointed out, clearly distressed. 'I had no *idea* he'd been worried about it all these years! Gloria didn't tell me all that stuff that Alain told you – about trying to persuade him the next day that it *had* happened, that he owed her further favours. We're not close friends. How could I have known?'

'All this hurt.' Sophie said. 'All this hurt because of one woman. It is very sad.'

'I wish I could have fixed things,' Ellie murmured. 'If I'd known, I would have.'

'At least I can tell Alain now,' I said with relief. 'Put his mind at rest. Is that okay?'

'Of course!' She straightened in her chair. 'And there's something I *can* do. I can tell Rupert. If I'd known about all those things she said to him when she left . . . I need to put him straight. Perhaps I should have done it a long time ago.'

I laid a hand on her arm. 'You don't need to do that, Ellie. I can tell him.'

'No. You already tried to tell Rupert what Alain told you, and he wouldn't listen. He would only think you're making excuses for your boyfriend.'

'Then I'll come with you.'

'I don't like to think someone could be so horrible to someone they once loved,' Sophie said as we dropped her at home.

'That's why love is best avoided,' Ellie pointed out. 'Too much pain. Too much potential for disaster.'

We drove on to *La Cour des Roses*. I got Ellie a glass of water and that's when I spied it, standing between a pot of paprika and a jar of homemade apple jelly: the ballerina figurine. It was balanced on one leg, the other looped up over her head. I walked over and plucked it off the shelf. I stared at the insipid, nauseating thing, then threw it in the bin. Good riddance.

When we knocked on Rupert's lounge door, he had just poured himself a shot of whiskey. Good. He was going to need it.

Slightly puzzled at Ellie's appearance, he filled us in on Bob's update on Jonathan's condition while we sat down, then looked at her quizzically.

'Rupert. I need to talk to you and I need you to listen,' Ellie said sternly, although her hands were shaking slightly.

'Er. Okay . . .'

Sensing something of import was happening, the dog came over from her favourite spot by the window to rest her head on his knees. I stared out at the dark shapes of the trees, swaying a little in the breeze, as Ellie told him her tale. His accusatory glare at me when he realised I'd confided in Sophie and Ellie turned slowly to resignation, then shock at Ellie's story, and finally anger.

Ellie had expected it. Braced herself for it, her knuckles white, gripping the chair arms.

'Why the hell didn't you tell me, Ellie?'

'Tell you what? I thought most of what Gloria told me was probably bollocks! I didn't want to interfere! I didn't think you'd thank me if I did. I didn't know you well enough.' Her eyes were rimmed red from holding back the tears. 'But for what it's worth, I'm sorry.' She stood to go, and without saying another word, she kissed us both and was on her way.

'Are you okay?' I tried carefully.

'What do you think?' Rupert growled at me.

'I would have thought you'd be . . . relieved.'

He barked out a laugh. 'Relieved? Relieved that my wife flirted with numerous men from the minute I bought this place? That she probably slept with a fair few of them? That she boasted about it to one of my *friends*?'

'Of course not! Relieved that she *didn't* sleep with one of your friends.'

'Not through lack of trying!'

'But she didn't succeed, did she?'

'Then why didn't Alain *say*?'

'Because he didn't *know*! That was what I tried to tell you yesterday, but you wouldn't listen! You heard Ellie. He was completely out of it. You must remember that night, Rupert, surely?'

'Yes. Doesn't change anything.'

'Why not? Gloria told Ellie he turned her down flat. Even in the state he was in. Doesn't that mean *anything* to you?'

'He should have told me. He could have saved me years of infidelity and heartache!'

'He didn't want to jeopardise your marriage, did he? Hindsight's a wonderful thing, Rupert. Think about that. Now, if you don't mind, I'd better go tell *him*. Maybe he'll appreciate the information more than you.'

I slammed out of the house and drove to Alain's in a turmoil of relief and upset and anger. As I pulled up at the kerb, I glanced at the clock. Ten thirty. Somehow, I didn't think Alain would mind.

He opened the door, wide-eyed. 'Emmy! Is everything all right? Jonathan, is he . . .?'

I laid a hand on his arm. 'It's not about Jonathan. Can I . . . Can I come in?'

I went through to the lounge. It felt like we should be curled up on the sofa together. Instead, he sat on the edge of the chair opposite.

'What's up?'

Without any preliminaries, I told him what Ellie had told me.

He listened intently and when I'd finished, he dropped his head into his hands while he absorbed it. When he finally looked up again, his eyes were moist.

'I can't tell you how good that is to know. To have an answer after all this time.' He managed a small smile. 'Not sure I'll be able to look Ellie in the eye for a while, though.'

'She doesn't think badly of you, Alain. She thinks Gloria acted disgracefully. That's why she fell out with her. She only wishes she'd known you hadn't remembered what happened. She could have put you out of your misery a long time ago.'

'Does Rupert know?'

'Yes. She told him.'

'And?'

'I think he's glad that nothing happened. But he's still hurt. He thinks you should have told him. He's upset that you kept it secret all this time.'

'But . . .'

I held up a hand. 'We both know the reasons. But he's hurting and he can't see it right now. I . . . I've done my best.'

'Thank you.' He gave me a questioning look. 'You must be glad, at least.'

'Glad?'

'That Gloria didn't get her wicked way with another boyfriend.'

'I suppose.'

'You *suppose*?'

'Alain . . . What Ellie told me doesn't change how I feel about this.' His face fell, and I hastened to explain. 'I can't deny it's a happy bonus, knowing you stood firm despite the state you were in. But I already understood what happened that night.'

'Then . . . Then why aren't we together?'

I let out a long sigh. 'Because this situation is bigger than you and me. I have Rupert to consider.'

He nodded. Gave me a brief smile. 'Thank you for telling me, Emmy. You have no idea how much it means to me.'

I smiled warmly. 'Yes, I do.'

I stood and he saw me to the door, laying a hand briefly on my cheek before I turned and left.

The next morning, Rupert studiously avoided catching my eye, slamming around the kitchen like a man possessed.

'Stop that!' I snapped. 'There are guests upstairs. They'll think the house is falling in.'

'Hmmph.' He moderated the slamming to clattering.

As soon as I could get away from him after breakfast was done, I went to hide in my room to phone Kate with yet another update, then continued to hide there, catching up with e-mails. There were several enquiries for bookings next year, and by the end of the morning, I'd transformed two of those into definites. Not bad for a morning's work. It seemed this sudden flurry was down to the Thomson clan, who had been busily posting photos of their accommodation and the gardens all over social media, even pictures of the breakfast and lunch tables, and saying how gorgeous the region was.

Risking Rupert's wrath, I knocked on his lounge door.

'I *told* you posting photos of food would work!' I announced as I waltzed in, before telling him the harvest we were reaping. 'Just think! Ten different groups of Thomsons here, all with their own individual groups of friends and acquaintances on social media seeing what we offer.'

He grunted. 'I hate social media.'

'Do you hate the results?'

'S'pose not.'

'Then cheer up!' I decided to take a chance. I wasn't convinced he was in the most receptive of moods, but Julia would only be here for two more days. 'Did you know that Julia Cooper runs a company that organises residential leisure courses?'

'No. So?'

'*So*. Maybe we could consider running activity weeks to help fill the early or late season. They're popular, and they can pay very well. Painting, writing, photography. Get an expert in, then let out the rooms to people who want to take part – but it would have to be fully catered. Lessons in the mornings, afternoons free to explore, then dinner with the resident expert.'

'And where would I find an expert I could afford?'

'Start with Bob and photography. You wouldn't even have to put him up here.' I turned my laptop towards him. 'Here's an example of a writing retreat. This is what they charge per head . . .'

'Bloody hell!' His jaw dropped. 'Really? Hmm. Maybe . . .'

The marquee arrived as expected not long after lunch, the van driver and his mate unloading long packages of poles, fat parcels of folded canvas and sacks of pegs, and piling them at the far end of the courtyard, next to the hedge.

By the time they'd finished that, sweat was rolling off them. Imagining they would have a long haul erecting it, I took pity on them and fetched iced drinks, for which they were grateful . . . and after which they waved, went back to the van, climbed in and turned on the engine.

'Wait!' I yelled, turning to Rupert. 'Where the hell are they going? Why haven't they set it up? When are they coming back?'

'They're not.' Rupert scrubbed a hand across his face. 'We have to do it ourselves.'

'*What?* But . . .'

'I ordered it last minute. The company had nobody to spare. It's a busy time of year with parties and weddings. There's a video on their website showing how to put this model up. I suggest we have some tea in the den and we watch it.'

We did. Our faces fell.

'We'll never do it before they get back from the jazz,' I pointed out. 'And it needs to be up by then, or nobody will be able to park. On the other hand . . .' I jabbed at my phone and thrust it under Rupert's nose. 'It's not forecast to rain tomorrow. We don't need a marquee.'

'A marquee was requested by the clients. It was included in the price we are charging them. It's here now, and it may as well go up.'

I huffed. 'Well, we're not going to manage it alone, that's for sure. We need muscles. Phone Ryan. Phone Bob.' I almost said 'Phone Alain', but stopped myself.

Rupert gave me a look. He knew. 'Four of us should do it.'

Hours later, the four of us were sweating so hard, we were wringing wet. The marquee was bigger than we thought. The courtyard was strewn with poles and canvas lengths. The dog weaved her way in and out of this exciting new obstacle course, getting in everyone's way. Rupert's laptop was balanced in the shade so we could watch instructions, then pause it while we tried to carry them out.

First, every last item had to be laid out exactly in position on the ground. Then, every pole had to go into the correct joining pole. Some of the joins were slightly bent, and Bob resorted to a mallet – sparingly, since we would be liable for any damage. Mainly, we had to rely on brute force – Ryan – but he was getting tired. My shoulders and arms screamed in pain from holding semi-constructed bits in position above my head while other semi-constructed bits were added to it.

Bob and Ryan, the two most laid-back people I had ever met, spent the entire time swearing like troopers, yelling in pain when they caught skin in the pole joints or banged thumbs with the mallet, and muttering colourful expletives at the dog.

And yet neither of them gave up until the job was done. It was a testament to how much they valued Rupert as a friend. You certainly wouldn't do it otherwise.

When it was stable and looking impressive with the tall hedge as a backdrop, we all collapsed in a stinky, sweat-ridden heap on a shady spot of the lawn, the dog flopping contentedly across us, and downed a couple of bottles of cool beer each before we found the energy to speak.

Bob broke the exhausted silence. 'Never again, Rupert.'

Rupert grunted.

'Shit!' Ryan suddenly sat up straight. 'Do we have to take it down, too?'

For some reason, we all found this hysterical, rolling around in the grass until our sides ached, bellows of laughter echoing through the garden and tears streaming down our faces.

Oh, this was what I loved about *La Cour des Roses* and the people who frequented it. Friendships where nothing was too much trouble. Crises that could be lessened by unity. Cool beer and loud laughter. Life could be a lot worse.

* * *

When the Thomsons returned from the final afternoon of the jazz festival, they were buzzing. Rupert made pots of tea for those who didn't have their own facilities, and they dotted themselves around the garden before worrying about what or where to eat that evening.

Julia invited me to sit with her and her husband. 'I wanted to thank you for everything, Emmy. I know we haven't spoken about it much – I didn't want to ask personal questions – but it's fair to say I've gathered that Rupert and Gloria had a rather acrimonious parting. Now I can relax a bit, I can imagine how hard it must have been for you two, not knowing what was going on and starting from scratch . . .'

'Oh, but . . .'

Julia laughed, and it immediately lifted all the strain from her face. This woman needed a holiday. A *proper* holiday.

'Oh, Emmy, I know you *tried* to hide the full extent of your ignorance . . .'

Robert was chuckling, too. 'You've done a grand job so far. The food's been superb, and it was so good of you to make sure we've had some meals together as a family. It would have been impossible, arranging places where all of us could go. Poor Julia's been a nervous wreck for weeks.'

I smiled. 'I'm sure. And I'm glad we've managed to accommodate and get round things between us. Have your parents had a nice time so far?'

'Wonderful. They've loved the jazz. We've just perched them on their deckchairs on the grass and made sure someone was always with them, and they've been in their element. They've loved driving along the lanes and taking in the scenery, and the family being together. It's been very special for us all.'

Robert smiled at his wife. 'I'm bringing you back here for a decent holiday next year, Julia, and I don't want any arguments.'

'You won't get any from me.'

'And we still have the party to look forward to tomorrow,' Robert pointed out. 'I bet Rupert's glad he's not catering for that!'

Frank and Sylvia came over to sit with us, Rupert with them, and we all shuffled around to accommodate them. 'How's your trip been so far?' I asked them.

Sylvia beamed, the thin skin over her cheekbones rosy with the sunshine. 'It's been such a lovely treat.' She reached across to kiss her daughter's cheek. 'And having everyone together . . .' She teared up. 'Well, I can't remember the last time we were *all* together like this.'

'Especially with Chris and his family at the other side of the world,' Frank said. 'I miss him.'

I swallowed hard, desperately trying to keep my emotions in check – happiness that everything had worked out for them, after all, and satisfaction that Gloria's ineptitude had been overcome and we had managed to make this work between us. I glanced sideways at Rupert and suspected he was thinking the exact same thing.

'And the party tomorrow sounds perfect,' Sylvia added. 'I can't think of a more lovely location for it. I have a new dress that Frank hasn't seen yet. I shall wear that.'

'I'm sure you'll look lovely in it,' I told her.

Frank leaned across to me. 'My wife would look lovely in anything.'

That evening, when I visited Jonathan at the hospital, he was half sitting up and there was a little colour in his cheeks, although he still looked tired. We chatted without him falling asleep, which was a major plus . . . or not, because then he could weigh in on my personal life.

'Why do you and Alain come separately?'

'You get more visitors that way.'

'That's a side effect, not the reason,' he wheezed. 'I may be ill and old, but I'm not stupid. I know something's going on. And I know something's up with Rupert, too. More than Gloria leaving.'

'Jonathan, I don't think . . .'

He caught my hand in his, the veins standing out like blue ropes under fragile thin skin. 'Listen to me. I've been nearly eighty years on this earth, and I only spent ten of them with someone I deeply loved. Those ten years meant the world to me, and they still do. The short time Matthew and I were given couldn't be helped. But this *can* be helped, I'm sure of it. Don't let pride stand in your way, Emmy. You'll live your life full of regrets and what ifs.'

Exhausted, he sank back against his pillow and closed his eyes.

I drove home with his heartfelt admonishment imprinted on my brain. But it wasn't pride that was the problem. It was the tug of war between the growing knowledge that I couldn't imagine not having Alain in my life and my loyalty to a good friend.

I told myself that I would get the Thomson stay out of the way and worry about it after that.

But as I tried to sleep that night, all I could think about was sitting at the back of Alain's house amongst the hydrangeas, sipping wine as the sun set across the rose field; Alain laughing over my grammar mistakes as I drooled over him in his specs; walking hand in hand along quiet evening streets; cycling past fields of corn and vines. Lying across his bed in the evening light, his hands working their magic.

I missed him so much. I'd been so busy being angry and upset, analysing and rationalising, telling myself I had to be sure and that there was Rupert to consider . . . But I hadn't listened to my inner voice at all. And now, in the middle of the night, it was screaming at me: *What if you lose him? What if it's really finished? Is that what you want? Is it?*

CHAPTER TWENTY-TWO

Up ridiculously early the next morning, I let the chickens out, roamed the garden with Gloria at my heels, then sat with my espresso on the Adirondack chair in my favourite hideaway corner, the dog's head in my lap, until Rupert came out to take her for a quick walk while I began on breakfast.

As I chopped yet more fruit – we seemed to have gone through a whole greengrocery department these last few days – I could only be grateful that our lunch provision was at least over with.

And the marquee hadn't collapsed overnight, which was a bonus.

As soon as breakfast was over, I drove into Pierre-la-Fontaine to collect the cake. With Jonathan's words still prominent in my mind, I couldn't help glancing up the street towards Alain's office, but I would gain nothing by bothering him at his place of work again. Besides, he'd already made it clear that he would like us to be together. The ball was in my court . . . and I simply didn't have time to play right now.

When the woman at the counter showed me the cake, I gasped. It wasn't a cake – it was a creation. Simple but elegant, with tiny gold rosebuds and delicate swirls and ribbons. So tasteful and so beautiful. I paid the balance with Rupert's credit card, wincing as I entered the pin number, and took charge of the boxed treasure with nothing other than complete trepidation. It was market day out there, which meant crowded streets and jostling people and a longer walk than usual back to my car.

I held the box in front of me as though it would break, gripping the ribbon handle like my life depended on it – but I needn't have worried. Everyone who passed me guessed there must be something special in that box, and I was given a wide berth. In the car, I placed it in the boot and stuffed old jumpers and a rug around it so it couldn't slide around, then drove home at half the usual speed.

La Cour des Roses was deserted when I got back.

'Where is everybody?' I asked Rupert when he'd duly praised the cake and my careful driving.

'The families with kids have gone to the zoo for the day. Tire them out a bit before the party. The rest have gone off sightseeing.'

'Crikey. Peace and quiet for us, then.' I let out a huge sigh of relief, making Rupert laugh.

'I'll take advantage and go to see Jonathan this afternoon, if that's okay with you,' he said. 'I should be back in time for the caterers coming.'

'No problem.'

Figuring I could spare an hour or so before starting to make sure everything was ready for the party, I took a lounger down the garden and sat amongst huge, floppy-headed, deep pink roses. I closed my eyes and breathed in their scent and dozed and woke and dozed again, the dog stretched out behind me in the shade, half in and half out of a flowerbed. Ryan would *not* be pleased at the dog-shaped dent in his flowers, but I figured she could do with an hour off from being nagged, too.

My bones melted in the sunshine, my blood warmed, my brain allowed thoughts and worries to buzz without stinging. And when I finally came out of my doze and allowed my senses to reorientate themselves before fully opening my eyes, I had come to understand that what mattered most to me about being here was the people. Rupert, Jonathan. Ellie, Sophie. Ryan, Bob. Alain.

I'd been concentrating so hard on my new role, desperate to improve *La Cour des Roses*, boost profits, pull us out of every difficulty that had come our way and anticipate future ones. To build my reputation in the community as a woman who could do that stuff, and do it well.

But the truth was, it didn't matter if *La Cour des Roses* hadn't made quite enough money *this* season. There was always next year. It didn't matter if the odd guest gave us a crap review. We would get good ones – far more of them. It *would* matter eventually if I couldn't get my business off the ground, and if I used all my savings. But I would have to ensure that didn't happen. Somehow.

Right now, what I cared about was Rupert not driving himself into an early grave after the stressful months he'd been through. Helping him come to terms with the aftermath of Gloria. Making sure I made time for all my new friends, just as they had made time for me. Finding a way, if it was at all possible, to reconcile Rupert and Alain, so that I could be with the man I wanted to be with, without feeling like I was betraying my best friend at the same time.

My much-needed break was ended by Ryan's arrival. He'd been roped in to string fairy lights around the patio and amongst the hedges and trees around the garden, depending on how far he dared stretch the tolerance of the electricity supply.

'How's Jonathan?' he asked me immediately.

'Stable, and a little better. I hope . . . No, I *think* he's going to be okay.'

'That's good.'

I went into the house to start dragging wine and soft drinks through to the kitchen from Rupert's lounge.

When Rupert got back from the hospital, he was a little pale, a little jittery.

'Is everything all right?' Alarm made my spine prickle. 'Is Jonathan okay?'

'Jonathan's fine, Emmy. Quite *chatty*, in fact.'

'That's good.' I registered his emphasis on 'chatty' and frowned. 'Are *you* okay?'

'Apparently not,' he grunted, giving me a hand carrying boxes and bottles through. I stopped him and moved to his little kitchenette to make tea. A bit forward of me, but at least we would have some privacy in there.

'What are you doing? I thought we were moving these?'

'We have time for a cuppa,' I told him. 'You look like you need one, and I probably haven't had enough to drink today.'

'Hmmph. I doubt tea will solve that.'

What on earth was the matter with him? I pushed him onto the sofa and handed him a mug, then sat next to him and nudged him lightly. 'What's up?'

'Nothing.'

I glared at him. 'Rupert, we have a big event tonight. You can't be like this. Get it off your chest now, with someone who's willing to take it and isn't a paying guest.'

'Can't.'

'Why not?'

'Because it's too close to home.'

'Ah. Well. Makes no difference. I can't see any other agony aunts around here at the moment, can you?' When he said nothing, I guessed, 'Has Jonathan been too honest again?'

'Beyond honest. He was quite belligerent.'

I smiled. 'That's good. Means he might be getting better.'

'Well, I can't say I enjoyed it. He gave me a stern talking to. Demanded to know what the hell was going on between us all. Wouldn't let it drop.'

'You . . . You told him?'

'Yes.'

I felt so relieved that he was finally ready to talk to someone. 'So what did Jonathan say?'

'He had to get a fair variety of swearwords out of the way first. That took a good five minutes. Jonathan and Gloria never got on, but even so . . .' Rupert stared at his feet. 'He was very sympathetic, but he was also very cross with me.'

'Cross with *you?*'

'Yes. For being so quick to give up on Alain's friendship. For what I was putting you through by doing that.'

'I don't want you making up with Alain for my sake. It would always be forced and false. If you choose to do that, it should be for *your* sake, Rupert. For a six-year friendship's sake.' When he said nothing, I wondered how far to push it and decided I had nothing to lose. 'Think about how much that friendship has meant to you. Think about *why* you're angry and *who* you're really angry with.'

He heaved a huge sigh. 'What Ellie told me, Emmy . . . You were right, it did alter my perspective. I remember how cut up Alain was about his wife leaving. I also remember he was pretty out of it that night. That's why we left him to sleep on the sofa.'

'But?'

'*But* there's still the *fact* of it, Emmy. I'm still angry at him for not telling me. For not saving me from . . . From everything that's happened since.'

'Would you have taken it kindly if he had? Would you have believed him? Or would you have believed your own wife? Would you have been happy if it had led to your marriage breaking up?'

'I know it's not *logical*. And I know it's a hell of a lot of blame to put on one person, but . . .' He scrubbed a hand across his face. 'I can't . . . My pride . . . God knows, Emmy, I have so little of it left where my disaster of a marriage is concerned.'

I nodded, scared to push him any further. He was wavering, I knew it. If I could bide my time, chip away at him . . .

I leaned in to peck him on the cheek. 'You've had a hard time, Rupert. And now with Jonathan . . .'

'Do you know what he said to me when I left?' he asked. 'He said, "How many years do you think I've got left, Rupert? You've been thinking I might die here in this hospital. *I've* thought I might die. Treasure what you have while you still have it, man."'

'Was he talking about Alain?'

'Probably, the sneaky old bugger. But I guess it could apply to a lot of things, couldn't it?'

And in a signal that the soppy moment and heart to hearts were over, he hoisted himself to his feet and carried on where we'd left off with the party preparations.

The caterers arrived not long after that, with tray after tray of incredible party food – and the dog was immediately banished to Rupert's quarters for the rest of the evening. When we'd helped them bring it all from the van into the kitchen, Rupert decided we had better ensure the same happened with the labradoodles when they got back with their owners.

His magic with lights achieved, Ryan sloped off before he could be asked to do anything else, as the caterers' van left and guests began to trickle back from their various trips and went off to shower and change into their glad rags.

Julia came into the kitchen to take a peek at the food and clapped her hands in delight. 'Perfect!'

'Where did you take Frank and Sylvia today?' I asked her.

'Saumur. Lots of sitting on benches by the river or the castle or the town, and cups of tea. I didn't want to wear them out.'

But as Frank and Sylvia ambled along the hall towards the staircase, they looked sprightly enough, and up for their big night.

As the two waiting staff the caterers had hired set themselves up at one end of the marquee with glasses and drinks, the van with the band arrived. When we'd greeted them and showed them where we wanted them to go, they began to haul out their instruments. Drums, bass, the whole caboodle . . . They started to set up at the other end of the marquee.

I turned to Rupert. 'I thought it was a five-piece band. There's only four of them.'

'Maybe the other one's been held up and will follow on. They didn't say anything.' He plucked at the sleeve of my T-shirt. 'Aren't you going to put a party frock on?'

I rolled my eyes. 'Who are you, my grandmother?' But I dutifully went to change into a dress and slap some make-up on.

As I did so, my heart was a little lighter and a little heavier at the same time. Jonathan had done a good job today – I could never have spoken to Rupert like that and got away with it, and he'd obviously got through to him a little – but it looked like Rupert was clinging on to his stubbornness by his fingernails, and I wasn't sure whether it was my place to intrude any further into his feelings.

Donald came wandering downstairs as I went back into the main part of the house. 'Are we having fish and chips?'

'Er. No, Donald, I'm sorry. It's party food tonight. There might be a prawn or two. Is that near enough?'

He wrinkled his nose. 'I can't find Patricia.'

'Is she in your room?'

'Which room?'

I took his arm and led him back upstairs. Patricia was in her robe.

'Oh, Emmy, I'm so sorry. I only left him for a minute while I had a quick wash!'

'Don't worry. I don't think he'd have got very far.'

'Used to be the top sprinter at school,' he muttered as I led him to the bedroom chair. 'Faster than that Jack Smith.'

I left them to it and went back downstairs. Rupert was outside, talking animatedly with the band. I'd never seen him in a jacket and tie, other than in his wedding photograph.

'You look very handsome,' I told him, smiling. 'What's going on here?'

'They're still one man down. Their clarinet player threw up an hour before they came here. They left him at the campsite and he said he'd follow on if he felt better, but he's just phoned them. He's stuck on the toilet and there's no way he can make it.'

'How much difference will it make?'

'They can still play. Apparently it's not like losing the drummer or the bass. They still have the keyboard and a sax player. But the sound won't be as good.' His shoulders sagged.

As did mine. 'Damn and blast.' I sighed. 'I . . . Sylvia and Frank Thomson have been married for fifty years – how many people achieve that? Ten different factions have driven or flown to France to celebrate it with them, one from halfway around the world. This can never happen again in their lifetime. Enough has gone wrong – or almost gone wrong – already. And we've put so much effort into it. I wanted it to be perfect.'

He squeezed my hand. 'You are *such* a soft touch.'

'Yes, well, you can't tell me you don't feel the same way.'

When he only grunted in reply, I scanned the instruments. 'Shame it wasn't their sax player that's ill.'

'What? Why?'

I searched his face. 'You know why,' I said gently. 'Maybe Alain could have played.'

Rupert's lips tightened into a thin line.

Sensing our despondency, the sax player began talking to Rupert again, lifting up the sax in one hand and the clarinet in the other, the rest of the band all chiming in with their opinions.

Frustrated, I demanded, 'What are they saying?'

Rupert looked at the ground. 'He says he can switch instruments depending on the piece of music. He plays sax *and* clarinet, so he'll switch to whichever is more dominant for each piece they're playing.'

'That's . . . Wait! He's a sax player, but he can play clarinet?'

'Yes.'

'So if he plays clarinet, they *are* down a sax player, after all . . .'

Rupert just frowned, but I knew he was softening towards Alain – he'd been touched by what Jonathan said about short lives and friendship, and the only reason he had for not making up now was pride.

'Alain told us he played with these guys a couple of times a few years ago.' I stood with my hands on my hips, the band looking on bemusedly. 'We have a chance to make this perfect for Frank and Sylvia.'

I turned to the sax player and switched to French. 'If we know someone who plays this,' I asked him, pointing to his sax, since I didn't know the word for the thing, 'is that good? And you could play that?' I pointed to the clarinet.

He answered in accented English to be kind. 'Maybe, but only if he plays jazz. And he may not know the songs we play.'

'He does know jazz. You played with him before. Alain Granger.'

The man frowned. 'Alain?' And then his eyes lit up. 'He is very tall, yes?' He held his hand way above his head to make his point.

I laughed. 'Yes.'

'If he could come, we could do *something*. It would be better than four.'

Rupert looked absolutely exhausted, and I wondered if I'd gone too far. 'Emmy . . .'

'Rupert, we've ascertained that they could make a better sound if Alain came. Whether you ring him is up to you.' I decided to push my luck – what did I have to lose? 'I'm sure Alain would be happy to do you this favour. That's the kind of friendship you have. I know you want to see him, really.'

'And how will that look? Me only speaking to him because I need a favour?'

'It would look as though you're willing to speak to him, which would be a step forward.' A couple of guests appeared on the patio. 'I need to get this party started. You can decide whether your pride's worth the loss of a good friend.'

When he stalked off to the house, I turned back to the band.

'Alain?' the sax player asked hopefully.

'I don't know. I'm sorry.'

'We will do our best, anyway.'

'Thank you.'

I wandered across the garden, weaving between the guests starting their special evening, hoping Rupert would see sense – but suspecting he wouldn't.

I took a deep breath and tried to focus on the moment. Ryan had done a fantastic job with the lights. They made the garden look so pretty. The guests were all dressed to the nines, ladies and girls in summer dresses, blokes and boys in jackets and ties. I got the waiting staff circulating with drinks. Once everyone was served, one of them could begin taking trays of food around, while the other manned the bar.

Rupert came back out, but I couldn't read his look – sulky or sheepish? He dutifully plastered on a smile as he began to circulate.

Once everyone was outside, the band began to play. As Alain had suggested, it was no cacophony of modern experimentation – just a mellow rhythm that floated across the courtyard and gardens.

Julia came across to where I was hovering near the drinks, in case there was a run at the bar, and gave me a tight hug. There were tears in her eyes. 'Thank you so much. This is so perfect.'

'You're welcome. That's a beautiful dress.' She looked a different woman in the floaty, floral number.

'And the woman in it is beautiful,' Robert said, joining us. 'Your eldest nephew wants to know if we can come back here as a family every year, my love.'

Julia laughed. 'Only if he wants to see me go even greyer than I already am. Where is he? I'll tell him *he* can organise it next time . . .'

They strolled off across the garden, hand in hand, and a pang of loneliness punched me in the gut.

I snuck a glass of wine before circulating, then grabbed a bottle and began topping up the guests, agreeing with their delight over the pink sunset and the sweet scent of the roses. As the band played on, I heard at least two jazz fanatics lamenting the absence of another wind musician.

I gritted my teeth and looked over as the clarinettist took up the sax again. He caught my eye and raised his eyebrows hopefully. I shrugged and shook my head, and suddenly felt that I had to stand back from all of this. I put the empty wine bottle down and made a beeline for the house.

It was cool and quiet, leaning against the bare stone wall next to the kitchen window. Even if everything worked out at *La Cour des Roses*, was it enough for me any more, without Alain?

As if in answer, I heard footsteps coming across the gravel from the lane and turned. I couldn't see his face in the bright lights shining from the house, but there was no mistaking his height. Or the instrument case in his hand.

I let out my breath on a long sigh of relief and hope. Rupert had called him. And maybe, just maybe, we could put this behind us, all three of us.

Alain didn't see me, but Rupert saw him. I held my breath as Rupert strode across the patio to the courtyard, reached out for a handshake, then draw Alain into a quick hug. I hardly dared believe that Rupert had made the call. And that Alain had accepted his plea for help.

As Alain started across to the marquee, I stepped out from the shadows of the house, and as though he sensed it, he turned back. 'Emmy.'

'Hi. Thank you for coming.'

'Did you think I wouldn't?'

'Rupert was worried it would look like he only called you because he needed your help.'

Alain shrugged. 'It's a start.'

I nodded. 'I want you to know . . . He's already beginning to soften a little, Alain, but it's taken a lot for him to do it. To call you.'

'I know. And of course you wouldn't have had anything to do with trying to persuade him?'

I arranged an innocent look on my face. 'Who, me?' I took a long look at his handsome face. 'And I also know it's taken a lot for you to come.'

He took his sax out of its case, then dared a kiss on my cheek. 'Duty calls once in a while. Do I at least get a beer?'

I grinned and went to fetch him a bottle. When I got back to him with it, the band had finished the number they were playing, and there were friendly greetings and a few minutes' discussion over which numbers Alain felt he could safely join in with before they were back in action. I stood at the bar and watched him adjust to their playing, tentative at first, then growing more confident as he got into it.

The sound was sexy. Alain was sexy, his lips at the mouthpiece, his long fingers at the keys, his shoulders twisting slightly to the music as he played. I didn't know much about it, but I figured he was pretty good for an amateur.

He was handsome and versatile and kind and forgiving, and I wanted to be with him more than I could ever express.

'Happy now?' Rupert was at my shoulder.

I turned to him. 'Yes. Thank you.'

'Will you . . . Will you and Alain get back together?'

I took a deep breath. 'I hope so. He wants to. I just couldn't . . . because of . . .'

'Because of me and him?'

'Yes.'

'Then you can feel free to go for it.' He nudged my arm. 'You're a good friend, Emmy. And I need to remember that Alain is, too.'

While I helped with drinks and food, cleared away litter, made sure the band got regular refreshments and took sneaky peeks at Alain playing, some of the family danced on the lawn, especially Sylvia and Frank – with each other, with their children and with their grandchildren. Dusk headed towards dark, and Julia came over to request that the champagne and cake be got ready. She asked for a drum roll and stood on the patio, where the family gathered around her.

Alain came to stand with Rupert and me, his hand lightly on my shoulder, and we hung back, waiting for the correct moment to pop the corks. Julia's speech was surprisingly short and to the point, thanking her parents for all they had done for their family over the years and wishing them many happy years to come. Her brother Chris told a short anecdote that made everyone laugh. The tent crowd sang a love song in folk style, for which the jazz band cheered and applauded good-naturedly. One of the smaller grandchildren read a simple poem she had written for them.

Already tired and tearful, it threatened to tip me over the edge into an emotional wreck.

And then Frank made a short speech. Struggling a little over his words, but with determination, he expressed his thanks to Sylvia, simply for being his wife. To his family for being a source of pride and joy and for arranging such a wonderful holiday at such a beautiful place. And to me and Rupert, for making it all happen.

The champagne was opened, the cake was presented – and oohed and aahed over – and, sadly, cut.

We had done it, and it had been worthwhile and appreciated. We couldn't ask for more.

Rupert plucked up a glass of bubbly for each of us and chinked his against mine.

'To us, Emmy, and to *La Cour des Roses*.'

'To us.'

And against Alain's. 'And to friendship.'

Alain smiled. 'To friendship.'

We sipped our bubbles, and then Alain joined the band as they began to play night-time music. I listened to him play, laughed at the antics of the children – now a little giddy or tired or both – and watched the dancing.

Rupert took my glass from my hand. 'One dance, Emmy?'

He led me onto the grass and held me lightly in a traditional ballroom stance as we moved around the lawn, allowing the music and the relief to wash over us.

I'd never been christened or baptised, so I didn't possess godparents. And I'd never thought much of it, or thought I needed any. But I figured I had an honorary godfather now, in the form of this man waltzing me around his garden, and I couldn't be more grateful for his presence in my life – and that his rift with Alain was showing definite signs of healing.

As the number ended, Alain tapped on his shoulder. 'May I?'

Rupert winked at me and went off to waltz a five-year-old young lady in a frilly party dress around the flowerbeds, much to her delight. We could hear her giggling sweetly, and it made us both smile.

'Shouldn't you be playing?' I asked him.

'They're doing a couple of numbers I don't know.'

'How convenient.'

'It is, isn't it?' He pulled me closer, and I rested my head against his chest as he guided us around the lawn between the other dancers and giddy children.

'Emmy, you do know I'm in love with you, don't you?'

The words murmured in my ear had my feet stumbling a little. I pulled back and looked into his face.

'I should have said it before, but I didn't want to scare you off. And then when I thought I'd lost the chance to say it . . . Well, I'm going to make up for it now. I love you, Emmeline Jamieson.'

His lips came down to meet mine in a kiss that was long and tender, as though he was frightened I would break. Or pull away.

I did pull away, eventually. Long enough to stroke my finger along the light stubble at his jaw, but not long enough to lose my nerve. 'I love you, too.'

His eyes widened, as though he hadn't dared hope I would reciprocate, and his Adam's apple moved in his throat. His hand snaked around the back of my neck to pull me back into a kiss, deeper this time, so it had my head spinning and my limbs weakening.

When we finally remembered we were at a public event – with children present – we shuffled apart a little and continued to dance.

As Frank and Sylvia brushed past us, Sylvia whispered, 'Looks like a keeper to me.'

I beamed back at her. 'I think you might be right.'

She lifted her hand to stroke Frank's cheek. 'I'm quite a good judge of these things, Emmy, though I say so myself.'

CHAPTER TWENTY-THREE

The next morning, Alain left early, knowing I had a busy day ahead.

Our goodbye kiss was relaxed – something that could not be said for our frenzy the night before, when we'd collapsed into my bed in the early hours of the morning, exhausted but desperate for each other; desperate to cement the reunion we'd begun in the garden, dancing through the twinkling lights, and to finally acknowledge that we were making love, not just having great sex. As we lay together afterwards, I'd promised myself that I would not be letting this man go any time soon.

After breakfast, I sat with Julia over a final coffee before she drove her parents to the airport. She was relaxed and amiable – the lines had lessened on her face, and she soaked up both the morning sunshine and Rupert's perfect coffee with equal pleasure.

'You are so lucky, living and working here,' she said.

'Ha!' I spluttered on my coffee, then laughed. 'I know I am, in theory. But as you've gathered, the last few weeks haven't been too peaceful. We've had quite a few . . . issues.'

'Because of Gloria?'

'Not all of it. But she didn't help matters.'

'But it's settled down now?'

'Yes.'

Julia smiled. 'I was hoping so, because I wondered if you'd ever considered running residential courses here?'

I hid a smile. 'It's crossed our minds, but we've never done it before.'

'I'd be happy to discuss it, Emmy, once I'm back in business mode. Would you be willing?'

'Of course.'

'Robert has asked Rupert about next spring, by the way. We want to come for a fortnight, and if my parents are well enough, maybe they could join us for a week of that.'

'Sounds wonderful.'

When they all left, there were hugs and quite a few tears.

'Hang on to that handsome saxophone player of yours,' Sylvia told me as she embraced me. 'He's madly in love with you. I could see it in his eyes.'

'Leave the poor girl alone,' Frank said jokingly as he ushered her into the car. 'Not everyone wants to be . . .'

'Consigned to fifty years of wedded bliss like us?' Sylvia finished for him.

Frank winked, and they were gone.

The marquee was taken down, with marginally less cursing and swearing than when it went up. The caravans and tent left the same day, as did Donald and Patricia – much to Donald's confused protests, bless him.

The only things I was truly pleased to see go were the portable toilet and the tambourine.

Only the Australians and Wendy's family remained, staying in the *gîtes* till Saturday, and then we would be on to non-Thomsons in the guesthouse – which, it occurred to me, would feel quite strange.

Rupert was quiet that afternoon, as we sat with a well-deserved beer in the garden.

'Are you okay?' I asked him.

'S'pose.'

'You should know by now that you don't get away with answers like that. What's up?'

'Other than that I've rung the death knell on my marriage and my wife turns out to have had very few redeeming qualities after all, and one of my best friends had to fend off her advances in our own home while the other best friend is barely this side of death's door?'

'Yes.'

He sighed. 'I'll be sixty soon.'

'When?'

'Sunday.'

'Why didn't you tell me?'

'Been trying to suppress it. I didn't mind hitting forty or fifty, but sixty feels distinctly over the hill and heading rapidly down the other side. Jonathan being so ill hasn't helped. A glimpse of mortality, I suppose.' He glared at me. 'And no, I don't need a pep talk, Emmy, thank you. But I know I've been acting oddly lately – or more oddly than even events here might dictate, anyway – and you deserve to know why. Now that you do, I don't want to hear another word about it.'

I nodded as my brain whirred. Rupert shouldn't be depressed about being sixty. He was healthier now, he had all his friends, he had Gloria (the dog) doting on him, Gloria (ex-wife) off the scene, his business was doing okay, and now that I was here, his workload was reduced. Somehow, I needed to show him that life was good, and it was the same whether he was fifty-nine or sixty. Not much of a tall order there, then.

My mother's call later that afternoon was perfect timing.

'Mum, can I pick your brain?'

'Of course. What's left of it. What do you need?'

'A list of games you played at birthday parties when you were a kid. And a list of party food too. Can you send it later today?'

'Yes, of course, darling, but what do you need that for?'

'It's Rupert's sixtieth and I want to throw a party. He was joking with a friend a few weeks ago about bob-a-job week and naff kids' party games, so I thought maybe I could take him back to his childhood. You're his age, so who better to ask?'

What I didn't add was that I knew my mother was the organiser of all organisers and would, if my luck was in, plan the whole thing from the suburbs of Birmingham and send it as a done deal – shopping lists, recipes, games instructions, the lot.

'No problem. Your dad's obsessed with getting the garden sorted before autumn, so it'll give me something to sink my teeth into.'

'Thanks, Mum. I appreciate it.'

And I did. Bossy mothers came in handy occasionally.

'How's your friend Jonathan?' she asked. 'Any better?'

'We think he's out of danger, but he's still in hospital. He's been so poorly, Mum.'

'Pneumonia's a nasty thing at that age, Emmy, but it sounds like he's coming out the other side. I'm so glad.'

'Me too. Thank you for asking.'

I spent the rest of the afternoon e-mailing the guests who would be here at the weekend to warn them there would be a party, which they were welcome to join in with or ignore, and desperately hoping that nobody came back with any objections. Then I set about phoning Rupert's friends and neighbours, roping Bob in to help me out.

That evening, I went round to Alain's. He handed me chilled wine and solicitously placed me in a chair at the back of the house, sitting next to me and taking my hand in his.

I closed my eyes and absorbed the quiet for a moment, appreciating the feel of his fingers entwined in mine.

'Things calmed down over there?' he asked.

'Yes, thank God. Honestly, I can't begin to tell you . . . It's been bedlam.'

Tongue in cheek, he asked, 'Is this something you're hoping to repeat every year, as a way of increasing the appeal and profits of *La Cour des Roses*?'

'Ha! It's something that I hope never to repeat in my lifetime. Portable toilets and caravans and tents? Nine vehicles jammed in the courtyard and on the lane, as well as ours? And I can't *tell* you how much food those people got through.'

His lips twitched. 'At least you weren't bored.'

'Oh, I would *so* love to be bored right now, believe me.'

'Boredom's overrated.' He raised a questioning eyebrow. 'How about a little stimulation instead?'

'Hmm. That could work, too.'

We took our wine upstairs, and Alain took his time, making sure I appreciated stimulation in all its glory.

'Feeling better?' he asked afterwards as we lay on our sides, our foreheads touching.

'Tired. But a nice kind of tired.'

'You've been overdoing things.'

'That's what Madame Dupont said. She thinks I should take time to smell the flowers and all that guff.'

Alain smiled. 'I don't suppose Jonathan told you how he'd only had ten years with Matthew and you should never live with regrets, did he?'

'Funnily enough, last weekend, when he was looking all weak and pathetic . . .'

We laughed. It was a wonderful thing – to be together, laughing and touching. It wasn't something I could take for granted.

'I love you,' I told him solemnly, wanting to be the one to initiate it this time.

He smiled. 'I love you right back. I was worried you might have only said it the other night because you'd been influenced by the fairy lights and the music and the champagne.'

I pouted. 'You mean I won't get those every weekend?'

I spent all my spare time between my usual duties reading through my mother's e-mail of games and food, adapting them to suit, shopping, then taking everything to Alain's to hide it away from Rupert.

On Friday morning, Rupert took a call that made my heart soar. 'That was the hospital,' he told me as he clicked off. 'They want me to go and discuss the possibility of Jonathan coming home.'

'Really?' Tears welled. 'They must think he's definitely okay then?'

Rupert smiled broadly. 'Must do. He's a tough old sod underneath all that limping and wheezing. I knew he wasn't ready to go yet.' But there was a tear in his eye, too.

We headed straight for the hospital, where the medical staff told Rupert that Jonathan could go home that afternoon, as long as he had help and someone checking on him regularly.

'What do you think, Emmy?' Rupert asked me. 'Can we do it?'

'I'm sure we can. Everyone will have to chip in. I'll set up a rota. And Jonathan will have to behave.'

He laughed. 'Do you want to be the one to tell him that?'

Saturdays were bad enough without all the extra subterfuge. For every new arrival greeted by Rupert, I'd had to wait until he was elsewhere, collar them and reissue an open invitation to the party. Most were fine, some even eager. One or two suggested they might go out for the day.

Madame Dupont offered to come early on Sunday to help, but I insisted she'd been invited as a guest and not for hard graft. I was only grateful she hadn't offered several of her chickens as a contribution.

My idea of putting on vintage British party fare had seemed a good idea at the time, but Mum's list of ingredients had to be seriously adapted to suit what I could obtain in a French supermarket, and my general feeling of inadequacy was not helped by Rupert's prawn salad, fish with perfectly steamed vegetables, followed by pavlova at the guest meal that night. All I could do was compare it to mini sausages on sticks in a panic. The only food item I was sure would be okay was the birthday cake Ellie had offered to bake – yet another facet to her that I would never have expected.

By Sunday, I decided I must have inherited some of my mother's social organisational aptitude, after all. I'd arranged for Jonathan to lure Rupert to his house for lunch and keep him there from twelve till three, during which time Alain and I ferried all the food and drink from his house to *La Cour des Roses*, while Ryan and his parents transformed the garden with garish bunting and balloons and Ryan set up what we needed for games.

I only just had time to smarten up before guests began to arrive at two forty-five as instructed, which was when I phoned Rupert to tell him there was a leak in a guest bathroom. He heaved a sigh and said he was on his way. As soon as he left, Jonathan would text Bob, who would go over there on his bike and bring Jonathan in Jonathan's car.

Rupert arrived to cheers and whoops.

'Emmy,' he growled. 'Is this your doing?'

'Yes. You said I was to say no more about it. You didn't say I couldn't *do* anything about it.'

Nerves fluttered in my stomach as I waited to see how he would take it. The trouble with surprise parties was that the surprise could be an unwanted one.

But he kissed my cheek, said 'Thank you for the party, love,' and went off to greet everyone with gusto, while I breathed a sigh of relief.

Ellie and Sophie had appointed themselves as drinks hostesses.

'I do not understand any of this food.' Sophie wrinkled her nose as she pointed at the array of halved melons turned upside down and stuck with cocktail sticks sporting combinations of cheese cubes, pineapple chunks, mini sausages and pickles; butterfly buns filled with blue buttercream (courtesy of Ellie); and a disgusting-looking trifle with enough cholesterol to kill an ox.

'This was the height of sophistication in my youth, I'll have you know,' Ellie commented mildly, sending them both into peals of laughter.

Ryan appeared, looking for a beer, and was quite disconcerted at the sight of scary Ellie giggling like a schoolgirl.

As he wandered off, bottle in hand, Sophie gave an exaggerated sigh. 'Well, I definitely would.'

'Really?' Ellie appraised Ryan's admirable backside as he walked away. 'Mmm. I can see where you're coming from. Bit too hunky for me, though. And three decades too young.'

'So what is *your* type?'

'It has to be the silver fox nowadays, whether I like it or not. Preferably lean and fit. Definitely no beer belly. But the main criteria are competence in bed, with no desire whatsoever to start proposing or anything equally ghastly.'

We cast our eyes around for likely candidates, but Sophie's gaze was distracted by Ryan again.

Ellie tutted. 'Oh, for goodness' sake, why don't you just make a move on him?'

'I don't know his type. I don't want to be rejected.'

Ellie and I both stared, gobsmacked, at the prettiest girl at the party by far.

'Do *you* know what his type is, Emmy?' Ellie asked.

'I . . . Er, he once said he likes women he can talk to and feel comfortable with. I get the impression he's not so bothered about them being too dolled up.' That was as far as I was willing to go on *that* subject.

I walked through the garden, saying hello to everyone as I weaved my way around the flowerbeds. It occurred to me that autumn would soon start to turn the leaves of the trees, and I looked forward to seeing what changes a new season would bring.

I dutifully greeted our mayor – Bob had advised me that it never went amiss to invite him to such things. He kissed me on both cheeks and told me I was clearly a born organiser, which boded well for my future business. The whole time I was talking to him, I was aware that most female eyes in the vicinity were upon him.

Jonathan was seated in the shade near the patio, with Bob and Alain to keep him company, and the dog secured around the chair leg in case she got too excited and stormed off on a mission to trip up all the guests or decided the feast in the kitchen was not to be ignored.

'Jonathan, are you okay? You're not going to get too tired?' I asked him.

'I'm fine, lovey. It's lovely to be out and about. Don't you worry.'

Madame Dupont came over, and she and Jonathan began a garbled conversation. They seemed to be enjoying themselves, and it allowed Bob and Alain to mingle for a while.

'Are *you* okay?' I asked Alain when he came over to steal a quick kiss.

'Yes. It's good to be here. To know I'm welcome.'

'You and Rupert are going to be fine. He values you as a friend.'

'I know.'

I squared my shoulders. 'Right. Time for games.'

I corralled the guests into some semblance of order. Nobody would be forced to take part, but thanks to the punch they'd enjoyed, plenty were game. Spectators lined the edges of the garden and we started with races, the flowerbeds and trees making the 'course' a little more exciting. The bean-bag (or in this case, rice-bag), three-legged and egg-and-spoon races were completed – the latter won by Madame Dupont, who had the iron control of a woman who could finish off a chicken without flinching.

With everyone loosened up, we moved on to the more risqué games.

Squeak, Piggy, Squeak involved adults, unfazed at being blindfolded, sitting on a cushion on someone's lap, asking them to squeak and trying to guess who they were. Since not everyone knew each other, it was made more hilarious with guesses like 'that chap with the glasses and the quiff' and 'the lady in the green dress with the impressive cleavage'.

Still on a blindfold theme, we moved on to Blind Man's Bluff, where people were allowed to stagger around trying to grope – er, I mean, tag – people, with similar outlandish guesses.

Since everyone now knew each other somewhat better than before, we formed two teams in a line, a balloon at the head of each to be passed to the player behind until it reached the back – using no hands. I was all for specifying a politically correct version, but the older team declared this to be for sissies and said that any body parts were allowed (bar hands).

If I'd worried about the party being a damp squib, I needn't have. Those of the generation who remembered such games were all for taking part, those bewildered by their antics were happy to watch and laugh, and plenty of younger guests were willing to take a leaf from their elders' book for a change.

'I see Sophie's got herself well positioned,' Ellie said wryly at my side as we watched.

Sophie had managed to get herself next in line to Ryan, and they were passing the balloon between them in a disturbingly erotic manner.

Ellie fanned her face. 'Is it my age or is it getting hot out here?'

With the older line winning hands down, a second game was declared, and Ellie and I were roped in.

Alain gallantly made sure he was behind me, so I only had to endure dubious movements with one stranger, and then it was our turn. I felt ridiculous as we manoeuvred the balloon between us. It didn't stop me wanting to duck out of the game and drag him behind the nearest bush, though.

We turned to watch the other team in time to see Ellie and Rupert engaged in combat with their balloon. I gaped as they wriggled against each other and exchanged coy smiles. Either Ellie *was* overheated . . . or she was blushing.

'Now, wouldn't *that* be an interesting pairing?' Alain murmured at my ear.

As everyone laughed and cheered, I felt a rush of happiness. I had a new life, a new man, and a best friend who was finally willing to forgive him.

'Happy?' Alain asked.

'Yes. Very.'

With *that* game over, I decided we needed a break and declared it time to eat. Thankfully, the food was well received – nostalgically in the case of some, and as a novelty for others.

Ellie and I placed candles on the cake to form the figures for sixty. We could have tried putting sixty candles very close together, but the lawn was dry and I didn't want to risk a conflagration. Lighting them, we carried it out to the garden and launched into 'Happy Birthday', with everyone joining in. And when that rendition had finished, the mayor and Madame Dupont began a French version, with Sophie and the other French guests joining them.

Rupert good-naturedly closed his eyes to make a wish and blew out his candles. I wondered what he'd wished for.

Jonathan hoisted himself up and very slowly ambled into the middle of the gathering, where Bob tapped the side of his glass for him.

'I'd like to propose a toast,' Jonathan said, as the chatter died down. 'Rupert has been my friend for six years now, and I'm sure many of you will realise that he's not exactly thrilled about being sixty. I don't know what he's moaning about. He ought to try being nearly eighty!'

A chuckle rippled through the crowd.

'I'm not going to make a long speech, but I do want to say this. People harp on about *carpe diem* – seize the day. Well, my friends, when you look at it from my side of life, you realise they have a point. Appreciate what you've got. Your health, your friends, your loved ones, your lovers. The fact is, life's too damned short.'

He raised his glass in Rupert's direction. 'As for this young man here, God knows he's had a hard time of it lately, but he's still made time to look out for his friends, to ensure his guests have a brilliant stay *and* managed to retain that dreadful sense of humour of his. He's always grabbed life by the horns, and I hope he will continue to do so for many years to come. To Rupert. Happy birthday!'

His sentiment echoed back from the crowd, and then he began to sing 'For He's a Jolly Good Fellow'.

I couldn't think of a more perfect way to sum it up.

Since nobody was showing any sign of wanting to leave, we moved on to the finale: tug of war. Typically, they insisted on men versus women, and the men won – but as everyone collapsed in a heap on the grass, nobody seemed to care.

Smiling, I picked myself up and dusted myself down. I was just thinking about clearing up in the kitchen when I felt a tug on my arm.

'Come with me,' Alain said.

'Where?'

'Somewhere quiet.' He dragged me off to the orchard.

'What are you doing?'

'Seizing the day.' He kissed me thoroughly. 'I'm so in love with you, Emmy. And I can't believe I'm lucky enough for you to be in love with me.'

My heart stuttered, and I reached out to link my fingers in his as a warm feeling of wellbeing flooded my system. 'Well, I am, so stop being so soppy. Have you been drinking?'

'Of course. A little. But I have also been inspired by Jonathan's speech.'

I frowned. 'Which bit?'

'I think it hit me at "life's too damned short".' He took my hands in his and dropped to one knee, right there on the grass under the shade of an old apple tree. 'Emmeline Jamieson, will you marry me?'

I stared down at him, my jaw open in surprise, my heart thudding against my ribcage.

'Since I can see you're speechless, I should add that I've never felt about anyone the way I feel about you. The thought that I was losing you was the most awful feeling I've ever had. The time I spend with you is the best I have, and when I'm not with you, I can't wait to see you again. Does that help?'

My mind raced at the same rate as my pulse. Was this too quick? Did we know each other well enough? Was it just a besotted thing that would fizzle out, or was it proper love?

I looked into those caramel eyes; stared at that mouth that I loved kissing; thought about his fingers linked in mine, knowing I never wanted to forget how that felt.

And said 'Yes'.

Alain had been holding his breath. It came out in a whoosh, but then he caught it again. 'Er – yes, that helps? Or yes, you'll marry me?'

I smiled. 'Both.'

And then his lips were on mine, and there in the dappled sunlight of the orchard, with his mouth working its magic, my body humming and my heart soaring, I knew for sure that no matter what life threw at me, my future lay right here.

LETTER FROM HELEN

Thank you for choosing *Return to The Little French Guesthouse*.

I have had so many lovely comments from readers telling me how much they enjoyed following Emmy's adventures in *The Little French Guesthouse*, so it has been a delight and a privilege for me to be able to continue her story as she, Alain, Rupert and friends negotiate the minefield of daily life at *La Cour des Roses* – romance, good times, bad times, heartache; as Emmy would say, 'the whole caboodle'.

I enjoyed exploring some of my secondary characters a little more in this sequel – especially Jonathan and Ellie. So many readers have said that *La Cour des Roses* seems like a real place to them. It does to me, too! I only have to picture it in my head, and I can imagine all my characters there.

If you enjoyed the read, I would love it if you could take the time to leave a review. It makes so much difference to know that readers enjoyed my book and what they liked about it . . . and of course, it might encourage others to buy it and share that enjoyment!

You can sign up for news about my new releases here:

www.bookouture.com/helen-pollard

You can also find me on Facebook, Twitter and Goodreads, and at my website and blog.

Thank you!

Helen x

f HelenPollardWrites

🐦 @helenpollard147

www.helenpollardwrites.wordpress.com

ACKNOWLEDGEMENTS

A massive thank you to my publisher Bookouture, who helped me bring life at *La Cour des Roses* ... well, to life! In particular, I would like to thank Oliver Rhodes for his faith in me, Natalie Butlin for all her dedication and hard work on my books, Kim Nash for her unerringly cheerful help with publicity, and my fellow Bookouture authors for their fabulous support and wicked sense of humour.

I wouldn't know where to begin in thanking my family. You have offered wholehearted support and put up with my lengthy absences glued to my keyboard in the attic, my moods, my exhaustion, my laughter, my tears. I couldn't have done this without you.

And while I'm on the subject of putting up with me, thank you to my close friends for allowing me to disappear for weeks on end, then listening so patiently to my ups and downs when we do get together!

A huge shout-out to the bloggers who have taken the time to read and review my books and spread the word. You are amazing and much appreciated.

And of course, most of all, a heartfelt thank you to my readers. You make it all worthwhile.